Quantum Spirit
Apocalypse

Sallie Haws

Austin   Los Angeles

Copyright © 2013 by Sallie Haws

All rights reserved. No portion of this book may be reproduced, stored in a retrieval system, or transmitted in any form or by any means electronic, mechanical, photocopy, recording, scanning, or otherwise without the prior written permission of the publisher.

Published in Austin, Texas by Fedd Books and in association with the literary agency of The Fedd Agency, Post Office Box 341973, Austin, TX 78734.

This book is a work of fiction. Names, characters, places, and incidents either are products of the author's imagination or are used fictitiously. Any resemblance to actual persons, living or dead, events, or locales is entirely coincidental.

Cover design by Amy Peck / www.goddess-studio.com
Book design by Mitchell Shea

Printed in the United States of America

First Printing: August 2013
Published in Austin, Texas by Fedd Books in association with
The Fedd Agency, a literary and entertainment agency,
P.O. Box 341973
Austin, TX 78734

ISBN-13 978-0-9894934-0-6

Dedication

To my family, without whom this journey would not have been possible.

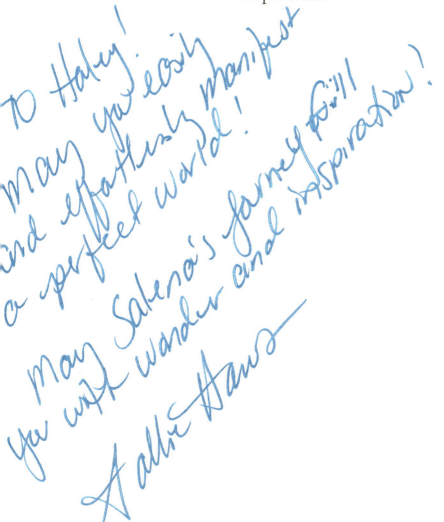

Acknowledgements

Quantum Spirit – Apocalypse is a dream come true . . . literally. However, the dream that inspired my story was only the beginning. You wouldn't be reading it today if it wasn't for the encouragement and support of my husband, Jim, my daughter, Marquise, my son, Terry, my sister, Amy, and my mother and father, Jackie and Terry Haws. Amy and Marquise spent countless hours reading, editing and offering suggestions and advice.

Thank you so much to Annie Turner for lending me your beautiful daughter, Katie, to be photographed by my husband for the cover of this book. My sister's perseverance and artistic talents made great use of Jim's photography and resulted in an exceptional design.

Without Jeane TuBears Jacobs' coaching and development on my earliest drafts, I may not have ever completed the manuscript. The final result you see was accomplished with the expertise and experience of my fantastic editor, Cara Highsmith, whose "Author Bedside Manner" was instrumental in helping me manifest my dream. Any mistakes you find are mine alone.

I am so filled with gratitude to everyone who freely pointed the way when I stopped and asked for directions. Thank you, Tom Hill, for introducing me to some invaluable connections, and Stephanie Sikora who provided me with medical insights and procedures. Bright Blessings and Big Hugs go out to my early, non-family readers — Jocie, Diana, Nancy, Tiffany, Becky, Jenny and Roger.

I hope you enjoy reading about Salena's adventures and journey as much as I enjoyed writing about it.

*Apocalypse: The imminent destruction of the world and the salvation of the righteous.
From the Greek "apokalupsis" that means lifting of the veil or revelation.*

Quantum Spirit
Apocalypse

CHAPTER ONE
Menarche

OMG! You'd think that with all my freaking psychic abilities I would have had more warning! I looked down at my messed-up bad kitty panties. Gaawd! I wrinkled my nose in disgust. Now what am I going to do? I mean I knew it would come sometime soon, but my friends, whose moon time had arrived months if not years ago, were already calling me a "late bloomer." In fact, it had become a kind of joke with my Sisterhood of the Silver Moon friends. I just thought I'd have some kind of premonition or something. Honestly, what good is it to be psychic and have a spirit guide you can actually talk to if she doesn't give you a heads up about important things like getting your first period during Eighth-Grade Algebra?!

"Next time Angeni shows up, I'm going to give her a piece of my mind!" I said out loud to no one in particular. *I could have at least come to school today prepared for this momentous occasion.*

Thankfully, I was the only one in the bathroom at the moment. I scrunched up my nose as my brain sorted through the rather fetid mix of smells that typically inhabited the girl's bathroom. The aroma of some kind of pine scented cleaning fluid permeated the other less desirable odors of what origin I had no desire to know. I looked around at the stall. No new scratched messages on the pink partition walls. I wondered randomly if AH still loved DP. With a sigh of resignation I started pulling the stupid little squares of toilet paper out of the dispenser to start cleaning up. I'm pretty sure it was some annoying old man who invented these totally aggravating paper squares. He probably never learned about female biology and the occasional need for a gob of toilet paper.

    I carefully removed my ruined underwear and held them between my thumb and middle finger. Grossed out, I looked around for a place to set them down temporarily. I didn't want to put them on top of the tiny pieces of rolled up toilet paper, dirt, hair and other unidentifiable stuff that was covering the floor. Suddenly, a swift surge of nausea engulfed me like being caught in an undertow from an angry wave. I closed my eyes when the disorientation and dizziness that followed almost knocked me off the toilet. No longer caring where I put them, I dropped the panties on the nasty floor and used the partition walls to brace myself. *Okaaay . . . I don't think that's normal. I know girls get cramps, but I didn't think they were like this. This isn't going well at all,* I thought as I slowly opened my eyes, which only added to my trauma.

    "Hey! Did somebody turn off the lights?" I asked the empty room as my voice echoed back to me. The bathroom had suddenly become very dark, and what was visible was extremely blurry.

My ears pounded as my heart began to beat faster and faster. I shivered as I broke out in a cold sweat, my panic rising. I never heard of blindness being a symptom of PMS!

"Salena?" A familiar voice called my name as the door to the girl's bathroom opened. A sigh of relief and unprecedented gratitude washed over me. My BFF, Keia, came to check on me.

"In here," I barely squeaked out between gasping breaths I took in an attempt to calm the tornado creating havoc in my stomach.

"Geez, are you okay? What happened?" She asked quickly stepping into the room and closing the door behind her.

"Umm… I don't think so," I managed to reply before the queasiness hit again, and I shut my eyes tightly and inhaled deeply to keep from losing my lunch all over the floor. "I," deep breath, "got my period," another deep breath, "but now I feel like I'm going to throw up," deep breath, "and I think I'm going blind!" I exhaled in a pitiful whine.

I looked up. The blurry edges of the bathroom stall door were moving back and forth. Then I realized Keia was talking to me because I heard her, but I couldn't understand her. It was like I was at the bottom of a pool while she was talking to me from above. My panic moved up another notch. I started to hyperventilate. Apparently, I was so special that my definition of PMS included not only going blind but deaf as well! Through the density of water in my ears and a shaking stall door, I thought I understood Keia say, "Open up!!!" I managed to slide the latch back. She stumbled in and looked at me.

"Oh, my God girl! What's happening to you?!"

I looked up, with tears streaming down my cheeks. Her words were muffled, but I sensed her concern as her blurry lips moved. I opened my mouth to tell her what was happening when I was assaulted again, this time by an excruciating migraine headache that caused what little eyesight I had left to be obscured by flashes of light like fireworks going off in my head.

"Help me!" I pleaded as those fireworks exploded in a fierce finale and everything went dark.

CHAPTER TWO
Outbreak

A beautiful meadow enveloped by craggy mountain peaks and flowing waterfalls surrounded me. Then consciousness slowly began to intrude upon my peaceful dream. I noticed a smell that didn't quite fit in with the environment. The last thing I remembered was being in the bathroom at school, but this didn't smell like the North Hall girls' bathroom at Swope Middle School in Reno, Nevada anymore. No, it smelled more antiseptic-like, and I was lying in a bed. I definitely wasn't home. My best guess was a hospital. Suddenly, I remembered that when I was in the bathroom, I couldn't see or hear. *No problem in the smelling department, it seems.* Blurriness floated around me in an array of strange muted voices and beeping noises. *Definitely, I'm in a hospital. How did I get here? Oh my gosh! I can hear again!*

    I concentrated on what else I might be able to hear. Soft rhythmic breathing was coming from near my feet. Somebody was sleeping in the same room with me! Then I got a whiff of a familiar mango citrus scent. *My mom is here!* The intoxicating aroma of roses wafted through the air, arousing my curiosity. A throbbing ache on the left side of my face, combined with the fact that I could only breathe through the right nostril, told me that something was stuck up my nose. I was dreadfully thirsty. My teeth felt like somebody had glued hairs on them, and I was afraid to move my lips for fear they would crack. *Not my best day.* I stretched my legs and received immediate negative, achy feedback. *Wow! Was I hit by a car after I passed out in the bathroom or what?* I rotated my ankles and stretched which released some of the stiffness.

So far, I could hear, feel my arms and legs, and smell through one nostril. I was apprehensive to open my eyes. *What if I was still blind?* My eyelids felt like they were attached to dumbbells; they were sealed shut. I lifted my hand to rub my eyes. A resistant tug on my arm kept my hand from reaching its destination. My other hand was free of any tethers, so I gently rubbed my eyes opening them one at a time.

"Mom?" My voice was barely more than a whisper and croaked unattractively like an ugly bullfrog. I tried to swallow. Saliva was conspicuously absent.

I heard her breathing hitch and a slightly incoherent "Mmm?"

"Mom? Are you awake?"

"Salena?" Her sleepy eyes found mine. "Oh! Thank the Heavens! You're awake!"

She stood up and grabbed my arm. "What's stuck in my nose?" I asked with a decidedly nasal voice as I gently felt the tube that had been shoved up inside it.

"It's a feeding tube. Don't pull it out," she said casually moving some strands of my hair off my face and then she gently gripped the hand that was examining the tube.

Looking past my mom, I examined my new surroundings. The downtown city lights of Reno twinkled through the darkened window. My dry lips cracked as they stretched into a grin. *I could see again!* Several vases of flowers supporting a multitude of roses sat on a table next to the chair where my mom had been sitting. I turned my attention back to my mom. Her dark brown hair was in disarray as odd strands of gold, stuck up in various angles, glinted off the brighter casino lights that pierced through the open mini-blinds. However, her unkempt hair wasn't the only thing I noticed. Surrounding her was the most amazing vortex of swirling colors! I was so startled by what I saw; I just stared at her with my mouth hanging open. The energy emanating off of her was mesmerizing. I had never seen anything like it before.

I wonder what that means? Am I seeing her aura? I've never been able to see energy fields around people before. I had seen ghosts and spirits, and carried on conversations all day with them, but they always only had a white glow around them that sparkled on occasion. I had never seen colors before. *Apparently my vision had come back and then some!* I wondered briefly if there was an on/off switch for this new "talent." I exhaled a deep breath, blowing a random hair out of my face. *Dang, I need to brush my teeth.*

Worried brows that were past due for a waxing, accentuated my mom's forehead. Tears welled up in her devoted stare as she absently tucked her hair behind her ears. Her red T-shirt and sweat pants looked like they had a rough night. It was obvious that she hadn't just come from the office.

"You okay?" I managed to croak out with a weak smile.

"I am now!" she leaned over me, placed her cheek against mine and breathed me in. Squeezing my arms tightly, she finished up with a kiss on my cheek. "I'm so relieved you're awake. I've been so worried!"

"Sorry," I sort of mumbled because my sticky tongue felt kind of fat. I was pretty sure the vacuum had backfired in my mouth while I was out. "Water?" I mumbled.

"Here. But just a bit," she said as she quickly poured water from a pitcher into a tiny plastic cup that was sitting on a bedside table. I watched the straw swirl around the rim. She held the straw where I could reach it and I sucked down the lousy tablespoon of liquid.

"Can I have some more?" I licked my sandpaper lips.

"Not just yet. Let me get the nurse in here," she said as she pressed a button.

"Does anything hurt?" Mom asked taking a hold of my free hand again.

"Umm, I don't think so, except maybe whatever is in my nose," I mumbled. I did a mental full-body scan. I could see and hear again. That was a relief. I didn't have a headache, and the unplugged other half of my nose was definitely working. I noticed that when I moved my lower body it felt as though somebody had glued my spine in place and put concrete boots on my feet. "What time is it?"

Mom squinted at her watch, "Two-thirty a.m. . . . on Wednesday. You've been in here for thirty-six hours. We've been worried sick. The doctors said you were in a coma, but they didn't know why, what caused it or if you would wake up!"

"What?! No way! It can't be Wednesday!" I exclaimed, and then gagged a little on the tube going down the back of my throat. "Gah! This nose thing is horrible!"

"Don't pull on that, young lady," said a woman who walked in wearing a nurse's uniform. Her nametag said she was Stephanie. "We'll get it out of you right away. You seem to be recovering quickly."

I spent the rest of the early morning getting poked and prodded, and then the fun really began when my doctors arrived for their morning rounds. They scanned me, x-rayed me, and took samples of every bodily fluid imaginable. Dad showed up sometime during the morning, but we didn't really get much of a chance to talk. I drifted off to sleep after lunch, finally free of every attachment but an IV.

The afternoon sun beamed through my hospital room window and I slowly pried them open, blinking rapidly to allow my eyes to adjust. Mom was reading in the chair where I found her when I woke the first time.

"Hey there," I said. Mom looked up at me and smiled. "How long was I out this time?"

"Not long. Just a couple of hours. It's almost three o'clock."

"Wednesday, still?"

"Yes," she smiled. "It's still Wednesday."

I stretched, yawned and rubbed my eyes. My mouth felt nasty again.

"So, I can't believe I missed a day and a half of school because I got my period. How totally wrong is that? Mom, when you got your first period did you go into a coma?"

"Don't be silly. You think this had something to do with getting your period?"

"Duh," I said. It made perfect sense to me. "It wasn't like I drank a potion I whipped up in Science class."

Mom scrunched up her face at me. "Very funny. You didn't slip and fall, and hit your head? "

"No, no slipping or falling occurred. Unless, I hit my head when I fell off the toilet after I blacked out, but then that would have been the result of the blackout not the cause. This totally had something to do with getting my period. I'm sure of it," I said with conviction.

"Salena, just because one happened right after the other doesn't necessarily mean that one caused the other. It's highly unlikely. Women have been getting their periods since the dawn of time, and I've never heard of it being the cause of a coma," my mom said with exasperation.

"Just because it's never happened before, doesn't mean my initiation into womanhood has to be like the rest of womankind. In fact, it almost seems fitting that getting my period would turn into some city-wide spectacle since I'm the last person who wants to draw attention to herself," I grumbled.

"Maybe somebody at school slipped something into your soda during lunch," my mom said completely ignoring what I felt to be perfectly sound reasoning.

"Really, Mom? I mean do you seriously think that Keia, Leah, or Katrina slipped me something like a date-rape-drug during lunch? They so don't swing that way, and neither does Sam. I'm not convinced he swings our way at all," I said scrunching my eyebrows together in feigned concentration.

"Honestly, Salena," my mom said in exasperation. "You know I didn't mean Sam or the girls. I see the coma didn't cure your sarcastic tongue."

"I know, right?" I said as the door opened and I heard the unmistakable footsteps of my father, James Hawthorne, coming into my room.

"You know, right, what?" He said as he quickly approached my bed. My dad always had a presence that I could feel when he walked into a room. At five foot ten, he wasn't usually the tallest guy in a crowd, but as a professor of Quantum Physics at the University of Nevada Reno (UNR), he had that commanding confidence about him. His charcoal hair had thinned out so much that he liked to tell everyone that he had "pink highlights." He couldn't bring himself to shave his whole head (even though it is so popular now) because he really liked his hair, what he had left of it anyways. Behind his wire-framed glasses, the bright sparkle in his gaze increased in intensity when he spotted us, but to my surprise that wasn't the only bright light I saw. Dominant fire and flame colors surrounded him as an irrepressible energy flared. His energetic field kept building up and then bursting, little sparks of color flying off. I felt as if I were watching my own little volcano erupt.

"Our daughter's sarcastic tongue survived her ordeal," my mom replied as she walked around the end of my bed to give my father a hug and a kiss. My parents could be so mushy sometimes. As they embraced each other, I watched in unabashed delight as their auras increased in intensity and blended together. Bolts of clear red electricity shot out from their energy fields attracted to each other magnetically and intertwining together like a double helix. The gold and turquoise of my mom's aura blended, mixed, and vibrated with my dad's orange spectrum in such a passionate embrace. I flushed red like I had walked into their bedroom without knocking.

"Yo, people! Get a room!" I interrupted their reunion.

"Ahh, yes, I see. Well, I guess that being cured was probably too much to hope for," he said with a smile as he leaned down to give me a kiss on the forehead. "It's good to have you back, Moonling!"

"Hi, Daddy," I said. He looked down at me, his eyes searching for something as he picked up my hand and held on tight. "So, do you have a theory as to what happened to me? Mom and I can't agree," I said looking from my dad to my mom in hopes that he might support my theory.

"Why don't you tell us what you remember and then we'll fill you in on what we know," Dad replied.

"Ok," I proceeded to give them a run-down of the events in the school bathroom. "So now, it's apparently Wednesday. Since when is a coma a side effect of getting your period? That's crazy!"

"You're not crazy, little one, just special," I heard Angeni's voice before I saw her. *Better late than never!* My spirit guide slowly materialized and floated at the foot of the bed. Sometimes her "other worldly" glow was so intense it would make my eyes hurt, but today I noticed that I was seeing more around her than I had before. Either her energy had changed or my ability to see her energy had changed. It wasn't just sparkly and white anymore. Now I saw a bright and clear metallic gold mixing in with the white. It was beautiful! Her familiar compassionate and kind expression warmed the chill from my anxiety. I relaxed even more as I watched her ebony hair flow perfectly around her face and down to her elbows as if orchestrated by an invisible conductor. I guess being a full-time resident of the spirit plane means you don't have to worry about such mundane things as wind or static creating a bad hair day. I don't know where she was on Monday, but I was really glad to see her now.

"So special I'll have to ride the short bus?" I asked her.

"What?" Dad said, confusion causing his eyes to narrow and his brows to pucker.

"Angeni's here, Dad," I said to him.

"Hi, Angi," Dad said calling her by the nickname I had given her years ago while looking across my bed to the other side.

Mom's own psychic abilities allowed her to see and hear Angeni just fine. My mom decided the best use of her psychic gifts was as a supplement to her psychological practice, which made her very successful. Sometimes her clients' dead relatives or friends really helped to move the healing process along . . . and sometimes they didn't. Because her psychic experiences began when Mom was really young, she kept a close watch on me for any sign of the "Family Gift." I was extremely grateful that I could talk to her about all the strange things I heard and saw.

"She's floating by my feet," I said as Dad quickly looked to his left to try to acknowledge Angeni. Mom was not very successfully disguising her amusement.

"Does she know what happened to you?" Dad asked me and then turned to look in Angi's direction.

"I can't say for sure," Angeni said to those of us who could hear her as she shook her head. "It's too early to tell."

I grunted. *Could she get any more cryptic? She knows something, but as usual, she can't say. I wonder who makes up the rules over there.*

"Not really," Mom told dad. "At least nothing she can tell us at the moment."

"Okay," Dad said. "Well let's start with what we do know. After you passed out, Keia went out into the hall to yell for somebody to get help. She told us that she didn't want to leave you at all because she was so worried about you. One of the teachers heard her yell, your math teacher, I think. Anyway, your teacher rushed into the bathroom and then just as quickly left to go get the principal who called 9-1-1. He escorted the paramedics to the bathroom, and they rushed you here. The doctors have been running all kinds of tests and scans to try to find out what happened to you. They know that something is very different in your brain and your heart compared to most people based on the Functional MRIs they ran, but they don't know why it happened or what might happen after you woke up . . . if you woke up. They said they had never seen anything like it."

Dad sounded annoyed, a tone with which I had more than a passing familiarity. Being a physicist, Dad has a very structured and organized mind. He really doesn't like it when people can't explain themselves, or cop out with an "I don't know." He thinks that if you don't know, then you should at least have some hypothesis that you could support and test through a series of experiments. Yes, science fair projects at my house were just a ton of fun!

"Did somebody dress me before Mr. Green showed up to see my butt cheeks hanging out?"

"Don't worry Sistah! I totally had you covered!" I heard as Keia and Leah burst in the room. They both squealed, as only we girls can do, and exploded onto my hospital bed with giant grins and laughter, flying right through Angi. I don't think I'll ever get used to seeing that firefly sparkle shattering when humans pass through spirit energies.

"You're okay! You're okay! I just totally knew you'd be okay. You had to be. There just wasn't any other option!" Keia exclaimed. Then she stopped, gave me a hard look with a frown and half-heartedly slapped my shoulder as she and Leah scooted off the bed to stand at my feet. Angi had moved to hover next to my mom and dad.

"What was that for?" I asked Keia.

"For scaring me half to death. Don't you ever do that again!" she scolded me.

"Sure, okay. Next time I get my period I'll be sure to do a 4-1-1 over the school intercom letting everyone know to be prepared for my next scene stealing moment!"

"Oh, ha ha, yeah, you do that! We'd get to watch Victoria Love go into anaphylactic shock again in an attempt to steal the scene back from you!" Leah exclaimed in a fit of giggles.

"Yeah, there's nothing like being deathly allergic to a lack of attention," I said, with contempt thinking of my nemesis.

"You've been the talk of the school for the last couple of days," Keia said more seriously.

I moaned. "I bet. Let me guess. Miss Love was telling everyone I faked it all just to get attention."

"Yeah, pretty much. She's such a Ho. Can't handle anybody else making headlines," Leah chimed in.

"So, you got me dressed, maybe, before Mr. Green came into the bathroom?" I asked Keia hopefully.

"Well, I didn't put your undies back on you, those things were seriously gross, dude. I wrapped them up in a paper towel and tossed them in the trash. Then I got your pants back on, and even though you were going commando, you weren't doing any major exposure or anything. I was pretty freaked out, Salena. You were just lying there, totally passed out, and naked from the waist down. I did the best I could, but I think I was a little hysterical."

"Um, a little?" Leah sarcastically chimed in.

"Shut up. You weren't there. I did the best I could under the circumstances," Keia retorted.

"You did remarkably well, Keia," my mom replied in that calm, motherly type voice. "I'm so glad you went in to check on her when you did. She could have been there until class was over."

"Umm, thanks. What happened to you Salena? What did you mean when you said you thought you were going blind?"

I retold my story to Keia and Leah, while Mom, Dad, and Angi listened for any details I might have missed when I told them.

"Does that usually happen to girls when they get their first period?" Leah asked my mother.

"Um, no, Honey. That doesn't usually happen to anyone, and we're not convinced that's what caused Salena's coma either," my mom replied. "Don't worry."

"Yeah, sure. Okay," Leah mumbled under her breath. I don't think she was convinced. She's a late bloomer like me—the last one, now, in our Sisterhood.

As Keia and Leah continued to talk to my mom, I scanned my two BFFs with my new Sight. Their auras were dancing and mixing together in a happy, energetic symphony. A rush of love and gratitude for them swept over me and settled into my core. They were indeed more than just my best friends; they were my soul sisters.

Keia and I became fast friends in daycare. I think we were attracted to each other because we kind of looked alike. We both have light brown hair with streaks of golden highlights, although hers has always been just a little shorter than mine. Neither one of us has any real style or layering in our hair, it's all just one length all the way around except she has bangs and I don't. Little specks of gold randomly scattered throughout the iris of her eyes remind me of dancing stars. We've always been about the same height and weight even as we have grown up. I think half the clothes in my closet are hers and vice-versa. I noticed that Keia's aura was predominantly a soft glow of pale yellow with lavender rings that encircled her and gently pulsated. We were convinced that we were twins separated at birth, but our parents staunchly denied it.

Leah joined us in kindergarten. She's always reminded me of an extra large pixie, so much so that we sometimes call her Tink. In keeping with her pixie image, she cut her chestnut-colored hair like Alice in the *Twilight* movies. She styles it like Alice too, kind of flippant and fun. No matter how she shakes her head, her hair always lands perfectly back in place. It's really annoying. She's about four inches shorter than Keia and me; not to mention way skinnier too. As I said, she's a pixie. In fact, while Keia and I always seemed to default to being a witch at Halloween, Leah's fall back costume was always a one of those tiny magical creatures. Her pale skin, however, keeps her from the same sun-worshipping status as Keia and me. She just burns. I love to watch her when she's being clever or mischievous, her eyes light up like a Fourth of July sparkler. Leah's encompassing energy field pulsed with a rainbow of bright emerald green, forest green, and a yellow-green. They had both evidently come directly from school since they were still in their school uniforms.

The other two members of our "Sisterhood" were conspicuously absent. "Hey, guys, where's Sam and Kat? How come they didn't come with?" I interrupted.

"They so totally wanted to, dude," Keia informed me, "but Sam had his Tai Chi class and Kat's dad was pulling one of those tug-of-war custody tantrums again. She decided that the best thing would be to just go to her dad's today to save her mom from having another mental breakdown. He's really an ass. I feel so majorly sorry for Kat. Anyway, we promised that we'd give them both a full update when we got home." Leah nodded in support.

Sam Jung, our token male in the Sisterhood, had been Keia's best "boy" friend since birth. Their moms are really good friends and next-door neighbors. They were pregnant together and gave birth to Sam and Keia three days apart from each other. Sam is half Chinese and half Anglo-American. His Chinese mother dominated his genetics, so he has straight black hair that he wears above the ear with long bangs that perpetually flop in front of his dark eyes. He and Leah are continually arguing over who is taller. Due to his height and propensity to sit and study, he had always been a little pudgy until he started martial arts training. Now he loves to teach us the new moves he's learned. Sam is easily the smartest kid I ever met. I know that's kind of cliché, but it's true. He felt totally abandoned and left out when Keia, Leah, and I officially named the Sisterhood in fourth grade. He begged and pleaded for a year before we relented and invited him to be our honorary "sister." We may have to consider changing the name to the Society of the Silver Moon, especially if we ever want any more boys to join.

Katrina Drake joined our group in sixth grade. Her family moved to Reno from the Bay Area that summer, so we didn't know her for most of our elementary school years. Her African-American heritage was heavily influenced by her father's southern Baptist upbringing and her mother's California Catholic influences. Both her mother and father were products of interracial marriages, which gave Katrina the most gorgeous caramel-colored skin that I spend hours in the sun trying to achieve. What I love about her is that she is easily one of the most exotically beautiful girls at school and she never lets it go to her head. I wondered what colors I would see in her aura.

"Mom, Angi, do you know anything about auras?" I asked.

"Angi? Angeni's here?" Keia and Leah squealed.

"Um, yeah, she's floating next to Mom," I replied.

"Cool! Hi, Angi," Keia said as she squinted her eyes in yet another attempt to try to see her.

Angi smiled at Keia and Leah. "Auras?"

"Uh huh, since I woke up, I not only have my hearing and eyesight back, but my eyesight appears to be, umm, more enhanced than it was before. I'm seeing all these amazing colors and swirling energy patterns around all of you. That's an aura . . . right?"

At first nobody said anything and they just stared at me, but then they all started talking at once.

"Okay, Okay! EVERYBODY STOP TALKING!" I yelled, and they all stopped and stared at me again. "Look, I'll tell you more about it, but first I'd really like to get out of this bed, go to the bathroom and brush the disgusting hair off my teeth. I feel like I've been cleaning the cat box with my tongue."

"Eeew! Salena! You can be so disgusting sometimes!" Leah exclaimed.

"Yeah, well, how do you think I feel?" I retorted.

When I stood up, I wobbled a little, but my equilibrium restored quickly. With the help of my twin, I headed into the sterile bathroom. The white and graphite composite tile floor was cold on my feet. My, oh-so-attractive, hospital gown that tied in the back completely failed to cover my buns. I felt a discomforting draft before Keia pulled the gaping shirt closed behind me. Keia stood guard at the slightly ajar bathroom door while I took care of Mother Nature's call. After washing my hands, I set them on both sides of the white porcelain sink for support as I leaned in toward the mirror.

I only filled the mirror up about half way. I was way taller than a lot of the guys in school, especially those whose voices still sounded like girls. I shot up to five-five in sixth grade, but hadn't grown at all since then. I wondered if I would gain any more height. My almost fully-dilated pupils glared back at me with a jolt. In that moment, I discovered being in a coma wasn't the same as forty-eight hours of beauty rest. My own eyes kinda gave me the heebie-jeebies; it was unnerving.

Something had changed in me. I felt different. The mirror reflected my ancient Mayan blood flowing through my veins. The copper star of family legend encircled my dark pupils, and the points faded into an iris of various shades of khaki green. My maternal history was traced back to a priestess of the Mayan Moon Goddess, Akna-U, who was wed to one of the Spaniards that conquered the Mayans. My mom gives her credit for our psychic abilities that have been passed down through the generations. I tried to do a little research on the Mayan Moon Goddess a couple of years ago, but it seems her real name was lost to history as she took on the name and personification of Mother Mary after the Spaniards imposed Christianity upon the native people of Central America. My mom's side of my family has called her Akna-U for generations. Akna means revered mother and refers to the Goddess of Fertility and Childbirth and U means Moon. She's one of the reasons my parents decided to name me after the Greek Moon Goddess Selene. I'm very grateful they didn't decide to name me Akna-U. That would have been the worst!

Being the genetic mix of Spanish, Mexican, and Native American on my mom's side and mostly English on my dad's side, my natural skin tone is a nice golden color. I like it because I love the sun and I don't burn too easily. You would think that being named after the moon, I would prefer the moon and night, but that's not how it really worked out. Another reason I was named after Selene was as a tribute to my mom. Her name is Miakoda (although everyone calls her Mia), which means moon in one of the Native American languages. So, it seems I have a long familial history that connects me to the power and presence of the Moon.

I've always considered my relationship with my parents to be a little different from what most of my friends seem to have with theirs. No matter my age, my mom and dad have always treated me with respect and have given me the opportunity to freely express my opinion. They rarely ever stifled me, which may account for my over-zealous tongue. I tend to say whatever comes to mind with very little filtering.

I gazed at my light brown hair that was not quite long enough to cover my chest. My normal highlights were dull, probably because they were greasy, and there were random hairs going every which way except the way I wanted them to go. I sighed and blew my hair out of my face. I was really looking forward to a shower.

After brushing my teeth and seeing to the rest of my bathroom duties, I went back into the room, pushing my IV cart with me. Someone had turned on the television, and everyone was watching it intently. They didn't even notice I was back. Even Keia had bailed on her guard duty.

The images on the screen were dreadful. There were dead bodies, or what we assumed were dozens of dead bodies, encased in black bags lying on the ground distantly behind the reporter who was standing in front of a small village in the tropics someplace. A ticker tape ran along the bottom of the screen "Breaking News! Outbreak in Malaysia! Half of village population decimated by unknown disease!" The reporter on the TV was saying that the W.H.O. and the Malaysian Center for Disease Control had quarantined the village and its inhabitants until they could determine how the disease was spread. The bodies were bagged and moved to an outbuilding awaiting removal and transportation instructions. There are ten more villagers showing flu-like symptoms who are being quarantined and transported to a nearby medical facility. The villagers not showing any signs or symptoms are being asked to stay in the village under observation until further notice. I noticed several black body bags being carried into a building behind the reporter as he was finishing his telecast.

> *"The government of Malaysia is stressing the importance that its people not panic. They are directing all resources necessary toward identifying this illness as quickly as possible, and they ask for everyone's cooperation with authorities to prevent further spread of this disease."*

My dad shook his head and looked concerned as he clicked off the TV. "I sure hope they get a handle on that situation soon." The rest of us mumbled our agreement. After that uplifting moment, everyone's attention turned to back me, but my focus was on Angeni. She stared at me with her eyebrows and her lips pinched together like she was trying, yet unable, to find the perfect piece in a puzzle.

"What's up Angeni?" I asked her.

"Salena, I have a really bad feeling about that outbreak. I don't think that's the last we'll hear about it. Energetically it feels bigger than just a small village incident on the other side of the world. It's troubling me," she said as she trailed off and looked up as if listening to somebody from heaven.

"What did she say?" My dad asked for the benefit of the non-psychics in the room. My mom's face was filled with worry and concern as she repeated Angeni concerns to the group.

I had a pretty good sense about what Angeni meant when she said that it felt somehow "bigger." It felt as though a dark shadow had engulfed that brief newscast. I shuddered in an attempt to shake it off. Desperate to change the subject and inject a little badly needed humor, I asked, "So, what do I have to do to get expelled from this place?"

CHAPTER THREE
Enigma

It was several more boring hours before I was able to put on my clothes and check out of the hospital. After I went into as much detail about my new aura-scopic eyes as I could, Angeni did her usual disappearing act, and then Keia and Leah rather unsuccessfully attempted to do homework. In between various examinations, I ineffectively tried to locate the off-switch for my personal energy-viewing channel. Seeing people's auras was as mesmerizing as it was distracting. I was sure if I didn't figure out how to turn it off and on, I'd never be able to function in school. So, in between my doctors and the nurses trying to find some reason to keep me in the hospital, I attempted, to no avail, to figure out the secret formula.

    We had just finished a delightful selection of gourmet hospital delicacies for dinner (*NOT*), during which my father negotiated my release with my doctor. My doctor didn't want to discharge me, but Dad managed to convince him. Leah's mom, Lisa, an emergency room doctor at this hospital, stopped by to see me just as the food trays were being cleared out of the room.

"Hi Mom!" Leah said joyfully as she popped up out of her chair, left her books on her seat, and headed toward her mom. Doctor Lisa smiled at her daughter as she leaned her five-foot-seven frame over to give her a big hug and a kiss on the forehead. Her chestnut curls fell forward enough to shield the affectionate gesture.

"Hi Salena!" Lisa said as her hazel eyes scrutinized me from head to toe as only a doctor, who's also a mother, can do. "How are you feeling?" she asked me.

"Just peachy considering the circumstances," I replied as I gazed back at her, studying her aura. It was a swirling mix of bright emerald and turquoise flames dancing to their own silent song.

"I'm so glad to hear it!" She exclaimed looking at my parents sharing their parental concern. "I stopped by your room a couple of times during my breaks over the last few days. Leah wouldn't stop pestering me for status updates," she said as she looked pointedly at her daughter who only shrugged her shoulders. She then spotted Keia still sitting in her chair quietly watching us. Lisa crossed the room quickly to Keia and squatted down to be eye level with her as she placed her hands on Keia's knees. "Hi Keia. How's your mom? We sure miss her around here," Lisa said as she lowered her voice.

Lisa's comment reminded me that Keia's mom, Lesley Von Housen, had been the Executive Director of Reno General Hospital until about three months ago. Poor Keia was so stressed out watching her totally distraught mom go through the drama and trauma of stupid political crap at her work. Keia had explained to me that some years ago her mother's family had sold a portion of the ownership of the hospital to a big pharmaceutical company in Carson City called Trader Pharmaceuticals. They had promised money that the hospital needed to improve the facility and services, so Leah said it seemed like a good deal at the time. Mitch Trader, the founding big-wig and majority owner of Trader Pharmaceuticals somehow became Keia's mom's boss and then he maneuvered his son-in-law into an unearned (Keia's word) top management job in operations, or something like that. Anyway, a few months ago, Mr. Trader had somehow managed to fire Keia's mom and make his son-in-law the Executive Director. It was all very complicated, and I was just glad it happened at the beginning of summer so that the Sisterhood of the Silver Moon could support Keia without having to worry about homework.

"She's doing okay," Keia replied softly. "She loved this place and all the staff and patients. It's been hard for her to let it all go. Every day it seems like maybe it gets a little easier, though."

"That's good to hear. She is a great lady, your mom, and she was the best Executive Director of any hospital I've ever worked at." She glanced furtively over her shoulder at the door to be sure nobody else was entering the room or standing within earshot. "Tell her we all miss her," Lisa practically whispered to Keia. I watched the turquoise in her aura reach out and touch the pale yellow and lavender pulses of Keia's aura. It was like somebody put kaleidoscope glasses on me and kept turning the wheel.

"I will," Keia smiled, grateful for the kind words.

I was itching to go home. Lucky for me a rather cute orderly entered my room pushing a wheel chair. "Can we leave now?" I asked.

"Your chariot awaits, m'Lady!" The cute guy said with a smile, as I clambered into the chair.

There was a sudden affirmative babble in the room as all six of us headed through the door and poured into the hallway.

We were a chatty, energetic group as we headed past the nurse's station to say goodbye, when suddenly Keia and Lisa stopped in their tracks and stared straight ahead at a guy walking toward us. That nasty salty taste that happens right before throwing up suddenly crept into my mouth. It was quickly accompanied by a heavy brick feeling in the pit of my stomach and cold, clammy skin.

Now what was happening to me? I hoped I wasn't having some sort of relapse. Then I looked at the guy Keia and Lisa were intently watching. The first thing I noticed was the dark outline around him, a graphite membrane pierced by thorny black spikes. A collection of colors—dark and muddied navy and olive green— flowing in and out of a storm cloud, were suddenly engulfed by a foreboding tornado. The darkness of his energy field reminded me of an insatiable black hole that sucked up the light. It was probably that vampire-like power that was causing my nausea. *What a creeper!*

His negative energy was having the same effect

that Victoria Love's had on me. I remembered how, after an early encounter with Vicky in elementary school, Angeni taught me to mentally construct a kind of force field around me by visualizing myself inside a room surrounded by bright and shiny mirrors. Instinctively, I imagined reflecting his negative energy back to him and shielding myself at the same time. I felt instantly better and shook off the residual harmful vibrations.

This man really disturbed me, especially when I finally focused on his face, and he was smiling. It was a patronizing smile; the kind you imagine the wolf having in *Little Red Riding Hood*. He was really tall, like over six feet. His originally dark hair looked like he had stuck his head in freshly poured concrete and then shook out what he could. I didn't think he looked old enough to have that much gray hair. At least his salt and pepper hair matched his salt and pepper aura. He looked at me as if I was some kind of lab specimen he could dissect in Biology class. Then he noticed I was unabashedly staring back at him. His invasion of my personal space made me feel like there were a thousand black mountain ants crawling all over my body nibbling at my flesh.

"Hello, Mr. Black," I heard Dr. Lisa say drawing his attention away from me.

"Dr. Robins, aren't you supposed to be in the Emergency Room?" He asked her as he looked down his rather large hawkish nose at Leah's mom. His nostrils flared like he smelled something sour. Unfortunately for me, by sitting in the wheel chair, I had the bad luck to be just at the right angle to see the nasty hair in his nose. I looked from Dr. Lisa to Keia and saw these sudden spikes of a muddied red color erupting from around both of them. I could simultaneously feel and see their anger aimed toward this yucky dude. He must be the one who took Keia's mom's job. That gave me even more of a reason not to like this guy.

"I'm on my break and thought I'd see how my daughter's best friend was doing. I presume that visiting a sick friend during our break times is still permitted." Lisa said as she defiantly looked the man straight in the eye and dared him to disagree with her.

He reengaged his self-righteous smile. "Of course it is, of course," he said as he nodded and grinned. He made me feel as if I had been held captive for weeks as a fast food fry cook who was never allowed to shower. Then he looked down at me again. "You must be Salena Hawthorne," he said letting the "n" in Hawthorne run on for too long. His penetrating and patronizing glare made the hairs on the back of my neck stand on end. "Just out for an evening stroll with your friends?" He asked eyeing the vases of flowers in everyone's hands with intense curiosity.

"Uh, yeah, I'm Salena Hawthorne, and no I'm not out for an evening stroll. Why do you want to know?" I asked straightening my back against the chair and looking him directly in the eye.

"Well, I'm Todd Black, the Executive Director here at Reno General," he informed me as he matched my posture and then literally stuck his nose in the air. *Wow! This guy's a real piece of work.* I snuck a peek at the nurses in the area who were covertly watching this exchange. "If you're not out for a stroll, then what are you all doing roaming the hallways?"

"Mr. Black," my father intervened. "We are taking our daughter home now. It was kind of you to introduce yourself, but we'll be on our way."

"Mr. Hawthorne, I appreciate your desire to take Salena home, but I'm afraid we can't allow her to leave just yet," Todd replied moving his body in front of our group to clearly block the exit.

"Excuse me?" My father replied, his voice rising. "*Mis-ter* Black, Salena's doctors have signed her release papers. What authority do you have to keep her here?"

"I'm the Executive Director of this hospital, that's all the authority I need," he claimed.

"Well, that's nice for you. How do you know who I am, and why do you care if I leave?" I interrupted demandingly.

"Well, you're kind of an enigma around here," he looked at me to see if I understood what that meant, since he couldn't read my expression he asked me anyway. "Do you know what an enigma is?"

Seriously? Is this guy for real? My mom's a psychic psychologist and my dad's a physics professor. How stupid does he think I am? I'm thirteen not three! What a turd. "Umm, yeah, I think so," I batted my eyes at him for effect. "Isn't that what people who are full of crap use to wash out their poop chutes? Do you need an enigma, Mr. Black?" I asked in the highest pitched, dumb blond voice I could muster all while trying to look innocent and sincere.

There was a moment of stunned silence as what I said sank in, and then a riot of laughter erupted in the hallway not only from my entourage but from the eavesdropping nurses as well. I watched Mr. Black's eyes widen in shock until he realized he'd been played. Then anger flushed his face red while he tried to regain his composure. I saw a muddy crimson hue settle over his energy field. I decided anger looked like dried blood on an aura. My poor parents were flabbergasted at my behavior, so my dad reinserted himself into the conversation.

"Mr. Black," my father said with a slight cough to clear his throat. Todd turned his heated face toward my father as he continued, "I'm not sure what business it is of yours what my daughter's mysterious health challenges are, and I do not agree with your purported claim that you can override her doctor's release since you are clearly not one. If you don't mind, it's been a long three days, so we are going to take Salena home now." *My daddy, my hero.*

"Mr. Hawthorne, I assure you I do have the authority, but I will make an exception for now. I will be contacting you regarding bringing her back in for more tests very shortly. Have a good evening," he replied, his nose pointing toward the heavens. He looked around at my group with a flustered and annoyed expression on his face when he noticed Keia glaring at him defiantly with a triumphant grin. He hadn't noticed her before, and he suddenly looked very uncomfortable. I watched him turn around, nod at the nurses and then tilt his chin up as he walked away.

Mom and Dad wasted no time in heading toward the big electronic sliding glass doors that promised freedom. Once outside, I took a deep breath and savored the scent of autumn in the air. The Fall Equinox was only two days away. The evening was cool, but not cold and there was just a slight breeze that lightly touched a few strands of my unkempt hair. As I gazed westward at the mountains, I noticed that the sun had once again lost the Battle of Dusk to the night as the sky over the Sierra Mountains went from an aquamarine twilight to a deep indigo providing a majestic backdrop to a perfect half-moon. The parking lot lights violated the darkness and caused my eyes to constrict. When my dad brought the car around, I eased myself out of the wheel chair and thanked the cute orderly as I settled into the backseat. As soon as he was out of earshot, Leah and Keia converged upon me.

"That's was absolutely the most hilarious thing I've ever heard!" Leah exclaimed.

"Oh My God, Salena! That was totally epic! I wish my mom could have witnessed that. I can't wait to give her the play by play! It'll be better than Christmas!" Keia was laughing so hard tears were streaming down her face. "Todd Black is such a pompous ass! How did you ever pull off that insult with such a straight, innocent face?"

"It's just one of my many talents," I laughed.

"It's just a sharp tongue, that's all it is," my mother said with a half-hearted scold in her voice. "You'd better watch it. That wicked tongue might get you in trouble some day."

"How did we raise a daughter to have such little respect for her elders?" I heard my dad ask my mom as he opened the passenger side door of our car for her.

"I don't know, but I'm positive she didn't get it from me!" My mom dryly replied. Dad just chuckled and shook his head as he closed her door and headed around to the driver's side. I don't think my parents respected Mr. Todd Black any more than I did, and I was really hoping that Dad wouldn't agree to bring me in for more testing, especially if it involved Mr. Black in any way. Something about that guy set my teeth on edge.

CHAPTER FOUR
Vanishing Point

"We have a surprise waiting for you at home," Dad said after we dropped off Leah and Keia at their homes.

"Really? Awesome! What is it?"

"If we told you, it wouldn't be a surprise," Mom said.

"No, duh, but why say anything at all then? Why not surprise me completely?"

"Cause it's more fun to tease you a little," Dad explained.

"Entertainment at the expense of your daughter. You two are model parents," I grumbled squirming in my seat now desperately anxious to get home.

I noticed that the living room lights were on when we pulled into the carport. The double wood doors to the house were located across a sky-lighted, brick-lined entrance.

"Would my surprise be human?" I asked.

"Could be," My mom said with a mischievous smile.

I scrambled out of the car and over to the front door. It was locked, but I heard the latch click and then the door swung open. A very large, practically bald man towered over me with a giant grin spreading over his face. Dark brown eyes reflected his smile. My Uncle Jack reminded me so much of Vin Diesel that *The Pacifier* became our favorite movie to watch together. His big burly arms wrapped around me, squishing my face into his chest as he lifted me off the ground with a breathtaking squeeze. The room spun as he whirled me around.

"Uncle Jack!!!"

"Moonling!"

"What are you doing here?!" I asked as he set me back down.

"I heard my most favorite niece wasn't feeling well, so *here* is the only place in the world I had to be!"

"Jack Hammer! 'Bout time you got back here! How the Hell have you been, Bro?!" Dad said as they embraced in a big man hug complete with back slaps. Jack's last name is really Hammond, but when he joined the Army after college his call sign became Jack Hammer.

"Been good, man, but not as good as you," Jack said, his expression softening as he looked at my mom. I think he always had a thing for her. Dad and Jack were best friends growing up and then they were fraternity brothers in college. Mom and Dad met at UC Santa Barbara where they both went for their undergraduate degrees, it was Jack who introduced them.

None of the grown-ups talk about it much, but Jack's first and only wife died shortly after they were married. For some reason, he never got married again.

His parents also died a long time ago, and being an only child, we were the only family he had. Curious, I studied his aura. Through my new sight, Uncle Jack looked like he was a giant seed inside a freshly picked orange. I started to salivate as I imagined how good a glass of orange juice would taste about now.

"Jack, thanks for coming out! It's great to see you! It's been too long," Mom said also warmly embracing the big man. "Let's catch up in the living room. Can I get you a drink?"

"No thanks, Mia, I already helped myself. Made myself at home as you instructed. My bags are in the guest room."

"Perfect! I do think that James and I could use a drink though," she said while she headed down the single step that led into the dropped living room and over to the bar to pour my dad and herself a glass of wine.

"I'd like a glass of orange juice," I called to Mom.

"Help yourself! It's in the kitchen," she told me, not taking the hint. Scowling, I turned my attention back to Uncle Jack.

"How long can you stay?" I asked.

"Not long, I'm afraid. Just tonight and tomorrow night, little one."

I pushed my lower lip out in a well-practiced pout. "Bummer."

"I know, but we'll have a chance to watch *The Pacifier* together tomorrow, I promise!" he said.

"Awesome!"

We spent awhile catching up, and I told him what

happened to me and about my new ability to see auras. Both of my parents are only children, and since Uncle Jack never had any children, he considers me the closest thing he's ever going to get to a daughter, and I love him like an Uncle. It was so good to see him! His government job takes him away for so long, sometimes it is months or maybe a year before we see him again. He always tries to come to Reno at the end of November each year so he can celebrate Thanksgiving and my birthday with us. He completely spoils me rotten which is totally okay by me. I decided to let the grown-ups talk a little longer, so after kissing them all, I left to go get ready for bed and take that desperately needed shower, orange juice forgotten.

"Ahhhhhh!" I exclaimed as I flopped on my cushy mattress. It was so good to be back in my own bed, clean and in my favorite PJs. Leah and Keia assured me they would call the rest of the Silver Moon members and fill them in so I wouldn't have to. I was very grateful, although I was kind of dreading the re-telling of my story again at school. My mom, dad and Uncle Jack were hovering in my doorway.

"How do you feel?" Mom asked me.

"Great! Now that I've finally had a shower and my scalp stopped itching," I said. "I'm not super tired, but tired enough considering that I was unconscious for the last three days. Hopefully I won't have too much trouble falling asleep."

"Ok, good to hear. Remember we promised your doctor we'd keep you under observation tonight and all day tomorrow as a condition for being discharged today," my father said. "Mom will take the first night shift, and I'll take the second."

I was actually kind of disappointed that I wasn't going to be able to go to school tomorrow. "What about you, Uncle? Going to give up a few hours of your night to watch me sleep? That tops the list of exciting things to do in Reno on a Wednesday night!"

"It is a tempting offer, but your parents didn't want to give up any time with you," he said and almost managed to pull off a sincerely disappointed look. The only thing that gave him away was the sparkle in his eyes.

"Yeah, I'm sure," I said and turned to Mom and Dad, "Thanks for looking out for me. I feel fine, but it will be nice knowing you're here if I need you. Lucky for you that lounger is still in here," I said sweeping my hand toward the super cozy, yet slightly stained, recliner in the corner that my mom bought when I was a baby. When I was little I used to crawl up into her lap on that chair, and she would read me all kinds of stories. Although my favorites were the "Harry Potter" stories, they all had magic and adventure, and I was delighted and enchanted by each one.

I crawled under my sheet and comforter as mom settled into the chair for the first watch. She had her Kindle with a book light illuminating the page. Hopefully, it was a good book that would keep her awake for the next four hours. Dad was going to switch with her at 2:00 am. The clock said it was just a little after 10:00 p.m. when I closed my eyes with a sigh.

I was really happy and in a state of pure bliss. It was sunny and warm in this beautiful mountain meadow. Majestic, snow-capped mountain peaks jutted up toward the sky reaching for the heavens, and I was surrounded by my family and my Sisterhood friends: Keia, Leah, Katrina, and Sam. We were all smiling, laughing, and thoroughly enjoying ourselves. I heard the distant rush of a river and thundering of a waterfall, but the stream that ran through the meadow was quiet. I could see and feel energy coming up from the earth and radiating off of the abundant coniferous trees surrounding the meadow and the plush grasses with the vibrant wild flowers poking their petals out to face the sun.

Taking a deep breath of the fresh mountain air, a familiar scent of pine and grass mixed with bark filled my senses. I plopped down on my back in the middle of the meadow and looked up at the sky. The long grasses blowing gently in the slight breeze tickled my legs and arms. A scattering of small puffy clouds surrounded the gleaming sun. A jet pierced the clouds like an arrow shot from the Goddess Artemis, leaving a stream of smoke in its wake. Mom, Dad, and all my friends settled themselves down around me. We made our own sun with me at the center. The palpable energy from our circle pulsated through me. I felt so full of love, compassion, and gratitude for my friends and family, I thought I'd simply burst! It was blissful, until I heard something scratching at the edges of my thoughts.

The voice was familiar as it intruded into my euphoric sanctuary. It was my dad. I noticed he wasn't in the meadow anymore. He was panicked and yelling. I couldn't possibly imagine what his problem was. After all he was just here in the meadow with me only a moment ago.

The yelling got louder as my dream began to fade and I slowly regained consciousness. Comprehension of his words gradually started to sink in.

"Salena! Salena! Oh, my God! Salena! Where are you?!" I heard my dad franticly yelling as I opened my eyes.

He was standing right next to my bed looking down at me. I sat up rubbing my eyes. "I'm right in front of you. What's the problem? Geez, stop yelling. You'll wake Mom," I chastised.

"James! What's wrong?" My mother called as she ran down the hallway and came to a halt in my doorway. *Too late,* I thought wryly.

"It's Salena. She was just here and now she's gone!" He said as his voice cracked.

"Don't be silly, honey," my mom said in her professional psychologists voice. "Are you sure she didn't just go to the bathroom?"

"No, no. I swear it! I was just sitting here, watching her and she just disappeared. Literally, she just vanished!" He exclaimed.

"Hello!! Yo! Mom! Dad! I'm right here!" I yelled, waving my hands in front of their faces. Then I saw my hands. They were glowing. *What the Hell?* I started to panic; fear hit me like a giant frigid ocean wave, as the last vestiges of my wonderful dream faded away.

"What, in God's name, is going on?" My mom exclaimed as her eyes widened in shock while she looked directly at me. *I've been wondering that too,* I thought ruefully as mom rushed over and grabbed both sides of my face with her hands forcing me to look her in the eyes.

"How did you do that?" She asked in awe.

"Do what?" I asked sleepily with a slightly groggy voice relieved that she was touching and holding me.

"Disappear." Mom and Dad said in Dolby 5.1 surround sound.

"I disappeared? Seriously? As in, like, invisible? You couldn't see me? Or hear me? I was right in front of you!" The words poured out of me, the incredulity of it not sinking in.

"You were not in that bed when I walked in, and then I watched you materialize right in front of my eyes. It was like you were beamed in from the Starship Enterprise," my mom attempted to explain.

"That's exactly what it looked like," my dad chimed in, trying to wrap his brain around what was happening.

"Yo! Can you keep it down? You have guests that are trying to sleep here!" Uncle Jack shuffled into the room wiping his eyes.

"Sorry to wake you Jack, but our unusual daughter just vanished into thin air and then rematerialized," Dad explained.

"Interesting trick, Salena. Been studying magic and illusions lately?" Uncle Jack asked taking my latest oddity completely in stride.

I just stared at them. I was utterly speechless (which is very rare for me). Tears started to well up in my eyes as I tried to digest yet another freak-a-zoid thing that was wrong with me. How could somebody who wanted to be so normal be so completely abnormal? My body felt unusually heavy, hot, and sweaty as if I had just walked out of an over-heated buoyant ocean into the Sahara Desert in the middle of summer. I felt a headache coming on that promised to be a doozy, and I was desperately thirsty. *This sooo sucks!!* Then, I had a hopeful thought that maybe this latest experience wasn't my fault. Maybe my quantum physicist dad was using me as a guinea pig.

"Uh, no. I haven't. Not at all. I really don't have any idea what they are talking about," I answered Uncle Jack. "Daddy," I prefaced as I wiped at my tears and sniffed my nose, "are you working on some new transporter device at work you haven't told us about?" I asked hoping for a logical answer instead of an illogical scary mystery. Mom and Jack looked over at Dad expectantly. That thought apparently hadn't occurred to them.

"I'm afraid not, honey. I wouldn't have been so freaked out if it was some experiment I was testing," he said with a hint of a smile. "Not that I would test such a thing on my daughter anyway. It seems, like your new ability to see auras, you have developed another very unique talent to add to your repertoire. How did you do it?"

"I have absolutely no idea," I looked at him, my eyes begging him to believe me. "I was just dreaming. That's all. The dream wasn't anything special, nor was I doing anything intentional. I woke up because you were frantically yelling for me. I tried to answer you, and I waved my hands in front of your face, but you didn't see me. That was when I got worried that something was wrong. Then I apparently re-materialized, or whatever."

"The full-body MRI's the doctors did at the hospital were definitely not normal. They had never seen the sort of wide spread electrical activity that your brain and heart were emitting. That's why the doctors couldn't give us any prognosis while you were in a coma. They had no idea what they were looking at. Obviously something triggered some kind of cascade effect throughout your body that has given you abilities beyond normal humans," my dad explained.

"Yeah, I keep telling you that the 'something' was getting my period. I'm sure of it." I said, still sniffling.

"Well, if it was your period, we can't turn it off now, so we'll just have figure it out . . . somehow," My mom promised. "It's 4:30 in the morning, a little early for you to get up. Why don't we all try to catch a few more hours of shut-eye and we can reconvene at breakfast?"

"Okay, I'll try, but I have to admit, this really scares the crap out of me. I wish I knew why all of this is happening. What if I disappear again, and I can't or don't come back? Do you think that I was dead for those brief seconds? I didn't feel dead. My arm was glowing, but otherwise I felt pretty normal. I just don't know if I can take any more of these special surprises. I wish Angeni were here. Maybe she would have some explanation for this." I replied as my mom, dad, and uncle gave me a big hug. I looked at them and read the concern and love in their eyes.

"I'm sure she'll show pretty soon, and if she

doesn't know when you first ask her, it's likely she'll be able to find out for us," my mom said obviously trying to reassure me as well as herself.

"No worries, my little moonling," my dad said using his pet name for me while he stroked my hair. "With Angeni's help we'll definitely get this mystery solved." Since my dad's an über-smart scientist, I believed him.

To my surprise I was actually able to fall back to sleep for several hours. Dad continued to keep watch over me, so that helped.

"Good morning, sleepy-head," Dad said as I stretched my legs and feet hearing my ankle crack as I rotated it.

"Mornin'. Did I disappear again?"

"Nope. Not even a flicker," he said. Well, that was a relief. "Your mom and Jack are up. She's making breakfast and Jack is harassing her."

"Nice to know things are back to normal," I said sitting up in bed and letting my feet hit the floor.

"Yeah. It is. Do you want to take another shower before breakfast?"

"Yup!" I said as I padded across the room feeling the soft carpeting squish between my toes.

"Okay, I'll see you in the kitchen for breakfast."

I was blow-drying my hair when Angi materialize behind me in the mirror. She noticed that her sudden and unannounced entrance made me jump and tried to suppress her laughter. "Not funny," I scowled at her as I turned off the hairdryer and turned around to face her.

"Where have you been? How come you are always conspicuously absent when I need you the most? Is there such a thing as an angelic cell phone? If there is, how do I get one? I had another incident this morning. I need your help!" I said to her probably more whiney and annoyed than I should have been. None of this was her fault, after all.

I watched several emotions cross her sparkling face as I ranted away. Her initial smile at making me jump was replaced with annoyance and then concern. "What kind of incident?" She asked.

Her eyes widened in surprise as I told her about my latest adventure. "Well, if it's any consolation, I've never heard of anything like that being a symptom of impending death," she said in a half-hearted attempt to calm me down. It didn't really work.

"You've heard of this happening before, as in real life, not science fiction?" I incredulously asked. She was suddenly looking uncomfortable.

"Well, um, there are stories, but I'm pretty sure they really wouldn't or couldn't apply to you. You're too young . . ." she trailed off in thought.

"You know, Angeni, as cool as it is to have a guardian angel or whatever you are, you frustrate me endlessly!" I said as I slammed my hairbrush down onto the bathroom counter in aggravation. She jumped. I think it's kind of funny when you can make a spirit jump. She scowled at me.

"Salena, it's not my intention to frustrate you. As I've told you before, there are some things I'm not at liberty to tell you, and being a spirit guide doesn't make me omniscient! You know the future is unpredictable and malleable based on choices you make every minute of every day. I've told you before that each person comes into this world with a purpose, but the only one who can discover it is . . ."

"Me. Yeah, yeah. I know. You've said that before," I grumbled.

"I think your purpose has not only arrived on your door step earlier than most people, but it's actually trying to kick the door in!" She said with compassion and sympathy. That is just so not what I wanted to hear.

"Tell you what, I'll go back to the Otherside and ask around to see if I can come up with any answers that I can share with you. And, I'll try to come around more frequently, at least for a little while. You know time works differently over there, so I often don't know I've been gone so long. Does that sound like a deal?"

Like I had a choice, I thought. "Yeah, sure," I said. "It's a deal."

CHAPTER FIVE
The Sisterhood

My bare feet complained when I stepped off the warm squishy carpet onto the cool hard marble of the front entry floor. Breakfast was calling me, and my mouth was watering. I suddenly realized that I was ravenously hungry. I quickly crossed the ice-like tile toward the kitchen, catching a glimpse of the morning sun over the eastern hills through the big picture windows in the living room. The lack of clouds held the promise of another beautiful September day.

The delicious aroma of my mom's yummy fried eggs, cooked with butter and Marsala wine, topped off with parmesan cheese, enveloped me; it made my mouth water and my stomach growl. I tried to eat with some composure, as I told Mom, Dad, and Uncle Jack about Angi's visit, but what I really wanted to do was scarf it all down. Dad assured me he would do some research today while he was at work. Mom had to meet with a couple of clients, so Jack decided to stay home and babysit me.

We watched movies all day. Starting with *The Pacifier*. As fun as that was, I was desperate to get back to school with my friends. There was no way I was going to stay home again tomorrow too. Everybody called to check on me when they got home from school, but nobody came by to visit.

Even though my doctors wanted me to stay home from school on Friday, I managed, with a great deal of negotiation, to get my parents to agree to release me from house arrest. I just had to promise NOT to disappear again. I thought that stipulation was rather silly. I mean, it's not as if I was trying to vanish into thin air or anything. Thankfully, it was a quiet, uneventful, and perfectly normal night followed by a tearful goodbye to Uncle Jack. He promised to be back at the end of November for Thanksgiving and my birthday. I couldn't wait. Mom made my day when she told me she would drive me to school. I hated taking the bus.

Last year on the first day of seventh grade our bus took a different route than it had for elementary school. I was sitting in the first seat on the right hand side of the very full bus looking out the front window when I saw this guy riding his bike ahead of us. We approached a red light but he didn't appear to notice. I watched in horror as he sped out into the intersection and a car that appeared out of nowhere hit him head-on. I screamed and yelled at the bus driver to stop as I watched him fly off of his bike into the path of another car that ran him over. It was a gruesome scene and I was hysterical as I fumbled for my cell phone to call 9-1-1. As I brought the cell phone to my ear and looked up I noticed that the bus driver had indeed stopped the bus and was staring at me like I had four heads. I looked behind me at the now silent middle schoolers, who also were staring at me like I had gone crazy.

"The bicyclist! The car ran over him!" I cried, turned around and pointed to a completely empty intersection. There was no bicycle, no body, no car. I was mortified.

"But I saw it! I swear I did!" I turned to the kid sitting next to me, "You saw it? Didn't you?" I asked him. He just looked at me, scooted as far away from me as he could, and shook his head. That's how I earned my nickname "Psycho Salena" on the first day of seventh grade. Turns out that was the onset of my visual psychic powers. So now I could not only hear ghosts and spirits, but see them as well. Oh, joy! Angeni later told me I had witnessed some kind of Hell-Loop where bad people who died an untimely death and who had limited spiritual beliefs, are doomed to relive their death over and over again. More often than not the bus manages to time its arrival at that intersection so I get to see that scene play out day after day. Now I try to sit in the back of the bus on the other side.

Mom drove me to school this morning using a different route, so there was no risk in seeing the "Hell Loop." As I stared out the window, I thought back to the bus ride home from school on Friday of the same week I became Psycho Salena. A bunch of obnoxious eighth grade boys had blown up condoms and were batting them around the bus. Their behavior got the whole bus in trouble with the driver, and I got really pissed off. I slammed the door when I walked into the house and my mom rushed into the foyer to greet me.

"What's the matter, honey? Did you have a bad day at school?" She asked concerned.

"Yeah! The bus ride home was the worst ever! We have to have assigned seats on the bus now, because these stupid boys were throwing condiments around. Can you believe of all my luck that the crappy bus driver made my assigned seat right next to Victoria Love? God, could it get any worse?" I exclaimed with exasperation and frustration.

My mom raised her eyebrows in an attempt to display some concern. "Really? Condiments? Were they throwing ketchup, mustard, and relish? That must have been a real mess! No wonder the driver was pissed," she replied, barely containing her laughter.

"What?!" I looked at her as I realized what I said. "No! That's not what I meant!"

"Oh? Then what?" She asked innocently. "You don't mean *condoms,* do you?" as if comprehension was just dawning on her.

"Oh, Ha Ha, Mom. You're so funny, I forgot to laugh," I said trying to keep myself from smiling as I began to acknowledge the humor of the situation.

I smiled and shook my head at the memory. I was just grateful I hadn't yelled out "Stop throwing condiments!" to those boys on the bus. I might never have lived it down, especially after the ghost bicycle crash incident earlier that week. At least this year we don't have assigned seats anymore; but I still hate riding the bus, which is why I'm so grateful Mom decided to drive me to school this morning.

As we pulled up behind all of those hateful

mustard yellow coaches, which had already spit out their passengers, I noticed my group of friends clustered in a circle just to the right of the front entrance of the school. It looked as if they were struggling to find me in the mass of middle schoolers converging on the school's front doors.

"Thanks for the ride, Mom," I said as I planted a quick kiss on her cheek. "I'll see you after school." I reached behind my seat to grab my lunch from the backseat and then hopped out and ran toward my friends. My backpack was still in my locker.

"Keia! Leah! Sam! Katrina!" I yelled, waving my arms and quickly walking toward my group of friends.

"Salena!" I heard them yell back as they finally noticed me and started migrating in my direction. They were all talking at once and jostling each other to give me hugs as they enveloped me in the circle. The whole Sisterhood of the Silver Moon, all five of us, were present and accounted for, even our mister sister, Sam.

"Hey, Salena! You don't look any different now that you have officially entered 'Womanhood'," Sam said as he flipped his long dark bangs out of his eyes and looked me up and down.

"Good to know, Sam. Thanks for your expert appraisal," I dryly replied.

The "Sisterhood of the Silver Moon" had started out as our own little girls "club" whose main purpose was to give us a reason to get together on Saturday nights to gossip, paint our nails, and watch movies. As my psychic abilities grew from just being able to hear Angeni, to being able to hear and then see other ghosts and spirits, we began to wonder about the source of my gift and how it may or may not be connected to spirituality and magic.

None of us had been raised with any specific religion, so we started to investigate and experiment with various different spiritual practices, starting with Wicca. When Sam joined the group he introduced us to some of the spiritual practices of the Far East like Buddhism, Hinduism, and Taoism. My mom contributed some Native American concepts and traditions as well. This grew into a sort of mystical show-and-tell where each member of the sisterhood would bring something they had discovered to our Saturday night slumber parties that we could explore as a group, that is, when we weren't gossiping or talking about boys.

"Geez, Sam!" Katrina scolded as she playfully slapped his shoulder. "Of course she doesn't look any different! You're such a guy sometimes!"

"Really? Only sometimes? What am I the other times?" He asked defensively looking around at the group. Nobody answered.

Although Kat's parents are divorced, and her mom claims to be a recovering Catholic, Katrina is concerned that if her parents knew of our more "pagan" or spiritual earth-based interests they might forbid her to be our friend. For that reason, she has let her parents believe that our "Sisterhood" is nothing more than a more formalized clique. So, we are always sure to include some kind of girly pampering as part of our Saturday night ritual.

Leah and Keia, however, keep their moms fully in the loop about all the weird paranormal stuff I can do. I think Lesley and Lisa find some of my supernatural abilities fascinating even though one is a high-powered executive and the other a doctor. In fact, maybe because they are scientifically minded they like hearing about our explorations and experiments. Sam's family doesn't really practice one religion. They sort of have a combination of several philosophies that work for them. I don't really know how much of our fun he has shared with his mom or dad. Sam probably thinks that if he doesn't share a lot about what we do, then his parents won't wonder about why he prefers to hang out with girls rather than boys.

Sometimes Angeni would show up, and I would do "readings" for the group. I discovered that I wasn't the greatest "fortune teller." My "readings" had about a fifty percent accuracy rate. *Not exactly something to write home about.*

Katrina and Sam had gotten the full scoop on my recovery from Keia and Leia Wednesday night and again from me last night, although I had purposely omitted my disappearing act. I wanted to tell everyone in person and watch their reactions. All of the phone updates didn't stop Kat and Sam from peppering me with questions, though. "Are you okay? What happened? Are there any new test results?" And so on.

"Hey, Hey, HEY!!" I yelled to get them to shut up. "I don't have time to go over all of it with you now. The bell's about to ring," I told them when they had quieted down. "Let's all meet for lunch today and I'll tell you what I know, which isn't much."

"I didn't bring my lunch today," Katrina piped up. "So don't start without me, 'kay? I'll try to be the first in line at the cafeteria. Are we gonna meet in our usual place?"

"Yeah, same time, same Bat Channel," I said as we all started to head into the school just as the bell started ringing.

I heard Katrina mumble to Leah, "What's a bat channel?"

"I don't know other than it probably has something to do with Batman. You know Salena's dad is some kind of super-hero, sci-fi fanatic," Leah replied.

I watched my friends split off to navigate the river of blue and beige uniform-clad bodies in the hallways to their first period classes. I realized I was going to be late to class because I didn't have time to get to my locker before the tardy bell rang. So I decided to go visit our Principal, Mr. Green, and thank him for his help. He could give me a pass, and then I could go to my locker before English.

Mr. Green was happy and surprised to see me back so soon. He had heard that I had awakened from the coma on Wednesday and thought I would be out longer. I thanked him for his concern and help, asked him for a pass, and headed to my locker. After gathering what I needed for my next few classes, I headed into English. Everyone turned to stare at me when I opened the door. Yeah, that was awkward. I saw a couple of Victoria's friends whisper something to each other as dark muddy green aura rays spiked through their more dominant darker and murkier pinks, but I just smiled and walked up to Mrs. DeLuca to give her my pass.

As soon as I sat down, I knew I was going to have a problem. My assigned seat in her class was in the last row, and I had a perfect view of everyone's auras. I felt as though I was sitting behind a bunch of intensely lit Christmas trees ignited in a frenzy of disjointed colors. I couldn't see the board. If I couldn't get control of this, I was going to have to sit in the front row of every classroom. *Wouldn't that just be awesome? Not so much, no.*

Thankfully, the morning went by quickly despite the aura distractions. After each class I asked my teacher if I could move up to the front of the class for a while. I told them that my eyesight hadn't returned to normal after the coma, which was more or less the truth.

I made my way to the outside lunch area between the North and South Halls to meet the Sisterhood. We gathered around our favorite tree and waited for Katrina to show up. It wasn't long before I saw her exit the building and head toward us. Her curly black hair bounced away from her waist in time with her excited footsteps. She reminded me of a long-haired Halle Berry as I enviously watched her head toward us. She narrowed her dark brown eyes at us trying to determine if we had started without her. Although the energy field surrounding Katrina was a bright light pink with a blend of lavender, I noticed that her field didn't extend nearly as far outward as Keia's, Leah's, and Sam's did. I wondered why her aura wasn't as wide as theirs.

"You didn't start without me did you?" She asked

the group in a breathless voice.

"Nope. You're just in time for story hour," I said smiling. I proceeded to tell them about the auras. Keia and Leah listened patiently as I told Sam and Katrina about their own auras and then repeated what I had told Keia and Leah about theirs on Wednesday.

"That's pretty cool, Salena," Sam said. "Can you see your own?"

I frowned in disappointment. "No, apparently a mirror doesn't reflect energy fields. However, I did see my arm glowing yesterday morning when I disappeared," I said nonchalantly waiting to see who would react first. As it turned out, it was a collective response—a stunned silence and confusion blanketed everyone, and then they all reacted at once.

"What did you say?"

"Did you say you disappeared?"

"What? Come again?!"

"Wait, start over!"

"Okay. Okay," I said laughing at their reaction. Then I recounted the story about my vanishing act.

"Dang, Salena! You've become some kind of a Super Hero!" Sam exclaimed in awe. "You're just like Violet Incredible! That is SOOO cool!"

"So, how do you do it?" Keia wanted to know.

"Yeah, can you show us right now?" Leah chimed in.

"No, I can't," I replied as my eyebrows scrunched together and I pouted. "I have absolutely no idea how or why it happened. I'm not even sure where to start to make it happen again or if it *can* happen again!"

The conversation picked up in earnest as the group discussed this latest turn of events with theories, questions, and plans for how they could help me learn about my new "power."

"Whoa! Red Alert! Bitch Brigade Bird of Prey off the starboard bow!" Sam announced under his breath cocking his head in the direction of Victoria Love, Montana Moore, and Dakota Jensen who were heading right toward us. Sam's a Star Trek über-freak. He's even tried to teach us Klingon during a few of our sleepovers.

I'm pretty sure Victoria was either the result of some kind of Utopian Society test tube experiment or she's Mattel's first android Barbie. She's freaking perfect in every way, and she knows it. Perfect platinum blonde hair; perfect white teeth; perfect perky boobs; perfect tiny waist, perfect pouty lips, and a perfect GPA. Her parents should have named her Venus instead of Victoria. You could fill a swimming pool with the amount of drool the seventh and eighth grade boys drip onto the ground after she walks by them. Today, though, I noticed one thing about her that wasn't perfect, her aura. It was very ashy with a mix of muddied green, navy, and brick, and like Katrina's, it was really weak. It barely extended past her body. Victoria had some serious issues that she hid really well.

I turned away from Bitch Brigade and pretended to be in a deep conversation with Keia, hoping that they would ignore me, when suddenly Victoria screamed a high pitched, ear-splitting squeal and ran toward me. If the squeal didn't capture everyone's attention, her suddenly running towards me in obnoxiously high heeled shoes (which, by the way, were totally against the school dress code) was probably enough to do it. I decided that my disappearing trick would come in handy about now. I waited a moment, and nothing happened. *Of course not.*

"Salena! Salena!" She shouted my name even though she was only two inches away from my face. "Can I have your autograph pleeeeese!" She cried. Unbelievably she was able to raise her voice another octave, which left my eardrums vibrating. Her two friends were squealing in concert with her while waving a stupid white piece of paper in my face.

"Bite me!" Keia demanded as she stood up in front of me with her hands on her hips in a perfect Wonder Woman pose. *She's such a bad ass.*

"And risk putting a dent in one of your fenders?" Victoria taunted. "I just want an autograph from our resident celebrity, Psycho Salena," she gushed with sarcastic innocence as her fan club snickered. I rolled my eyes. Victoria's been calling Keia a car (because of Kia Motors) since second grade. She really needed to get some new material.

"Hey, Victoria, the man hole you climbed out of is missing their Love nest. Better hurry back!" Katrina entered the fray.

"Look, V, its Pussy Galore! She must not have had her Fancy Feast this morning, she's being kinda catty," Montana pointed and laughed at Kat.

I chimed in before Keia or Kat could react, "Victoria, there is no room for us in your solipsistic world." My voice was calm, yet it held just a touch of patronization. "We are no threat to you."

Victoria was momentarily silent as she stared at me with her eyebrows pinched together while my friends burst into hysterics. Clearly she was baffled. Keia had helped her brother, Tim, who is a Junior at Reno High, study for a vocab test last week. She couldn't stop laughing as she told us that the new word for Victoria was *solipsistic* because it meant "extreme egocentrism." I couldn't pass up the ripe opportunity to spring it on our tormentor. I was really hoping that one of her groupies would remember it later so they could look it up.

Miss Love finally collected her haughty demeanor, flipped back her perfectly coiffed, professionally bleached blonde hair, and said, "Of course you aren't, darling. You are insects—easily squashed!"

Proud that she got in the last word, she skillfully turned on her four-inch heel and started walking away. I held Keia back from wanting to tackle her as I watched Victoria and her Ladies-in-Waiting sashay across the quad waving at their courtiers along the way. I wondered how a girl with the last name of Love could be such a hateful bitch.

"How does she always get away with wearing those obnoxious shoes?" Kat asked Leah as she looked down at her regulation footwear.

"Heck if I know," Leah replied shaking her head.

The bell rang just a little after we had resumed our conversation and we decided to get together at Keia's house the next night to make me disappear, this time on purpose.

CHAPTER SIX
The Fifth Dimension

Unfortunately, even though they had two days to research my new "talents," my mom and dad were practically useless in helping me understand what was happening to me. My dad, being a super-hero fanatic and a quantum physicist, was so excited that his daughter is a real-life Violet Incredible, that when we sat down after dinner on Friday night, he reverted into scientist-speak and started firing questions at me. If I had known what language he was speaking, I might have been able to answer some of them, but sadly they don't teach Latin in school anymore. Thankfully, my mom finally interrupted him, ending my Roman inquisition. She convinced him to write down his questions and then rewrite them in English so we could all discuss them together. Dad got this wild look in his eyes, rubbed his scalp through his thinning hair, which caused some of those said hairs to stand up on end, and then sequestered himself in his office for the rest of the evening.

When mom dropped me off at Keia's on Saturday afternoon I lifted my face to the sun soaking in the heat and energy of the warm September afternoon. I watched a slight breeze pluck one of only a few red leaves from a tree in Keia's front yard. I was nervous and excited at the same time. We had been planning the ceremony we were going to do tonight since yesterday. On one hand I was hoping that it would work, but on the other hand I was kind of scared. *What if I disappeared again and then couldn't get back? Would I die? Really pleasant thoughts, Salena.* My mind was racing as I rang Keia's doorbell.

"Hi Salena! It's good to see you up and about. I'm glad you're okay," Keia's older brother Tim said with a smile as he opened the door. Whatever I was thinking fled like a scared rabbit out of my brain the moment I laid eyes on him. *Wow, I really had it bad.* I felt myself flush and stammer my thanks as I looked down at my feet. My toenails needed painting, and I forgot to shave my legs.

"Keia! Salena's here!" Tim yelled back into the house as he smiled indulgently at me. He's known that I've had a major thing for him since about the fifth grade, but he's never seen me as anything more than Keia's little friend. Although, he is sixteen, so I don't know what I expect him to think of someone three years younger. I snuck a peek at him with my new eyes. His aura was a gentle pulsing mix of silver and a clear red. As pleasing as that was to gaze upon, it was his physical attributes that always got my blood pumping and tied up my tongue. He transformed a couple of years ago from this lanky boy into a tall, athletic, yummy package. His light brown, top-of-the-ear length hair has golden highlights from his devotion to water sports, and he could so totally pull off the cute puppy dog look that make my legs go all wobbly. I wished for the millionth time that I could do more than mumble incoherently in his presence. Thankfully, once again, my BFF saved me from making a complete ass out of myself.

"Hi, Salena!" Keia gushed as she grabbed my hand, ignored her brother, and pulled me into the foyer of her house. I looked back at Tim and gave him a sheepish smile as Keia dragged me up the circular staircase to the second story chatting the whole way. "Katrina and Sam are already here, and Leah's on her way. I've got everything ready in the game room for us to cast our circle tonight. This is going to be so awesome!"

"Glad you think so," I muttered. "Honestly, I'm a little scared," I said looking in her eyes, letting her know that I was being honest and not sarcastic.

"Yeah, I can understand why you might be feeling that way," she said compassionately. "But, we'll all be there for you. We'll keep you safe." She said with determination, and then asked, "Do you think Angeni will show?"

"I don't know. . . . I hope so," I replied.

The door bell rang and then we heard Tim yell, "Keia! Leah's here!"

Keia leaned over the balcony looking down into the foyer. "Hi, Leah. Come on up. Thanks, T!" She said, finally acknowledging her brother.

Keia's game room was a large bonus room that was above the garage. It had a couple of big windows that looked out over the street, and one open to the back yard. To my left as I walked into the room, the wall had floor to ceiling built in cabinets except for the large open space that housed the flat screen TV. The couch that was usually in the middle of the room was pushed against the far right wall to make room for the ten-foot diameter circle that Keia had laid out with string. She had taped it down to the carpet in several places to make it keep its shape. Appropriating her brother's compass to accurately identify the four directions, she set candles to clearly mark those spots. *She's taking this circle-casting thing pretty seriously.*

Sam and Katrina were sitting on the couch when I walked in. "Hey Guys," I said to them as I took in all of Keia's preparations.

"Hey, Sal!" Sam replied while Katrina waved at me. "I worked all last night and all day today on aura research! I found a dozen books online, some you could even download, and I have all of these great websites that you can use too. Did you know that there is a camera that takes pictures of auras? It's called the Advanced Kirlian Aura Capturing System. Pretty cool, huh?" His enthusiasm for this subject raised the energy level in the room, collecting everyone's focused attention.

"Very," I agreed. "Did you happen to find any information in your research on how to turn the darn thing off?" I asked him, not to dampen his enthusiasm, but that's all I really wanted to know about auras at the moment.

Sam had opened his mouth to continue his

lecture on auras based on his research, and then shut it when he realized what I had asked him. "Ummm, no. I didn't. Sorry," he said as the wind left his sails.

I felt his drop in energy immediately. "Oh, Sam. I'm sorry. I appreciate all the work you did, really. I didn't mean to be bitchy. It's just hard to get used to this thing. It's very distracting. You can show me everything later, okay?"

"Okay!" He said smiling and happy again.

"Sam that research on auras is awesome and will be really useful. While you were doing that, I was figuring out the best way to cast this circle," Keia said as she took charge of this little get together. She was really excited to tell us that based on our astrological signs, we each represented one of the four elements. Sam and I were both fire signs, which align with the South. However, since I was going to play the part of Spirit and be in the center of the circle, Sam was going to represent Fire at the southern point on the circle. Keia is a Pisces—a water sign—so she'll be located at the western point. Our earth representative for the north is Katrina, who is a Virgo, and Leah, our resident Scorpio, is the air element of the east. It was interesting to me that Keia and Sam were born only three days apart, but they had different Zodiac signs. Keia is a total Pisces, and Sam is a pretty good representation of an Aries, at least based on all the horoscopes the Sisterhood had read over the years. I'm a Sagittarius, and, so far, I think I'm fairly typical.

I had worn a comfortable pair of white denim shorts with a cute red v-neck t-shirt. I kicked off my flip-flops so I could sit cross-legged in the center of the circle. After closing the blinds, shutting off the lights, and lighting several candles, Keia handed out pieces of paper to each of us to recite as we "called in the directions." We all sat down in our designated spots.

Leah, signifying the east went first. "I represent the east and air. I am the embodiment of the breath of the living, the oxygen that fills our lungs, and the winds that transport life. I add the power and purpose of the air to this circle of light, love, and compassion."

In unison, we all said, "Welcome east and air!"

Sam was next. "I represent the south and fire. I am the embodiment of passion, perseverance, and intention that heats our core, fuels our focus and ignites our imaginations. I add the power and purpose of fire to this circle of light, love, and compassion.

We chimed, "Welcome south and fire!"

Keia continued, "I represent the west and water. I am the embodiment of the purification and healing power of the oceans and reservoirs, of rain and snow, and the core element of our bodies that nurtures and cleans. I add the power of water to this circle of light, love, and compassion."

"Welcome west and water!," we all said in unison.

Katrina followed Keia, "I represent the north and earth. I am the embodiment of the nurturing, stable, healing, bountiful energy of the land, plants, and animals. I add the power and purpose of earth to this circle of light, love, and compassion."

We all responded, "Welcome, north and earth!"

Then it was my turn. "I am Spirit. I am the

embodiment of the Holy Spirit, the Great Spirit, and our connection to Spirit. I add the power of Spirit to this circle of light, love, and compassion."

"Welcome Spirit!," everybody chorused. Then there was silence. The only sound in the room was coming from a refrigerator in the corner and our collective breathing. I closed my eyes and tried to imagine myself as invisible.

Nothing. I didn't feel anything. Cautiously I opened one eye. None of my body parts were glowing. *Well, Dang! When I want glow, nothing happens.*

"Do you feel any different?" Sam asked me.

"No. We're missing something, obviously," I replied.

"What do you remember about your dream?" Keia asked.

"Not much other than being totally at peace, happy and contented, surrounded by you guys. Anybody have any ideas as to what to try next?"

"What if we all visualized you going invisible?" Leah suggested.

"Maybe, but I'm pretty sure you weren't doing that in my dream. It can't hurt to try though," I said. So we all closed our eyes and concentrated on me disappearing. After a minute or two, I opened my eyes again. "I'm still here," I said, stating the obvious.

"Did Angeni give you any hints at all?" Katrina asked.

"Nope. I haven't seen her since Thursday morning in my bathroom."

"Maybe we should try electro-shock therapy,"

Sam said with a devious grin.

"Great idea Sam!" Keia said. "We just happen to have one of those machines in our garage! I'll go get it!"

"Do you have anything she can bite down on so she doesn't swallow her tongue?" Leah asked, playing along.

"Keia, do you think your brother will let us borrow a couple of his leather belts to strap her hands down?" Katrina said stifling a giggle.

I rolled my eyes at them. "Yeah, you guys are so funny. Any other brilliant ideas?" I asked when finally I saw Angeni appear behind Leah's head.

"Hang on a sec," I said to the group. "Angi's here."

"Hi Angi!" They all said in unison. She smiled at them, and then looked at me.

"Thanks for coming. We were going nowhere fast," I said.

"I'll try to make this quick. From what I found out, which wasn't a whole lot, you're not going to die," she said to me.

"Good to know. Thanks," I replied.

"The next part is a little more vague. I think the key to all of this is love," she said.

"Isn't love always the answer?" I asked. *Seriously? What was I supposed to do with that amazing insight?*

"No . . . I mean yes, but that's not what I meant," she said, shaking her head in frustration. "You asked me in the bathroom Thursday morning if I had ever heard of anybody disappearing like you did. I told you that I would try to find out an answer that I could share with you."

"Yeah, and that answer is *love*? That's not an answer Angeni, that's an emotion."

"Look, in order to intentionally disappear, I believe you need to find your love connection to the divine spark within you," she told me with an absolutely straight face. I looked at her dumfounded and blinked my eyes a couple of times. I waited for her to continue. She didn't. The only love connection I was interested in was one with Tim, but somehow I didn't think that was what she was talking about.

"So I need to find a love connection with the Creator? Isn't that, I don't know, a bit presumptuous?" I repeated. I was pretty sure I had no idea what she was talking about.

"What are you talking about, Salena?" Leah asked me in a whisper.

"Hang on. I'll tell you in a sec," I whispered back.

Angeni gave me an exasperated look. "A connection of pure love with the Goddessence within you, yes," she patiently tried again. "As you sit there in the middle of the circle, imagine a giant funnel coming off the top of your head pulling energy down from the heavens. Then imagine these large, healthy roots reaching down from your center deep into the Mother Earth and pulling her energy up through you like sap. Visualize and feel those energies combining and intensifying and filling up your heart and then imagine it spreading throughout your whole body. That's your spark and your love connection to the divine," she said with a smile on her face.

"Oh," I said. "Sounds easy enough when you put it that way."

"You'd be surprised at how hard it is for most people. I'll stick around over here in the corner for a little while" she said.

"What's easy enough, Salena? What did she say?" Leah asked again.

I summarized our conversation for them, and then we settled down to try again. The room was warm and my core temperature rose in anticipation of this next attempt. We all took a couple of deep breaths to center ourselves. Instead of having everyone focus on me turning invisible, I asked them to visualize sending me love. To my astonished delight I was able to observe the energetic results of the Sisterhood's meditations. Everyone's auras mingled together in a weave-like pattern that was gently pulsing all around us, above and below. It was as if we were safe inside a giant protective glowing bubble. *Awesome!*

Closing my eyes, I concentrated on what Angeni had told me to do. I focused on feelings of love, gratitude, forgiveness, and happiness as I visualized pulling the energies down from the heavens and up from the earth. Emotionally, I felt centered, relaxed, and elated, but I didn't feel any different physically. Breaking my concentration, I opened one eye to look around at the group. Kat's eyes were open and she gave me a sheepish smile. Obviously, I hadn't disappeared yet. I huffed in frustration. That caused everyone else to open their eyes.

"What'd ya break the meditation for?" Sam

asked.

"It's still not working," I needlessly pointed out.

"Patience, Salena. Don't be in such a hurry," Angeni said from the corner of the room.

"Try imagining yourself back in the meadow from your dream before you start funneling the energies," Keia suggested.

"Yeah, and add deep concentrated breathing in with that. Imagine sucking in the Goddessence with each inhalation, and that it is filling you up. That's more or less what they teach us in Tai Chi," Sam added.

"Okay, let's all breathe together," I suggested as I closed my eyes and took a long loud deep breath.

With each protracted inhalation, I imagined Divine Love filling me up. I visualized myself in the middle of the meadow. I remembered the soft blades of grass, the scent of pine and dew-damp Earth, and I heard the soft rumbling of a creek. I relaxed into the visualization and the breathing. A slight tingling began down my back behind my heart; I felt the electric impulses start to spread when my curiosity got the best of me. I ever so slightly opened my right eye to look down at my arm to see if it was glowing. The slight tickle on my back vanished as soon as my thoughts veered away from the meditation. *Darn! Lost it again! But I think I got closer that time!*

"Salena, slow down. You were getting there that last time. You started to fade out ever so slightly. Let go of any fear and believe in yourself. You can do this. You've already done this!" Angeni coached.

The Sisterhood was doing their part. Their eyes

were closed, even Katrina's. Committing to my success, I closed my eyes and breathed deeply. This time I actually felt as if I'd fallen into the warm, soothing, empowering embrace of the Divine Feminine, and the energetic, vastly intelligent and safe cocoon of the heavenly father. I was truly 'At-One' with both of them.

My body started to tingle, at first in that same spot on my back behind my heart and then the sensation rapidly spread throughout my body. I'd swear somebody had plugged me into a light socket. Every nerve in my body was firing all at once, and I felt like I had suddenly lost thirty pounds. *Was I floating?* I opened my eyes to see if I was still on the floor when I heard Katrina gasp.

The vibrant, multi-colored pulsating dome enveloping our circle had increased in intensity and color. I somehow just knew that the dome went through the floors and could be seen from down below. It looked like what I'd expect to see if I was inside a ginormous energetic Easter egg. I stood up and looked around.

"She's gone!" Katrina's eyes were big as saucers. I guess she didn't really believe that I would disappear because the color had drained from her face as she stared wide-eyed and slack-jawed at the center of the circle. The others opened their eyes in awe. I felt the strength of the circle fluctuate with the drop in energy, and the vibrancy of the colors dimmed as the group's anxiety increased causing the contraction of their auras.

Then I noticed the woman. She was standing just outside the circle with her hands clasped softly in front of her and a smile on her face. Looking down at me from her slightly greater height, she held me captive with her clear blue gaze. Kindness poured out of her, so much in fact, that I could almost see the energy she was generating as well as feel it, even through the circle. Her softly flowing cream-colored skirt and a fuzzy azure sweater accentuated her casual and easy demeanor, as though she always hung out in a stranger's game room on Saturday nights. Although her clothes looked normal, she definitely wasn't. She was glowing and sparkling, as if someone had just dumped a whole jar full of gold glitter all over her and then turned on a strobe light. She was shimmering just like . . . (my eyes drifted down to my arms and legs) . . . ME!

"Hello, Salena." She greeted me with a smile. "My name is Amalya Gaian. Welcome to the Fifth Dimension."

What the heck! I looked past her to Angeni who had moved from her corner over closer to the circle to look for me. She looked denser and more solid now than she usually does. I could barely see through her. "Yo! Angeni!" I called waving my hands at her. "Can you see me? Hello?" She didn't respond or make eye contact with me. *Huh, apparently, Angeni can't see me either, that's odd.*

I could feel the panic beginning to rise in the group as they realized, much to all of our surprise, that we had been successful. I looked at my friends with concern, wishing they would just chill out. A slight haze of ash began to settle over our dome that felt heavy and a little cold, like a wet blanket. I guessed that was how "worry" was being manifested energetically, and I shivered slightly. A musical voice interrupted my examination of the circle.

"Don't be afraid, Salena. This is a beautiful and wondrous place where there is nothing to fear," Amalya explained to me. "I am your ambassador and guide."

I glanced down at my feet expecting to see ruby red slippers on them because clearly I had landed in Oz. "How do you know my name?" I asked her, glad that she hadn't called me Dorothy.

"We know a lot of things here. All of which I'd like to share with you, if you'll let me," she said with a very kind smile and exactly the same tone of voice that I imagined a fairy godmother would use. Her clothing wasn't working for me at all. She should have on a big poofy ball gown and a magic wand. *Bippity, Bobbity, Boo!*

The vibration of Leah's voice penetrated my skin as she called for me, "Salena! Please come back!"

Sam yelled, "Hey, Girl!" as if I was down the street. "We're starting to worry!" He put his arms into the middle of the circle and swept them around. His arms went right through me, which made me stumble and shudder. It felt so cold! I was beginning to lose my grip on the peaceful centeredness I had achieved. My friends' anxiety and fear had become my own.

Amalya began to fade away as I thought I heard her say, "I'll be waiting for you to return."

I rematerialized in the center of the circle, much to the relief of all my friends who rushed in to hug me. The first thing I noticed was that I felt heavy, hot, sweaty, and desperately thirsty. Just like the first time. I was beginning to see a pattern here. There was apparently a price to be paid for my disappearing act, that seems to be inter-dimensional travel. *Who knew?*

After I drank several glasses of water and took some ibuprofen for the headache that followed the dehydration, the Sisterhood of the Silver Moon spent the rest of the night going over and over what happened in minute detail.

Then, we painted our toenails.

CHAPTER SEVEN
The Grand Tour

Leah's mom, Dr. Lisa, dropped me off at my house on Sunday after Keia's mom, Lesley, stuffed us all with French Toast, sausage, and cantaloupe. I was so full I felt pregnant with a food baby. Mom and Dad were both sitting in the living room reading when I waddled through the front door.

I excitedly filled them in on what had happened the night before. The concept of another dimension that existed beyond our perceptions delighted and fascinated them both—my mom from the spiritual-psychological side, and my dad from the scientific side. Of course they had a gazillion questions that I couldn't even begin to answer. My discussion with them was almost a complete repeat of the aftermath of last night. I thought about getting the words "I don't know" tattooed on my forehead.

After they finally exhausted their questions, I headed to my room. I had some homework to do and I wanted some time to myself to process everything that had happened to me in the last week. It was all so overwhelming! I really hated being the center of attention. All I ever wanted was to be liked and respected and to fit in with my peers. How does a person "fit in" when weird things keep happening to them? I was grateful that my friends and family think my weirdness is cool, and I was happy that this was 2012 and not the 1600's when people with my "talents" were burned at the stake.

Before I decided to tackle my English and Math homework, I sat on the floor in my room with my back resting comfortably against the side of my bed. The steel-blue shag carpeting tickled my calves, and golden rays of autumn light streamed in from the windows behind my head. I closed my eyes and took several deep, cleansing breaths. Imagining my Heaven funnel and Earth roots reaching and pulling the Goddessence into me, I focused on the feelings of love, gratitude, and peacefulness swirling and coalescing into my heart and then spreading throughout my body. I began to feel lighter and noticed the same tingling sensation I had last night. I opened my eyes.

Last night I hadn't really noticed how the room and the things in it looked different. Everything that wasn't living had its own platinum energy field. My desk and chair glowed, but the energy didn't pulse and it didn't extend very far out from the object itself. I looked at the plant hanging from the ceiling next to my closet and it had a vibrant pulsating green energy field that had little sparkling stars within it. The energy coming off of the plant was far stronger than what was coming off of the inanimate objects. I stood up, turned around and looked out the window at the trees outside. The sheer magnitude of the energy I saw coming off of the landscape enchanted me.

"It's beautiful isn't it?" A soft voice said behind me. I jumped and whirled around to see Amalya standing in front of me. Today she wore violet capri leggings with a matching tunic top that sported a large butterfly created out of sparkling inset crystals. The sunbeams and warmth emanating from her had me wishing for a pair of Ray-Ban's.

"Um, yeah, it's incredible. I've never seen anything like that before," I replied.

"There isn't any way to see hyperphotonic emissions in the Third Dimension. You might be able to see their energy signatures from time to time, but not with the full force and impact that is in the Fifth Dimension," she explained.

"Hyper-fo-what?"

"Hyperphotonic Emissions – The vibrancy and energy that comes off of organic material." She explained.

"Oh . . . Um . . . That sort of sounds like something out of Star Trek. How about I just take your word for it? So, about this Fifth Dimension thing," I said. "What happened to the Fourth Dimension? How did I skip that?"

Amalya smiled at me. "You didn't. You've been living in the Fourth Dimension for most of your life."

"Uh, Amalya. I thought that I was living in the Third Dimension. I mean, 3D is a big thing in movies and everything."

She laughed. "So it is. You are correct. Maybe it's

better to say that you've been living in both dimensions, simultaneously. The Fourth Dimension shares space, time, and matter with the Third Dimension. What separates the people who also exist in the Fourth Dimension versus the people who are confined to the Third Dimension is their state of mind."

"So my 'state of mind' is different from the rest of the world? No wonder I'm called Psycho Salena," I said frowning as I chewed on my lower lip.

Amalya shook her head. "No, I'm sorry. I don't think I'm explaining this very well. Think of it not so much as a 'state of mind' but more like a belief system. There are people who are polarized by humanity's differences, who believe only in the limitations and lack in the world rather than opportunities and abundance. Those people are solely three-dimensional. Does that make sense?"

"I guess so," I replied as I decided that grownups like Todd Black—the hospital administrator who had taken Keia's Mom's job—probably could be considered strictly Third Dimensional.

Amalya continued to explain. "People who are truly stuck in the third dimension are not open to the full range of power that comes from centeredness, purpose, connectivity, love, and peace. People who also move within the Fourth Dimension are more loving, tolerant, open-minded, and forgiving. They aren't subject to the tendency toward exerting their will on others and need for control."

"Oh," I said still trying to absorb everything she said, and understand why it was important. I mean I'm not really sure how determining that Victoria Love was a Third Dimensional would help me deal with her during lunch break.

"Okay, so I think I'm getting your description of the Third and Fourth Dimension, but you're in the Fifth Dimension. Are you dead?" I asked her.

She had a light musical laugh, "No, not at all. I'm very much alive, like you. In fact, I was born here in this dimension."

Born here? Seriously? That's interesting. I wish my dad were here to ask more intelligent questions. Maybe I should grab a pen and paper and take some notes. I intended to walk over to my desk to grab a piece of paper, but instead I did what could only be described as glided, like I was ice-skating. *Okay, that was really weird.* I reached down to my desk to pick up a pen and a pad of paper, but my hand went straight through the desk. I yanked my hand back with a startled yelp.

"Here in the Fifth Dimension we vibrate at such a high frequency that we can penetrate through any matter that was created with a lower vibrational frequency. You're really floating over the floor, not standing on it. Anything we need or want we have the ability to manifest instantly from the energy of the earth and sun. Here," she said as she held out a pen and a pad of paper to me that she didn't have in her hand a second ago.

"Seriously? That is so cool! That's magic! You can do real magic in this dimension?" I asked awe struck again as I accepted the paper and pen. This was blowing my mind in epic proportions. She really was my fairy godmother.

"I suppose the way you define magic, yes. But we don't consider it to be magic because it isn't illusion or a trick. Everyone has the ability to manifest instantly. We shape and mold the energy we require to meet our basic physical needs so that we can spend the rest of our conscious time on intellectual, artistic, and spiritual pursuits."

I was wondering if I was ever going to understand the whole of what she was talking about. "Um, okay. So if you were born here, how did I get here? I mean, I'm just a thirteen-year-old girl from a small city in Nevada who hasn't even gotten her first kiss yet. I'm about as far from an intellectual spiritualist as it gets!"

Amalya's aqua marine eyes sparkled as she laughed. She then glided over to me, put her arms on my shoulders, which surprisingly felt very solid, and said, "That is a very good question! We are not quite sure we have all the answers yet because we haven't been able to really talk to you. That is why I'd like to take you on a tour of my colony and introduce you to some friends of mine who are very, very wise and might have some of the answers you seek." I wondered idly if she was going to be introducing me to Master Yoda.

"Are you ready to go? Don't worry, I'll have you back before dinner," she said to me.

"I guess," I said, homework forgotten. I did have the presence of mind though to look down and make sure I still had clothes on. I was very happy and relieved to see I was fully dressed. I didn't understand how that was possible, but I wasn't going to question it now.

"Great! This time we'll travel in tandem since I know where we are going. But to get anywhere on Earth in this dimension, you only have to visualize it and hold the intention to be there," she explained to me as she enveloped me in a big hug and my bedroom vanished.

I think I blinked, but I'm not sure. Instantaneously we were in the middle of this giant meadow, surrounded by tall trees and even taller mountains, some of which still had snow on them. For some reason this place felt familiar to me. I frowned as I tried to chase the elusive memory around in my head. Suddenly, I realized that this was the same mountain meadow that I dreamed about in the hospital and at home, only that one was empty of people, this one wasn't.

There were buildings placed here and there, seemingly without any order or design consistency. Although it looked slightly chaotic, it didn't look messy. There were no streets, cars, or shops, or anything that would resemble a thriving community. There were a couple of groups of people sitting in circles, others who were just talking to each other, and still others who were sitting alone. One thing all the people had in common was their energy fields. They all looked like freaking brightly lit stars that had mega-watt rays of silver and gold luminescence shooting out of them. They reminded me of Fourth of July sparklers. I wondered if my aura looked like that too.

"Welcome to the Sierra-Nevada Colony of the Fifth Dimension," Amalya said by way of a formal introduction.

"Thanks," I murmured as I watched a small group of sparkler-people, adults and kids, move towards us.

"Salena Hawthorne, this is Douglas Downing and Diana Pyne, two of our community Elders, and Cherie and Gregg Stanton," Amalya introduced the grown-ups first.

Thankfully all of the manners training that I endured at the hands of my parents took over as I responded automatically. "Pleasure to meet you," I said with a smile as I shook their hands and then resisted the urge to curtsy.

"The pleasure is all ours," Diana responded.

"Here with the teen welcoming party is my niece, Illiana, Diana's daughter, Opal, Douglas' son, Zander, and Gregg and Cherie's son, Jace and his younger sister . . . Where's Jaz . . . ?" Amalya stopped and looked around.

"Here! I'm here!" I heard the voice before the body popped in. "Ohh, m'gosh! Salena! It's you! It's really you! I can't believe you're finally here," she gushed while she jumped up and down, her short black curls bouncing with her. Jace rolled his eyes, but I couldn't help grinning at her unabashed welcome.

"Yes, Jaz. Salena is finally here. Jazwynd meet Salena. Salena, this is Jazwynd, Jace's little sister," Amalya finished her formal introductions as I shook Illiana's, Opal's, and Zander's hands.

Illiana's hair was the first thing I noticed about her. It flowed down to her hips in waves of spun bright gold. I noticed that she was taller than me when I looked up into her pale aquamarine eyes. Annoyingly, her pale skin was absolutely flawless. Apparently abandoning any connection to natural hair coloring, Opal's head was covered in a short, spiky bright pink mop. It sort of matched the rose colors radiating off of her aura. Opal and I were more evenly matched in height, and we both looked a little down on Jazwynd. Zander definitely got his height and coloring from his dad, Douglas, who stood a head above me with bronze-toned skin and short dark hair.

There was no doubt that Jazwynd and Jace were related. He may be a foot taller than his sister, but their coloring was identical. Jace's emerald eyes thoroughly captivated me as he reached out his hand to welcome me.

As soon as our skin touched, Jace's energy literally magnetized to mine. It jumped from him to me when our hands connected and then wrapped around me in a purring embrace. I don't think he was expecting it either, because he looked at me with a startled, rather quizzical expression and then smiled. *Oh, boy, I was in trouble now.* My insides turned to mush. I made a fist with my left hand to keep it from shaking as my stomach did a complete roller coaster loop.

Jace's sun-kissed complexion was highlighted by distinctive cheekbones and a squared off chin. His physique was, well . . . perfect. A sudden random thought of running my fingers through his short wavy hair hijacked my brain and I had to swallow quickly because I think I started to drool. I was feeling tingles in places I didn't even know existed! As soon as Jace let go of my hand, I felt like a piece of me was missing, like someone had unplugged me, and I was running on battery power.

The adults were smiling at us kind of knowingly and the kids curiously. I quickly looked down at my feet hoping nobody would see the feverish heat washing over my face. Jazwynd saved the moment by being almost oblivious to, or at least totally disinterested in, whatever it was that just happened between Jace and me.

"Salena, it's so totally amazing you are here. Ever since Amalya told us about you, I've kind of been watching you, hoping that you'd figure it out soon and come visit," Jazwynd blurted rapidly.

"Way to be a Fif-D stalker, sis," Jace teased.

"No! Not like that!" Jazwynd shot her brother a dirty look. "I wasn't stalking you," she looked beseechingly at me.

"That's okay. What's a 'fifty' stalker?" I asked.

"Not fifty, as in 5-0, but Fif-D as in Fifth Dimensional. You are a Third Dimensional –Thir-D, and we are Fifth Dimensionals – Fif-D's!" She explained. "Your Silver Moon friends are so cool! Can I be your first Fif-D member?"

"Umm. I guess so," I replied looking around at the other kids who were watching Jazwynd with slightly indulgent expressions. "So, Jazwynd, that's a pretty unusual name. How'd that come about?"

I heard Zander cough and say under his breath, "Here we go!" Opal, Illiana, and Jace laughed. Jazwynd ignored them all as she rolled her eyes.

"Oh, my gawd! This is just so TMI, but when my parents were symbing for me, there must have been this totally ginormous Jasmine bush nearby because my mom says all she could smell during 'that time' was Jasmine on the wind. It's just so totally wrong that I'm always having to tell people about my moment of creation," Jazwynd stopped and looked pointedly at her parents. "I mean, really, what were you guys thinking? Don't you know that kids can't even imagine their parents doing *that*, never mind how embarrassing it is to tell other people about it?" She tried to look outraged as she finished her rant, but everybody else just smiled at her. They must be familiar with this particular reaction from Jazwynd.

"So, just call me Jaz, please," she asked.

"Sure, Jaz. Can I ask you a question though?"

"Ask away."

"What's symbing?"

Jaz's face flushed, and her mouth dropped open, but nothing came out. One of the other kids snorted.

"Symbing is short for 'symbiosis', Salena. In the Fifth Dimension, it's how we merge with another soul to invite in a new spirit and create a new life," Diana told me.

Opal leaned over to whisper to me. "It's more or less how we have sex here."

"Oh," I laughed as my eyes connected with Jace's and my face suddenly heated up again. "Okay. Good to know."

"I'm not sure how we managed to get on that

subject so soon upon your arrival, so I think we should move on," Amalya said, attempting to keep some sense of decorum. She began telling me about everyone's role in the community, starting with herself. "In addition to being the New-Arrival Ambassador for North America, I am also the Educational Envoy for the North American Fifth Dimensional children under the age of eleven. Our children get their education in a more "experiential" way. Each morning I teleport between all of the North American colonies, gathering the children, and then I deliver them to various locations around the world based on their lessons for the day. Then I collect them in the afternoon and bring them home. I don't chaperone the older kids because they have done this enough to know how to get where they need to go."

My thoughts were racing around what she was telling me. I had more questions than I could articulate, but I didn't want to interrupt. So I continued to listen politely as she talked about the rest of the adults and kids, but my ears really perked up when she started talking about Jace.

"Young Jace here wants to be a chronicler of the Akashic Records, so his education thus far has taken him to some of the most historic places on Earth."

I watched his eyes light up as Amalya explained Jace's career path.

"That sounds cool. My mom said the Akashic Records are the energetic recordings of every spirit's incarnation. Is that what you're talking about, um, chronicling? Like a librarian or something?" I was having a really hard time imagining that this really hot guy wanted to be a librarian.

"Well, sort of, but not really. They are called the Chronoscenti, and it's one of the most prestigious jobs a Fif-D can have. Before you can even think about an apprenticeship, you have to be fluent in all of Earth's languages written or spoken in the last 2,000 years, and then after that you get to study ancient linguistics. I'll tell you more about it the next time you visit, okay?" Jace said.

"Yeah, sure. No problem," I replied, pretty sure he was gently trying to blow me off. He must have read my thoughts or something.

"Seriously, Salena. I mean it. I really want to spend some time with you to tell you more about it. Is it a date?"

Jazwynd, Opal, and Illiana's eyes popped open as the three of them stared at him as if he had four heads.

"Umm . . . yeah? Okay. It's a date. My next visit would be good. Anytime . . . really . . . That'd be awesome." *Wow, babble much, Salena?* Suddenly, the creamy, yellow with brown-striped pebbles at my feet were utterly fascinating.

"It was really great meeting you, Salena. I've got to go meet up with somebody, but I'll see you around," Jace said as he nodded to the group and then reached out and gently grabbed my upper right arm. Again, his touch was nothing short of electrifying. I think every nerve ending in my body was standing at attention.

My neural soldiers assumed the "At-Ease" stance as soon as Jace gently removed his hand and slowly walked away. *Dang that boy has some serious mojo!*

Peeling my eyes away from Jace's disappearing back, I brought my attention back to the group. Jaz was fidgeting, bouncing one leg up and down, like she had to go to the bathroom or something. Opal whispered something to Illiana, and she nodded. Both had rather perplexed looks on their faces as they watched Jace walk away.

"Can I stay with you while you give Salena the tour?" Jazwynd asked the adults, looking beseechingly at each one. The grown-up Fif-D's did that non-verbal eye-contact communication thing and then nodded.

"Sure, Jaz, you can tag along. I'm sure Salena would appreciate your company," Diana said smiling. Jazwynd squealed her delight causing the adults to wince. "Opal, I'd like you to join us too if you can," she said to her daughter.

"Sure!" Opal said grinning at me. "I can translate the adult-speak for you," she whispered to me. I gave her a grateful smile.

"It was a pleasure meeting you, Salena," Cherie said. "Gregg and I are going to head back to the house now and leave you in our daughter's capable hands. Be good," she reminded Jazwynd with a smile. I thanked them and then watched as they clasped hands and then vanished. I guess they didn't feel like walking.

"Hey, Salena, Illiana and I have some homework to do for our Metaphysio class so we need to get going. It was great to meet you!" Zander said.

"Yeah, Salena! We'll see you around, 'kay?" Illiana agreed.

"Okay, bye!" I replied enthusiastically to Zander

and Illiana before they vanished and then leaned over to Opal, "Metaphisio?" I queried.

She laughed, "Yeah, Metaphysiology. It's the study of fifth dimensional physiology." I thought that sounded like a rather dreadful subject and didn't inquire further. Silently, I wished them luck.

Amalya decided to tag along for a little while, so my Fifth Dimension tour group consisted of Diana, Douglas, Amalya, Jazwynd, and Opal. Douglas took charge and gave me a tour of the colony and explained the various buildings and homes that made up their little town. Every building was a manifestation of one or more person's thoughts, and they could be moved or changed to meet the needs of the individual or group. It was, as Leah would say, totally awesome amazing. I was majorly impressed, but Jazwynd and Opal for the most part looked bored. I tried to write things down so I could remember to tell my parents later, but I could barely hold the pen steady enough. Amalya was right. Her friends were super über smart.

The tour ended in what I guess could be considered the town square. It was a park-like setting in the middle of the colony, and we were standing just outside of a large white domed gazebo.

"Shall we sit down?" Diana asked as a round table, complete with six chairs, suddenly appeared under the Gazebo.

"Douglas and I have an errand to run really quickly, so we are going to leave Salena with you for a few minutes," Amalya said to Diana as I watched two chairs disappear as quickly as they arrived.

"No problem, we will take good care of her," Diana replied before Amalya and Douglas disappeared.

"Do you have a word for that?" I asked the group as I sat down in the chair.

"A word for what?" Opal asked.

"The appearing and disappearing act that people and things do all the time around here," I said sweeping my arm toward the now empty space where Amalya and Douglas were just standing.

"Yeah, we call it apparating and disapparating," Jazwynd snickered as she tried to keep a straight face. Opal snorted.

"Seriously?" I asked. I thought J.K. Rowling had made up that word.

"No," Diana replied, shaking her head slightly at Jaz and pursing her lips. "It's just called teleportation when people do it. The appearance or disappearance of objects is simply materialization or manifestation, or dematerialization or unmanifestation."

Opal rolled her eyes. "Mom, you're so . . . I don't know . . . *scientific*. In all seriousness Salena, us kids do refer to teleportation as apparating or disapparating sometimes because we love Harry Potter," Opal explained just slightly sticking her tongue out at her mom. I liked watching how these Fif-D kids interacted with their parents. In some ways it was similar to the way my Thir-D friends and I do, and in other ways it was very different.

Diana smiled indulgently at her daughter despite Opal's previous cheekiness. She was slightly shorter than me, and unlike her daughter, had less dramatic sandy blonde hair that curled around her face between the bottom of her ears and her chin, which accentuated her creamy and flawless glowing complexion. Nobody in the Fifth Dimension had any warts or pimples. Must be nice.

"Diana," I said, rather shyly. "I have an issue I was hoping you could help me with."

"Sure, Salena, I'd be happy to help. What is it?"

"When I woke up from my coma, I could suddenly see auras and it's really distracting. Is there a way to turn that on and off?"

Her laugh had a tinkling musical tone that I'm pretty sure I couldn't emulate with years of practice. "We call that Ocular Dynamic Resonance, or O.D.R., and, no, there isn't a way to turn it off. It's a natural ability we all have here in the Fifth Dimension. It helps us identify and classify the energy of everything in our environment."

Opal leaned over to me and loudly whispered, "Not to be confused with odor," she said wrinkling her nose for effect. "That word still means the same thing here." This time it was me who snorted.

"Ocular Dynamic Resonance? Really? That's a mouthful," I said smiling over at Opal. She was totally cracking me up.

Diana's laugh washed over me, making me smile. "Yes, so it is. The good news is there is a way that you can learn to focus your eyes so you don't feel like a cat chasing a laser light," she smiled at me as I laughed. "Here, I'll teach you."

She showed me how to focus my sight

intentionally on an object, and then how to let my eyes drift a little so the ODR lost some of its significance and faded into the background.

"This will work on Thir-D's auras or light bodies as well as our Fif-D ones," she explained to me.

"Really? That'd be great. Your energetic fields here remind me of sparklers on steroids. I want to wear sunglasses when I'm near you people so I won't burn my retinas."

Smiling she said, "Look at me and then let your eyes drift and then adjust. My light should dim to a manageable level," she instructed. It took me several tries, but I finally got the hang of it.

"What do you do all day if you don't have to work and make a living?" Turning to Opal and Jazwynd I asked, "You guys still go to school, right?"

"Not exactly. We don't go to a *place* called a school. The world is our school, so we go all over the planet and learn different things from different Fif-D masters," Jazwynd said.

Opal picked up the explanation, "As Amalya was explaining earlier, sometimes it's in a class environment, and sometimes it's just one-on-one with the instructor. One time, during one class I had, all we did was observe a Third Dimensional class being taught."

"After our formative education, once we are adults we can do anything we want to. That is the beauty and blessing of living in this dimension. We aren't limited by money, social status, body type, or gender in doing anything that we are interested in. We can manifest with a thought anything that has been created in any dimension at any time," Diana explained.

"Anything? Wow. I wouldn't even know where to start! But, even if I wanted to be an Olympic gymnast, I don't really have the build for it," I said with a frown as I looked down at my chest and stomach.

Diana smiled at me with that indulgent "teacher" smile. "Our bodies vibrate at such a high frequency that we don't get sick, ever. If I wanted to become a mountain climber, I just refocus my body self-image on the physique I need to be able to scale Mt. Everest, and I will have created the muscle mass to support me. However, I still have to *learn* to mountain climb. This dimension is all about learning and experiencing new things without having to worry about satisfying our basic survival needs or overcoming physical limitations."

I stared at her, blinking. My jaw was slack, perpetually in awe. Now I know what those poor deer feel like when a car is coming at them in the dark. "So, um . . . do you have any old people here?"

Diana laughed. "Yes, but they don't necessarily *look* old. Our cells don't break down, so we don't age the same way Third Dimensionals do. The people who do look older have been here a long time and want to look more distinguished or wise, so they choose the gray hair look. They could choose to look twenty if they wanted to."

"So is Jace actually younger or older than he looks? How old is he anyway?" I asked, stealing a peek at Jaz, hoping I sounded casual, but wanting to steer the conversation back to more interesting subjects.

"No, he's not really younger or older than he

looks. Young people are discouraged from manipulating their bone, muscle, and genetic structure until they are fully and naturally grown and have been taught how to make any adjustments safely. He's seventeen."

Seventeen, huh? That's only a year older than Tim is, but four years older than me. He probably thinks I'm just a little girl. I thought, suddenly depressed.

"How old are you guys?" I asked Jaz and Opal in an attempt to make it look like I wasn't just focusing on Jace.

"I'm eleven and she's fourteen," Jaz volunteered. "Illiana and Zander are fifteen."

"So, Jaz, um . . . tell me about Jace. Is he going to be like, I don't know, um . . . graduating soon? Do you graduate here?" I tried to appear nonchalant, but my face started to heat up before the thoughts formed into words.

"What's there to tell?" Jaz rolled her eyes and took a deep exasperated breath. "He's my annoying big brother. No, we don't really call it graduating here, we Ascend," she said lifting her nose in the air looking snooty. "Eighteen is the 'Age of Ascension' in the Fifth Dimension, and Jace is walking around like he's 'All That' thinking the world revolves around him, which, of course," she said shaking her head, her curls bouncing, "it doesn't."

I wanted to ask more, but Amalya suddenly "apparated" behind Diana. She manifested a chair and steered the conversation in a different direction. Amalya explained that feelings of fear, jealousy, hatred, revenge, and the like did not and could not exist in the Fifth

Dimension. She told me that was how and why I had rematerialized back in the Third Dimension so quickly the first two times. I had become afraid. If I ever focused too long on a low vibrational thought or emotion in the Fifth Dimension, I would quickly rematerialize back in the Third Dimension on the same spot where I was standing in the Fifth Dimension.

"That would not be a good thing," she told me. "The Sierra Nevada Colony is located in the mountains a long way from any Thir-D road or building."

Now that was a sobering thought.

CHAPTER EIGHT
Home Coming

Amalya taught me how to travel the way Fifth Dimensionals do. She had me close my eyes, visualize my bedroom and say, "I am home in my bedroom." I opened my eyes. True to her word she had me back before dinner. Time in the Fifth Dimension is also a very different thing. It's fluid, like the energy they manipulate. Apparently Fif-D people are still tied to sunrises and sunsets, but the time in between can be slowed down or sped up depending on the needs of the person. I felt like my visit lasted many more hours than just the two that had passed according to my bedside clock. I thanked Amalya for her time and the tour. She said to come back soon, that there was still a lot for me to learn. *Duh, that was the understatement of the century.*

It wasn't difficult to come up with the negative or fear thought I needed to lower my vibrational frequency so I could rematerialize in the Third Dimension. I suddenly remembered I had a vocabulary test *and* a math test tomorrow I hadn't studied for yet, and that was all it took. I felt myself becoming weighted down by the Third Dimension again. Only this time it was ten times worse than ever before. I stumbled out of my room and across the hall to the bathroom to douse my head under the sink and guzzle two large glasses of water. I took a couple of aspirin too to help combat the squeezing vice that somebody had just put over my head. Shaking and dizzy, I steadied myself with my hands on the counter and took deep breaths waiting for it to pass. It took awhile, but finally went away.

I walked out into the foyer and noticed that my parents were still sitting in the living room reading. "Hey," I said.

"Hey," they replied not looking up at me.

"Did you get your homework done?" Dad asked absently continuing to look down at whatever he was reading.

"Umm, no. Not exactly," I said.

They both finally looked up at me. "Well, Salena, if you weren't studying what were you doing? Messing around on Facebook?" Dad asked me with that annoying dad-tone.

"No, I, um, was getting a tour of the Fifth Dimension," I said with a bit of a wince because I knew what was coming.

My parents did not disappoint. At first they were mad (actually Mom was kind of hysterical) that I didn't tell them what I was going to do, and that I didn't get my homework done. Then their curiosity got the best of them and they wanted to know everything I found out. I reached into the pocket of my pants to see if the note I created in the Fifth Dimension survived the downgrade in vibration. It seemed logical to me that if my clothes survived going back and forth, then any object that was on me or connected to me when I crossed dimensions would survive the vibrational shift. I was very excited to find my note in my pocket, and surprisingly it was legible! I wondered if my iphone would survive. I kinda doubted it because electronics seemed to be hyper sensitive to energy surges, and if going to the Fifth Dimension wasn't an energy surge, I didn't know what was. Maybe I'd try it on one of the old cell phones we had shoved away in the kitchen junk drawer.

I was glad to see Angeni morph into shape in front of the fireplace as I began my story. Now I wouldn't have to repeat myself later. I got comfortable on the white living room couch across from my parents who were occupying the facing club chairs, and I started telling them about what I had learned.

"The Fifth Dimension, it seems, is another state of existence for humankind; a more evolved state of existence. Apparently there are two kinds of people who live there—those who were born there and those who ascended from the third/fourth dimensions."

Dad was really curious about what exactly the fourth dimension was since there was so much theory and speculation in the scientific community. He was completely enthralled as I recounted what Amalya had told me.

"Salena, this is incredible! There are several different Fourth Dimension theories put forth by physicists and spiritualists that don't all mesh. The one that resonated with me the most is what I refer to as the psychological state of mind theory." Mom smiled and nodded at him. I guess they'd had a discussion about this subject sometime in the past. *Who knew?*

"Anyway, my hypothesis is that all possibilities exist in the space and depth of the mind, and that we just have to be willing and open enough to access it!" This stuff really excited my dad.

"Yes, James, I could see how you and Amalya are saying the same thing. By being open and accepting of new ideas, thoughts, people, and possibility there is less judgment and polarization to interfere with full discovery." Mom was nodding as she summarized. "It works for me." Mom and dad turned their attention back to me and motioned for me to continue.

I described how Amalya teleported me to the colony and about meeting the elders Douglas and Diana and all of the other kids. I included Jace in my story as just one of the group. I didn't feel the need to go into the explosion of sensations that happened when he touched me. No, I kept that to myself.

"Apparently, I'm not only 'special' in the Third Dimension, but also the Fifth Dimension as well. The Ascended Masters, the elders told me, are only able to achieve the Fifth Dimension level of existence after years of spiritual study and development, and once they arrive in the Fifth Dimension are not willing or able to return to the Third Dimension." Mom leaned forward and tucked her hair behind her ears, as I took a sip of water. Dad drummed his fingers on his leg, impatiently waiting for me to continue.

"I guess after somebody works their whole life to

achieve that goal, going back to their previous existence would seem like a failure. Those born there do not have the capability to lower their vibrational frequency enough to exist in the Third Dimension. So, lucky, special me—I am the only one who has ever been able to go back and forth." I rolled my eyes. Dad stopped drumming his fingers and rubbed his eyes without taking his glasses off.

"I must have caused quite a stir over there. Amalya said that she felt my arrival on the aetheric when I first disappeared. She described the aetheric to be like a blanket of energy that wove itself through everything on Earth. Much to her surprise when she first arrived at our house, she discovered that not only was I a kid, but I had already rematerialized in the Third Dimension. She started to follow me after that, which was why I saw her the second time at Keia's house."

"Do the elders know how you suddenly came into this ability for inter-dimensional travel?" Dad asked me, reeling from the notion that his daughter held some of the secrets to the universe that physicists and philosophers had been debating for centuries.

"Not exactly. It definitely had something to do with the coma and some kind of 'quantum chemical', whatever that is, reaction that unlocked the spiritual doorway in my heart. I just needed to find the door and open it. Oh, hey! Did you know that we have another brain in our hearts?" I asked.

"Yes, that's been scientifically proven, but its function and purpose hasn't been clearly defined . . . yet," Dad explained.

"Well, I can tell you that when I visualize the joining of the Divine Feminine and Masculine energies in my heart, I kind of, like, open this portal and I disappear. I told Diana and Douglas that I thought getting my period triggered the quantum chemical reaction. They said it was possible," I said as I looked triumphantly at my mom. She raised her eyebrows at me and gave me a nod finally surrendering to my argument.

I excitedly told them about how the people in the Fifth Dimension manipulated energy to create anything they needed when they wanted it. I described the transient nature of the buildings and clothing. Everything was created with thought. They lived in a mountain valley because it was surrounded by natural power. That's their primary energy source. It was mystical, amazing and awe-inspiring.

"Yes, the Fifth Dimension is one of pure energy, love, and connection to the Divine," Angeni piped in. "I didn't think you had gone there, Salena, because you are so young and not exactly focused on spiritual pursuits. When I gave you that advice at Keia's house, it was an experiment. I was rather shocked that it worked," Angeni said. My mom repeated her words to my father. "I can follow you there now that I know where you've gone. It's just a matter of changing my vibrational frequency. Isn't there something else about the Fifth Dimension that you need to tell your parents?" Angeni asked me pointedly. My mom raised her eyebrows at me and again translated for Dad while she waited for me to respond.

"Um, yeah," I slowly started. "Apparently

negative emotions or energy patterns cannot exist in the Fifth Dimension. That's why I reappeared so quickly the first two times. Dad freaking out when I was in bed and then my friends panicking and calling for me the second time caused me to be afraid which instantly brought me back to the Third Dimension," I told them.

Angeni looked at me with an expression that clearly said, "Go on." When I hesitated, she said, "Tell them the rest," I gave her a dirty look as Mom looked at me expectantly.

"Ok, well, um, Amalya told me that if I ever get afraid or whatever while I'm in the Fifth Dimension I'll rematerialize in the Third Dimension exactly where I was in the Fifth," I blurted that out quickly hoping my parents wouldn't freak. Mom and Dad looked at each other, alarm spreading across their faces as comprehension started to sink in.

"That sounds dangerous, Salena," my dad said. "At thirteen, I'm not so sure you have very good control over any of your emotions, especially now that you are experiencing hormonal changes." Okay, yeah. That was probably an understatement. "As easy as it sounds like you can travel around over there, what if you get afraid and rematerialize in the middle of the mountains?" He asked worriedly.

"Well, I thought I'd immediately sit down and begin the visualization that Angeni taught me and go back to the Fifth," I explained like I had given it a lot of thought. "I really don't think you need to worry. I mean, the Fifth Dimension is all about good, positive, loving things. What could possibly upset me over there?"

We continued the discussion as we headed into the kitchen to start getting dinner ready. Dad turned on the TV while I helped Mom pull out the ingredients to make my grandmother's awesome amazing meatloaf. The local five o'clock news was on, and the outbreak in Malaysia was the top news story, again.

> ...*Officials believe they have been successful in containing the mysterious outbreak that occurred last Tuesday. There have been no more reported deaths, but many patients showing symptoms of the common cold, have not improved. They are being kept under observation in the isolation ward of a hospital in Kuala Lumpur. Other village members who were exposed have shown no symptoms. Officials have refrained from commenting on the possible strain of flu, but it has not been linked to H1N1 or the Bird Flu. In a related story, closer to home, Trader Pharmaceuticals, located in Carson City, Nevada has pledged to commit as many resources as necessary to find a treatment. Mitch Trader, executive chairman and founder of Trader Pharmaceuticals was interviewed outside his home this afternoon,*

the reporter said as the station switched to the interview with Mitch Trader.

I tuned out and turned my attention to the meatloaf ingredients. I so totally didn't care what Mr. Trader had to say.

CHAPTER NINE
Doom Buggy

On my next visit to the Fifth Dimension, Jace was true to his word and we spent what felt like hours together, discussing the Akashic Records and the Chronoscenti. Elaborating on what I already knew from my mother, he reminded me that the Records are the energetic recordings of every soul's journey from the time it decides to leave its point of origin to experience life as a separate entity until it decides to return Home. Every thought, word, and deed is recorded in these records for every incarnation of every soul. The really amazing thing is that the Records are stored inside crystals. The Akashic Chronoscenti, he explained to me, are the Master Chroniclers and Keepers of the Akashic Records. It is one of the most highly respected and prestigious callings in the Fifth Dimension, and that's what Jace wants to do when he grows up.

I could tell he was definitely passionate about it. I wasn't sure it would be my calling if I was a Fif-D, but he could talk to me about it all he wanted. I didn't care what he was saying; I just wanted to be near him. Like a junkie, if the moment seemed right, I'd touch him gently and quickly just so I could get that quick rush of energy that only seemed to come from contact with him. It was a little addictive and I was too embarrassed to ask anybody about it.

I got to know Jace and Jazwynd's parents a little better. The Stanton's had a home near the center of the colony. Gregg and Cherie chose to look about age forty —old enough to have a seventeen-year-old son, and young enough to be . . . well . . . young enough, I suppose. Light blonde hair framed Cherie's face and curled under just above her shoulders. At five-foot-five, I could look directly into her emerald eyes that matched Jace's perfectly. Her petite frame was a nice contrast to her husband's more muscular and stocky build. Gregg decided he didn't need hair, so he shaved most of it off. From what little of it he let grow, I determined that Jace and Jazwynd got their dark hair from their father. At five-foot-eleven he towered over Cherie and me in a protective and totally non-threatening way. His gentle brown eyes were a gateway to his compassionate nature. They welcomed me into their family like I was another one of their children.

The following Sunday morning, I made my third foray into the Fifth Dimension. The Sierra Nevada Colony kids and I decided to venture out past the perimeter of the colony a little way. They took me to their favorite meadow and conjured up some chips, salsa, and sodas. It was a beautiful fall day in the Sierra Nevada Mountains, but I could smell the approaching winter on the air. We sat in a circle, snacking and slurping, in the middle of a mountain meadow and talked about interesting things and it was a nice time. But, if I'm being honest, I was getting a little bored.

"What do you all do for fun around here?" I asked the group.

Illiana looked up from the stalk of grass that she had been twirling in her hand, and smiled at me. "We go to Disneyland," she said with a mischievous glint in her eye.

"Yeah! Let's go!" Opal exclaimed in a vigorous nod that made her now green hair bob up and down. I wondered idly what had happened to the pink color, and how Diana felt about this new look.

"That would be totally epic!" Jazwynd exclaimed jumping up right after Opal.

"I'm down with it," Zander said standing up. He looked down at Jace and extended his hand. Jace grabbed hold and hauled himself up intentionally trying to bring Zander down on top of him.

"I'm in!" Jace said deftly blocking Zanders' playful retaliation punch.

"Seriously? Disneyland?" I asked, as Illiana and I stood up together.

"Where are we going to start?" Jazwynd asked as she grabbed my left hand and Jace *Yay!* grabbed my right. Our group had formed a circle and were now all holding hands.

"How about the Haunted Mansion?" Jace suggested, looking at me. I hoped that meant he wanted to ride with me on the Doom Buggy during the tour.

"The Haunted Mansion it is!" Zander said, and all at once we teleported.

The last time I was at Disneyland was about two years ago and anybody with personal space issues would have to have been rushed to the hospital. I noticed immediately upon rematerializing in front of the Haunted Mansion that attendance was definitely down. There wasn't even a line. As a group, we herded ourselves into the first room, deftly avoiding the few Thir-Ds that were also on the tour. I was strongly urged not to touch a Thir-D when I'm in the Fifth Dimension. Apparently, they feel really cold. Sadly, Jace had dropped my hand shortly after we arrived, but Jazwynd still had a hold of me.

"Stay close to me, okay? I'll show you what to do," Jaz said. I wondered what exactly she meant. After the initial opening scene, we waited until the Thir-Ds had moved into the hallway before we followed them down to the Doom Buggy loading area. We had divided up into three pairs, two-by-two. Illiana and Zander were first in line. A pang of disappointment shuddered through me when I realized that I would be riding the Doom Buggy with Jazwynd instead of Jace. He was riding with Opal.

"Keep a hold of my hand, Salena. When we see an empty carriage, I'll teleport us into it. Once inside we need to create an energetic anchor to the buggy so it doesn't just pass right through us. Okay?" Jazwynd looked at me.

"Um. Sure?"

"Just don't let go of my hand. I'll keep you with me until you get the hang of making your tether. You really don't want one of these things to go through you.

It feels awful," she warned. She had my full attention now and I let my romantic thoughts of riding with Jace through a dark amusement park ride fade away.

"Okay, here we go!" Jazwynd said as we blinked from the loading platform into an empty carriage. She had us perfectly positioned inside the buggy so we weren't actually touching anything.

"This is so totally awesome! I love it!" She exclaimed. I was beginning to realize how awesome it was too. "Okay. I'm going to color my tether now so you can see it." Sure enough a bright white cord appeared that connected the front of the buggy to Jazwynd's belly. It reminded me oddly of an umbilical cord.

"Normally the energetic tie is invisible because it is just pure energy surrounded by the intention to keep connected to this machine, and usually when we are sitting in a moving vehicle we tether ourselves to the seat and our root chakra. It gives a whole new meaning to having a stick up your butt!" She laughed at her own joke. "But you wouldn't be able to see that, so I'm doing it this way. I wanted you to see what it looked like so you can imagine your own, and know how to attach yourself to a moving Third Dimensional vehicle or object. As a Fif-D you can't ride any rides at Disneyland by yourself unless you know how to do this!" She grinned at me. I smiled back at her, trying to enjoy the ride and listen to her at the same time.

"Your turn," she said nodding her head at her umbilical cord.

"So what do I do again?" I asked. Jaz rolled her

eyes at me.

"Pay attention, Salena!" She scolded me, snapping her fingers. "In your mind's eye, create a cord or rope of energy that you anchor to the front of this buggy, then stretch it to anchor with your solar plexus chakra and set the intention to keep you connected until you release it."

"Wait, a chakra is an energy center on the body, right? Show me where you want me to anchor it, again..." I asked.

"Here," she reached around with her right hand and placed her fist just above my belly button. "This chakra here is called your Solar Plexus Chakra. Anchor it here."

I imagined an energy rope connecting me to the buggy and sticking at both ends. I felt a slight pull, but I wasn't sure I did it right.

"Now imagine it white for me, so I can see it," Jazwynd instructed. My mind's eye turned my rope white. Except, it wasn't exactly a rope. It looked more like a piece of dental floss. Jazwynd cocked an eyebrow at me and struggled to contain her mirth.

"Hmm, good job Salena! Not bad for your first try," she said still trying unsuccessfully to stifle her giggles.

"Shut up, Jaz. I'm working on it!" I said closing my eyes, furrowing my brow as I tried to concentrate harder.

"I think it's great, Salena. If you ever get a nasty buildup of energetic tartar on your teeth, you know just how to cure it!"

"N-O-T helping!" I said trying to be mad at her for teasing me, but I couldn't. I imagined a thicker rope with a giant anchor on each end. My rope thickened okay, but it had way too much slack in it.

"That's better Salena, but it's too loose. Imagine it to be more like a pole than a rope," she suggested.

"Okay, one energy pole coming up!" I said and slightly changed my visualization. I knew I had done it right because I suddenly felt solid in my seat, sort of how it feels when I put my seatbelt on in the car.

"You did it! That's perfect, Salena!" Jazwynd exclaimed. "Okay, I'm going to release mine now, so keep a hold of my hand. You're going to hold us both in."

I whipped my head to the side to look at her, eyes wide open and pulse accelerating. She recognized the panic in my eyes. "Don't be afraid!" She said quickly and I felt a rush of energy from her through our hands. Oh, yeah. Suddenly rematerializing on a ride in Disneyland in front of a bunch of Thir-Ds might not be such a good idea. Although on this ride, they might think I was just part of the experience. Her energy push did the trick through. I wasn't panicked anymore.

"It's okay, really. If I didn't think your tether would hold us, I wouldn't let go. And if something does go wrong, I can make a new connection really fast for us. Okay?"

"Okay."

I saw her umbilical cord disappear and we didn't budge.

"I did it!" My grin stretched from ear to ear.

"Yes, you did! Awesome job, girlfriend!" Jazwynd and I high-fived with our free hands. "And just in time too, because the ride is almost over," she said nodding to the mirror in front of our buggy. We couldn't see ourselves in the Third Dimensional mirror, but the hitchhiking ghost was there.

I practiced making my energetic anchor for the rest of the afternoon as we teleported in and out of "Pirates of the Caribbean" (The Johnny Depp doppelganger is hot!), "Radiator Springs Racers," "Splash Mountain" (Yes, Fif-D's do get wet!), "Space Mountain," and several others. The few rides where I was able to sit next to Jace made the experience all that much more exhilarating, especially if I managed to be able to sit close enough to touch him. Sadly, though, he didn't give any indication that I had the same effect on him that he had on me. My final test for the day was the "California Screamin'" rollercoaster where the group made me ride by myself using the root chakra tether. After that thrilling ride, it was time to head back. Hand-in-hand, with grins from ear-to-ear, we formed a circle and they all teleported me home.

We arrived as a group in my parent's foyer. I could hear the TV in the family room blaring and mom cooking dinner. The reddening sky told me I was right on time.

"Thanks for bringing me home, guys. That was so much fun! I can't wait to do it again. I can't believe we can go anywhere in the world with just the blink of an eye! Thank you, Jazwynd for showing me how to make the tether. That was, I don't know, just amazing covered in awesome sauce! I wish my Thir-D friends could meet all of you!" Yeah, I was gushing.

After saying goodbye to me each one popped out until only Jaz and Jace were left.

"Should we wait for you to descend?" Jace asked. "Do you need any help with a negative thought to lower your vibration?"

"Sure, I'd like you to wait, I think. Umm, I have a pretty good library of bad thoughts, I'm sure I can dig one up from somewhere," I replied.

"Okay, Salena," Jaz said, wrapping her arms around me and squeezing. "Come back soon!"

"Yeah. That was fun today. It's good having somebody new in the group," Jace said as he put his arm around my shoulder in a casual, buddy, sort of way.

I guess he doesn't think of me as anything more than a little girl, like his little sister. I mean, how could he really? I'm not only four years younger than he is, but I'm also a Thir-D, which makes me mentally more like twenty years younger. I could never be cool enough or cute enough to interest a guy like that. I'm so stupid and silly. What was I thinking? Gawd! I probably looked like an idiot today. I'm so embarrassed! He probably knows why I kept touching him. Really, could this be more humiliating?

That internal rant was all it took to bring me down as I watched Jace and his sister slowly disappear while my body heated up, my legs became jelly, and I was suddenly dying of thirst.

Welcome back to the Third Dimension.

As the end of October approached, schoolwork intensified because the first quarter was finishing up. I wasn't able to get back to the Fifth Dimension because too many projects and reports were due, and I was falling behind.

One great thing about living in Nevada is Nevada Day. The state celebrates its induction into the United States by giving us a school holiday on the last Friday of October. Coincidentally and happily, that means we get a three-day weekend around Halloween.

Even though Halloween was on a Wednesday this year, we weren't going to miss having fun over the three-day weekend. The Sisterhood especially likes to do a ceremony at this time of year to celebrate Halloween, but also the ancient Celtic holiday of Samhain, (pronounced *sow-win*). Samhain literally means "summer's end" and was celebrated by the Celts as an opportunity to give thanks to the gods for the harvest. It was also believed that this was the time when the spirits of the people who died though the year were given passage to the next existence. Whatever spin society has put on this holiday over the centuries, it is the period when the veil between the worlds is thin and communication with spirits and ghosts is at its easiest.

In past years, I managed to find a few ghosts who hadn't crossed over, so we would entertain ourselves well into the night with ghost stories told by real ghosts.

We had this year's celebration all planned and ready for Saturday night at my house. I asked Angeni to show up in case I couldn't find any ghosts who wanted to or were able to come. Ghosts can sometimes have BIG issues.

The only thing that might spoil our fun this year is the stupid flu outbreak from Malaysia, now named the "Blue Flu" because the people who have died from it mostly turn black and blue, like somebody looks after they've had the crap beaten out of them from the inside out. *How gross is that?* Apparently the "Black Flu" name didn't catch on because it was too close to "Black Death"—the name given to the Bubonic Plague. I guess some talking head thought that "The Blue Flu" sounded catchy because it rhymed. I was thinking that a deadly disease really didn't need its own slogan, but nobody asked me.

Unfortunately, the Malaysian flu outbreak hadn't been contained as well as they had hoped. There had been exponentially more cases of it appearing all over the world, even here in Northern Nevada. From what little I could gather from the newscasts, it seems they still don't have any idea how it spreads or why it infects some people and not others. Apparently the people who have died from it are coming into the hospital with acute hypoxia (lack of oxygen in the blood) that has terminally damaged some essential body part like the liver, lungs, brain, and so on; it runs the whole gamut of organs throughout the body. Hypoxia isn't normally contagious, it usually happens when people do something like hiking at high altitudes without first acclimatizing, there are usually ways to treat that. Not with this version of it though. The doctors and scientists are totally baffled. The only thing that links the deaths is the speed at which it kills, the lack of oxygen in the blood, and the way the body looks after death. *Yuck*. My dad's even been staying late at the University for the last couple of weeks lending his brain to a bunch of other über smart people who are all trying to help find answers.

The Center for Disease Control was issuing warnings right and left, and the Washoe County School District was calling every night with a decision about having students attend school the next day. Although Leah's mom, Dr. Lisa, had been super busy at the hospital, most of us kids think the grownups are totally over reacting as adults tend to do when the media gets a hold of anything. Everyone was in a panic over the Swine Flu a few years ago, and nothing really happened except for the poor little piggies getting such a bad rap that they changed its name to H1N1.

At first we teenagers were celebrating. "Yahoo! No School!" Then we had a rare adult moment. We realized that if we didn't go to school over the winter, we would have to go to school over the summer. Nobody wanted that . . . at all. Even worse, we might have to re-take this school year over again. It never occurred to us that some of our classmates might not even survive the pandemic. No, that was too preposterous to even consider.

As odd as it sounds, now we all wait for the recorded phone call every night from the district, and then cheer if school is going to be open the next day. We don't mind going to school as much now, even if everyone has to wear the oh-so-attractive facemasks all day and sanitize our hands as we enter and leave every classroom. I'm kinda bummed because I had just bought this totally cool new vampire-red lipstick, and now I can't show it off.

I woke up Saturday morning to the radio disc jockey informing his listeners that the Governor had called off the Nevada Day Parade. He didn't want to risk the Blue Flu being spread. I grudgingly got out of my nice warm, comfy bed to start setting up and decorating for the party. The Sisterhood of the Silver Moon were all coming. To my delight and horror, Keia had invited her brother, Tim, and his best friend, Connelly Kenyon, who Leah totally had the hots for, and they said it sounded like fun! So now butterflies on steroids were zipping around in my stomach, I couldn't decide what to wear or how to do my hair! I tried to help my mom clean up, but I was strung up tight like a starving humming bird frantically flitting from flower to flower.

"Salena!" My mom had to yell because I had my earbuds in, blasting party-prep music.

"What?!" I stopped, unplugging myself.

"You are completely spazzing out and driving me crazy," she scolded me. "Why don't you go into your room and take a chill pill?" My mom's eighties lingo comes out when she's flustered. I didn't have the heart to tell her that nobody says "spaz" or "chill pill" anymore.

"Okeydokey," I said with a smile as I grabbed my dusting cloth and skipped back toward my room tossing the rag into the laundry room before launching myself onto my bed. Mom was right; I was wound up tight. I could probably use a little meditation to calm my jitters. I hadn't been to the Fifth Dimension in a while, so I thought I'd pay them a short visit too. The thought of maybe seeing Jace again created new butterflies that overpowered the Tim butterflies. Geez I was fickle.

I pulled my phone out of my pocket and placed it on my bedside table, fluffed up my pillows on my bed and sank into the downy comforter. It was like sitting on a puffy periwinkle cloud. I took a deep breath, let it out, and gratefully began to relax. My meditation routine started with taking several deep breaths. With each inhalation I visualized the Goddessence filling me up from the tips of my toes to my hair follicles. Then I imagined my heaven and earth vortexes equally infusing my heart with divine love.

Before too long, I began to feel the familiar sensation of being in the Fifth Dimension, and I opened my eyes. Amalya was pacing back and forth in front of my closet.

"What are you doing here? Is everything okay?" I asked her.

"Thank the Divine you finally showed up!" She exclaimed as she glided over to me and grasped my hands. "You have to come with me right away!"

"Why? What's going on?" I asked again as I stood up out of bed.

"The world needs you," she said as she wrapped

me in her arms and my bedroom vanished.

CHAPTER TEN
Conclave

Amalya brought me to a stop in a large round room with a domed ceiling. The luminescence of the walls and ceiling reminded me of the buildings I had seen at the Sierra Nevada Colony, although I was pretty sure I hadn't seen this building there from the inside or the outside. We stood almost in the middle of the sphere at the front end of a raised oval-shaped platform that I assumed was a stage. There were several rows of chairs in a stadium type of set up that ascended from the platform in the shape of a fan. The slightly translucent honey onyx walls glowed from within unexpectedly generating a warm, soothing atmosphere. The light coming through the domed ceiling sparkled as it filtered through thousands of glass blocks. As I looked around the room, there were too many people to count, and they all stared at me. I saw some young dude, who got a good look at me, nod to some other guy. After they had a brief verbal exchange, the young dude disappeared.

"Where are we?" I hissed under my breath to Amalya.

"In the Grand Canyon Colony's Fifth

Dimensional tribute to the Navajo's Hogan," she quickly whispered back.

"Wow, thanks! That explains it all," I replied rolling my eyes. "Why is everyone staring at us?"

"You've become somewhat famous in our world, Salena. Everyone wants to meet the young lady who can cross over worlds," she told me still whispering.

"Don't you think I'm a little underdressed for the Fif-D version of a Debutant Ball?" I questioned as I slid my open hands down my body from my boobs to my hips, proudly showing off my standard house work outfit of paint stained jeans and an old, holey T-shirt. "And, what does this have to do with . . . how did you put it? Oh, yeah, the world needing me?"

"This isn't your introduction into Fifth Dimensional society," she replied with irritation, until she got a good look at my outfit, "But I can see where some better clothes might be more suitable for the occasion. To change your clothes simply close your eyes, picture in your head an outfit that you would like to wear, and then say strongly to yourself, "I am wearing this clothing now.""

"Sure, I can try that, but I still don't know what to 'imagine' because I still don't know WHAT the occasion is!!"

"Oh! Right! Sorry. We discovered how the Blue Flu got past the quarantines and we want to show you how it happened. We've called this 5D Global Conclave of representatives from colonies around the world to introduce you and the plan we have. Historically, we have been able to track and observe Third Dimension global calamities, but we've never been able to intervene or help in any way. Now, for the first time ever, there is somebody who can carry our message and knowledge back to the Third Dimension," she finally explained.

"Me?" I asked, although I already knew the answer.

"You," she replied with a maternal smile. "Go ahead and get changed now. It looks like people are starting to arrive."

Even though I technically didn't have to undress, I wasn't about to stand in the middle of this auditorium trying on different imaginary outfits. I hopped off the platform and found a somewhat secluded area off to the side. I imagined into existence a little dressing room that surrounded me complete with a three-way mirror. After trying on a few different ensembles, I decided that an off-white peasant skirt with a green tank top and wide gold belt would have to do. I pulled my hair out of my house-cleaning ponytail, leaned over, scratched my scalp and then flipped everything back. I smiled at myself in the mirror. I'm not gonna lie. This instant-manifestation-clothing thing was way cool. I could totally get used to this.

I dissolved my dressing room and looked around at the now practically full amphitheatre. I recognized only a few people who were standing, and not yet sitting, in the front row: Douglas, Diana, Amalya, and Jace's mother and father, Cherie and Gregg. After seeing his parents, I looked around eagerly to see if I could spot Jace or any of my other Fif-D buddies, and was disappointed when I didn't.

"Ladies and Gentlemen!" A big booming voice came from the center of the stage and reverberated around the room. Everybody quieted down. "Please take your seats. Our guest of honor has arrived, and we should get started," the man said. I had no idea what his name was, but Merlin, Gandalf, or Dumbeldore came to mind immediately. He so perfectly represented a stereotypical wizard that I was absolutely sure he tried to look like that on purpose. The long white hair and beard were perfect as were the small gold half spectacles he balanced on the end of his nose. Long flowing robes and a pointed hat were the only things that were missing. I guess he liked how he looked in a tailored charcoal colored business suit better. Maybe he wore the robes when he was lounging around his house.

"As most of you know, I'm Agnus Deverell, Elder of the Grand Canyon Colony. Welcome! This conclave was called in response to recent discoveries pertaining to the flu pandemic that is now spreading throughout the Third Dimension. We have an unprecedented opportunity to aid humanity through this crisis with the help of this young lady, Salena Hawthorne," he reached out his hand in my direction and gestured for me to join him on the stage. I shot a pleading look to Amalya who just mouthed "Go on," and shooed me toward Mr. Deverell. Slowly, I navigated my way up onto the stage to stand next to him. His grandfatherly smile and the twinkle in his eyes suddenly reminded me of Santa Claus, and I relaxed a bit. He winked at me before he began speaking again.

"Thank you, Salena, for joining us." I just smiled

and nodded, completely at a loss for words. I really wasn't given a choice up to this point anyway. "Now I would like to introduce Diana Pyne, one of the Elders of the Sierra Nevada Colony who accepted Salena into their community."

Smiling, Diana stood up and walked onto the platform, "Thank you. Agnus," she said, to the room, then turning to me, "You can go back and sit with the others if you like, Salena."

Relieved and full of gratitude, I thanked her and went to sit next to Amalya. My pulse started racing and butterflies twirled around in my stomach when Jace suddenly materialized in the seat next to where I was going to sit. Inexplicably happy and uncontrollably nervous, I made my way to the seat between Jace and Amalya. As soon as I barely brushed up against him, our energy fields reached out to touch each other's, which electrified the butterflies already doing somersaults in my abdomen. I didn't know if I wanted to throw up or dance. *Doesn't he feel that too? And, if so, how does he ignore it so well?* I wondered.

"Since she first arrived in the Fifth Dimension around the Fall Equinox, it has been my absolute pleasure to know Salena," Diana began. "She has shown incredible resilience and courage to come visit our dimension several times since she first discovered her ability to transcend." I squirmed uncomfortably in my hard plastic seat as the attention of the room transferred to me.

Diana continued, "Salena allowed us the opportunity to examine and question her extensively, and this is what we've discovered. She is the first person from the Third Dimension, as far as we know, whose spiritual doorway unlocked at the onset of puberty. Through focused meditation, she discovered that balancing and joining the masculine and feminine energies, she was able to locate and open the divine passageway in her heart. This allowed her to change her vibrational frequency to a high enough level to reach the Fifth Dimension." I heard clothes rustle and chairs squeak amid an increase of whispers. The back of my scalp started to tingle with the intense focus of so many eyes on me. I slipped down a little in my seat.

Diana's speech kept going. "However, what makes her different from the ascended masters who have made the journey here and from those of us who were born here, is that when Salena becomes afraid or focuses on one of the low energy thoughts, she re-materializes in the Third Dimension. Unlike us, she does not just dissolve away and cease to be able to exist in this reality." A sudden rumble of voices erupted behind me at that last statement.

"What does she mean you dissolve away or cease to exist?" I whispered to Amalya.

"Shhhh, I'll tell you later," she told me. Initially irritated, I quickly changed my mind when I realized that I didn't want to suddenly get afraid for her and then re-emerge in the middle of the Grand Canyon.

The room quieted down when Diana resumed speaking. "The Akashic Chronoscenti discovered how the Blue Flu thwarted the efforts of the Malaysian Government to keep it contained. It seems that a pharmaceutical firm headquartered in Northern Nevada may be the culprit. The Chronoscenti would like to have Salena access the Akashic Records on the chance that she may know any of the people involved," she stated as the room rumbled again, this time louder, with the voices of people talking and exclaiming. I heard words such as *unheard of*, *impossible*, and *ridiculous*, and "She's just a child!," "What are they thinking!," and "Too risky!" Feet shuffled and chairs scraped. My body temperature rose as the energy inside the Hogan increased in intensity.

Diana noticed that somebody had their hand up. "Clarence, do you have a question?"

"Thank you, Diana, for acknowledging me," he said as he stood up. Clarence looked to be about the same age as my parents, although his light brown hair hadn't started receding as much as my dad's. His small flat nose made his eyes look bigger than they really were. At over six feet tall, thin, with an angular face, he kind of reminded me of a praying mantis. At least he wasn't green. That would've been really creepy. He projected his voice so the whole room could hear. "This is highly irregular. The whole reason for this dimensional reality is to experience a higher level of existence – an existence without the negative emotions that limit spiritual growth. Why would we want to consider opening the doors of communication to the Third Dimension and put our existence in danger?" Clarence's ears drew back and his eyebrows crept upward as he scanned the room quizzically, looking for agreement, and then sat back down. I followed his gaze around the room and watched some people nod in and others shake their heads. More whispering ensued.

"Your concerns are valid, Clarence. Thank you," Diana replied. "That's exactly why we've called this meeting here today. The choice to open the communication between the dimensions is not risk-free, so we felt that we needed to call this caucus and give you all the opportunity to understand what is at stake here." The audience quieted down. Diana, once again, had their complete focus.

"The pandemic is spreading fast and could potentially derail all of humanity's evolution. Salena's appearance on the scene at this moment in time is not by chance. The synchronicity of this alignment is not something to be ignored. In discussions with the Chronoscenti, and the Elders of The Grand Canyon and Sierra Nevada Colonies, we believe that the Fifth Dimension has a role to play in the cosmic shift of consciousness that is rolling through the Third Dimension now. If the results of this pandemic are serious enough, it could set the Third Dimensional world back centuries." Diana barely got the words out of her mouth before the room erupted in excited voices. I saw some people get up and move over by other individuals with whom they continued their conversation in earnest.

Diana let the room continue in their discussions for several minutes before she started striking a spoon on a glass that I know she wasn't holding earlier. The room quieted down again as the glass and spoon disappeared. "Ladies and Gentlemen, I want to give you plenty of time to discuss this turn of events with each other and we will have that time soon. It was important that you see Salena, and know that she truly exists; but, she doesn't need to stay here for our discussions, and she doesn't need your permission to enter the Akashic Records since she was already invited by the Chronoscenti. Amalya Gaian and Acolyte Jace Stanton will accompany her to Niaca." *Holy Crap! I'm going to the Akashic Records with Jace and Amalya?!* Eyes wide open, expressing my bewildered surprise, I turned to look directly at my smiling and nodding companions.

The Sierra Nevada Colony Elder continued to speak over our non-verbal conversation, "I am hopeful that by the time Salena returns from that visit, we will have come to a consensus regarding our involvement in the Third Dimension's latest global crisis." On that note, the room erupted in a cacophony of voices. I watched the audience break off into discussion groups and the chairs disappear and reappear to accommodate the people who created them.

"Come on, let's go outside before we leave for Niaca," Jace grabbed my hand to lead me toward a door that wasn't there before, Amalya trailing in our wake. Once outside of the Hogan, the majesty of the Grand Canyon's walls with their luminescent earth tone colors, a whooshing from the Colorado River and the distinctive cry of a red-tailed hawk stopped me cold. A rush of energy from the surroundings poured into me so effortlessly I felt like purring. Then I remembered what we were doing there.

"Okay, spill," I said to Amalya and Jace. "What

did Diana mean when she said you 'cease to exist'?"

"All right, I'll start," Amalya began. "I've already told you that fear, hate, greed, jealousy, etcetera cannot exist in this dimension, right?"

"Yeah, that's how I go back home, I use a fear thought," I said, and then realized that sounded somehow wrong. I shouldn't have to be "afraid" to go back home.

"The end result is that you are no longer in this dimension, correct?" She prompted me.

"Yeah, go on," I responded.

"Well, the same thing basically happens to us, except that we don't technically rematerialize, in another dimension. We simply dissolve and evaporate into the spirit world," Amalya attempted to explain. My jaw dropped and my eyes opened really wide.

"So you DIE?" I asked thinking that over population wouldn't be a problem in the Third Dimension if people died every time they had a negative thought. In fact, having a population at all might be a problem.

"This physical form ceases to exist, yes, but our spirits are eternal, they never 'die.' You need to remember that on this dimension nobody lacks for anything, ever. All we need or want is available for us to create. Nobody has more than or less than somebody else. There is no disease or illness because there is no fear or stress. When we have learned what we came here to learn, we can choose to, what we call, 'evanesce' – which means to turn to vapor. The risk that Diana referred to is that if we become emotionally involved or attached to somebody from the Third Dimension we run the risk of involuntary evanescence."

Involuntary evanescence, huh. I suppose that is one way to put it. I just looked at her with my mouth impersonating a hungry Venus Fly Trap and my eyes repeatedly blinking. I was very grateful for the abundant energy coming from the canyon; it was helping me maintain my objectivity. I firmly decided I wouldn't think too hard about what Amalya had just said until I was back in the Third Dimension where I could worry about them to my heart's content.

"So the caves where the Akashic Records are located are in a place called Niaca?" I asked.

"Yes," Jace replied as he scrunched up his face. I got the feeling that he wasn't happy about something. "I told you that the Records are stored in crystals, and that's true it's just not the whole story. They are stored in these giant selenite crystals that are located 1,000 feet below ground under the Niaca Mountain in Mexico. Not only were they buried deep in the ground, they were immersed in very hot, magma heated water. Twelve years ago, the company that had been mining the land for lead, silver, and zinc pumped the water out of the Akashic cave and discovered the giant crystals. Thankfully, the crystals don't have any significant third dimensional commercial value and their sheer majesty has inspired the company and scientists to preserve them."

"They really have no idea what they've stumbled upon, do they?" I asked thoroughly enchanted by Jace's story. I made a mental note to Google Niaca when I got back home.

"No. Thankfully the records can't be accessed physically in the Third Dimension like they can in this dimension and the ones beyond this one. Some Third Dimensional Spiritual Masters have accessed them through Fourth Dimensional altered states of consciousness and have written about their experiences, but they haven't physically entered them like you are going to do," he replied.

"What?! Back up a sec. What do you mean like I'm going to do?"

"The Chronoscenti want to show you how the virus was spread. They found the energy signature of the person or persons involved and believe that if you watch the events unfold, you may be able to help. In order to do that, you have to enter the Akashic Records," he told me.

"So I just go into the cave and a Fifth Dimensional IMAX Theater appears?"

"Um, no, not exactly," he paused, breaking eye contact with me and looking up as if he was trying to access the far reaches of his brain. "You get energetically transported inside the crystals," he winced as he told me, bracing for my reaction.

"Oh, Hell no! Seriously? What drugs are you on dude? I don't think so! I am so not merging with a rock!" I exclaimed. "I have a Halloween party to get back to. My mom's probably having kittens about now wondering why I've been gone so long. I don't have time to get all metaphysical with crystal!"

"When you leave here, I'll go back and tell your

mom where you've gone," Angeni said suddenly from behind me. An involuntary shriek escaped me as I jumped and turn to face my spirit guide. *Dang, I hate being startled. How does Angeni always know where to find me?* I asked her once and she told me that she implanted a psychic GPS in my brain while I was sleeping. *She thinks she's so funny.*

Recovering quickly, I put my hands on my hips. "Do you know what they want me to do? And you think I should do it?!"

"Yes, Salena, to both of your questions, I do," Angeni replied in her soothing, gentle voice. "The Akashic Records are not just stored in any old rocks, they are stored in Selenite gypsum crystals. Selenite got its name from the Greek Goddess Selene, just like you, which, by the way, is not as coincidental as it might seem. Remember, I told you that I felt the happenings in Malaysia were somehow 'energetically bigger'? Well, I knew I wouldn't be getting that 'sense' of it if you weren't going to be somehow involved. Your life purpose is all wrapped up in this global event. I think the Chronoscenti know this as well, which is why they have invited you into their treasured sanctum. By the way, it is quite an honor and privilege to be able to enter the Records, don't turn down the invitation lightly."

I blew a few stray hairs out of my face. "Oh boy, oh boy," I mumbled as I sorted through everything I heard and tried to make a decision.

"You'll still be back in time for your party," Jace piped in. "Time, as you and I know it, doesn't exist inside the Records. You can experience somebody's whole soul journey in a matter of seconds of 3D time."

"You know all this because you want to be a Chronoscenti?" I asked.

"Yes, and the Chronoscenti know the life path I've chosen. It's because of my studies and being your friend that they agreed to allow me to accompany you to the Records, but not inside them. I've never been there before. This is such an amazing opportunity for me, Salena! Please say you'll go!" He pleaded as his verdant eyes sparkled with the intensity of multifaceted emeralds. I was a complete goner. Like I could deny him anything? Only then did I realize I carried on that whole conversation with him without tripping over my tongue or looking down at my feet.

"Okay," I sighed, resigned to my fate. "I'm in."

CHAPTER ELEVEN
The Akashic Records

Amalya, Jace and I landed about thirty-five feet in front of a tunnel that had a rectangular white sign above its entrance with the name "Rampa San Francisco" painted in the color of midnight. Two scantily clad, fine-looking warrior-type dudes stood at attention in front of the creamy walls of the arched entrance. Their star-like auras easily identified them as Fifth Dimensionals, but I had no idea why they were dressed identically in crimson-colored loincloths, balancing matching red-feathered headdresses on their heads. They each held a round silver shield and a spear. I raised my eyebrows at Amalya and quickly lifted my chin in their direction silently asking her, *Who are they?*

"The Akashic Sentinels," she told me. "They keep watch over the access to the Records, and like to dress as Aztec Warriors. It adds an air of mystique and ceremony to the job, but basically they just function as receptionists for the Chronoscenti," she said with a smile. "But don't tell them I said that!" She added conspiratorially. Jace and I laughed. Even though this was an active mine, I didn't see any Third Dimensionals milling around. Maybe they didn't work on Saturday. We made our way over to the Sentinel on the right.

Amalya addressed Sentinel One, "Please let Chronoscenti Jacqueline Cosgrove know that Amalya Gaian, Jace Stanton, and Salena Hawthorne are here to see her. She's expecting us." He nodded at his partner and vanished. I barely had time to switch my weight to the other leg before he reappeared.

"She'll be with you shortly," Sentinel One reported. True to his word a woman materialized in front of us at the entrance to the tunnel. Her chest length sparkling white hair glittered in the late afternoon sun adding brilliance to the blinding rays of her energy field. A floor-length sapphire velvet robe flowed around her in perfect undulating waves of fabric while crystals studding the material winked at me with startling intensity. Her deep, sparkling eyes that matched the color of her robe perfectly accented her flawless pale skin and thin pink lips. I squirmed as her omnipotent eyes penetrated through to my core. Suddenly feeling naked and exposed, I looked down and was relieved that I was still dressed.

"Chronoscenti," Amalya and Jace said in unison as they brought their hands together in reverence at their chest and bowed their heads. They formed a Lotus flower with their hands and fingers, which was obviously a formal greeting that they forgot to teach me.

"What are you doing?" I whispered to Jace.

"It's called a Mudra. Just copy me, hurry!" He whispered back.

I quickly tried to imitate them. The Chronoscenti nodded her approval when we looked up.

"This must be Salena Hawthorne," she said as she walked around me looking me up and down. I resisted the urge to cross my arms to guard my personal space. "Young, very young. Naive, untested, innocent too, eh? In every way, yes?"

I couldn't tell if she was asking a question or stating a fact, but either way, my cheeks started tingling as they turned beet red. *Jace and the sexy sentinels so totally didn't need any confirmation that I am still a virgin.* The Chronoscenti stopped in front of me, lifted my chin with her finger so I could look her in the eyes. She mesmerized (or was it hypnotized?) me. I had never looked into anyone's eyes and seen the depth of knowledge and experience as hers had. She radiated love, compassion, and humility. I trusted her completely, instantly.

"I am Jacqueline Cosgrove, you can call me Chronoscenti or Lady Cosgrove. I will be your guide while you are inside the Records. Follow my lead and my instructions and you'll do just fine," she said to me holding my gaze steadily as she spoke. "The Akashic Chamber is hyper-heated due to the magma that runs beneath it. In the Third Dimension, humans can't last more than ten minutes in there without some kind of protection. But, don't worry, the heat of the cave won't bother us in this dimension, and once you are inside the Records, you don't even know the chamber is there. The scientists and miners do not work on the weekends, so we'll have the place to ourselves. Any questions?" she asked as a gazillion of them bombarded my thoughts even though I felt my head shaking "no" in unison with Jace's and Amalya's. *What was with that?*

"Ok, then. Let's go." Lady Cosgrove smiled as we all held hands and the "Rampa San Francisco" sign disappeared.

The next moment I found myself inside a chamber of awe-inspiring giant crystal beams and formations that I could only describe as something like Superman's Fortress of Solitude. This chamber was easily the size of a basketball court. There were hundreds of ginormous semi-translucent crystal pillars haphazardly jutting out from the floor and ceiling. In the center of the chamber sat a remarkable formation of selenite that unmistakably resembled a giant lotus flower, its unfolding petals frozen in a crystalized tribute. I quickly made the connection to the Chronoscenti greeting. The flower and surrounding shards glowed from within, piercing the complete darkness with its soft soothing light. The intense heat may not be noticeable in the Fifth Dimension, but the slightly rotten egg, sulfur smell, caused by the magma managed to transcend dimensions without much trouble. The stench forced me to take shallow breaths and made my eyes water.

Looking around, I noticed that there were four other Chronoscenti present in the chamber. They positioned themselves around the crystal lotus in a diamond shape that reminded me of the ceremonies the Sisterhood of the Silver Moon had done. "Are they going to cast a circle?" I asked Chronoscenti Cosgrove, totally curious now.

"Yes, it is the only way to enter the Records from this Dimension since we still have a physical body. The energy from the circle casting raises our vibrational level, which allows us to enter the Records in spirit form through the Crystal Lotus, the portal into the Akashic Records," she explained. When she pointed at the giant clear stone lotus flower in the center of the room, I was totally captivated. Dozens of selenite petals easily reached almost six feet high, spreading out and encircling the core giving the flower an almost twelve foot diameter. There was absolutely no doubt in my mind that this chamber was created by design and not by accident.

"Are you ready to begin?" Chronoscenti Cosgrove asked me.

"I guess," I said. The only thing I was sure of was that I wasn't sure I was ready. Still inside the radius of the circle, Jace and Amalya sat on a selenite beam that easily had room for two. Another pillar had either grown or fallen against the beam, which formed a perfect backrest. If they could get used to the smell, I decided they'd be pretty comfortable while I was inside the Records. "Wait!" I stalled. "If Jace and Amalya are inside the circle won't their vibrational frequency get raised too?"

"That's a good question, Salena, but no it won't for two reasons. They need to be connected to the portal, and the intention and focus of the energy from the other Chronoscenti will be on you and me," Lady Cosgrove answered. "Shall we?" She asked reaching out for me to take her hand.

After wiping my sweaty hand on my skirt, I placed the palm of my right hand in her left. Joined together, we moved in front of and faced the crystal portal. *My hand is sweating again. What if it slips out of her hand before we're completely inside? Oh, geez, I didn't think we were supposed to feel the heat in here? I'm sweating everywhere!* I thought nervously as I felt beads of perspiration chase each other down my back. I quickly wiped my forehead with the back of my free hand before anything dripped into my eyes. I took several deep breaths, trying to calm myself even though the air smelled, and even tasted, a little rank.

"Grip the left side of this petal with your left hand. I'll grip the right side of it with my right hand. This will connect us while we are inside and we can communicate to each other telepathically," she instructed. "Okay?"

I nodded mutely as I gripped the crystal petal so tightly my knuckles turned white.

"You don't have to hold on so tightly, Salena," she said to me. "Try to relax a little, but don't let go. After the other Chronoscenti close the circle, we will shut our eyes and say with powerful intention 'I am entering the Akashic Records'."

"That's it? That's all I have to say?"

"Yes, why?" Chronoscenti Cosgrove looked at me curiously.

"Well, I guess I thought that I'd learn some cool spell in Latin or something."

She laughed and smiled at me. "I'm afraid not.

Besides, it's not what you say, but how you say it that matters. And, we like to keep things simple around here."

The other Chronoscenti began to cast their circle. Instead of candles, crystal bowls of varying sizes sat in front of each of them, and in their hand was a wand-like Surdo mallet that had a silicone head instead of rubber. They were using that to "play" the crystal bowls.

The Chronoscenti calling in the East direction used his wand to play the smallest glass vessel. It created a beautiful tonal vibration of sound that permeated through my whole body making me tingle. The remaining directions were all called in the same way, each Chronoscenti continuing to play their bowl until all four had synchronized together to form a wondrous perfectly blended harmonic convergence. Chronoscenti Cosgrove called in Spirit and with that, we both closed our eyes, and said the magic words, "I am entering the Akashic Records!"

I was floating . . . disembodied . . . weightless. I sensed that I still had a body, but I couldn't see my limbs or torso. I remembered hearing someplace that this was how amputees felt after their arm or leg was removed—they still could "sense" their missing limb even though it wasn't there. The space surrounding me appeared to be a large white room with indistinctive puffy, cotton ball walls. The foggy atmosphere made everything slightly blurry, yet I could see millions of twinkling multi-colored lights shining through the haze. Looking up I gazed upon a perfect luminescent full moon shining above me. I somehow knew that was the portal in and out of this world.

I heard Lady Cosgrove's voice in my head say, *"This way"*, and a tug on what I sensed was my hand. Thankfully, I didn't feel the need to overanalyze my lack of a physical body and followed her pull toward a small red star. Somehow we funneled into that star, lights flashed quickly past me, and then we stopped and images appeared around me.

His name is Trystan Jones, I heard the Chronoscenti's voice floating around my mind. We are in Singapore right after the outbreak in Malaysia occurred. Trystan is driving across one of the two main roads that cross over the water into Malaysia.

We had hitched a ride in someone's head and were watching his past—live from his perspective. Wicked.

It was very late at night, or very early in the morning, depending on how you look at it. The road was quickly disappearing in the rear view mirror as Trystan drove toward Malaysia. I could hear his thoughts as clearly as if they were spoken aloud and he wasn't paying a lot of attention to the road. The conversation he had with this boss earlier in his office continued to replay in his head causing his palms to sweat and little beads of perspiration to form on his brow.

"Jude Bonaparte here," his boss said in greeting when he answered his phone.

"It's Trystan. I think we may have an incredible opportunity here, sir," he said getting right to the point.

"I'm listening," Jude replied pushing a little more interest into his tone.

"There's been an outbreak in Malaysia, in a small village not too far across the border from here. I think I can get tissue and blood samples from the victims which would give Trader a huge head start on a treatment or maybe a vaccine," Trystan explained.

"Excellent news, Mr. Jones. We'll give you a finder's fee and a cut of the profits. Take all of the standard precautions . . . and don't get caught."

"Yes, Mr. Bonaparte. Thank you," Trystan replied.

"Don't thank me until you get your money. Good luck Mr. Jones," Bonaparte grunted as he hung up the phone.

Trystan came back to the present as he crossed the Malaysian border. It wasn't too long before he turned off of the main road and headed down a winding dirt road that seemed to lead to nowhere. I could tell his mind kept going back to the money. He kept fantasizing about how he would spend it and was practically salivating over thought of the millions he could make. Suddenly, his car's GPS jolted him back to reality, "You have arrived at your destination," it said.

He now focused on the task at hand and found a flat area, with lots of cover from bushes, where he could hide his car. He covered himself from head to toe with the kind of gear you'd see on a Special Ops agent or a prowler—then grabbed his medical kit and headed into the jungle surrounding the backside of the village. He approached the settlement from behind the building where they had stored the bodies.

He came upon the morgue shed and

congratulated himself on his expert use of the handheld GPS. As Trystan came around to the entrance of the building he spotted a couple of patrollers roaming near the front of the community. We were treated to Trystan's internal struggle, longing for one of the cigarettes the guards were puffing on as they wandered back and forth, then reminding himself he had quit for good this time. Carefully watching his steps, he slipped noiselessly into the shed. The mask he wore didn't protect him from the rank odors that assaulted him and his stomach heaved from the reminder that the room was full of dead bodies. He moved quickly, picking the first bag he found and squatting down to unzip it.

Being inside Trystan's head, I was so focused on what he was thinking, doing, and smelling that I almost missed the black vaporous cloud that erupted from inside and around the bag when Trystan jostled and unzipped it. The smoke-like murkiness reminded me of exhaust from an old Chevy truck that seriously failed its smog check. It shrouded Trystan and then slowly dissipated. At that point it occurred to me that I was simultaneously seeing through Trystan's eyes AND my own eyes. Although I'd been watching, hearing, and smelling things through Trystan's senses, I still had the use of my own Akashic Records version of eyes. (*That is SO cool!*) I know Trystan didn't see that cloud because he didn't have any thoughts about it at all.

Did you see that black cloud come out of that bag? I telepathized to Lady Cosgrove.

Yes, I did this time. It escaped my observation the first time I watched this scene, she admitted.

Do you know what it was? I asked as I watched Trystan taking blood samples and extricating tissue samples as quickly as he could.

No, I've never seen anything like it, Chronoscenti said. *So do you think you've ever met this Trystan Jones fellow?*

No, he's not familiar to me. But unless he's traveled to Reno, I doubt I would have ever met him. I've never been to Singapore before.

Okay, let's fast forward now to the next person he meets. You've seen how Trystan got the samples out of quarantine. Somehow his business associate contracts this disease and he is the one who is responsible for spreading it around the world.

I felt a tug on my non-existent hand and we sped off, colors and images flashing by me like I was riding a rollercoaster at night. We came to a stop in a huge room where floor to ceiling windows looked out on the city of Singapore, easily thirty stories below, and the ocean beyond. Daylight shined in through the coated windows making the sky look like a giant tanzanite gem with clouds mimicking the reflections of light caused by the stone's facets. A very large dark cherry wood desk sat between Trystan Jones and the door to his office. It was almost completely clear except for a computer monitor and a picture of him with some lady. I also noticed a business card holder full of his Trader Pharmaceutical cards that proclaimed his title was Executive Director.

Where and when are we? I asked.

In Trader Pharmaceuticals Singapore office two days after Trystan acquired the tissue samples.

"Come!" Trystan said gruffly in response to a knock on the door. His clammy skin made him shiver even though he'd overheated earlier and removed his jacket. He cleaned off his desk in preparation for going home right after this meeting. He thought it was the lack of sleep the last couple of days that had made him feel so exhausted.

A heavy-set, sixty something man, stepped through the door with a big grin on his face. "Trystan! Good to see you again! How are you enjoying your expatriation to Singapore?!" The man bellowed.

Trystan winced. Mr. Marc Malicki, Trader Pharmaceutical's Vice President of Global Marketing, could fill a room with just his voice, let alone his presence. At six-foot-one, he towered over most people and had tree trunks for arms left over from his college football days. Marc still had a full head of hair even though it was mostly fading into a tarnished silver. He always seemed high strung and stressed. Malicki made it sound like Trystan's decision to move to Singapore was some kind of punishment. In reality, Trystan was thrilled with the opportunity to leave his meddling ex-wife in the States while he and his mistress, turned second wife, moved to Singapore to start a new life. Trystan stood up and went around the desk to greet Marc and give him a handshake.

"We are enjoying Singapore a great deal! Thanks for asking," he said as he shut his office door behind Marc.

"So, I understand you got the samples that we needed." Malicki stated getting right to the point as he popped an antacid in his mouth, chewed, and absent-mindedly rubbed his chest.

"Heartburn?" Trystan asked, nodding to Marc's telltale gesture.

"Yeah," he replied with resignation. "Always."

"That sucks, man," Trystan commiserated. "Yes, I delivered the samples to our lab here yesterday. They have already started to work on them. I don't have any preliminary results for you at this point, but I have a great deal of faith in our lab techs. They'll figure it out shortly and we'll be able to get started on live testing very soon," he confidently replied.

"That is good news! I would like to talk to you a few minutes about the marketing strategy I'm developing for the launch of this treatment," he said as he walked over to the small conference table to the right of Trystan's desk.

Using my own Akashic eyes I realized I could see Marc Malicki's energetic field. It makes sense that it would record people's auras too since the Records are an energetic recording of a soul's journey. Mr. Malicki's light body reminded me of that Todd Black guy at Reno General. Like Todd's, Marc's dominant color was #2 lead pencil gray, with sporadic shoots of charcoal sticking out like gnarled, burned tree roots, and a few other colors that were so dirty they were begging to be washed.

Suddenly and very silently I watched a black bubble of what looked like crude oil float over to Marc and splatter against his aura. The globule came from Trystan's direction. I had a sudden memory of all those poor birds and sea animals that got covered with oil and suffocated when that drilling rig collapsed in the Gulf of Mexico. I shuddered even though I didn't have a body to shake. I stopped listening to them talk as I watched what the oil splat was doing to Malicki's aura. The pulsing blob stuck itself just under his chest, and it just sat there throbbing.

CHAPTER TWELVE
Contagion

Did you see that?! Please tell me you saw that black oozing bulbous thing that landed on Marc's aura under his chest! I begged the Chronoscenti.

Yes, child, I see it too. And before you ask me again, no, I didn't notice it the last time either. I guess I was paying too close attention to what they were saying and not truly observing them. You have a gift for looking at situations from a little different perspective, Salena. I was right to recommend that we show you these events, she said with approval. I felt my face get warm, and then wondered how I could possibly blush if I didn't have a face.

Hmmm, it looks like it attached itself to his solar plexus chakra, she pointed out.

Chakra's again. I'd learned a little about two of them at Disneyland, but I think it was only enough to be able to make the tether. I was pretty sure I was missing some important stuff. *Lady Cosgrove, I have a very basic knowledge of what Chakra's are, but I think I'm missing a lot of info. Can you explain them to me again? Especially the one you just mentioned, the solar plexus chakra?*

Of course. The Chronoscenti responded. Her

thoughts started transmitting to me with more of a lecture type tone, as if she were suddenly standing in front of my classroom. *Although human beings have many chakras, there are seven main ones that we focus on. Starting at the very top of the head and moving down the center of the body, the chakras are: The Crown, Third Eye, Throat, Heart, Solar Plexus, Sacral, and Base/Root. The quick definition of a chakra is that it is a swirling energy center that permeates through a spot on the physical body. They are considered to be the focal points for the reception and transmission of energies throughout the physical and auric fields. The black blob, as you call it, on Marc has attached itself to his solar plexus chakra. That chakra is the energy center that governs the stomach, liver, gall bladder, and nervous system.*

I wondered if the black exhaust escaping from in and around the body bag was somehow related to the gross pulsing oil bubble sitting below Marc's chest. *Is there any way we can see what Trystan's energy field looks like?* I asked her.

Yes, there is. We'll catch a ride on Marc next. I wanted to show you that it was he who was really responsible for spreading it around the world anyway, although we weren't quite sure how he got infected and how it was transmitted. I guess we just assumed that it was either an airborne virus, or transmitted by touch, she said as she tugged my hand, and I was on the night roller coaster ride again.

This time, though, we stopped briefly in the foggy room with the blinking Christmas lights before we headed for another star, this one was yellow. We funneled through that one like we did the first one and then stopped when we were back in the same office, except in this case everything was now from Marc's perspective. How weird is that? I'm not gonna lie, it's totally freaky.

Looking at Trystan through my eyes and Marc's point of view made the energetic version of my stomach clench, and as impossible as it sounds, I broke out in a cold sweat. Attached to his aura, right under his chin, sat a very fat, solid black, bulbous body that looked frighteningly like a black widow spider. Dozens of writhing and pulsing charcoal tentacles had stretched themselves out over his whole body. I couldn't tell where the spider's tentacle-legs disappeared and the web began. The stomach clench became outright nausea when I realized that the web could continue to grow until he was completely encased in it, just like a spider preserves its prey. (*Ok, Eeewww! OMG that is SO disgusting!*) I remembered my seventh grade science class when we learned about how a spider wrapping their prey in its web, then pumps the bug inside full of something that made it dissolve which allowed the spider to suck the cocoon dry.

The parts of Trystan's energy field that weren't obscured by the webbing looked similar to Malicki's, except with maybe more obsidian mixed in with the dirty slate and muddied colors. *Geez, Trader Pharmaceuticals seems to hire only people with dirty and dark auras.*

Chronoscenti, didn't you say that it's only been two days since he took those samples from the village? I asked.

Yes, that's right. When I watched Malicki's journey the last time it was after he left Jones' office. I never saw Trystan again. I would have definitely noticed those ebony webs if I had come back to this exact time. I have never seen anything like this before in all the years I've been chronicling the Records. It's very disturbing. Salena, did you notice that the concentrated area of blackness on Trystan is different from where it is located on Marc? It's sitting on Jones' Throat Chakra, she said.

Honestly, I hadn't noticed that until just now. I was too busy grossing out thinking about how it looked like LOTR's Shelob was going to feast upon Trystan. What does the Throat Chakra do? I asked.

It governs the bronchial passageways, the voice, lungs, and alimentary canal, she informed in a perfect teacher's voice.

Is it important if I don't know what the alimentary canal is? I asked really not wanting to have to remember any more than I already had been given today.

She laughed softly. *No, I guess not. Does it matter if I don't know what LOTR's Shelob is?*

Seriously!? I gaped at her even though she couldn't physically see me. *You've never heard of The Lord of the Rings? Shelob? The big, black, nasty-ass spider that captures Frodo and wraps him in her web?*

Oh, yes! I've definitely heard of The Lord of the Rings. I read those books once. An interesting and rather chilling analogy, Salena, she acknowledged. *Have you seen enough? Do you want to go back?*

Honestly? I think I've seen more than enough, but I'll stick it out a little longer. If it's okay with you, I'd like to continue on with Malicki to see if we can find out more about how this disease is spreading. I think we may be on to something.

I sensed her approval through our telepathic connection. A rush of warm and soothing tingles trickled down from my energetic head to my toes when she said, *You are a courageous young lady Salena. While we are still inside Marc, let's fast forward to when he is waiting in the lounge before he catches his flight to China.*

I felt the slight tug on my hand as she pulled me, once again, into the Akashic slipstream. We stopped inside a very large room decorated with dark wood paneling, marble tables, and leather oversized chairs and couches.

Malicki got a drink at the bar and walked through the lounge looking for a spot to settle down. The lounge was surprisingly crowded which forced him to pick a seat that wasn't as isolated as he wanted. He let out a deep sigh as he sank into the soft leather seat. He was exhausted.

How long has it been since the meeting in Jones' office? I asked Lady Cosgrove.

Three days, she replied.

I wonder what his energy field looks like now, I said to her. *Wow, check out the lady's aura across from him!* Whoever she was, she radiated all kinds of positive power. Her primary color was a clear luminescent gold metallic that shot out from her like the sun and would have blinded me if I had real eyes. A vibrant orange danced around the gold and mixed brilliantly with a splash of violet.

Yes, she has a lot of spiritual and physical energy. Clearly she is very intuitive, artistic, and magical. She is very outgoing and courageous, but could be suffering from a slight eating disorder, probably always on a diet or something, the Chronoscenti told me.

Seriously?! You were able to read all that from her aura?

I asked in awe.

Ye . . . ssss, she said starting at a low note and carrying the "s" as she raised her voice to a higher tone, *You weren't?*

I . . . um . . . well, I am still getting acquainted with what all the colors mean. Sam gave me some books, but I haven't made a lot of progress in them. Honestly, it has just felt more distracting than useful, so I more or less tried to ignore it, I grudgingly admitted.

I swear I thought I heard her tsk me. *Salena, you better get up to speed pretty quickly on reading energy fields. It looks like that may be the only way to see this infection. Your ability to help diagnose people in the Third Dimension will be critical,* she said.

I will, I promised. *Look, there goes a black bubble heading toward the woman,* I said as we watched the floating blob move away from Malicki. I expected it to splat on her aura the way the one from Trystan had onto Marc's, but as it approached the outer edges of her energy field one of the golden rays shot out and zapped it like a bug zapper does to moths. I actually heard a slight zzziip sound and saw a little puff of dark smoke replace the bubble and then dissipate. *(Now that was badass!)*

Salena, do you realize what we just saw happen? The Chronoscenti prompted me, her voice inside my head sounded excited and reverent at the same time.

Umm, we saw the auric equivalent of a bug zapper? I asked. She laughed at my analogy and was eager to lead me to a better understanding.

Yes, but more importantly we may now have a clue as to why some people are not getting the disease, she said.

Because they have a golden aura? I asked trying to follow her reasoning.

Not exactly. I think it may be more likely that the people with immunity don't have any shades of gray or black in their aura. People with dark energy fields have an abundant amount of fear accumulating in them, and solid ebony indicates an inability to forgive or long-term harboring of bitterness and resentment. Black spikes in auras draw or pull energy into themselves, she was thinking "out loud" for my benefit, projecting her thoughts.

So you're saying that those charred branch-like spikes I saw jutting out of Trystan and Marc are physically attracting those nasty crude oil bubble blobs? I speculated.

Almost, Salena. What I think may be happening, is that the bubbles are attracted to energy fields in general, which would account for the one floating toward the lady across from Marc. But the dark areas allow the blobs to find a place on the aura to attach and then grow, it "sucks them in," if you will.

I waited for her to continue, silently chewing on all the thoughts racing through my mind as I watched a couple more crude oil bubbles float away from Malicki. Another one headed toward the woman across from him, and it suffered the same fate as its predecessor. Yet another kept going, floating away, getting smaller and smaller in diameter until it just vanished. *Huh, I guess they don't have a very long shelf life*, I mused.

Yes, I saw that. It makes sense if you think of a black aura absorbing energy around it. If these bubbles are a negative energy contagion, they would be self-sustaining only for as long as their individual power lasted. If they don't attach to a host, they would eventually eat up their own energy and dissipate completely, like a parasite.

Her transmitted thoughts went silent while I struggled to remember what I learned about parasites in my science class. The image of a big blood-sucking tick came to mind and I shuddered.

Thankfully, the Chronoscenti's voice interrupted my train of thought. *Salena, we have discovered some very important things here. I'll report our findings to the Fifth Dimensional Conclave when we get back. I suspect somebody from there will want to do some scientific research to prove our hypotheses.*

After all those years in elementary school, I finally have an idea for the most awesome science project, and we don't have to do one in eighth grade. That's just wrong.

The Chronoscenti's telepathic voice once again put a stop to my rambling self-dialog. *Let's jump ahead a few weeks to a meeting that Malicki attends in Carson City. In your third dimensional timeline this meeting was about a week and a half ago. In accordance with our original intention for bringing you in here, there could be someone at the meeting you might recognize. Maybe now that we have a better idea as to what is happening, you might be more effective in communicating with them.*

I didn't have time to question her or comment on my ability, or lack thereof, to "communicate" with somebody from Trader Pharmaceuticals before I felt the now familiar tug and speeding-train-through-a-lighted-tunnel sensation of time traveling through the Akashic Records.

Still attached to Malicki, we came to a stop inside

a very large room whose second story windows looked out at the snow-capped Sierra Mountains. We did have a little bit of snow a week or so ago. I didn't think that much of it had stuck around. The room was totally dominated by a ginormous conference table made from dark cherry wood with inlaid granite. About thirty leather high-backed executive chairs surrounded the table—one-third of which were occupied by men. (*Wow, not a single woman was in this room.*)

At the far end of the room, high on the wall, were three sixty-inch monitors. The face of a man I'd seen on the news was staring at me from the monitor in the center. He said he was sorry he couldn't be there in person, but his wife decided at the last minute to go visit her family in Washington State, so he figured it was the perfect opportunity to get away with his assistant on his yacht to "get caught up on his contracts" he said with a wink. All the guys in the room guffawed and made some lewd remarks at his unspoken message.

At the opposite end of the room sat a tall, balding man who looked like he may have been an athlete once, but couldn't be bothered anymore. What was left of his platinum hair collected just above his ears. He reminded me of a concrete gargoyle with his stern and unyielding expression and his dominantly charcoal energy field. I was grateful I didn't recognize him, but he was obviously some big shot, or he was just acting like one.

So, I'm guessing we are in Carson City now, I said to Lady Cosgrove.

Yes, at Trader Pharmaceuticals Headquarters, she

replied.

Who is the dude at the head of the table?

Mr. Jude Bonaparte, the President, the Chronoscenti said.

I remember that name! That's the guy who sent Trystan to the village to get the samples! I thought the guy on the TV Screen, Mr. Mitch Trader, was . . . um . . . like, the Main Man here. He's been on TV a whole bunch trying to convince us that he's going to save us all.

I'm not sure about their company structure, Salena. But, I think you can pretty much assume that as the owner, Mitch Trader is deeply involved in the company, even if he isn't President.

Well, if our guess is correct, it won't be long before Trader Pharmaceuticals is looking for a new President. Check out his aura. I've never seen such a dark shade of charcoal. Occasionally, I saw a moldy brick and dirty navy, but the dominate color totally reminded me of smoke from a house fire. I looked around the room and noticed that some shade of muted dirty gray was the prevailing color of everyone's energy field except one guy.

He sat slightly detached from the main body of the group closer to the TV screen. His pure white, abundant hair was carefully and conservatively styled. His periwinkle eyes held a degree of compassion that was noticeably absent from the other attendees at the meeting. His energy field was bright metallic silver mixed with soft lapis and pale amber pulsating in and out. Despite his seat at this table, I was pretty confident he wasn't a member of the "In" crowd. I wondered why he worked for them.

Marc Malicki was sitting a few seats down from Mr. Bonaparte's left side. I changed my focus from energy fields to faces as I looked across the table and totally unexpectedly recognized the man staring back in our direction. Katrina's dad was here! I knew he was some kind of product liability lawyer, and that he divorced Kat's mom last year because he couldn't stop sleeping around. I haven't seen too much of him because Kat is more frequently with her mom than her dad due to his travel schedule. That was okay with me, though, I never really liked the guy. From what Kat has said, she's really mad at her dad for being so mean to her mom. She's been coming to school lamenting almost every day about dire threats her dad throws at her mom and how her mom breaks down, sobbing. It's totally stressing Katrina out.

Chronoscenti, I didn't think there was even a remote possibility that I would know anybody in this company, but I actually do. The bald African-American guy sitting across from us is the dad of one of my best friends; his name is Dean Drake.

That's terrific, Salena! Do you think he'll be open-minded enough to listen to you?

I thought about Katrina's reluctance to tell her parents what our Sisterhood does on occasion with our mystical explorations. I seriously doubted that Dean Drake would even give me the time of day, much less listen to me. And once he found out more about my "New Agey" abilities, he may forbid Katrina from being friends with us at all. *From what little I know about him, I doubt it*, I replied.

Well, we can talk about it later, Lady Cosgrove said.

It looks like Malicki's infection has spread in the last three weeks if the amount of spores he's hatching has anything to do with it.

Chronoscenti Cosgrove was right. About a dozen crude oil bubbles were heading away from Marc. I felt like I was in some kind of slow motion paint ball fight where Malicki was the only one with a splat gun loaded with black paint. I think that Mr. Bonaparte was the first one hit and then the other dozen bubbles also found their mark. The only one who didn't get hit was the white-haired guy.

I focused briefly on our host's thoughts. Marc wasn't paying much attention to the meeting. Most of his internal dialogue centered on the fire raging in his stomach coupled with the occasional bouts of nausea. He was thinking he had never had such a bad case of indigestion and was concerned that he had a bleeding ulcer. The appointment with his doctor couldn't come soon enough. This trip had really taken a toll on him. He was exhausted.

Your friend's dad has been infected. The spore attached to his Heart Chakra, the Chronoscenti's voice in my head prompted me to look across the table at the now standing and pacing Dean. Sure enough, one of Malicki's black paint balls scored a direct hit over Dean's heart. I couldn't say I was surprised though. Dean Drake's aura was easily the darkest in the room, charcoal and obsidian dominated any other colors. His energy field looked like an angry pent up thundercloud before it unleashes a tornado.

Slowly the consequences of what I was looking at began to cascade through my brain. Dean Drake is

Katrina's father. He's infected now. It won't be long before he's contagious. If Katrina has any ash in her aura she might catch it. I struggled to remember what Kat's energy field looked like, but it wasn't coming to me. Suddenly, this disease wasn't something happening half-way across the world causing the adults to overreact, nor was it only impacting people who I thought kinda deserved it. Mr. Drake was bringing this disease into my sisterhood. I had to get home. Now.

CHAPTER THIRTEEN
Symbiosis

Lady Cosgrove, please get me out of here. I need to get home, ASAP! I urgently telepathized.

"Okay, Salena. I'll take you back right now," she said and pulled me away from the Carson City conference room. Almost instantly we were back where we started, in the ephemeral star room where the foggy atmosphere made everything slightly blurry, yet I could still see the millions of twinkling multi-colored lights shining through the haze. I looked up and saw the full moon portal shining brightly above us.

Are you ready? She asked me.

Almost, I just have one more question about the stars in this room, I said.

Go on.

Do the colors of the stars mean anything? I asked remembering that Trystan's was red and Marc's was yellow.

Of course they do. You haven't learned by now that all colors have meaning and an energetic resonance? And that reminded me of my failure to embrace my new Sight over the last month. I mumbled a rather incoherent affirmative response.

Inside the Akashic Records soul stars resonate the energy of the spirit depending on which dimension they currently inhabit and where they are in their cycle of existence within that realm. Green, yellow, and red are third dimensional colors. Green means the person is alive; yellow emanates from terminally ill or dying souls; and red represents people who have died, but haven't crossed over to the 'Spirit Dimension.' Azure and lavender are Fifth Dimensional colors. Azure tells me that they are alive and lavender reflects a person who is approaching his or her time to evanesce. The white stars are souls who inhabit the spirit world and are either spirit guides or are awaiting reincarnation, and the bright luminescent golden stars are angels, she informed me.

So, Trystan's dead? And Marc is dying? I asked confirming what she told me.

Yes, Trystan died about a week ago. It's kind of odd that his star is still red, but not everybody crosses over quickly. Some never do. All the ghosts in your dimension have red stars. And yes, Marc is going to die, she explained in a very clinical manner.

What color is Dean Drakes star? I asked with a sense of foreboding.

Let me see, she said and she went quiet for a moment. Then she perfunctorily answered, *Yellow.*

(Oh, crap!) Suddenly I was even more anxious to get out of the Akashic Records. *I'm ready to leave now*, I told her with an even greater sense of urgency.

Okay, exiting is almost like entering. Look up at the portal and say with conviction and intent, 'I am exiting the Akashic Records'. We'll do it together on three, ready? One, two, three!

Rematerializing in the Fifth Dimension from the Akashic Records was almost as uncomfortable as reemerging in the Third Dimension from the Fifth. After being completely disembodied and weightless, putting my body suit back on felt like I was being stuffed into an über cheap wool material that itched like crazy and was two sizes too small. I stumbled away from the Crystal Lotus breathing heavy and scratching my arms and legs in an effort to eliminate the prickling, poking, and stretching.

"Salena, are you okay?" Jace asked me, concerned.

"Yeah, give me a sec," I panted.

Once the disorientation subsided and my skin stopped feeling like I was rolling naked down a hill of weeds, the memories of what I'd learned inside the Records came flooding back along with a rush of fear for Katrina and her family.

"Oh, God, Jace! I have to get home!" I cried desperately. "It's Kat, she's in danger! Her dad. He's infected. I have to help them!" I stammered pleading. I was reaching out to Jace when his eyes got big with concern.

"Salena!" He yelled, although I could barely hear him. "Don't be afraid!" He cried as he reached out for me.

"What?!" I yelled because his voice sounded so far away. And then it hit me. *OH NO! OH CRAP! OH CRAP! OH CRAP! I am reentering the Third Dimension!* I started to feel the overwhelming heat and humidity of the Crystal Cave creep over my skin, making me sweaty and clammy. Everyone in the cave started to become translucent and ephemeral. Panicked, I grabbed for Jace's outstretched hands. Instantaneously I was infused with an energetic pulse of pleasure that vibrated from my toes up my legs through my abdomen filling the core of my being. This indescribable exhilarating pressure built up from my center as if every chakra locked into perfect alignment as it filled with tingling hot energy until it reached the very top of my head and burst open in a mind-blowing, multi-synaptic explosion of pure contentment that left me shaking, weak-kneed, and breathing hard. *OOHH!! MY GOD!! WHAT WAS THAT?!* I exclaimed inside, trying to keep the smile from consuming my face as I reveled in my current state of pure bliss. Then I realized that Jace's arms were wrapped tightly around me and he, too, was shaking.

"Salena, I'm sorry. I didn't know what else to do. I'm so sorry. Please forgive me. It was the only way I could think of to save you. I'm so sorry," he kept saying that over and over as he buried his head into my neck.

I slowly opened my eyes. The "Rampa San Francisco" sign was above Jace's head. We were out of the caves and back on the surface. All five of the Chronoscenti were watching us along with Amalya and the two sentinels, so I was definitely still in the Fifth Dimension.

"What happened? Why are you apologizing? I was fading into 3D, but you stopped it somehow…" I asked Jace as I looked up into the depths of his verdant eyes. I was more content at this very moment than I had ever been before. I never wanted it to end.

Unfortunately, it did. Jace gently put his hands on my waist and pulled me out of his embrace and let me go. I instantly regretted the separation as my energy dropped, then he grabbed my hand and that instant connection reignited, sending shivers throughout my body once again.

"I . . . uh . . . I . . . uh . . . ," Jace stammered as his face flushed and his emerald eyes begged me to understand. I gave Amalya and the Chronoscenti a look of complete incomprehension. Lady Cosgrove finally took pity on us.

"He symbed with you. He did it to raise your vibrational energy and take your mind off of your fears to keep you in the Fifth Dimension" she explained. I saw Jace wince and look down at his feet when she said that.

He symbed with me? Huh? I thought Opal said symbing was how the Fif-D's had sex. I didn't just have sex with Jace, certainly not by any definition I'm familiar with. Jace is so distraught and embarrassed, so something must've happened. All I know is that whatever he did not only worked, but, dang, I'd do it again in a heartbeat. It was totally epic!

"Okay, so you 'symbed' me," I said to Jace tilting my head so I could try to look him in the eye. "What's the big deal? It worked. I'm not a steam-baked, 3D Salena. Why are you so sorry?" He just looked at me, completely mute, shaking his head with tears forming in his eyes.

"Have you ever heard of Symbiosis, Salena?" Chronoscenti Cosgrove asked me gently.

"Um, sorta, I guess. Opal . . . um . . . told me it

was . . . um . . . how Fifth Dimensionals have sex?" I said stumbling over my words, heat flooding my face. I heard Jace utter a little moan. "But Jace and I didn't just have sex! I mean, we couldn't have. He . . . he just . . . uh . . . hugged me and brought me back up to the surface.

"Opal, it seems, only gave you a fraction of what Symbiosis means in the Fifth Dimension. Third Dimensional 'Sex,' as you referred to it, is only part of symbing. Symbiosis is literally translated as 'together life,' and in this world it's how we create new life. By joining our minds, bodies, and spirits with our partner we experience the ultimate pleasure of joining two souls and, if we choose, we can bring a new life into this world," she explained in a very matter-of-fact manner. I looked at her, blinking, with my mouth hanging open, momentarily speechless. Naturally, that didn't last long.

"Well, I can tell you for sure that we definitely didn't do that kind of joining together, nor did we invite in any spirits, between the Akashic Chamber and here. So I must be misunderstanding you." I said completely confused.

Amalya picked up the conversation. "Full symbiosis here is the joining of the physical body (sex in the Third Dimension), the mind, and the spirit. What Jace did was join his mind and spirit with yours, not his body. However, if any part of symbiosis is done to another person without their permission, it is considered one of the highest offenses that can be committed in this dimension. That is why Jace is so upset and has been repeatedly asking for your forgiveness."

Oh, wow! I thought, comprehension finally leaking into my befuddled brain. I had a bazillion questions I wanted to ask Amalya about their "Symbiosis", but I figured my Fif-D S.H.A.R.E. (Sexual Health And Reproduction Education) class would have to wait until we didn't have an audience. I looked back at Jace. I swear he looked more pale and faded than he did a few minutes ago.

"What's happening to Jace?" I asked Lady Cosgrove.

She looked at me with compassion, "He's entering the first stage of evanescence."

"What?! Oh, my God. Jace, Jace look at me. I forgive you. I totally do. You so saved my sorry butt back there . . . and . . . and . . . ," I lowered my voice to a whisper so only he could hear me and grabbed a hold of his biceps. "It was the most awesome amazing thing I've ever felt," I said blushing furiously. At that moment I felt a rush of energy from me pour into Jace that returned him to his normal vibrant state, and then instead of feeling drained from the outpouring of energy, I felt even more energized, happy and content. *Geez! How'd that happen?*

"The power of Forgiveness, Salena," Amalya said knowingly. "Pretty cool, huh?"

"Yeah," I said, wondering if she could read my mind.

"Thanks, Salena," Jace said, his enchanting eyes lighting up with his gorgeous smile.

"Any time," I said and I totally meant it. I think I

started to melt.

Now that all the crises seemed to be over, I suddenly remembered what had caused them in the first place. At least this time I managed to keep my fear in check. "I have to get home, guys. My friends are in trouble."

"Jace and I will escort you home," Amalya said.

"Awesome! Thanks!" I replied as I walked over to Lady Cosgrove and gave her a big hug. "Thank you for taking me into the Records and being such an amazing guide!"

She returned my hug with a fierce one of her own. "You are most welcome, child. Any time. Oh, I almost forgot. I have something for you," she said as she reached into a hidden pocket of her sapphire robes. She pulled out a piece of crystal that fit into the palm of my hand. "Here is a piece of one of the selenite crystals from the cave that broke off a long time ago. I infused it with some of my energy so it will glow in the dark. Consider it a gift from the Goddess Selene, and a token of our appreciation for the great work we did together today."

I thanked her profusely and gave her another hug telling her I'd treasure it always. I quickly imagined pockets into my skirt and slipped the precious crystal into one.

Jace, Amalya, and I arrived safely back in the foyer of my house. The living room was full of people. *Looks like everyone has arrived for the party, I thought.*

Angeni, my mom, and dad were talking in one group. I noticed that my parents' auras were weaker than I'd seen them before, and that their energy fields had a light dirty blueberry colored veil covering them.

"Your parents are worried about you," Amalya pointed out.

"Is that what that dirty blueberry color means?" I asked.

She nodded. "The kids aren't worried, but they are getting impatient."

Leah, Keia, and Kat were sitting on the couch together, but it didn't seem like Katrina was participating too much in their conversation. The boys, Sam, Tim, and his best friend Connelly, were doing some male bonding on the couch across from the girls. It looked like Sam was showing them something on his iPhone—probably a new app or something. Occasional flares of orange-fire would erupt out from the kids' auras.

"I'm guessing orange flares are a sign of impatience?" I asked Amalya.

"Yes . . . sort of. They are just excited about this evening's activities and are anxious to get started."

"Well, then I guess I shouldn't keep them waiting any longer," I said.

Suddenly shy again, I turned to face Jace, looked down at my feet, took a deep breath, and then looked up at Jace. "Thank you for saving me," I said quietly to him with a sheepish grin on my face.

"Thank you for forgiving me," he said as he took both of my hands in his and gave me a soft, gentle, and quick kiss on my unsuspecting lips. I was startled, but in a totally good way, and it sooo didn't last long enough!

Swaying on my feet, I was pretty sure that counted as a first kiss. *Oh, Wow. Oh Boy. Oh My. Oh, Yes!* All I could really think about was, *I got my first kiss! I got my first kiss! I got my first kiss!* It was totally the best kiss ever. So what if I didn't have anything to compare it to. He smiled at me, cupped my chin in his hand and gently rubbed my cheek with his thumb.

"Don't be a stranger," he laughed.

Frantically trying to remember how to speak, I finally managed to mumble something that sounded like, "Uh, no. No, I won't be."

"Seriously, come back soon, Salena. I want to bring you up to date on the discussions at the Conclave. I'll be back at our Colony later today. Have a nice Halloween party," Amalya said and both she and Jace vanished.

I whooped and jumped up in the air giving it a good punch! Spinning around and hugging myself, I was absolutely giddy with excitement. *How do I come up with a negative thought to help me descend when I'm so dang happy?*

That was just so amazing. All of it! The symbing . . . the kiss! Wait until the Sisterhood hears this! OMG! Is he my boyfriend now? I wonder if I should consider us "Facebook Official" and change my relationship status. Since he doesn't have a Facebook page everybody will tease the crap out of me for having an "imaginary" boyfriend. So, maybe the FB thing is out.

What if he's not really my boyfriend? I mean we partially symbed and everything, and then he kissed me. But it's not like he officially declared anything, or asked me to be his girlfriend, or even expressed his undying love or something. Maybe he's just being nice. Maybe he doesn't really like me at all . . . Oh, that did it. I'm feeling the Third Dimension coming on.

There's nothing like obsessing over a hot guy to crank up the fear factor.

CHAPTER FOURTEEN
Operation Aura Cleanse

Ow! Ow! Ow! Crap that hurts! The longer I'm in the Fifth Dimension the more painful it is to come back to the Third. I thought as I finally solidified in the foyer. I heard somebody yelp as I fell down on my knees.

"A little help here, please," I managed to eek out between the uncontrollable shakes, dripping sweat, and dizziness. Everybody rushed toward me at once, all talking at the same time. Much too belatedly I remembered that I had changed my clothes in the Fifth Dimension. Panicked, I quickly looked down, and to my enormous relief I still had on the outfit I had created before the Conclave. I stuffed my hand into the pocket of my skirt and found the crystal Chronoscenti Cosgrove gave me. *YES! Everything survived the journey back!* Then I heard my dad's voice above everybody's.

"Get her two large glasses of water!" he commanded somebody as he picked me up and carried me down the living room steps to his recliner. He was kneeling on the floor next to the chair smoothing the hair away from my face. "You were there for a long time today, Moonling. We were starting to get worried."

"I know. I'm sorry, but it really wasn't my fault. Amalya swept me up in my room and took me to this big meeting, and then I went spelunking inside these giant crystals. Our world, this Dimension, is in deep doo-doo, Dad. The Blue Flu, it's not organic. It's energetic." My words tumbled out of my parched throat as my brain tried to engage my tongue in an effort to regurgitate everything I had learned today. My big brainiac dad just looked at me like I was speaking Russian or something. "You don't believe me?"

"It's not that I don't believe you; I don't understand you," he said as he handed me my first glass of water. It tasted so good as I gulped it down past my dry lips.

"Okay, sorry. It's a long, complicated, and rather disturbing story, which I'm afraid is going to take precedence over the party. And, I think we are really going to need help from the medical community. Leah and Keia, are your moms home tonight?" I asked, and they both nodded at me. "Can they come over to hear this story so I only have to tell it once?" They both hopped on their cell phones, while I finished guzzling my glass of water and reached for the second one.

"Angeni told me a little about where you were and what you were doing, but even she was starting to get worried about you. She was just about to go find you when you showed up," Mom said to me as I drank down the second glass.

"I know. I'm sorry," I said again. "Oh, Sam! I have another research project for you!!" I said smiling at him. He had moved back to his spot on the couch.

"What's that?" he asked.

"Chakra's. I think they may be important in fighting this disease."

"I'm on it, Sistah!" Sam said as he leaned over to a backpack that was lying on the floor and pulled out his iPad. I looked up from Sam and spotted Tim and Connelly staring at me like I was a movie star.

"What's up guys?" I asked them as Keia and Leah bounced back into the living room announcing that their moms were on their way.

"How . . . how did you do that?" Tim asked me.

"Do what?"

"Suddenly materialize out of thin air!" He exclaimed. "That's . . . That's . . . "

"Weird, not normal, strange, wicked, sick, freaky, awesome?" I tried to help him find the word.

"Yeah, that about sums it up. You've, um, got quite a, ah, unique talent there," Connelly said smiling. I smiled back with a slight laugh. Connelly's mischievous bright eyes reminded me of the sky on a cloudless day. His ear length blonde curls gave him a casual fun look that matched his personality. He was stockier and shorter than his best friend. I could totally see why Leah had such a thing for him.

"Yeah, it is that. I guess I just assumed you might have heard more stuff about me through Tim. Otherwise I wouldn't have just suddenly appeared in the middle of the room out of nowhere."

"Are you a witch, like, for real?" Connelly asked. I laughed.

"Well, I suppose in some places I might be called

that, but no, I don't consider myself a witch. I don't cast spells or conjure up anything." *At least not in this dimension.*

Turning to Keia, I asked, "You didn't tell your brother about my new super powers?"

"No Duh!" Keia said indignantly. "We agreed it was a Sisterhood secret, remember? Although, Leah and I did tell our moms," she admitted sheepishly while Sam, Leah, and Kat were all nodding in agreement. "Tim's known about your psychic abilities since the whole Psycho Salena fiasco, but I didn't tell him about what happened to you after, you know, the coma incident."

"Sorry I questioned your secret keeping ability, but I have a feeling the whole world is going to know about my new abilities pretty soon."

"Yeah, my mom kept asking how your recovery was coming along after your coma, and it just didn't feel right not telling her the truth. Especially after the first ceremony at Keia's and everything," Leah confessed. "I'm not sure she really believed me at first, but she came around eventually."

"So guys, are you still interested in sticking around?" I asked Tim and Connelly.

"Heck, ya!" Tim said.

"I'm game," Connelly agreed.

"Great! I think I'm going to need all the help I can get. Leah, could you please fill Tim and Connelly in on what's been going on so they are up to date before your mom gets here?"

"Sure," she said giving me a pointed look that I

couldn't interpret. "Let's go into the kitchen and I'll catch you up."

Katrina sat on the far corner of the couch facing me and quietly watching the commotion in the room. She was more withdrawn tonight than I'd ever seen her. I tuned in my Sight and looked her over. A significant amount of dull platinum had crept into her energy field. There wasn't any black at all, so that was a relief.

"Kat, have you been afraid of something recently?" I inquired.

She looked at me, startled that I'd ask her a question like that. "Just the usual stuff, why?" she answered.

"Your aura has accumulated a lot of gray since I first saw it. I know it wasn't there before. Has your dad been acting funny lately?"

"Well, I've been afraid for my mom. Dad was being such an ass to her this month. I mean more so than normal. And then, I was supposed to go over to Dad's last weekend, but he wasn't feeling well, so I stayed home. Letting me stay with my mom was definitely not normal for him. Any time he can legally keep me away from her, he does, no matter what he's got going on," she admitted.

"Has your mom seen your dad in the last week and a half?" I asked.

Kat's expression clearly communicated she didn't understand why I was questioning her so much about her parents. "She went over to see him today to pick up more post divorce papers," she said as she rolled her eyes. "He's burying her in legal bull poopie, because he can. Why are you suddenly so interested in my parents?"

Damn! I'm too late! Now what do I do? Kat isn't infected, but her mom might be. Shoot! Shoot! Shoot! I thought and agonized about what to say next. "Umm . . . Kat . . . I . . . uh . . . "

"Spit it out, Salena. If you've got something to say, say it!" Kat said frustrated with me. The doorbell rang. I never appreciated the saying "Saved by the Bell" more than at this moment.

"I'll get it!" Leah said as she emerged from the kitchen with Tim and Connelly trailing behind her. Her mom and Keia and Tim's mom came into the room. Lesley's dark hair complimented her olive skin and skimmed the top of her shoulders. At five-foot-two, both of her kids were already taller than she was.

Dr. Lisa was several inches taller than Lesley. She had pulled her curly chestnut hair back into a ponytail, which accentuated her high cheekbones. Dark circles under her eyes reflected the stress she's been under at the hospital since the outbreak.

I scanned Dr. Lisa's and Lesley's energy fields quickly to make sure they were clean. Thankfully, they weren't infected, but Lesley's had some ash like Kat's, and that concerned me. I quickly looked over everyone else for any signs of gray, and to my immense relief I didn't see any.

The grown-ups exchanged the usual adult greetings and my dad invited them into the living room.

"I thought the kids were going to have a Halloween Party tonight, complete with real ghosts and everything," Lesley said. "I wasn't expecting to be invited."

Dad cleared his throat. "Well, ah, Salena apparently made a very interesting discovery on her inter-dimensional travels today, and she insisted that what she has to tell us is more important than the party. I remember when I was thirteen, nothing was more important than a Halloween party, so we are all very anxious to hear what she has to say." Dad said with a slight smile and a wink.

"Leah has been telling me about Salena's adventures, but she never mentioned that they had anything to do with the Blue Flu before," Doctor Lisa commented.

"Until today, they didn't," I said.

"Please, everyone, take a seat," my mom said.

Everyone found a comfy spot to sit as I began my story. Even Angeni stuck around the whole time, hovering in a corner. The Halloween celebration forgotten, the energy in the room had shifted from a casual party atmosphere, to a one of heightened awareness and anticipation that this group was at the precipice of something big, something powerful . . . something that could impact the whole world. I had everyone's undivided and rapt attention as I led them through my journey and the discoveries the Chronoscenti and I made.

Mom was fascinated with the Chronoscenti's use of the crystal bowls as a way to raise our vibrational levels. Dad was squirming in his seat trying to analyze and understand the science behind the existence of Akashic Records and how they worked. Dr. Lisa asked a few questions when I got to the part where Malicki was infected by Jones, then she asked Leah to get her a pad of paper and pen so she could start taking notes. Before I got to the part about Kat's dad, I warned my friend that this was why I had been asking questions earlier.

Her stricken look brought tears to my eyes. "You're sure he's infected?" She asked mascara tears streaming down her cheeks. I nodded mutely.

"He's got one of those disgusting spider-like things wrapping its . . . its web around him?" She sobbed.

"Oh, Kat!" I exclaimed as I got out of my chair and wrapped my arms around her. "I'm sooo sorry. I don't know how far along the infection is now. I just saw the bubble land and stick on your dad ten days ago. I've only seen one person with the web-like thing. So, maybe not," I said as I tried to ease her mind, but I knew in my heart that he probably did. *This just totally sucks the big one!* I blew out breath I didn't know I had been holding, letting out a sad sigh.

"You think my mom's infected too, don't you?" Kat said in a defeated voice barely above a whisper.

"I don't know. It depends on several factors. I would know if I saw her though," I said.

"So, you look at her, then what? You don't have a cure, do you?" Kat's voice changed from defeated to slightly angry. I could see the muddied red of anger beginning to materialize in her energy field.

"No, not exactly, but I figured that with the help of everybody here we might be able to find one. I do know there is no way I can do this on my own," I looked around the room at the faces that stared back at me. Mom looked as if she didn't recognize me—as though I had suddenly grown up in the minutes it took me to tell the story. Dad was beaming with pride. Dr. Lisa was tapping her chin with her pen while she bit her lower lip and looked up at the ceiling. Lesley looked at me with a slight smile on her lips and kept subtly shaking her head. Tim and Connelly had the same expression on their faces the whole time—one of astonishment and incredulity. Keia, Leah, and Sam were all looking at me with open expressions of determination and support, like they were just waiting for the next adventure to begin. It was Kat's blood shot eyes beseeching me to help her that flamed the fire of my determination to make a difference.

"Chronoscenti Cosgrove told me the Fifth Dimensionals would be putting together a task force to study the disease, especially now that we know it's energetic and not organic. The next time I go back there, hopefully they will have more answers. In the meantime, while I was inside the Akashic Records I saw two people with bright, vibrant auras who didn't have any shades of gray or black, either repel or destroy the virus. The good news about that is that not everybody is at risk. By focusing on positive, loving thoughts and releasing and letting go of fear and hate, we can resist and fight the disease. So, at the very least, I think we need to start by strengthening the energy fields of this core group so we can maintain our immunity," I said more or less thinking out loud.

"Do any of us have cruddy auras?" Tim

wondered as a worried frown crossed his face.

"Only two of us, Lesley and Kat," I said as I looked compassionately at them. "But the good news is that the gray is pretty light, and there isn't any black."

"So, if we release our fears the negative energy will go away?" Lesley inquired. I didn't have an answer for her, and then I saw Angeni nodding and heard her say, "Tell her that is exactly what has to happen."

"Um, yeah. My spirit guide, Angeni, says that has to be done."

"Did she tell you how to do it?" Lesley asked. I looked over at Angeni. She smiled at me. "I think you already know, Salena, but I'll help you along. Forgiveness and love."

Oh, Yeah! I suddenly remembered how I had brought Jace back by forgiving him. But that was so easy! I wasn't sure the forgiveness that Kat and Lesley needed to do would be that simple.

"Forgiveness and love is what is needed to clean the darkness from our energy fields," I said trying to put some authority into my voice that I didn't feel I had. I saw the acceptance of the truth of my words in the faces of everyone in the room.

"I've been pretty angry and unforgiving toward Todd Black and the Reno General Board of Directors for the despicable and cowardly way they ran me out. I'm sure that's why my aura could be ashy. I've been very afraid about what's going to happen next," Lesley confessed. Keia, who was sitting next to her mom, put her hand over her mother's and gave it a squeeze.

"I've been afraid for my mom because of the

divorce. She's not handling it well, and she's getting more and more depressed," Kat revealed to the group.

I looked at my mom for help. "Lucky for us we have a psychologist in the house. What's next, Mom?" She gave me an exasperated look.

"Oh, goodness Salena! Healing deep-seated hurts like those can sometimes take years in regular psychotherapy. We don't have that much time . . . ," my mom replied, although I could tell she was sorting through options in her head.

"I think I have an idea as to how we can help with the love part," Leah spoke up.

"Let's hear it!" I encouraged her.

"Well, Salena, do you remember when we cast our circle the first time you deliberately tried to go to the Fifth Dimension?" She asked and the Sisterhood members in the room all nodded. "Didn't you say how you could feel the love being poured into you from us? You said later that you think that trip was easier than subsequent trips because of our love and support," Leah said smiling proudly.

"Yeah, you're right, Leah! Great memory! What do you all think about casting a circle tonight with Lesley and Kat in the middle?" I was excited. *This just might work!* "I also have another idea. It's something Lady Cosgrove said to me before we entered the Records. I was surprised that the words we needed to say weren't more complicated or in some ancient language, and she told me that it isn't necessarily what we say but HOW we say it, that matters. Conviction and purpose puts the how behind the what," I told them, wondering where the heck I was getting this stuff. It felt right, though, so I just went with it.

"So, are you saying that when Mom and Kat are inside the circle they could say something as simple as 'I forgive' as long as they really mean their words?" Keia asked me excitedly.

"Yes! It's the easiest thing we can try. And there is absolutely nothing to lose if it doesn't work," I enthusiastically replied. "Lesley, Kat, do you think you're up for giving it a try?"

"Sure, I guess," Lesley replied.

"Yeah, me too," Kat agreed.

"Can I ask a question?" Connelly queried, raising his hand.

"Sure," I smiled at him.

"What is 'Casting a circle'?" he said. I heard Tim whisper to him, "Thanks, dude, I had no idea what the hell that was either."

"Lesley and Lisa, do you know what we mean by casting a circle?" I asked them.

They looked at each other, smiled and nodded. "We were both big fans of P.C. and Kristin Cast's *House of Night* series that you girls turned us on to, so I think we have some idea," Lisa spoke for the two of them.

"Sam, would you please explain the process to Tim and Connelly while I go get candles and other circle stuff?" I asked. "Oh, and we may need to move the furniture out of the way."

"Yes Ma'am!" Sam said as he saluted me. "Gentlemen if you would join me in the dining room for a debriefing on 'Operation Aura Cleanse' I can prepare you for our upcoming mission."

"'Operation Aura Cleanse,' dude?" Connelly said as he put his arm around Sam while they headed up the stairs that led to the dining room. "Way to make this girly stuff sound more important and manly!"

It wasn't how I was expecting the Halloween Party to be; it was way better. After their debriefing, Tim, Connelly, Sam, and Dad pushed all the living room furniture to the sides of the room while I scarfed down some pizza that had been ordered earlier. The sun had set about an hour earlier, so the candles lighting the living room flickered aimlessly casting shadows on the walls. Light from a practically full moon gave the room a soft glow. Basking in her light, I sent off a silent prayer to the Moon Goddess Selene for the success of our ceremony this evening. Taking a deep breath, the scent of the dying fire from the fireplace tickled my nose and mixed with the variety of fragrances emanating from the candles.

Everyone gathered in a circle in the living room. The eyes of the newcomers were lit up with curiosity and a touch of trepidation over casting a real circle and doing a real ceremony this close to Samhain/Halloween. Leah grabbed a yellow candle and found her spot representing the air element and the east. The red candle, symbolizing fire, disappeared into Sam's hands as he placed himself at the south. With a grin on her face Keia grabbed the blue candle, signifying water, and bounced over to the west. My mom picked up the green candle and took Kat's earth spot at the north because Katrina and Lesley joined me in the center. Tim,

Connelly, Dad, and Lisa filled in the forty-five degree (quarter) points between the directions.

"Are we ready to begin?" Mom asked. Enthusiastic nods and smiles came from the Sisterhood members, the others responded more subtly. "Leah, we will start with you in the east, please begin."

"Guardians of the east, I call upon you to protect these healing rites of ours." Leah recited her portion of the ritual, invoking the elements, closing with "So mote it be." Leah's musical voice danced upon the air enchanting us while she lit her yellow candle. Lisa's expression first registered surprise and then pride in her daughter's oration. Tuning in my Sight, I watched Leah's auric field expand to twice its previous size, connecting with Tim's and Connelly's who were standing on either side of her.

The deep voice of Sam Jung resonated throughout the room. His invocation raised the room's vibration and my temperature. The timbre of his new "adult" voice still surprised me. He sounded so mature and masterful. I felt the intensity of the Fire Element engage when he lit his candle and observed Sam's aura expand and connect with Connelly's and Dad's.

Keia's enchanting voice flowed over us, and her face glowed in the light of her candle flame. As she completed her incantation, my skin prickled with the refreshing sensation of walking into a cool pool on a hot day. Her energetic field rippled outward like waves in a pond and intertwined with Dad and Lisa's.

Mom's turn was next. Her steadfast, soothing and nurturing voice filled the room, rooting us to our spots.

She has a significant connection to the Earth, and through my Sight I saw it respond enthusiastically to her call. Her aura filled up, starting at her feet, with the colors of the earth, and then radiated out to connect with Lisa's energy field on her right and Tim's on her left. She reminded me of a Thanksgiving cornucopia. After she lit her candle, she smiled at me and then winked.

Taking a deep cleansing breath, I began my part of the ritual. My voice felt strong and full of conviction. I looked up at my raised arms above my head and saw the dome of pulsating light that was weaving around us complete and then snap shut its circular enclosure above my head. I felt as though I was standing inside a soap bubble, looking at the world through a translucent and constantly changing veil. The waves of loving and positive energy undulated repeatedly toward us as we stood in the middle. My skin tingled relentlessly as my light body tried to expand more to absorb all the potency it could.

I brought my hands down and lit my white candle. "The circle is closed," I said.

Lesley, Kat, and I turned to face each other and sat down cross-legged. Holding hands we made a small circle inside the big one. "Okay everybody, please close your eyes. Take a deep breath, and as you exhale visualize sending waves of turquoise energy to surround Kat and Lesley. Imagine it washing away any dirt or stains and cleaning their auras. After you've done that three times, breathe naturally and quietly, hold the vision of clean and pure teal or white halo surrounding them,"

I instructed. I closed my eyes and took a deep breath, exhaling slowly. I heard the rest of the group follow suit. I felt the tension in the hands I held slowly dissipate as I repeated the deep breath two more times.

Breaking the silence, I opened my eyes to read my notes I had placed on the floor earlier. I could see the blue-topaz energy enveloping the inner circle, but it wasn't able to penetrate the weak and tarnished energy fields of my friends. Undaunted, I pressed on.

Speaking out loud, I said, "I now invoke the blessing ability of peaceful, powerful, spiritual energy to manifest within this circle. I now accept right action, higher spiritual preeminence, and great mindfulness within this sphere. I now name this a sacred space and know the holiness of this space is full of the potency for creativity, clarity, and healing. This sacred space feeds our spirits, and fills us with insight, and wisdom."

"Kat and Lesley, please repeat after me," I whispered to my inner circle. "I am here to purify and cleanse the past from my physical and energetic being."

"I am here to purify and cleanse the past from my physical and energetic being." Lesley and Kat repeated in unison.

"I release myself from any past events, people, or places that have caused me harm or people who continue to cause harm to me or my loved ones." I said and then they reiterated my words.

"My spirit and aura are clean and balanced, and I forgive the past. Specifically, I forgive . . . ." I stopped there indicating they should fill in the blank. Mesmerized, I watched Kat and Lesley's light bodies as they each echoed me and then inserted a name. Their words of forgiveness and intent somehow released the lock that was stopping the healing energy from the group. A rush of sparkling turquoise swirled up, in, and around the occupants of the inner circle. Awestruck, the now pulsating, vibrant, and untarnished auras of Katrina and Lesley danced enthusiastically before me. *We did it!!!*

"Oh my God! We did it! I wish you could all see what I see! It's so beautiful. Your auras are cleansed and beautiful!" I said to Kat and Lesley, tears springing to my eyes in reaction to the rivulets I saw streaming down their faces. The three of us stood up, and then we all put our hands in the air and gazed up at them.

"Please repeat after me," I said somewhat breathlessly. "I am strong; I am powerful; I am balanced; I am protected; I am healthy. I am surrounded by the light of the Goddessence that protects me and keeps me from harm. I am light, I am love. So mote IT BE!" The fervency from the crescendo of voices reverberating out of the circle was probably felt throughout the Fifth Dimension.

Rapture. That's the only way I can describe the look on everyone's faces. They were glowing with an inner radiance, like the Selenite crystals did inside the Records. I'd never seen this happen before. The moon had moved and was no longer shining through the window. So, it wasn't lunar light shining in the windows reflecting off their faces—it was a glow coming from within everyone's heart.

After we finished the ritual and reopened the

circle, you could've stuck a fork in me, I was so done. The kids decided to stay the night. The girls crashed on the floor of my room, and the boys took the still cleared living room floor. Doctor Lisa said she would be back tomorrow to talk to me some more about how to better diagnose the disease. I yawned and said "Sure, but not too early."

My bed never felt so good as I crawled into it. The last thing I remember thinking is that Operation Aura Cleanse succeeded beyond my wildest imagination!

CHAPTER FIFTEEN
Spirit Battle

Sunday morning came earlier than I expected, and I totally didn't want to get out of bed. My iHome clock said it was 10:08. I seriously considered going back to sleep until the delicious aroma of French Toast funneled into my nose, making my mouth water. Looking down at my floor, Leah still had a pillow over her head, but Katrina and Keia's sleeping bags were empty. Carefully navigating my way out of my room, I managed to make it to the bathroom without running into anybody. I was examining my blood-shot eyes and my greasy ratted hair in the mirror when it hit me. *Holy Crap! Tim is in my kitchen! I can't go in there looking like something the cat dragged in!* Shower first. French Toast later.

    Only thirty minutes had passed before I walked into the kitchen wearing these totally cute leggings and soft tunic top that I bought last weekend that I was certain made me look like I was in High School. I felt sophisticated and mature except for my wet hair. I decided not to dry it because I couldn't stop salivating over the smells luring me to the kitchen. I had barely walked into the kitchen when Katrina's cell phone rang.

"Hi Dad!" She said happily answering the call, and then her smile disappeared. "Oh, hi Wilkins. What are you doing at Dad's?" I watched her eyebrows lift, her mouth drop open, and pain blanket her eyes. "What?! . . . No! That's not possible! Mom was just with him yesterday and he was okay. Who else is with you? . . . Dr. Randall? He's treating him at home? Why isn't he in the hospital? . . . They sent him home?? . . . Oh, God!" Katrina's agonized expression caused my heart to constrict as I watched tears stream unchecked down her cheeks. "Yes, I'll get there as soon as I can. I'm sure I can get Salena's parents or Keia's brother to drive me over there. Thanks for calling me, Wilkins." Katrina's wet and bloodshot eyes locked with mine as she sniffed her runny nose and hung up the phone. I handed her a tissue.

"Thanks," she said as she honked into the Kleenex. "That was my dad's assistant, Wilkins Stone. My dad had a heart attack this morning," she said looking down at the soiled tissue in her hand. "The hospital said his oxygen levels were too low. He has the Blue Flu and they couldn't do anything for him. They sent him home rather than putting him in quarantine. His private doctor is with him at his house. Dad's been asking for me. I have to get there as soon as possible," she murmured.

"Will you come with me? To my dad's?"

"Of course I will."

I scarfed down two pieces of French Toast as fast as I could before we headed to Mr. Drake's mansion. My dad drove us. Kat and I sat in the back seat of the Expedition while Dad quietly took us to her father's house. I held her hand in as her waves of grief ebbed and flowed.

We stopped briefly at the guard-gated entrance to Sierra Pines Country Club where Katrina's dad lived. When the guard saw Katrina, he waved us through. The giant house echoed as we walked through the unlocked front door. I had been over to Katrina's house a few times before her parents divorced, but not since. It now had a rather vacuous empty feeling. The lively energy of Katrina and her mom was definitely missing.

"You must be Mr. Hawthorne," a man said as he strode toward us, hand extended.

"Yes, and this is my daughter, Salena," Dad replied. While he shook the man's hand, I tuned in my Sight and gave Wilkins the once-over. I decided you couldn't work for or be near Katrina's dad without being afraid in some manner. Mr. Stone's weak and gray aura was infected, but he wasn't contagious. Dad would be safe enough around him, so I kept my observation to myself.

"I'm Wilkins Stone, Mr. Drake's assistant. Thank you for bringing Katrina over so quickly. Kat, your dad is in his bedroom with Dr. Randall and the nurse. You can go see him right away. Mr. Hawthorne, you are welcome to wait in the living room. Would you care for anything to drink?"

"Just some ice water would be good, thanks," Dad replied. While Mr. Wilkins and my dad went into the living room, Katrina and I headed up the grand staircase to the master bedroom.

I stopped Katrina before we entered her dad's bedroom and looked her over. The gray was still gone, but her energy was low. Remembering that I had grabbed Lady's Cosgrove's crystal before leaving the house, I pulled it out of my purse and grasped it tightly. My hand tingled at first, then I felt the same sensation travel up my arm and permeate throughout my body. I wished I could see my energy field in the mirror. I had a sense that it had expanded considerably.

Taking Katrina's hands in mine, clasping the crystal between us, I closed my eyes and took a deep breath. As I exhaled, I visualized sending her a vibrant flow of energy through our connection to infuse her aura with Love and Light so she would be strong enough to repel any spores from her dad that got close to her.

"You look good," I smiled at her.

"No gray?" She asked.

"Nope, just remember. Don't be afraid. I'll be right there with you," I said, giving her an encouraging squeeze. Hand in hand, we entered his room.

Dr. Randall and the nurse gave Katrina and me a nod as they quietly left the room. "We'll wait in the hallway," the doctor said softly as he pulled the door behind him leaving it just slightly ajar. I quickly checked their auras and, lucky for them they seem to lead rather fearless lives.

Turning my attention to the area above and around Mr. Drake was shocking and very disturbing. If I didn't know what I was really looking at I would have sworn that somebody had come into the room before us with a bubble wand blowing black oil bubbles all around Katrina's dad. They completely surrounded him. I shuddered and resisted the urge to tell Kat not to get too close. *No wonder Wilkins was infected!* I sent up a silent prayer that the Chronoscenti was right about fearless energy fields.

Then I made the mistake of looking down at Kat's dad with my Sight still engaged. My stomach clenched as beads of perspiration broke out over my body giving me the chills. I couldn't see Mr. Drake – at all. He reminded me of a burned Egyptian mummy. The black writhing tentacle-web-leg things had completely encased him. Then, to make matters worse, I spotted the source of the black bubbles. The throbbing and pulsing spider-like body that was sitting on his heart chakra pooped out spores in a rhythmic beat. My hand flew to cover my mouth and I watched in horror as Shelob spread her seed.

"Daddy?" Kat said as she let go of my hand and approached his bed. He cocked his head slowly in the direction of her voice.

"Kitten? Is that you?" Mr. Drake replied his hoarse voice was barely above a whisper. He opened his eyes only half-way and very slowly as if the weight of his eyelids was beyond his capacity to lift them.

"Yes, Daddy, it's me. How are you feeling?" Katrina pulled a chair up next to his bed, grabbed his hand, and then sat down. The heart monitor on the other side of the bed beeped irregularly as I focused on the bubbles surrounding Kat. To my relief, she was repelling them so far.

"Not good, baby. I'm so tired, so tired," he said as he closed his eyes again. "I have no idea how I got this. I was being so careful . . ."

Kat turned around and looked at me with the question of "Should I tell him?" written across her face. I shook my head left and right, silently saying no. I knew it wouldn't make any difference anyway.

"I want to tell you something," he half whispered. "I know I haven't been the best father, especially lately with the divorce . . . " He paused and took several deep breaths. This was costing him energy he didn't have. "But I want you to know that you are the best thing that ever happened to me and that I love you, Kitten."

"It's okay Daddy, I forgive you," she said which immediately caused her energy field to expand, pushing the spores further away from her. "I love you, and I'll be here to help you get better. I promise," Kat said choking back a sob, tears tumbling down her face.

"Don't . . . think . . . I . . . will . . . get . . ." the word "better" made it past his lips but didn't have any voice behind it. He squeezed her hand with the last of his strength and let out a long breath. The heart monitor stopped beeping as I watched a straight line appear across the screen accompanied by a long uninterrupted tone.

"Daddy?! Daddy! Don't leave me!!!" Kat pleaded with her father frantically looking from him to me. Immediately the door to his room swung open with the doctor and nurse rushing in. I grabbed Kat, pulled her out of their way into the corner where we could unobtrusively watch what was happening. I hugged her tightly as she sobbed.

I had never seen anybody die before. I was morbidly transfixed on the activities around Mr. Drake's bed. The black bubbles were somewhat displaced by the amount of energy emanating from the bodies surrounding Kat's dad, but they still managed to drift toward the two new energy sources. The spores didn't have any better luck with the doctor or nurse than they had with Katrina. In fact, the nurse had a lot of gold in her aura, which was literally zapping the damn things! I wanted to jump up and down and cheer!

Doctor Randall grabbed those paddle things off of the monitor and placed them over Dean's heart. The nurses said "Clear" and Mr. Drake's chest jumped up from the bed, but his heart didn't start again. The spider stopped pooping crude oil turds, but I didn't know if that was because Mr. Drake was dead or because it just received a jolt of electricity. The medical team tried one more time to start his heart, but they were unsuccessful.

Then I began to hear a sound that made my teeth clench and my eardrums vibrate. I blinked in horror as I realized the earsplitting sound was somehow coming from Mr. Drake. Kat crumpled down to the floor with her back against the wall, hugging her legs, sobbing into her hands as I plugged my ears with my fingers. It didn't do any good, and then I realized I was the only one in the room who could "hear" it. The shrieking wail of acute agony pierced the atmosphere along with rays of light briefly shooting out of slits in the tentacle webbing. Pure white sparkly light beams were trying to reach through the openings with tortured screams and then they were sucked back in. This happened repeatedly, over and over in various spots all over his body. But, each time the light beams tried to escape they had less and less extension before the tentacles would close the gap. *WTF!!! What the hell was happening?*

Since I can see ghosts, I expected to see his. So I waited and watched as the shrieking continued to abate into eventual silence. I waited, and waited. Dr. Randall and the nurse continued to try to revive Mr. Drake to no avail, yet his apparition never appeared. Smaller and smaller rays of light still randomly pushed through open spots in the shroud although their activity slowed down considerably.

"He's stuck in there," Angeni said as she materialized next to me. Her eyebrows were furrowed, and she had an inscrutable look on her face.

"What do you mean by that?" I whispered to her, trying not to call attention to myself. She didn't answer me and just continued to stare at Mr. Drake her jaw moving back and forth like she was chewing on something. I stared at her, waiting for her to respond. Finally, I couldn't stand it. "Angeni? What do you mean?"

She shook her head like she was trying to shake off an unpleasant memory. "His soul can't get out. It is fighting to get out but it can't get past that stuff that's wrapped around him. I'll bet that's what's causing the bruising that all the Blue Flu victims have in common. It's a postmortem battle of the spirit against the cage of the body."

"What happens to a spirit that can't escape its body?" I continued to whisper. Her eyebrows raised and she looked at me intensely for a moment.

"I don't know, Salena. I've never heard of that happening before," she said to me with a touch of worry in her voice that she didn't try to hide.

"Ah, hell, that can't be good," I muttered out loud.

"Salena, who are you talking to?" Katrina asked me as she emerged from her crying spell. Her voice was all nasally from all of the stuffiness that comes from sobbing. I pulled a bunch of Kleenexes out of the box on the nightstand and handed them to her.

"Angeni," I replied as she blew her nose.

"What can't be good? Did she say something about my dad?" She asked looking at me with bloodshot eyes and tear-stained cheeks. There wasn't any way in hell I was going to tell her that her dad's spirit was trapped inside his body. I shot Angi a distraught look. She just sadly shook her head—sooo not helping.

"I'll catch up with you later. I've got to check a couple of things," Angeni said as she misted away.

"No, um, she, um," I stammered. "She was talking about . . . um . . . something that's going on in the Fifth Dimension," I said hoping she'd buy it for now. I'd have to tell her the truth sometime, but I couldn't bring myself to cause her more pain or worry at this moment. "Come on, let's go find my dad. Would you like me to call your mom and tell her what happened?"

Katrina nodded solemnly as we headed out of the room in search of my father. We didn't have to go far because he was heading down the hallway toward us with a look of concern on his face. Mr. Stone sped past us and into the master bedroom as I rushed into my dad's arms and squeezed him tightly. I soaked up his masculine energy and love, extraordinarily grateful for his presence. Dad hugged me back with a fierce intensity and then turned to Kat and wrapped his arms around her tightly as fresh new tears streamed down her face.

"We're here for you, Kat—Salena, Mia, and I. Anything you need, anything at all. Just ask," Dad said as he rubbed her back. "Was he contagious?" he asked me in a low conspiratorial whisper.

"Yeah, but her energy was fearless and strong. She's okay, at least from that standpoint, anyway," I told him. Relief flooded through his light lapis eyes before he closed them and took a deep breath. "I told Kat I'd call her mom to let her know what happened."

"I called to check in with her when we arrived, Moonling. She asked me to bring Kat home when we were done. Let's all go downstairs, and I'll call her back and then I'll call home too," he suggested.

"Okay, thanks," I replied putting my arm around Katrina as we headed back down the staircase to the living room. I led her over to the supple leather couch while dad pulled his cell phone out of his jacket pocket.

A few minutes later, Dad strode toward us with determined steps. "Okay, girls. Are you ready to go now?"

"Yeah, there's nothing left for me here," she mumbled under her breath.

With Kat between us, we walked slowly out to my dad's car. I climbed into the back seat with Katrina and we mutely watched houses and buildings of all shapes and sizes go by, wrapped up in our own thoughts as we drove down the Mt. Rose Highway to the 395. I barely paid attention as we exited the freeway and headed up McCarran Boulevard before turning on Plumas towards the Ridgeview Apartments located on the Lakeridge Golf Course.

The pit of concern for Kat's mom, Trinity, grew heavier and heavier in my stomach. I recognized this foreboding sensation. It was part of the psychic package I was born with. Dreading what my Sight would reveal about Trinity when we got to her apartment, I took a deep breath to clear the edges of nausea that were creeping into my abdomen. Considering how contagious Mr. Drake was today, I couldn't imagine that he was a whole lot better yesterday, and if Trinity had any ash in her energy field . . . well, I had no idea what I'd do. I focused on sending loving thoughts to Kat and her mom while we drew nearer and nearer to our destination.

Trinity was waiting for us outside her apartment door when we pulled up. I first met her about the same time Barack Obama was running for President. The way she looked and carried herself reminded me a lot of Michelle Obama. They shared a similar skin tone and hairstyle. Sadly, the divorce had taken a toll on Trinity and the woman approaching us now had unkempt hair haphazardly pulled back into a ponytail and a make-up-free face that accentuated the dark circles under her eyes. She rushed over to the car and opened Kat's door practically pulling her out of the car and into her arms —comforting her as only a mom can. I climbed out the rear passenger side door and came around the back of the car. As I focused on Trinity's aura, a wet blanket, heavy and cold, settled over me. I shuddered and wrapped my arms around myself as I gazed upon a nasty black ink stain right below her belly button.

    I suppressed a yelp so I didn't draw Kat's attention. The only good news was that the gray in Trinity's energy field was light, like fog, instead of dark and foreboding like a thundercloud, and there were other more positive colors such as rose and emerald that swirled around each other. Although no black, except for the ink splat, was present, and it wasn't crapping out any babies (thank goodness), my Sight revealed her anger in the muddied crimson color flaring in and out like a sentient fire. I was completely stuck. Frustrated, I chewed on my lower lip as thoughts tumbled through my brain. *I can't bear the thought of Katrina losing both her mom and dad. I hope Angeni has some ideas or maybe the Chronoscenti came up with a solution already. We could try the cleansing ceremony. Shelob quit pooping spores when they tried to shock Mr. Drake's heart. Maybe electro-shock therapy would work.* I imagined Sam inventing an aura shock therapy gun, like a Star Trek phaser, and, suddenly, there I was in a Tomb Raider outfit running around obliterating the aura-sucking spiders. With that image in my brain, I snorted at my absurdity and shook my head profusely in a desperate attempt to clear my thoughts.

Dad had climbed out of the car as well, so while Kat and Trinity were consoling each other, I made my way to my father. "Trinity is infected, Dad," I said in a painful whisper. "I haven't a clue what to say to Kat. I know she's going to ask me. God this sucks!"

"I know, baby. I know," he consoled me by pulling me into a big hug and rubbing my back. "Is she contagious?"

I shook my head. "No, not yet." Hearing that, Dad made a decision.

"Ladies, I think you should go inside and spend some time together. You need to take solace with each other for a little while, and I need to get Salena home. Kat will you call us later and give us an update on how you're doing?"

Kat looked over at my dad and me with a blank yet shocked look like she was having trouble translating English. "Yeah, yeah. I'll call you later, Sal," she spoke slowly, as if she didn't understand the words coming out of her mouth either.

"If you forget to call, I'll call you," I assured her and gave her one more hug before walking back around to the front passenger seat. I heard Trinity thank my dad for bringing Katrina home, and then we watched them shuffle back to their front door with their arms around each other and their heads hanging down.

CHAPTER SIXTEEN
The Society of the Silver Moon

A harmony of male and female voices surrounded me when Dad and I entered the house. The scene in the living room gave me a déjà vu, the same people who were there last night were still hanging out; even Dr. Lisa and Keia's mom, Lesley, had come back over.

"Hey there!" I said loud enough to get everybody's attention, stepping down into the living room.

"How's Kat doing?" Keia asked.

"Did her dad infect her?" Leah inquired.

"What about her mom? Did she get infected too?" Queried Dr. Lisa.

"Are you okay?" Mom asked before she enveloped me in her arms. I breathed in her familiar citrus mango scent deep into my lungs and relaxed into her embrace.

"Honestly?" I mumbled into her shoulder. Mom nodded her head. "I don't know. I'm so overwhelmed with everything. Something really bad happened when Mr. Drake died, Mom. Even Angeni kinda freaked out."

"Come sit down and tell us about it. Maybe

together we can come up with some ideas for what to do next, and hopefully that will take some of the burden off of you," Mom said.

My audience settled in the living room as I related my observations surrounding the death of Dean Drake. My eardrums vibrated at the recollection of his spirit's screams. I wrapped my arms around myself shuddering at the memory. The mood was somber when I finished telling them what Angeni had said about Mr. Drake's spirit being trapped and fighting to get out.

Throughout my recap, Tim looked at me with focused intensity, giving me his full, undivided attention. I don't remember him ever watching me like that. When I caught his gaze he lifted both of his eyebrows and gave me a lopsided smile. *That's weird.* I felt hot little tingles crawl up from my stomach to my neck. I resisted the urge to fan myself. Tim is so dang cute! Then my conscience suddenly kicked in. *What about Jace?* It scolded me. *What about him? He's cute too*, I reminded myself.

"Yo! Salena! Focus girl!" Leah interrupted my obsessing. My face heated up as my focus returned to the topic at hand.

"Sorry," I said looking down in an attempt to corral my galloping thoughts. "Where were we?"

"I would like to summarize what I've heard from you in the last twenty four hours, Salena, to help me figure out the best way to diagnose and treat this disease," Doctor Lisa said. Everybody nodded for her to continue. "Okay. People with gray and/or black in their auras are susceptible to infection. Once infected, by something that resembles a crude oil bubble which attaches to a chakra, the disease appears to start by deoxidizing cells in that chakra region which causes those related organs to shut down. The hemoglobin in the red blood cells reduces the transport of oxygen throughout the body resulting in people suffocating and then dying. At some point in the growth of the infection, the core body of the disease begins to release spores that can spread the infection while it wraps tentacle-like webbing around the person, which after death prevents the person's spirit from moving on. Did I miss anything?"

I heard Connelly mutter "Holy Crap" under his breath while I shook my head and said, "I don't know about deoxidization and hemo-goblins, but all the other stuff is right."

Lisa laughed, "That's hemo-*globin* not hemo-goblin. Hemoglobin is a protein in red blood cells that carries oxygen, not a goblin which is an evil, mischievous mythical creature."

"Yeah, okay. If you say so," I replied as she continued.

"One of the major challenges facing the medical community regarding the Blue Flu has been that all of its victims died from some form of virulent hypoxia that causes what appears to be random organs in the body to fail. The only thing linking the deaths is cyanosis where fingers and lips turn blue in some patients, a low overall oxygen level in the blood, and then bruising that appears all over the body after death.

When you saw Dean get infected you said that the spore landed on his heart chakra, correct?" Doctor Lisa asked me.

"Yes. Chronoscenti Cosgrove specifically commented on that," I replied.

"Today he died of a heart attack. I'm betting that's not just coincidence," she explained. Nobody argued with her. "I think the most interesting connection you helped me make today, Salena, is that *oxygen*, which is carried by the red blood cells to various body parts, is what those organs convert into *energy* to perform their functions. What I find to be more than just a bit coincidental is that when a person's aura is tainted with the Blue Flu it appears to poison their body's ability to create or properly utilize the oxygen or energy our systems need."

"The 'Blue Flu' isn't really an influenza illness at all then, is it? Not by the real classification of a flu virus, anyway," Keia's mom, Lesley, asked.

"No, it's not, and the scientific community has known that for a few weeks, but the catchy name stuck. Based on Salena's report, I think the Black Plague sounds like a far better description," Dr. Lisa replied. "But, no matter what we call it, until a cure can be developed, we need to devise a way to identify people who are infected with it, and only allow medical personnel to treat them who have 'fearless auras'."

"Easy, peasy, lemon squeezy," Keia said sarcastically.

"Actually, Keia, it might be easier than we think," Sam piped in. We all looked at him expectantly. "Salena, do you remember when I first told you all about the research I did on auras?"

"Yeah," I replied feeling slightly guilty that I hadn't been more appreciative of his research, and that I had virtually ignored my new ability for the last month.

"Well, there's this camera that takes pictures of auras. There is always one at the Psychic Fair every year, so maybe somebody has one in town we can borrow. We could test it to see if it works as good as Salena's vision, so she wouldn't have to work the check-in desk at the hospital every day," he said smiling at me.

"Dude, you go to the Psychic Fair every year?" Tim asked Sam.

"Um, yeah, my mom drags me there, but it's pretty cool though," Sam replied, a little blush creeping over his face.

"That's a really good idea, Sam. I'll check it out," Lesley said sending her son, Tim, one of those "Mom looks" that communicates annoyance and exasperation at the same time.

"Anything we try to communicate to the medical and scientific communities surrounding these discoveries will be debunked," my dad pointed out.

"Yes, James, that's true. However, if we are able to show unprecedented success in diagnosis and treatment, they won't be able to debunk it for long," Dr. Lisa countered.

"How are we going to keep Salena from becoming the poster child for this campaign? I'm not having my daughter dissected on the Ten O'clock News," Dad said.

Nobody had an answer for that one, and I'm not gonna lie, it made me squirm in my seat. I hated being the center of attention, and this situation was ripe with potential to put me smack dab in the middle of a ginormous clash between science, religion, politics, and big business. So NOT where I wanna be.

Angeni chose that moment to materialize behind the couch. The light streaming through the windows behind her was visible through her translucence. My mom and I noticed her at the same time.

"Hello, Angeni, it's nice of you to join us," Mom said looking in Angi's direction. Everyone in the room turned to look at her even though they couldn't see anything.

Angi responded with a slight smile, "It's good to be here, but I'm afraid I don't have very good news."

"She says she doesn't have very good news for us," my mom repeated. "Okay, Angeni, let's hear it."

"I went back to the Spirit Realm with the discovery that Salena and I made regarding Dean Drake's spirit. As I suspected, what happened to him was unprecedented before the Blue Flu. Sometimes souls don't cross over quickly and spend a little time as ghosts before they finally cross, so no one in the spirit realm noticed that the victims of this disease hadn't arrived yet. It didn't occur to anybody that they couldn't cross over and that they might be stuck in the Third Dimension. This disease has ramifications beyond the third dimensional existence. It could severely impact the long term spiritual evolution of humanity."

God! This just gets better and better! I stared at her

trying to wrap my brain around what she just said. Thankfully, Mom had the presence of mind to repeat what Angeni had said to the group.

"Do they know how to cure it?" Dr. Lisa asked hopefully.

"Yes and no," Angeni replied. "Humanity has always had the power within them to cure any disease and create any existence they choose. The Fifth Dimensional people are proof of that since they live in that existence every moment of every day. Since the Blue Flu is a disease created from and propagated by fear, it stands to reason that love in its purest and divine form would cure it; that is the 'yes' part of the answer."

"Hang on, Angeni, let me translate," Mom interrupted. She stood up from her recliner and paced around the room telling everyone what my spirit guide said. I could tell she was very anxious about what we just heard; Mom doesn't normally feel the need to walk around while she is talking. She spends a lot of her time with her therapy patients' deceased loved ones helping them to cross over. She has a great deal of empathy for those lost and/or stranded souls. When she finished, Angi continued.

"The 'no' part is that despite all of the teachings and knowledge that is available to the Third Dimension, being able to conquer fear through the power of love still eludes most people. I think we need to find a way to give the masses some kind of method or process that will provide them with a perfect example to follow in order to achieve the state of mind or belief necessary to abolish this disease."

As Mom relayed Angeni's message to the group I watched the kid's faces and saw disbelief move into confusion, which was then replaced by concern and finally determination. It began to slowly dawn on my friends and me how critical and daunting our task had become. How in the world could a small group of middle school students from Reno, Nevada, with the support of a few parents and siblings, succeed where so many spiritual masters had failed?

"Sure, Angeni, no problem, we'll get that knocked out before dinner," I commented drily rolling my eyes. Everyone laughed a little, slightly releasing the tension in the room.

Tucking her brown hair behind her ears, Lesley stood up. We all looked at her expectantly. "The good news is that we know a lot more than we did two days ago!" Her bronze eyes glowed with an intensity I hadn't seen before. "And, we know how to increase people's immunity, now. It's a great start! We'll just take this one step at a time and with help from the Fifth Dimension and Angeni, we'll find a solution. I know we'll figure it out!"

I'm pretty sure Lesley was a cheerleader in high school. She had an amazing way of motivating people. She packs a lot of power in that five-foot-two frame of hers, no wonder she ran that hospital so well. Keia and Tim looked at their mom, smiling proudly. I not only felt, but also saw the energy level in the room rise.

"I think the patient for our first trial should be Trinity," Leah chimed in. "We have to help Kat any way we can!" Everyone agreed that, if Trinity were willing, when we had our first idea for a cure, she'd be our initial test subject.

"I'll give her a call and set up a time to meet with her in the next couple of days," Mom volunteered. "Salena, James, are you two hungry? The rest of us ate before you got home. I have some sandwiches in the kitchen."

"I'm starved," I said jumping up from the couch.

"Me too!" Dad agreed following mom and me into the kitchen as conversation continued behind us.

Shortly after I took the second bite of my sandwich, Tim sauntered into the kitchen.

"Hey, Salena," he said to me with a slight lift of his chin and a smirk on his lips.

"Hey," I mumbled back with my mouth full of sandwich.

"What you did last night for my mom and Kat . . . " he began.

"Yeah?" I said after swallowing.

"That was pretty bad ass, just sayin'. Like, um, I mean, thanks for what you did for my mom," he said.

"Uh, you're welcome," I replied debating on whether or not to take another bite and slightly flummoxed that Tim was really talking to me. My dad grabbed his sandwich, winked at me, and followed my mom out of the kitchen.

"So, yeah . . . you've got some pretty cool powers, huh?" Tim continued.

"I guess," I replied in what was undoubtedly a brilliant response for a tongue that has an uncanny ability to tie itself into knots when in the presence of

Tim Von Housen.

"So, are you going as a superhero for Halloween?" He asked grinning at me. I laughed which helped ease my self-consciousness.

"No, I hadn't really thought about it. We were going to do our Halloween celebration last night, but it kinda got usurped. If I put a costume on, I'm usually a witch."

"That works!" He said with an adorable smile that made my heart speed up like I just drank ten Red Bulls. "Witches have cool powers too! Why don't we all go Trick-or-Treating as a group on Wednesday? You, me, Connelly, Keia, Leah, Sam, and Kat? It might make a fun distraction from this totally messed up Blue Flu crap. I'll drive," he offered.

"Hey, Timothy, are you bothering my BFF?" Keia said bouncing into the kitchen.

"Naw, he's just suggesting we all go Trick-or-Treating together to get our minds off of this, you know, stuff," I told her.

"That'd be cool. You and Connelly going to become official members of the Sisterhood?" Keia asked, bumping his shoulder with hers. A flash of panic crossed Tim's face.

"I've been thinking about that," I interjected before Tim could reply. "Should we consider changing the name to The Society of the Silver Moon so it's gender neutral?"

"That sounds good to me," Tim said smiling.

"You so totally don't get to vote," his sister pointed out.

"What are we voting on?" Connelly asked as he walked into the kitchen with Leah and Sam trailing behind him.

"You don't get a vote either," Keia told him.

"Changing the name of the Sisterhood of the Silver Moon to the Society of the Silver Moon to make it more gender neutral," I told everyone.

"Yeah, Tim wants to join but his delicate male ego can't handle being in a 'Sisterhood'," Keia poked at her brother.

"I didn't say I wanted to join, you assumed that just because I suggested that we all go Trick-or-Treating together," Tim defended himself.

"Guys, guys, chill" I said trying to get Keia and Tim to settle down. "By now, everyone who has been participating in this little adventure is part of our group since we have this mission we are on to save the world. It's not like we're an official organization with membership cards or anything."

"I'm good with it," Sam said.

"Yeah, me too," agreed Leah who was surreptitiously stealing glances at Connelly.

"Okay, I'll ask Kat what she thinks when I call her later. So, do we all want to go out together Wednesday night? Tim said he'd drive," I asked. Everyone chimed in with their form of agreement and started talking about their costumes. I took that opportunity to finish my sandwich and send some intentional healing thoughts in Kat's direction.

Everyone finally left after our action plan began to take shape. I sat on my bed running through the decisions we made today. Starting tomorrow, Dad and Lisa would inform their peers about what we learned and see how many might be willing to believe without proof. Lesley, with help from Sam, would look into an Aura Camera option for diagnosis. Mom said she would contact Trinity and reach out to the local psychic community to see who else might have the same ability to see auras as I do. Although Mom is psychic and can see ghosts and spirits, she doesn't have my same ability to see auras. Angeni can see energy fields though, so she and mom worked out a temporary diagnosis relay system between them and Lisa. Angeni can spot the infected people, tell mom, and then mom will tell Lisa. First, though, they planned to identify the nurses and doctors who have immunity. It's hard for Angi to hold the low vibrational level necessary to be seen in this dimension for too long, so she was going to try to recruit some additional help from the spirit realm.

    The faster we could come up with a cure, the better off we would be – which is the part of the plan where I came in. I would go back to the Fifth Dimension. Suddenly, the memory of Jace's kiss popped into my thoughts and my body got warm and fuzzy. Then immediately following that memory, I got all jittery from excitement about going Trick-or-Treating with Tim! I realized, slightly shocked, that I was starting to like Jace as much as I've always liked Tim! And, now of all times, when Tim finally noticed I'm alive!! Frustrated, I let out a sigh that caused my lips to make a raspberry noise. I had no idea what I was going to do about either one of them. I was in desperate need of some alone time with my BFFs to talk about it. I hadn't even had a chance to tell them what happened with Jace yet!

Ted Nugent's "Cat Scratch Fever" suddenly blasted out of my phone, startling me out of my reverie and jolting me back to reality. *That is Kat's special ringtone. As she promised, she is calling me back. It is time to tell her about her mom.* I sighed as I stared at my phone. I felt my energy drop as a wave of sadness and trepidation flowed through me. *I am way too young for this kind of responsibility. It's just so not fair . . . for either of us.* Taking a deep breath, I answered her call.

CHAPTER SEVENTEEN
Metaphysics 101

I realized at school on Monday that none of the precautions the district was taking to protect the kids from the spread of this contagion would work. This plague of fear wouldn't be thwarted by masks or obsessive hand washing. All of the hand sanitizer in the world wouldn't stop the black orbs from sticking to your aura.

    I was so distracted by reading the energy fields of my teachers and classmates that I didn't pay much attention in class. One teacher who was new this year was infected pretty badly. Sam convinced him he should go home and rest. Tuesday, on the way to second period class, I literally bumped into Vicki Love in the hallway dropping all my books on the floor. She and her sidekicks taunted me as I collected my things, and when I looked up at her, I noticed that Vicki's sacral chakra had a black bulbous hitchhiker. Montana sneered at me and kicked the last book out of her way before I had a chance to grab it. I watched them walk away from me wondering how much longer Vicki had to live.

    Wednesday night was the best! The Halloween

celebration with Tim was TOTALLY awesome! I had the most amazing time ever! Even though the whole group of us went, Tim walked and talked with me the most of anybody. He even kicked Connelly out of the front seat so I could ride shotgun. His costume cracked me up. It was a stuffed magnet with little yellow chicks stuck to it that he wore around his neck. There were plenty of real and fake ghosts wandering the streets with us. I tried to ignore the real ones. Only one person who answered their door was infected, but, thankfully, not yet contagious. I made a note of their address to give to my mom and dad. I was relieved to see that the disease hadn't spread too widely in this area of Reno, at least not amongst those who opened their doors to Trick-or-Treaters.

Mom, with the help of Kat, managed to explain to Trinity the true cause of the Blue Flu. Trinity agreed to be our first test subject, but I think she decided to do it more out of humoring her daughter than actually believing us. The sooner we could start experimenting on her the better, especially considering how quickly this disease spreads and kills. Therefore, Mom, Dad, and I thought that a trip to the Fifth Dimension with the hope of bringing back a cure would be worth me missing a day of school.

I decided to get an early start on Thursday and got up at the same time I normally do. Although temperature doesn't seem to have the same impact on me in the Fifth Dimension as it does in the Third, I decided to dress for Reno's weather and put on a new pair of jeans that had sparkly stones decorating the pocket along with a long-sleeve multicolored tunic that had a handkerchief hem. I told Mom and Dad I was getting ready to leave and closed my bedroom door.

"Salena?!" Mom yelled outside my room.

"Yeah, Mom?" I said as I opened the door.

"I love you, baby. Be safe," she said circling me in her arms. I felt as though she had somehow joined our heart chakras and then poured pure energy into the center of my being. A heat wave blossomed out from my chest and filled me with pure mommy love.

"I love you, too."

The energy boost from Mom made it easy for me to connect to the Goddessence this time. I stood in the center of my room with my arms up and palms toward the sky and my legs firmly planted hip width apart and took a deep breath, pulling the divine feminine and masculine energy into the core of my being. I opened my eyes to see Amalya standing in front of my closet door smiling.

"You're getting better at that," she commented.

"Mom gave me a boost before I started. Have you been waiting for me?" I asked.

"No, I've been monitoring your progress, so I knew you were planning on coming over this morning. I decided to come meet you. We have a lot to discuss, so I thought I'd take you directly to where we are meeting," Amalya informed me.

"Okay, take me away," I said as I grasped her hand and my bedroom vanished.

We materialized inside a warm, wood-paneled

room that had large picture windows on the north, east, and west walls. I recognized the Sierra Nevada Colony meadow outside. Through the north window I could see Mount Lassen, and through the west window, the creek that ran through the meadow was clearly visible. The east window looked out over the meadow and expansive sky. The southern wall had a ginormous rock-faced fireplace. The oval shaped room accommodated a large similarly shaped Brazilian Cherry wood conference table in the middle. I recognized almost everybody seated around the table. I smiled and nodded at Chronoscenti Cosgrove, Douglas, Diana, Jace's parents, and then my pulse jumped when I laid eyes on Jace too!

"I think you know almost everyone here," Amalya said. "I'm not sure that you were ever formally introduced to Chronoscenti Cosgrove's husband, Chronoscenti Terrence. He was in the cave when you and Lady Cosgrove went into the Records." I recognized him and performed the customary reverent mudra greeting. His salty hair made him look wise and distinguished, yet his aquamarine eyes sported permanent laugh lines against his unmarked light peach skin. The twinkle in his eyes told me he loved to laugh, enjoy life, and have fun. I liked him right away.

"I don't think you had the pleasure of meeting Chancellor Hart Williams who is the Fifth Dimension's medical and scientific leader and Hierophant Jana Tarini, our spiritual leader," Amalya introduced as they shook my hand.

I've gotten used to the Fifth Dimensionals having light bodies that shine like stars, but by comparison Jana was a freaking sun! I blinked and squinted when I looked at her just like when I walk outside at noon on a cloudless day. I was tempted to materialize a pair of sunglasses, but thought better of it since nobody else had a pair on. I wondered how anybody got any sleep in this dimension since everyone's auras were so dang bright.

Once my eyes adjusted, I could finally see Jana at the center of her aura. She instantly reminded me of a forty-something version of Princess Jasmine from "Aladdin," except with shorter hair. Her almond-shaped, bright copper eyes matched the golden rays of light that shot out around her. Her gentle compassionate smile put me immediately at ease. I felt as though I had been granted an audience with the Goddess herself. I resisted the urge to kneel in front of her and ask for her blessing.

Chancellor Hart Williams I thought looked like most old guys, since they all kinda look the same to me. His thinning silver hair had a few peppery streaks running through it and he had a full white beard. The wire rim glasses completed his look. He would probably have totally intimidated me if he didn't remind me so much of my father. Like my dad, Chancellor Williams exuded confidence and intelligence, yet I sensed an openness and lack of judgment in him that encouraged me to want to learn as much as I could from him.

I wandered around the table saying hello to everyone individually. I gave Lady Cosgrove a hug. Our experience in the Records created a strong connection between us. I saved the best for last—Jace. He smiled at me; his sparkling eyes reminded me of a drop of water catching the sunlight on a blade of grass.

"Hi," he said.

"Hi."

"Hey . . . um . . . I was . . . wondering if . . . maybe, after this meeting, I could . . . like, take you to dinner?" He stammered. I felt my face getting warm.

"Really? Yeah, sure. That'd be fun!" I think my heart skipped a beat. With both of us sporting silly grins, we each found a seat at the table. Full glasses of ice water manifested in front of each person.

"Let's get started," Chronoscenti Cosgrove said and everyone at the table turned to look at her expectantly. "Thank you, Salena, for coming back and joining us for our first Metaphysics 101 class. Since your visit last weekend, we have discovered a great many things, as I know you have as well. Amalya kept watch over your discoveries and activities, so we are up to speed with what you know. We were impressed with how you were able to cleanse your friend's auras to increase their immunity. That was good work." She smiled at me. I smiled back, murmuring my thanks, feeling a little swell of pride over her praise.

"We confirmed the hypothesis that people who have fearless auras are immune to the Blue Flu. One other interesting thing we learned is that the darker the aura the faster it kills and the more contagious it becomes. Infected individuals who have a minimal amount of light gray are exhibiting symptoms like chronic infections, allergies or headaches, but the infection doesn't spread throughout their energy field, nor does it become communicable. For those people it appears to be causing very annoying symptoms, but they don't seem to be at risk of dying as long as their level of fear doesn't increase. We found one person who got infected and then managed to cleanse their light body of negative energy. They weren't able to rid themselves of the contagion, but it seemed to go dormant and ceased to cause any chronic physical ailments."

"So, are you telling me that Kat's mom, Trinity, won't die?" The excitement racing through me felt like somebody had just lifted a 200-pound weight off my shoulders.

"Yes, that's right, Salena, as long as she doesn't increase her level of fear. It definitely gives us more time to find a cure for her and people like her." Astonished at how much lighter I felt, I couldn't wait to get home to tell everybody.

"So, it sounds like you don't have a cure to give me, yet, right?"

"No, we don't, and we won't. The Blue Flu can't exist here because disease cannot manifest at the frequency level that permeates the Fifth Dimension. Everything and everyone here vibrates the highest levels of positive energy. The frequencies emitted by all of the negative emotions or thoughts are the source of all disease. This means we don't have any way to formulate or test any cures. Therefore, we are going to give you some recommendations today based on our combined knowledge, but you and your friends are going to have to do the testing on your own," Lady Cosgrove explained.

"Okay, I guess that means I'll be taking a bunch of notes," I said as I visualized a spiral bound notebook and a pen which instantly appeared in front of me. So cool.

It seemed that several hours passed as one idea after another was introduced to me. As the sun moved across the sky shadows traversed the ground. The group didn't just tell me stuff, they taught me stuff. Most important, I thought, was that I learned about the Goddessence energy that permeates everything. The energy has been called Adamantine Particles by some spiritualists or more recently the God Particle by some scientists. It's what the Fifth Dimension taps into to manifest all that they need. It's in the Third Dimension too, Thir-Ds just don't know how to access it as quickly or use it as accurately or abundantly.

The two Chronoscenti traded off teaching me about the different healing properties of various crystals and stones. They spent a lot of time explaining the uses and benefits of Selenite Crystal, Quartz Crystal, and Citrine for healing and energy work.

Chancellor Williams subjected all of us to a quantum physics lecture that I'm sure my dad would have given anything to attend. Me though, not so much. I have to grudgingly admit that when he talked about the connection of quantum physics to physiology especially as it related to potentially treating the Blue Flu, I took careful notes and asked a lot of questions. For the most part, though, I trusted in the fact that the energy existed and that it can do what everyone says it can do, I really didn't want to know the science behind it, but I listened politely anyway attempting to take notes for my dad's benefit. Hopefully he will be able to translate my phonetic spelling for most of what the Chancellor said. I decided during our lunch break that I really didn't miss a day of school after all.

That afternoon Hierophant Tarini got her turn to teach, and she was by far the most interesting person who spoke. We were all enthralled. She shared examples of metaphysical healing methods that have been employed for centuries, and she told stories that gave me a whole new appreciation for history. I know I wasn't the only one in the room who learned something either if the rapt expressions around the table were anything to go by. I noticed somewhere along the line, Jace and Amalya had also started taking notes.

"My head is so full, I think it's going to explode, and my hand feels like it's stuck in this position," I moaned to the group, held up my crinkled fingers holding the pen, and they laughed. No sympathy with this crowd. "You all have given me some great ideas on how to help the living, but what about the dead? There are still souls cocooned inside dead bodies or fused to their ashes." The mood in the room sobered up. Nothing like being a party crasher.

"Yes, we are aware of the fate of the souls in the bodies that have perished since this plague was unleashed," Jana said softly. "At this point we don't have an answer for that one either. Our initial focus was on helping the living. Because learning to overcome fear through love, compassion, and forgiveness is the foundational purpose of every soul who chooses to incarnate in the Third Dimension, there were some in our dimension who questioned getting involved in your dimension's problems at all."

Jana stopped for a moment, took a drink from her glass of water, and then continued. "However, that was before it was discovered that the Blue Flu was trapping souls. The higher dimensions of the spirit and angelic realms were as surprised by that turn of events as the rest of us, so we were told that whether we liked it or not, we're helping find a solution. Nothing ever surprises anybody in the angelic realm, so this is really big." There were confirming nods around the table. *Wow! Angeni and I really stumbled onto a universal crisis. No wonder she was so worried.* It was a little disconcerting to know that now I not only had the attention of the Fifth Dimension but also the Spirit and Angelic realms. No pressure.

"Nobody is even sure, yet, how the disease got started in the first place. The Chronoscentis have been charged with researching that through the Records. In any case, freeing those trapped spirits is not your problem at the moment. We're here today to give you ideas on how you can help the living so you don't have as many souls to save later," Jana looked at me with a half smile teasing her lips.

"Me? So I don't have as many souls to save later? Seriously?" My eyebrows actually started to ache with the pressure of holding them up. "You guys are just so not funny," I said shaking my head and looking down trying not to give them the benefit of my smile.

"Seriously, Salena, we don't want you to worry

about those entities now. Yes, they are trapped, and yes, we have to do something about it. However, it is not our priority. As you are beginning to understand, time doesn't work the same way for the other dimensions as it does in the Third. Those trapped essences will not realize how long in 3D time they have been confined. They are in stasis. They can't stay there forever, but for now, they are not really suffering per se," Lady Cosgrove offered in an attempt to soothe my concerns.

"Dean Drake's soul screamed like somebody was pulling his toenails out one by one and then used them to scrape down a chalkboard. That sure didn't sound painless and not suffering to me," I commented not necessarily wanting to contradict Chronoscenti Cosgrove, but feeling compelled to inform everyone of what I experienced.

"You are correct, Salena," Jana responded. "For those spirits who initially discover they are trapped, it is very troubling and painful. They have just separated from their Third Dimensional existence, and they are innately compelled to move on. The inability to do so causes them deep distress, but they eventually quiet down, and there is no more pain."

I looked at all the kind and compassionate faces staring back at me and decided to take their advice and worry about it later. I couldn't do anything without their help and guidance anyway. I let out a deep breath that I didn't know I was holding. My silent agreement was acknowledged around the table.

"Ladies and gentlemen," Diana spoke up. "I think we have talked Salena's ear off enough for today, and if the pages of ink in her notebook are any indication, it looks like she has plenty of things she can work on with her friends to develop a treatment for the Blue Flu. Maybe we should call it a day."

Murmurs of agreement were followed immediately by breakout sessions and sidebar conversations. Jace and his parents wandered over to the northwestern corner to discuss something, so I decided to go sit on the hearth of the fireplace and take a moment for myself. I wondered again how come I was able to be here, in this dimension. *Why do I, of all people, have these special talents? How did I become the one singled out to save the world? Who volunteered me for this destiny, anyway?* I muttered to myself letting the warmth of the fire seep into my core.

"I can feel the weight of your ruminations from across the room." I looked up into the compassionate sapphire eyes and gentle smile of Chronoscenti Cosgrove. "And I see it reflected in your light body."

I smiled at her. "What *does* my aura look like?"

"You haven't been told?" She asked as I shook my head. "It's predominately a brilliant luminescent honey color like Jana's. Yours just isn't quite as strong as hers because you are so much younger. Jana is in her last physical incarnation. She is headed to the angelic realms after this lifetime."

"Golden energy fields fry the nasty fear bubbles," I commented remembering the nurse in Dean Drake's room and the lady at the airport.

"Yes. Gold is the color of enlightenment and divine protection. You are being guided by your highest good, inner-knowledge, and connection to the Goddessence. You are not only immune to the Blue Flu, but you are its worst enemy. So, my dear, what's weighing on you so heavily?"

"Just wondering who volunteered me for this crappy detail," I fussed. Lady Cosgrove sat down next to me on the hearth and gently took my hands in hers.

"You did, child. You chose this path for yourself for this lifetime. As we all do," she told me. I looked at her, blinking, processing what she said. It rang true through my core.

"Figures. The one person I can't blame without taking all of the responsibility," I said wryly.

"I'm going to tell you something that might help you understand yourself a little better. After you left last Saturday, I was curious about you. So I went back into the Records and followed your soul star into your previous incarnations," she told me holding my gaze with her intense eyes. *Holy Crap! I didn't know she could do that!* I thought as I swallowed. "Genetically you know that you are the descendant of what you call a Mayan High Priestess, yes?"

"Uh, yeah. That's what my mom told me."

"Well, young lady, she is not only your ancestress, she is you. That embodiment was one of your earliest incarnations. You chose to be born into this time and place with the abilities you have to help humanity through this shift in consciousness. This is your most powerful and last physical incarnation. You have a lot to accomplish in this lifetime, so your gifts blossomed very early." Inwardly I laughed at her choice of words. I'm not sure I would call them "gifts," and they didn't blossom, they erupted.

"Why didn't Angeni tell me this a long time ago?" I wondered, feeling a little betrayed.

"It's possible that she doesn't know, and there are sometimes things that the Guides cannot tell their charges because of the whole 'free will' thing. Part of why we choose to incarnate is to experience what happens to us when we make certain decisions. She may not have been given access to your life plan for the simple reason that if she doesn't know, she can't interfere or tell you what to do even if you ask her to."

"So, how come you can tell me this now, when she can't?" I was not quite ready to let Angeni off the hook.

Chronoscenti Cosgrove smiled and her eyes got a mischievous glint in them. She leaned over and whispered conspiratorially to me. "Because I went into the Records and looked at your soul's journey through every existence, physical or otherwise. I didn't read, nor do I have access to, your current life plan. I only observed you for a short while as you worked on it during your last sojourn in the spirit realm. That's one of the benefits to being a Chronoscenti."

I couldn't decide whether knowing all of that about myself made me feel better or worse. Letting go of Lady Cosgrove's hands I stood up and paced in front of the fire, patting my legs with my hands as I walked. *Now I have nobody I can blame but "muah" for all the "fun" I've had the last thirteen years. That just sucks. It's so much easier to blame somebody else for all your trials and tribulations than to have to take responsibility for yourself. Geez, I guess I was gonna have to just wo-"man" up and learn to listen to and trust my "higher-self." Oh joy. Can't wait.*

CHAPTER EIGHTEEN
Twin Flames

"You ready to go?" Jace asked pulling my attention away from my thoughts.

"Yeah, sure," I replied. Turning back to the Chronoscenti I said, "Thanks for telling me that stuff. Honestly, though, I'm not sure that knowing I'm the one putting myself through this makes any of it easier." I scrunched up my nose like I smelled something stinky. She laughed at my expression.

"Don't worry, child. You'll do fine," she said putting her hand on my shoulder and giving it a squeeze. Remembering my manners, I quickly made my rounds to the rest of the people in the room expressing my gratitude. After I told Amalya I'd be in touch, I picked up my notebook and then Jace grabbed my hand.

"Come on, Salena, let's blow this popsicle stand. I'm starvin'," he said and the room was gone.

The bright sun, warm air, and slight aroma of brine and fish told me we were no longer in the Sierra Mountains where the afternoon shadows had vanished into the blanket of twilight. I took a deep breath and slowly let it out savoring the scent of the ocean through my body. The endless waves crashed on the beach in front of us leaving foam and glistening sand behind as the water receded. Behind me, an almost sheer wall of lush, tropical plants surrounded large areas of multi-faceted and variegated smooth-looking stone that stood as testament to the eons of interplay with the ocean. Wherever we were, we were alone in both the Third and Fifth Dimensions.

"Where are we?" I asked Jace breathless from the majesty surrounding me.

"At the beach," he said grinning.

"No, duh, dude!" I playfully slapped his arm. "What beach? Where?"

"The Big Island in Hawaii. This beach is inaccessible from land, and because of the wave action, not a lot of boats anchor out there. This is one of my favorite places in the world. I thought I'd share it with you," he put his hands on my waist and looked down at me. Yeah, that made me all hot and bothered, which of course, was totally visible on my now cherry-colored face.

"It's beautiful! Thank you!"

"I thought you deserved a break from all that serious mumbo jumbo back at the colony. Are you hungry?"

"Yeah."

"Then dinner is served!" he said turning me around. In front of us was a round table sporting a red and white checkered tablecloth and a matching red umbrella. The cushions on the chairs coordinated perfectly. The table was set for two and a lush green salad sat at each place, along with a glass of ice water and a Coke. Completely enchanted, I squeaked in surprised delight, clapped my hands, and oohed and aahed as I walked around the table admiring his handiwork. Just behind our seats a large lava boulder stuck out of the sand. I set my notebook down on it and turned to look at Jace. While I had my back turned, he had changed his clothes to shorts and a Hawaiian shirt. He smiled at me with a lopsided grin.

"You like?" He asked me.

I looked him up and down as I raised my eyebrows. "Yeah, I like." I said sporting a mischievous grin and nodding my head. I was totally charmed and nervous at the same time. My logical brain hadn't caught up with my emotional one yet. On one level I was so comfortable with Jace, I felt we had known each other for years. In reality, though, we've barely spent any time together . . . certainly not alone . . . like this.

Smiling and blushing at the same time, he shook his head. "I'm talking about our picnic at the beach," he clarified.

"Oh, that! Yes, it's amazing! I don't know if I'll ever get used to everything that can be done in the Fifth Dimension with just a thought. What else is on the menu?" My mouth began to water. I was hungrier than I initially thought.

"Whatever you want, although I was kinda hoping you liked lobster," he replied.

"I love lobster," I said smiling. "Hey, Jace, can you turn around for a sec. I'd like to change my clothes too." He gave me a quizzical look, but did as I asked. I quickly reformed my jeans and long sleeve tunic into a Hawaiian sundress, and because I thought it would be totally silly, I made my dress out of the same material as Jace's shirt. My tennis shoes disappeared and the soft, warm sand gently sifted through my toes. When Jace turned back around and saw my dress, he laughed happily.

Dinner was delicious and created completely by his thoughts. Jace explained to me that once something is invented or created and named in any dimension, the energetic recipe, schematic, or plan is permanently imprinted into the aetheric or Goddessence and is then available to be recalled into existence at any time. That's how he created our dinner. When we were through with our Bananas Foster dessert, Jace cleared the table. Literally. Everything vanished and in its place was a big red blanket that spread across the sand. Now that was the way to do the dishes! Jace sat down on the cover and patted the space next to him. I took the hint.

"I want to show you something." The look in his eye and shift in his energy communicated that this was going to be something serious. He turned to face me sitting cross-legged. Ignoring the butterflies that started zipping around in my stomach, I mirrored his position tucking my dress under my knees, suddenly glad I had thought to make it ankle length instead of a mini. "Hold my hands. Now close your eyes and take a deep breath. As you let it out, focus on your connection to your core." I did as he asked, finding it easy to get centered because of the abundant energy surrounding us here. "Okay, now open your eyes."

Above each of our clasped hands two double helix-shaped, polished silver and luminescent gold ribbons of energy rippled together in a seamless balance. They swirled sinuously together, timed perfectly and harmoniously in their own choreographed dance. Their appearance and movement somewhat reminded me of how my parent's auras had joined together in the hospital when I awakened from the coma.

"Jace, what am I looking at here?" I asked, a little nervous about what I was going to find out. I could feel the ribbons of vitality pulsating through me. I was absolutely sure that our heartbeats were joined and beating together in perfect harmony. As I realized this, my pulse sped up which was immediately reflected in the double helix dance between us.

"Our energy fields."

"Uh, huh . . . and . . ." I prompted.

"And, how they are connected to each other . . . part of each other," he said prompting me to shift my gaze from the dancing DNA to his emerald eyes. That made sense to me on some deep emotional level; only my logical brain wasn't processing very well.

"And that means . . ."

"It means that . . . uh . . . , it means that we are . . . um . . . Twin Flames," he blurted out. He was obviously struggling to get across what he was saying to me, but I couldn't make it any easier for him. I had no idea what he was talking about.

"What's a Twin Flame, Jace?" Startled by my question, he looked at me with wide eyes. The shifting of his focus caused the ribbons of energy to slowly dissipate. "I'm sorry. I'm not trying to make this difficult for you on purpose, but I really don't know this stuff. I wasn't raised in the Fifth Dimension where metaphysics is taught in elementary school."

Jace let go of my hands, rubbed his eyes and blew out a deep breath. "Okay, I'll do my best to explain twin flames to you." He stretched his legs out and rolled onto his side, propping his head up with his hand. I did the same. It was more comfortable than sitting cross-legged.

"The other name for Twin Flames is Twin Souls. Initially created at the same time, they are, simultaneously, the other half of each other's soul and a complete soul individually. Kinda like the way identical twins are formed from the same egg and sperm that split off into two separate people. We each have only one Twin Flame. It is said that Twin Flames don't share too many lifetimes jointly, that they only come back together in their last physical embodiment."

"So you think you and I are twin flames?" I asked flattered but not quite buying it.

"I don't think, Salena, I know. I just proved it."

"With the dancing double helix energy ribbons?"

"Yes."

"Why does that prove it?"

"Because they were attracted together like magnets, fit together perfectly, and they formed the double helix when they came together. DNA is the code of the Divine."

"Who told you they thought we were Twin

Flames? Or did you know this from the first time you met me?"

"No, I didn't know, but Douglas, Diana, and Amalya were suspicious. They knew something was up the way our energies mixed when we first met. But I think the kicker was when we partially symbed," Jace said, his face turning the color of the blanket. The memory of that incident still made him uncomfortable. "Chronoscenti Cosgrove said that's not easily achieved without mutual consent unless there is at least a soul group connection. The ease with which we connected told her there might be something more between us. She confirmed it when she traveled your soul star. She taught me how to perform that little demonstration to prove it to myself and you."

"What's a 'Soul Group Connection'? I mean, I've heard of soul mates before, but not a Soul Group Connection."

"Well, while we have only one twin flame, we can have many soul mates. Soul mates come from our Soul Family or Soul Group, and we have many lifetimes of experience with these people in various types of relationships like siblings, friends, parents, and spouses. Our soul mates incarnate with us to help us grow spiritually, therefore we have a deep love and divine connection to those people," Jace said.

I began to wonder if I was ever going to visit the Fifth Dimension without something, or everything, making my head spin. I laid on my back and gazed up at the azure sky watching the seagulls surf the currents of the wind, my brain swirling madly through what Jace just told me. *Holey Moley! Now what am I supposed to do? How do I assimilate this into my world? Jace is my freaking Twin Flame?! My perfect soul complement, the other half of my spirit? Really? Could our future in this incarnation be any more problematic?* I closed my eyes in a slow blink, and then opened them slowly holding Jace's gaze.

"What does that mean for us, Jace? Are we like, soul-star-crossed lovers or something? We're from two different freaking dimensions. Romeo and Juliet have nothing on us. I can't stay here forever, and you can't come to the Third Dimension with me."

Jace placed a soft finger on my chin and turned my head towards him, and cupped my cheek with his palm. "I honestly have no idea what it means for our future, but right now all I care about is our present." And then he kissed me. Gentle and tentative at first until I responded with a heat and passion I didn't know I had in me. At that moment I let go of all the bazillion bytes of information I had tried to absorb during the day, all of the responsibility I felt for the Third Dimension, and all of the potential complications the future might bring. My energy field burst open without those restraints and uninhibitedly joined with Jace's. My body was on fire inside and out. Energy, pure and divine, filled me up until I felt like I couldn't contain it any longer. It was the most exotic and erotic experience I had ever felt, and we were still fully clothed. Good thing too, because somebody cleared their throat above us.

My eyes shot open and my heart practically pounded out of my chest. Jace rolled himself to a seated position squinting up at the sky. I could barely make her out with the sun shining through her, but she was there, hovering above us. At least she had the decency to look a little contrite.

"Gawd, Angeni! Can't you at least knock?" I scolded her, pushing myself up while trying to make my irritation wash away the heat I felt in my face.

"Sorry kiddo, but your mom sent me to look for you. They are getting worried," she said.

"Really, you couldn't have just, like, I don't know, peeked in on me, without interrupting, and gone back to tell them I'm fine?!" I stood up and brushed off some sand.

"Sorry, sweetie, they wanted me to tell you it was time to come home. They might have freaked out if I went back and told them you were making out on a beach in Hawaii and couldn't be disturbed."

"Oh, ha ha! You're really funny, you know that? I thought you were supposed to be my spirit 'guide', the operative word here being 'guide' not babysitter."

"Salena," Jace said quietly touching my arm. "It's okay, really. We weren't doing anything wrong."

"I know, it's not that. It's just that I don't want to go back and face all that crap back home. I'm not ready to go." I pouted.

"It's okay, Jace, I'm used to Salena taking her frustrations out on me," Angeni said smiling. I narrowed my eyes and shot her a dirty look. I was tempted to stick my tongue out at her, but I thought that might invalidate my babysitter comment.

"I'm sorry, Angeni, but you know how much I

hate it when you sneak up on me," I said hanging my head in remorse.

"Apology accepted," she said.

"Will you go back and tell my parents I'll be home soon, please?"

She looked at Jace. "I'll get her home safely," he promised.

"Okay, but I'll be back if you don't come home soon."

"Of that, I have no doubt," I said giving her the shooing motion with my hands.

Alone together again, I shyly looked up at Jace. "Sorry about that."

Jace laughed. "There's nothing to apologize for Salena. I had a great time!"

"Yeah? Me too!" I said. Jace grabbed my hand and pulled me off of the blanket, which then disappeared. We walked over to the holey, black rock and picked up my notebook. Jace wrapped his arms around me, and I embraced him back. Smiling, I looked up at him. He kissed me again, and I closed my eyes reveling in the soothing caress of our compatible energies.

When I re-opened my eyes, we were in my bedroom. *Now that was the best way to travel!* I thought. "That was . . . nice."

"Yes . . . it was," he smiled. "I should get going. Don't stay away too long."

"Uh, Jace. Does this Twin Flame thing make us, like, I don't know, um, in an official relationship or anything?"

"Do you think it should?" He asked.

I took a deep breath and let it out as a sigh. "I think it would be so cool to be in an official relationship with you, but we live in two different *dimensions!* And, in all honesty, there's this guy in the Third, named Tim, that I've liked for, like, ever. And he just noticed that I was actually alive. I like you both, a lot . . . I'm so confused." I said looking down at my feet.

Jace tilted my head up so I could look him in the eyes. "Jealousy is one of those emotions linked to fear that can trigger evanescence in the Fifth Dimension, so we aren't raised with the same preconceptions about relationships that you are in the Third. I know you have feelings for Tim, since he is part of your soul group, I would be very surprised if you didn't. There is likely something that you are supposed to learn from him in this lifetime. I can't keep you from experiencing whatever that is."

"Wait! What? Tim's one of my soul mates?" I questioned.

"Yup, everyone in your expanded 'Society of the Silver Moon' is. So, for right now, I think that we need to take our relationship each day or moment at a time. When we are able to spend time together we rejoice in the moment and learn all we can. It's really all we can do for now."

"Are you sure you aren't just, I don't know, like waaaay too mature for me?"

He laughed. "Maybe. You bring up a good point. We might have to cool it for a while until you grow up a little!" He teased as I gasped in feigned shock at his taunt and blew him a raspberry; he stilled it with a kiss.

"Take care of yourself, Salena. I'll see you soon," he said and was gone.

CHAPTER NINETEEN
Trinity Trials

I shifted the sundress back into the jeans and top I was wearing earlier (those were my favorite pants), and transported myself to the family room and kitchen. I wanted to reappear in here so my parents knew that I was home, and I could quickly lie down on the couch. I noticed that it was very dark outside when I glanced out the sliding glass doors to the patio, and breathed a heavy sigh. Due to the duration of my stay in the Fifth today, this reentry was bound to be painful. Searching for a fear thought to obsess about, I finally settled on what might happen if we couldn't figure out a cure. *How many people would die because I wasn't good enough?* Yup, that did it. I began to feel heavy, sweaty, and thirsty.

Good god it hurt! I heard my mother gasp as my legs gave out and I crumbled onto the couch, moaning. Mom rushed over to me from the kitchen sink, and Dad followed her with two big glasses of water. I didn't say anything for a moment, taking deep breaths while I let the dizziness pass. Then I began to shake uncontrollably, like I had a high fever or something. I was really hoping that I wasn't going to lose my lobster dinner.

"This was the longest she's been gone. Even longer than last Saturday," Dad commented to Mom as they waited for me to open my eyes.

"I wish we had some way to communicate with her other than through Angeni. I'm not sure she is aware of the passage of our time over there. She said it does work differently," Mom replied.

"Well, I for one, am glad that you can communicate with Angeni and she is able to find Salena, no matter where she goes. I consider that a real blessing." Dad said. Then he noticed my binder. "What does she have in her hand?" Dad asked as he reached down to grab my notebook. I opened my eyes and smiled at them.

"Notes from the 5D version of a college prep class I took today," I replied with a hoarse voice. "They tried to give me all kinds of ideas on how to treat the Blue Flu, but they didn't give me a cure for it. It can't exist in the Fifth Dimension, so they can't run any experiments." Dad took a seat in one of the recliners across from the couch and started to read my notes.

"Can you drink this yet?" Mom asked me handing me a glass of water.

"Yes, thanks," I said propping myself up. The water tasted really good as I drank it all down and began to feel more normal again. "Sorry I was gone so long, again. Jace took me out to dinner, and . . . I . . . uh . . . got distracted. What time is it anyway?"

"8:30 p.m." Mom replied.

"Oh, I didn't mean to make you worry. I had no

idea," I said, sheepishly. "Is there still school tomorrow?"

"Yes, although more and more teachers are calling in sick. I think they are about at the tipping point. Principal Green called and said that your teachers would be giving you all the information for how they are going to continue their class over the internet through Skype and such. They have been working on multiple solutions district wide for just this potential scenario. I think Monday will be the district's first attempt at public home schooling." Dad informed me.

"What about UNR?" I asked.

"Yeah, we are doing the same thing. It's probably best that people avoid getting together in large public venues for awhile."

"Well, I do have some good news. Chronoscenti Cosgrove told me that the lighter gray the aura, or the less amount of fear a person has, the slower the disease spreads throughout their body, and rather than causing quick suffocation, it just makes the person sort of chronically ill with recurring infections. Also, the disease doesn't become contagious with those individuals. Simply put, the more fear-based a person is, the faster the infection spreads, becomes transmittable, and kills. I was excited when I heard that, because it means that we have more time to treat Trinity, and she might not die!" I explained.

"That is good news, Salena. Lesley was able to get access to an aura imaging system from a company out of Southern California. She explained to them a bit about what you had discovered and why we need it.

They are going to let us use it on loan to see if it will allow the rest of us to see what you do and assist with diagnosis. It will also give us the ability to record the healing sessions we try with Trinity. The company is very interested in the results of our tests. If it works, they won't be able to keep up with the demand for their systems. Lesley said it shipped on Tuesday, so she should be getting it tomorrow. We all agreed to start at 8:00 a.m. on Saturday at the Von Housen's."

"That's great news, Mom! Do all the kids know?"

"I think so, but you might want to check your phone for any email or text messages."

"You took some excellent notes here Salena. Mind if I keep reading this for awhile?" Dad asked me.

"Knock yourself out, Dad. I'm wiped. If I'm gonna go to school tomorrow, I need to get some sleep." Feeling the weight of the Third Dimension fully settled in my body now, I slowly stood and headed to bed.

Queen Victoria and her sycophantic (word supplied by Sam) ladies-in-waiting were noticeably absent from school on Friday. I didn't really miss them, but I was both morbidly curious and sadly dreading finding out if Victoria's infection had spread, despite her solidly grey aura. Not that I didn't trust the Chronoscenti's word, but I wanted to see for myself. I guess I'd just have to wait until Saturday to see if the contamination in Trinity's aura had stayed the same or gotten worse.

The mood was somber at school, and I noticed more and more ashy energy fields. The horrible irony of this plague was that the wider it spread, the more fear there was to feed on, which only perpetuated the problem. We were running out of time to find a cure and tell people what the real cause of the Blue Flu was. I was so frustrated that I just wanted to scream.

The best part of the day was when I was able to tell Katrina and the rest of the original Sisterhood that her mom has a good chance of surviving and why. Kat was so happy she was in tears and kept hugging me and laughing. After that, I kept my friends fully entertained as I relayed the events of the day before, including the juicy details of my date with Jace.

Mom, Dad, and I pulled into the Von Housen's driveway promptly at 8:00 a.m. on the first Saturday of November. Tim opened the door and smiled at me. I was proud of myself for looking him straight in the eyes and smiling back. The rest of my team was already gathered in the family room waiting for us as we joined them.

"Hi Mia and James," Lesley said. "There's fresh coffee and some pumpkin bread in the kitchen. Help yourself."

"Oh, thank heavens!" My mom gushed and grabbed my Dad's hand leading him into the kitchen. The doorbell rang and I heard Tim welcome Trinity and Katrina.

"Sounds like the gang's all here. Why don't we head upstairs?" Lesley said leading the way. "Lisa and I thought we'd set up everything in the game room over the garage. We've got room to move around in there."

We all headed up the circular staircase and walked

down the hallway to their game room. The furniture was once again moved out of the way, but this time in the center of the room was a hospital gurney and a bed-height table with a laptop that had a little camera, a weird hand-shaped pad and a separate flatscreen monitor. Directly kitty-corner across from the laptop table there was also a video camera sitting on a tripod. I was impressed. Somebody had been busy. I sure hoped that the Aura System was able to show what I see, otherwise I didn't know how to prove that what I was seeing was real.

"Salena, Kat and your mom have been telling me about some rather bizarre abilities that you claim to have," Katrina looked at me questioningly.

"Yes, ma'am. What they are telling you is the truth, and I really hope you believe me."

"Knowing you as I have over the last several years, I can't think of any good reason for you to make any of this up; but, is it okay if I remain skeptical and adopt a 'wait and see' approach to what we are going to do today?"

"Yes. Just remember, if you can't believe in me, believe in the love that you and Kat have for each other, and believe in your daughter. She wouldn't have asked you to do this if she didn't believe it was important."

Trinity cocked her head and looked at me as if seeing me for the first time. She nodded her head slightly and said, "Okay. I'm ready. Where do we start?"

"I'll be your chauffer, this evening. If you'll kindly climb aboard," Connelly swooped down in a bow to Trinity and pointed to the gurney. She laughed, took off her sweater, and climbed onto it. Lisa looked very official in her doctor's lab coat.

"Lisa, Sam, and I spent quite a bit of time playing with this yesterday afternoon and evening to get it set up. I think you'll be pleased Salena. It seems to work pretty well," Lesley said. "Trinity, just place your hand on this pad and your aura will show up on the screen. We've picked the full-body shot so we can see all of your chakras as well." We all gathered around to see what would happen.

I noticed that the colors on the screen were softer and more muted than what I could see. The monitor showed Trinity's light body to be more like a puffy multi-hued cloud and didn't include the more vivid and striking rays of colored lights that I saw. Excitement coursed through me as I realized that the colors on the computer aligned very closely with my Sight! Elated, I told the group that the program was pretty accurate.

"Now look at her Sacral Chakra, the second one from the bottom. Do you see the black spot there?" I pointed to the screen. Everyone nodded and murmured in astonishment. "That's the infection. On the screen it's barely the size of a period. However, what I see on Trinity is about the size of a silver dollar. By the way, it hasn't grown at all in a week. Which is totally awesome," I smiled at Trinity and Kat who beamed a movie star smile back to me. "Also the screen shows the gray to be more of a muddied white, but the difference between gray and white in my eyes is very significant and they mean two very different things. So far I've only seen white in the auras of people in the Fifth Dimension and spirits. Nobody here has white in their energy field today, so I can't show you the difference."

I continued, "An infection the size of Trinity's may be hard to spot if you didn't know where to look, however I'm pretty sure that the severely infected and contagious people will be easier to diagnose with this equipment. On the guys I saw in Singapore, the black pulsing spider-like bodies of the virus were bigger than my fist. We'll need to find a more infected person than Trinity to really be able to show that what we are claiming is actually true."

"With your mom and Angeni's help last week we have identified several people in the hospital who are severely infected. Now that we can see Trinity's infection, we can proceed with attempting to treat it today. If we are successful, I should be able to convince at least one of the patients we've identified to try our new procedure. Mia, can you and Salena meet me at Reno General tomorrow and we'll see if we can drum up any volunteers? I think if we show them their aura, we might have people lining up!" Dr. Lisa said to the group.

I looked to Mom for confirmation and she turned to me, nodding. "Yes, I believe we can manage that," my mom said.

"So, are we ready to begin the healing session?" Dr. Lisa asked. Everyone in the room nodded. "Okay, Salena, where do we start?"

"Well, I've been giving this a lot of thought over the last couple of days. I even had Mom take me down to the stone store near the airport yesterday, and we picked up a few different crystals. I figured every little bit would help. I thought we'd start with what we know does work and that's cleansing Trinity's aura of fear. The Fifth Dimensionals said the guy they saw who got rid of the fear in his energy field still had the infection, but it had gone dormant. So if nothing else works, at least we can prevent Trinity from having any of the ugly symptoms," I explained. "Trinity, we are going to surround you in a circle and focus on sending you loving and healing energy. You have the harder part. You have to repeat a powerful statement of forgiveness that you firmly believe and fill it with intention and purpose. You have been afraid of something or somebody for some period of time and that fear has accumulated in your light body. Do you know who or what it is that you need to forgive?" I asked her gently.

Trinity creased her brow in a worried frown as she looked around the room. She really didn't know any of us very well, and we were asking her to open up and share very intimate stuff with us. Her eyes settled on her daughter, and I knew then that she was mostly worried about what Katrina would think of her if she revealed her deepest fear. Kat picked up on her mother's distress, walked up to the gurney, and took her hand.

"Mommy, I love you, no matter what you say. I've already forgiven Daddy for how he treated you and me. He's gone now anyway, so by not forgiving him and holding it all in, you're only hurting yourself. Trust us with this. Trust me," she said. My eyes were stinging as I felt tears forming. Blinking rapidly to try to keep myself under control, I noticed that none of the other females in the room were having any better luck than I was. Even the guys were glassy-eyed.

"My sweet girl, how did you get so wise?" Trinity asked Kat as she reached up and touched her daughter's cheek wiping off an errant tear. "So what do I say?" She asked looking at me, then my mom and then Lisa.

Lesley answered her, "Alright, what we said last weekend was 'I am here to purify and cleanse the past from my physical and energetic being. I release myself from any past events, people, or places that have caused me harm or people who continue to cause harm to me or my loved ones. My spirit, soul, and aura are clean and balanced, and I forgive the past. Specifically, I forgive . . . ' and then Katrina and I filled in the blank."

"Uh, okay. That's a lot to remember," Trinity replied. "Can you write it down for me?"

"Already have! Here," Lesley said as she handed Trinity the piece of paper from which she had been reciting.

"Trinity, since we are trying to cleanse your aura and cure your infection, I'd suggest that we amp up the forgiveness statement. So where you start saying, 'Specifically, I forgive' continue with something like 'I forgive Dean Drake for causing me pain. I forgive Dean Drake for causing Katrina pain. I forgive myself for any mistakes I've made. I release the fear. It is gone.' Or something like that," my mom suggested.

"I think I can do that," Trinity said as she looked at her daughter and gave her hand a squeeze. "Will you please add what you just said to this piece of paper?" Trinity handed the paper to Mom who quickly wrote down her suggestion.

Trinity looked at the piece of paper that mom handed back to her, took a deep breath and said, "Okay, I'm ready. Let's do this."

"Sam, will you start the video camera?" I asked

"Sure, and the Aura program also allows us to record the aura as well. Want me to get that going too?"

"Really? That'd be great!" I told him.

"I'm on it!" He replied as the rest of us took our places forming a circle around Trinity. "Remember to keep your hand on the sensor pad the whole time, okay?" Sam told Kat's mom and she nodded.

The original members of the sisterhood took their usual places in the circle and the rest of the group filled in at the midpoints. I stayed in the middle with Trinity to represent Spirit. My dad and Dr. Lisa (the two scientists of the group) decided to observe.

We began by calling in the directions and welcoming the elements into our circle just as we did in the earlier cleansing ceremony. I stood behind Trinity's head and gently placed my hands on her Crown Chakra at the very top of her head as I invited Spirit to join our circle. I marveled at the energetic dome we had created around us, noticing the energy today was just as strong as it had been last Saturday.

"This circle is closed," I announced. "Okay everyone, just as we did last week, please close your eyes. Take a deep breath, and as you exhale visualize sending waves of turquoise energy to surround Trinity.

Imagine it washing away any dirt or stains and cleaning her aura. After you've done that three times, then breathe naturally, quietly hold the vision of Trinity with a clean and pure teal or white energy surrounding her as you repeat to yourself: You are light. You are love. Release your fear and forgive. I love you, over and over while Trinity says her part," I instructed.

We all closed our eyes and breathed deeply. I felt Trinity relax a little through my connection with her through her crown chakra. Just as before, I invoked the blessing ability of peaceful, powerful, spiritual energy to manifest within this circle. After that I led Trinity into her forgiveness statements.

After the second time through I heard Lisa whisper to my dad, "James, do you see that?"

"Remarkable," Dad whispered back. I opened my eyes and looked at Trinity's light body now cleansed of all the fog, which allowed her normal rose and emerald colors to be more vibrant and dominant. As pleased as I was to see that, I couldn't help noticing that the black spot below her belly button was still there. We were definitely missing a key element in this process, and I had no idea what it was.

"Trinity, your aura is cleansed! You did it! There's no more muddied white!" Dr. Lisa exclaimed. I noticed Lisa was definitely more excited this time than she was last week when we cleansed Lesley and Kat's auras. I guess seeing truly is believing.

"It is?!" Trinity exclaimed looking down at herself attempting to see her own aura. Realizing that was futile, she looked over at the computer monitor.

"Wow! It does look different! That wasn't so hard. I do feel so much more peaceful and less stressed. Thank you, Salena. Kat, honey, that was amazing!" Her radiant smile lit up her face.

"I know! I felt so good after the cleansing ceremony last weekend too. It was awesome!" Katrina concurred.

"Yes, I am so excited that worked a second time. We have a good process now for helping people increase their immunity to the Blue Flu. But, unfortunately, we didn't get rid of your infection, Trinity. The black spot is still there. We are missing something. Dad, you reviewed all my notes from Thursday, what would you suggest we try?" I asked him. He walked over to pick up my notebook from the table where he had set it.

"Let's see. The Chronoscenties instructed you on the healing power of quartz crystal. Why don't you try placing the quartz crystal over the dark energy location and see if it absorbs it," He suggested.

"I don't think that will be enough, James," my mom said. "The crystal will be a good receptacle, but I don't think the infection is going to randomly decide on its own to go into the crystal. Something needs to direct it," my Mom added.

"What if we visualize the nasty splotch, like merging into the crystal?" Leah suggested.

"Yeah, that might work. Mom, you willing to go for it?" Kat asked.

"Baby, I am more than willing to rid myself of any residual negative energy your father left with me.

Going forward I'm focusing on the most positive and beautiful gift he ever gave me, and that's you!" Trinity replied.

"Intention and belief are the most powerful thoughts we have to be able to make this happen. So we need to focus and purposely visualize the charcoal smudge going into the crystal, but most importantly we need to *believe* it can," I said as I placed one of the quartz crystals I bought yesterday right on top of Trinity's sacral chakra.

We all closed our eyes and took several deep breaths to center ourselves, and then visualized the splotch, as Leah aptly called it, merging with the crystal. And . . . nothing happened. Well, almost nothing. Energy swirled around the infection, but it didn't move.

"Dad? Any other suggestions?" I asked, letting out a frustrated sigh.

He flipped through my notebook, and gave us some more suggestions. Those didn't work either. After a few more hours and several failed attempts, we decided to take a break. The level of frustration we were all beginning to feel had negatively affected the energy in the room. We opened the circle and released the energy.

Lesley went down stairs to pull out some lunch stuff. While we filled our bodies with food power, we discussed what we would try next. Our resident Physics Professor (a.k.a. my dad) was in his element, and he had a captive audience.

"Alright, let me see. Chancellor Williams talked a lot about the ubiquitous field of energy that runs through everything. Quantum physicists in the early twentieth century tried to call it ether, but that name has fallen out of favor and there isn't one name yet that everyone agrees upon because once proven scientifically, I believe it will be the convergence of science and spirituality. In any case, according to the Chancellor, it is this energy, Salena you call it the Goddessence, that is the source of all creation in the Fifth dimension. It is also in this dimension; we just haven't figured out yet how to use it," Dad said thinking out loud.

"Dad, seriously, that's really interesting and all, but could you, like maybe, get to the point?" I prodded. Dad's annoyance with my impatience was communicated loud and clear with the single look he shot my way.

"I'm thinking here, Salena," he commented drily.

"Yeah, I know. I can see the smoke rising from over here," I teased. That earned me the *very* annoyed dad look.

"Mia, a little help here, please. Your daughter drives me to distraction," Dad pleaded with Mom who laughed and shook her head at me.

"I actually do have some thoughts about how we might take everything we tried this morning and punch it up a bit," Mom said and now *she* had our undivided attention. "We've proven that forgiveness is the essential ingredient to cleansing an aura, but what is the key to healing fear?" We all looked at her, waiting for her to continue.

"*Love*. Love is the cure for fear. The Goddessence is love—our focused and unwavering belief and knowledge that we are part of, and not separate from, the Goddessence—NOW. That we are LOVE—right NOW—that we are whole and healed right NOW. That is the 'something' I think we were missing."

That raised everyone's energy, and suddenly there were several excited conversations going at once. Eager to test my mom's idea we all headed back upstairs, turned on the equipment, and reacquired our places in the circle. Mom asked each person to close their eyes and take a deep breath filling their core, and let it out completely carrying away any and all negative thoughts or energy. We repeated that two more times and then we cast the circle again.

We were getting good at it. Everyone's voices were full of conviction and authority. I watched the elements respond quickly and everyone's auras expand wider and faster. I could feel the joy and excitement radiating off of the group, now that they saw with their own eyes the results of our work in cleansing Trinity's aura this morning. I knew, from someplace deep inside me that I was meant to be a part of this process and to awaken this group to the invisible, incredible capabilities of the Metaphysical world. I shook off any lingering doubts about my ability to help make this happen. I was given a gift and the responsibility to teach others about this gift. Everyone here trusted me and believed in me. I needed to take that trust and belief and channel it into the healing process. It was time for me to fully embrace my potential and find a way to lift up the world, starting with my friends.

I closed the circle and completed my part of

invoking the blessing, when Tim spoke up, "I can feel the energy this time, Salena. It's like all my senses are heightened and I'm warmer, like I've been wrapped up in an electric blanket on a cold night," he said before we started the new part of the ceremony.

"Yeah, me too," Connelly agreed with his buddy. "I didn't notice it before, but it's definitely there this time." I smiled in response to Connelly's sloppy grin that spread across his face.

Keia rolled her eyes at her brother, and then smiled at him, happy that he "got it." "Took ya long enough!" she teased. The smile he gave her was full of brotherly love, but the mega-watt smile he sent sailing in my direction made my knees go weak.

Sam chimed in as well. "Yeah, dude. I know what you mean. The first time I felt it, it was like my body had gone on red-alert. Not in a bad way though, it's just like, suddenly I was hyperaware of everything around me. It's cool!"

"It makes me feel like I can accomplish anything," Leah agreed, catching Connelly's eye and then looking away.

Lesley looked at Keia and Tim with pride. "I know what you all mean. It's a little different being part of the outer circle rather than in the middle, receiving all the energy. Last week I felt like somebody had plugged me in. This time, it's a little different because I'm more focused on giving than receiving, yet it feels just as . . . incredible. Thank you, for including me."

With that single statement of gratitude, the energy in the circle increased to almost a palpable level for me. *If this is going to work, now is the time!* I thought.

"Let's get started, shall we?" I asked.

The outer circle and I started to repeat Mom's idea of a new chant that turned our cleansing ceremony into a healing one. "I am love. I am light. I am compassion. I am divine. I am pure Goddessence. It's already done. Trinity Drake is whole. Trinity Drake is perfect. Trinity Drake is healed. It's already done."

While the circle was chanting, Katrina's mom started to continually repeat the mantra my mom gave her, "I am love. I am pure goddessence. I am compassion. I am divine. I am whole. I am healed. I am love. It's already done."

After a few rounds of chants, I moved to Trinity's side and put the pointy end of a three-inch quartz crystal shard on top of the smudge stuck on her sacral chakra. I closed my eyes and visualized pulling the negative energy into the crystal, like a vacuum cleaner sucks up dirt. I had a brief sensation of stuck sluggishness like when you are trying to suck a large chunk of ice cream through a straw when drinking a milk shake. Then I felt the energy give way. Opening my eyes, I saw the blotch lift off of Trinity's energy field and funnel into the crystal! No longer clear, the quartz stone looked like a thunderstorm was raging inside of it.

CHAPTER TWENTY
Reality Testing

"Did we get that?!" I asked excitedly. "Please tell me we got that!" Dad was standing over the computer clicking the mouse.

"Yes! We got it! That was amazing Salena!" Dad beamed. Everyone whooped and hollered.

"Let me see that crystal, Salena," Trinity whispered in a reverent voice as she held out her hand. I placed it in her palm. The temperature of the crystal had dropped several degrees from room temperature almost immediately after capturing Trinity's infection.

"Incredible," she said, tears streaming unchecked down her cheeks. "Why is it so cold?"

"Fear has the lowest vibrational energy of all emotions. As molecules slow down, so does their temperature. Take water for instance. At its lowest and slowest vibrational rate it's ice, at its highest and fastest it's steam." Dad scientifically explained. Trinity looked from the dark crystal to my dad and then to me. Shuddering slightly, she handed it back to me quickly releasing it.

Trinity's tears triggered Kat's as they continued to

repeat words of gratitude and love to us and the divine universe. Lesley was telling her two children how much she loved and appreciated them. Connelly and Sam were remarking how cool it was to see the crystal fill up. I quickly brought everyone's attention back to me so we could open the circle and start celebrating. I think we watched the replay of Trinity's cure about twenty times!

Sam couldn't wait to get back home to begin making the Blue Flu Treatment Video that we planned to create. He grabbed a copy of the video, said his goodbyes and headed next door to his house. Our idea was to put the video and testimonials everywhere on the internet we could think of and link those to our website and blog. We had already purchased *BlueFlu.edu* as part of our plan. Sam's strategy was to make this information go viral . . . pardon the pun!

I looked down at the now smoky quartz crystal in my hand and wondered what to do with it. I guess I could ask Amalya or Diana the next time I'm Fifth Dimension. After making arrangements to meet up at the hospital the next day, we all headed home.

Reno doesn't get a lot of rain, and this had been an especially dry fall season. The wind had picked up bringing with it a biting cold from the north, but the sun shone brightly through the little wisps of clouds. As

I stared out my bedroom window at our backyard trees, I noticed their sunset colored leaves determinedly stuck to their branches shuddering in the breeze. I checked my phone. Leah texted me that she and her mom were going to meet us at the hospital at ten am. Keia and her mom really wanted to go, but Lesley didn't feel very welcome there after the way Mr. Black and his buddies had treated her. Sam had texted me earlier that he had finished editing the video and transcribing the ceremony and to check my email. I used the hour and a half before we had to leave to retrieve Sam's work and prepare myself for the big presentation.

Lisa and Leah met us in the lobby when we arrived and ushered us into a conference room where there were several other doctors and nurses waiting for us. We all took seats around the conference table. Leah and I sat next to each other. We were feeling a little awkward being included in this room with a bunch of grownups we didn't know.

"I would like to introduce Miakoda, James, and Salena Hawthorne," Lisa said to the medical personnel seated around the table. A few of you met Mia last week when she helped me identify and diagnose some of our patients. For those of you who didn't meet her last week, she is a psychologist with a private practice here in town. James is a physics professor at UNR and Salena goes to school with my daughter, Leah, who I believe you all know." There were welcoming smiles and nods around the table. "Salena, James, and Mia, these are the doctors and nurses I approached after your original discovery last weekend, and I have already brought them up to speed on our success from yesterday. They are very interested in seeing the video," Lisa continued as I handed her the flash drive. One of the nurses there was the same one who took care of me when I was recovering from the coma. Nurse Stephanie winked and smiled at me as Lisa handed the flash drive to her. She plugged it into the USB port of a laptop sitting on the conference table and worked to get the video launched.

There were shocked murmurs around the table when they saw the once clear crystal turn stormy grey, and then I brought out the crystal and quickly passed it around the table. Nobody wanted to hold it for long. The crystal was cold, almost freezing, and that wasn't because I had put it in the freezer. It also looked more like a lava rock than a quartz crystal now because it was dark, muted, and lifeless. The thunderstorm had gone dormant.

"Did you bring the aura visioning equipment?" a younger male doctor asked my dad. The guy's nametag said he was Dr. Daniel Yates.

"Yes," my dad replied. "It's all here in our bag. Also, here is a transcript of the ceremony that we performed. We might be able to improve upon it with practice, but for our purposes today, I think we should try to duplicate it as closely as possible in order to verify the results. If you have three patients who are willing to give it a try today, Salena brought several crystals with her. Also, I think each patient should have a different person using the crystal so we can hopefully show that this procedure works no matter who is part of the process," my dad said as he passed out the instructions.

"I just want to say that we appreciate your open-mindedness to try this metaphysical treatment. I have to admit, I was skeptical at first too even though I'm Salena's father and am fully aware of her unique capabilities," Dad looked apologetically at me and my mom.

This time a lady, Dr. Jennifer Ryan, spoke up. "We are willing to look at anything that will help cure or at least treat people with this illness, Dr. Hawthorne. And based on what you just showed us in this video, I am very excited about our opportunities to make great strides in that direction, even if it does fly in the face of western medicine," she smiled at her peers who returned it in kind. "It so happens that we do have three patients who have agreed to give our metaphysical therapy a try, and I can tell you that if it is successful, they will be lining up out the door. With Mia's help last week, we identified over a hundred patients in Reno General alone who are infected with the Blue Flu. A few didn't survive through the end of the week. Nothing we have tried seems to be working. Blood transfusions are helping a little by postponing the inevitable, but it certainly isn't curing the problem. We've also tried a hyperbaric chamber. The disease seems to stall when the patient is inside it, but once removed it picks back up where it left off."

"Well, there's no time like the present," Dr. Yates said as the rest of the team smiled and nodded. "Let's give it a go, shall we?"

The first patient was a woman in her mid-forties. She looked like an older version of Victoria who had definitely had her share of plastic surgery. Her expertly dyed hair hung limply around her make-up-free face. Despite the obvious surgeries, she still had creases that appeared to be permanently carved into a perpetual sneer. She had an oxygen tube in her nose and every breath she took was labored. Through my eyes, she appeared to be about fifty percent infected. Her light body was a mix of tarnished silver to freshly poured concrete. There was no doubt that image was everything to this woman who obviously worked out and spent hours in a tanning booth each week. The colors in the rest of her aura were muddied and told me she was judgmental, superficial, and insecure; I wasn't surprised she was infected. Her heart chakra housed the black widow body that was just beginning to eject small spores.

"What the hell are you doing here?!" a familiar voice in the corner exclaimed. Startled out of my examination, I turned my head to the occupied chair sitting in the corner of the room. No wonder this woman reminded me so much of Victoria, she must be her mother. Sitting in the corner of the room, looking pretty ragged out was none other than Victoria Love herself.

"V, darling, I've agreed to try this new treatment Dr. Ryan told me about. Don't be rude," her mom replied.

"But, Mom, that's Salena Hawthorne, the psycho freak at school I told you about," Victoria rose from the chair and whispered loudly enough for everyone in the room to hear. Puzzled, Mrs. Love looked questioningly at Dr. Lisa.

"Mrs. Carmen Love, I'd like to introduce the Hawthornes and my daughter, Leah. It was Salena, Leah, and her friends who brought this treatment to our attention," Dr. Lisa said. "It's a rather unconventional treatment, but it isn't invasive at all. It merely requires you to believe in its power to heal you. Are you still willing to let us try this on you and allow us to videotape you?" Lisa asked her. Mrs. Love looked to her daughter for input.

"It's up to you, Mom. I told you, she's a freak."

"Despite my daughter's ill-mannered advice, I believe I'd still like to give it a try," she said and Lisa handed her some forms to sign. Looking me and Leah up and down she commented, "You two seem very young to have discovered a new treatment for this flu. How is that possible?"

Leah looked at me rather helplessly, so I answered her. "I have the ability to see people's energy fields, Mrs. Love. I discovered that the Blue Flu was being spread from aura to aura. We've brought this computer program that captures peoples light bodies on the screen so you can see what I see. The biggest difference between the Blue Flu and every other type of disease is that this one is spread energetically not biologically. Therefore, the more positive mental energy and belief you can put into this procedure, the better your chance of success," I told her.

"All right," she said, although I could tell she was still more than a little skeptical.

I explained to the group what I saw before my

dad set up the system. Victoria's Mom was so much more infected than Trinity was that I was hoping it would show up clearly on the computer. Dad also brought in a thirty-two inch display to attach to the laptop and set up the whole contraption on a mobile cart he borrowed from the hospital.

"If you'd put your hand on this pad here, we can show you your aura," I told her as I moved the hand pad closer to her. Mrs. Love gently laid her palm on the pad and looked at the computer screen questioningly. Once again the aura visioning system showed a fairly accurate representation of what my Sight picked up. A collective gasp was heard from the group of people in the room as the full impact of her infection was displayed on the screen. It didn't capture the spores she was excreting, but that didn't really matter for our purposes.

"Oh, my Lord!" Carmen exclaimed as she stared at the screen, tears forming in her eyes and spilling down her cheeks. "That looks awful," she whispered. "You have a way to remove that?"

"Yes, we do," Lisa replied. "However, it requires as much of your belief and participation as it does ours." Lisa went on to explain the healing ceremony/procedure to Mrs. Love whose eyes got big.

"That sounds a bit heretical to me. I've always been a good Catholic woman," she explained to the group. I grabbed Leah's hand and we headed to a corner of the room. I didn't want to have anything to do with this discussion. I'd let the grownups work it out. My mom picked up the conversation at this point.

"You are right, this procedure incorporates more than solely Christian beliefs, Mrs. Love. In fact, in does a pretty good job of blending many spiritual beliefs and practices. The concept is to combine the powerful energies of the whole universe and the potent elements of nature to clear away the negativity that is currently affecting you. Many of our dominant religions today do a good job of polarizing people and programming them into believing that there is only one right belief. However, by accepting, combining, and balancing the positive principles of all spiritual practices we give this process the most chance for success. The choice to continue is still yours. There is very little risk to giving it a try," my mother gently explained.

I cleared my throat loudly to get the groups attention. "Mrs. Love, Victoria is also infected with the Blue flu, although her infection hasn't spread as much as yours. I'd like to recommend that she be included in your ceremony." Both Leah and Victoria looked at me completely startled.

"I'm infected too?" Victoria squeaked.

I nodded. "Mrs. Love, can I show you and your daughter her aura?" Victoria's mom nodded mutely. I showed my nemesis where to put her hand on the pad. Her ash colored aura filled the screen with a definitive black spot over her Solar Plexus Chakra. It had grown over the last week, but not exponentially.

"You knew?! You knew I was infected and you didn't say anything? You should have said something. You should have told me!" Victoria ranted hysterically quickly removing her hand from the sensory pad.

"You wouldn't have listened to anything I said anyway, Vicki," I snapped back at her. "I know what you and your friends think of me. You would have called me a freak and dismissed me."

"Girls, that's not helping," Dr. Lisa interrupted. "Shall we proceed with the matter at hand?"

Carmen looked at the monitor that was still displaying her daughter's tarnished aura, crossed herself with her free hand and sighed deeply. "Okay. Let's get this done. V, I would like you to join me, please." She pleaded as she held out her hand. Victoria didn't hesitate to grab it and hold on tightly.

I wasn't going to participate directly in this session as I did with Trinity's. We really want to see how well it works with different people using the crystal. Leah's mom decided to be at the center with Mrs. Love and her daughter. That was okay by me anyway. I rather doubted Vicki and I could get past our feelings for one another to really bring in the love necessary for this to work. Dr. Ryan closed the door to Carmen's private room and the nurses, Stephanie and Julie, rolled her into the middle. The doctors took the north and south points and the nurses took the east and west points. My dad manned the computer screen, and Mom joined Leah and me in the corner. To my surprise Angeni materialized next to me just before we got started.

"I'm glad you showed up," I whispered to her. "I'm a little nervous. I sure hope this works."

The doctors and nurses reviewed their parts and reviewed with Mrs. Love and Victoria their part of the ceremony. I held onto mom's and Leah's hands as we watched in silence. They cast the circle. I watched the auras of the doctors and nurses weave together into a powerful azure and aquamarine sphere with bolts of energy radiating inward. *So far so good!*

Dr. Lisa began her part as Spirit. She invoked the blessing ability of spiritual energy to manifest within the circle. After she finished, Mrs. Love chanted her words of forgiveness. The spider had stopped expelling black spitballs and I noticed some contraction of the infection and clearing of her aura. Dad could see Mrs. Love's energy field output increasing on the computer screen.

"It's working, keep it up," I said to the group, and I saw a rise in energy from everyone as doubts slid away and belief replaced them.

I nodded to Lisa as she maneuvered one of the two crystals I had handed to her earlier, like she would a scalpel, severing the links connecting the body of the infection to Mrs. Love's energetic field. She then placed the crystal over Carmen's heart chakra and closed her eyes and imagined the negative energy going into the crystal. Nothing happened at first, and I saw Lisa open one eye to check as a frown spread across her face. She looked over at me.

"Imagine the crystal as a straw that you are sucking on that has some large piece of ice stuck in it, but don't put your mouth on it. Keep sucking until it releases, then it should flow into the crystal," I instructed her, then under my breath, "I hope."

Dr. Lisa closed her eyes again and did as I said. I watched her cheeks suck in and vibrate. Then the crystal started to darken as angry storm clouds flowed into it and off of Mrs. Love's aura. I stared as the tentacles that had wrapped themselves around Mrs. Love funneled into the crystal like a long piece of spaghetti does when it gets sucked into a mouth.

"You did it!" My dad exclaimed to the group looking from the now burnt-looking crystal in Lisa's hand to the computer screen.

"We sure as hell did!" Lisa exclaimed quickly checking Carmen's oxygen saturation on the monitor, confirming its steady rise. Mrs. Love was crying, looking into each smiling face of the medical personnel surrounding her.

"I'm cured?" She asked.

"Yes," Lisa said gently as she placed a hand on Carmen's shoulder.

"Can you do V now?" Carmen asked.

"Of course," Lisa replied. The circle members repeated the same thing for Victoria. Surprisingly, clearing her aura was more difficult than cleansing her mother's. She had difficulty formulating her thoughts into words. I really don't think she wanted to say out loud what she had to because I was in the room.

Angeni spoke to me and mom, "Victoria is a very angry person who needs to forgive a lot of people, but first and foremost she needs to forgive herself."

I decided to try to make it easier for her by focusing my thoughts and intention on sending her love. That wasn't as easy as it sounded, all sorts of reasons why that was a bad idea kept entering my brain. Then I realized I needed to forgive Vicki. So I closed my eyes and took a deep cleansing breath. Surrounding myself in sparkling crystalline energy, I said to myself, *I forgive Victoria Love and clear the past between us. So mote it be.*

Vicki's first words of release and forgiveness were tentative and she was really struggling. I decided this would be a good time to pass on Angeni's advice.

"Vicki," I said gently, causing her to open her eyes and look at me. "Try forgiving yourself first."

Her eyes opened wide, tears spilling out unchecked, as she silently acknowledged the necessity of what I suggested. "I forgive myself," she said gasping for air as she sobbed.

Then, a dam broke. Vicki let loose with a cathartic rush of emotion and tears as she forgave her mother, her father, and some other man named Edward. I don't know if he was a relative or not, but whoever he was, he had damaged Victoria in ways I really didn't want to know about. Flashes of her memories played in my head causing me to cringe. I don't have that happen very often, thank goodness. This time though that elusive psychic ability gave me an insight into Vicki that changed my whole opinion of her. I could also tell from the striking angry reds in her energy field that Edward was the source of the fear that consumed her.

It was an intensely personal moment of sobbing and tears between Victoria and her mom. I was mesmerized as I watched mother and daughter bond through the processes of forgiveness and love. The energy in the room was now so tangible that I could almost taste it. I wiped an unexpected tear from my cheek as I watched the crystal in Lisa's hand that she had used on Vicki turn to a tarnished silver color.

Victoria and her mom weren't the only ones healed by their ceremony. I was too. I no longer hated or resented Victoria, and I no longer feared her either. I felt a great deal of compassion for Vicki and her family after discovering the pain that Edward guy caused them. Her strength and courage to face that in this group of relative strangers and "freaky" onlookers truly impressed me. I still didn't like Victoria, but I couldn't hate her either.

"Is that it? I'm cured now too?" Vicki asked.

"Yes. Your auras are no longer infected with the Blue Flu, and they've been cleansed of fear. As long as you hold onto what you've learned and truly embrace the forgiveness you experienced today, you'll be immune," I said. "Go ahead and put your hand on the sensor and see for yourself," I replied. They both did so, astonished that they could no longer see any black at all.

The doctors and nurses opened their circle, wheeled the head of the bed back against the wall and started to compare notes. I told them that I saw their auras intermingle and weave together as they formed their circle. I was convinced that helped to focus the energy that facilitated the healing. Everyone was very eager to try it again. Mrs. Love wanted to go home with her daughter, but the doctors told her that they'd like to keep her under observation for one more day and she reluctantly agreed.

As we were heading out of the room, Mrs. Love called me aside.

"Thank you for what you did for me and Victoria, young lady. You have been given a very timely gift it seems. You are very special," she said to me. *You don't know the half of it*, I thought, but out loud I just said, "You're welcome, and thank you."

The healing team was moving down the hall when Vicki tapped me on the shoulder and motioned for me to follow her. "Thank you," she said. I just looked at her blankly. "You didn't have to do that for me, especially after the way I've treated you lately. Sooo . . . Anyway . . . Thanks."

I didn't respond immediately as I held her gaze, determining her sincerity. Finally, after she started to fidget under my scrutiny I replied, "You're welcome, Vicki. I'm glad I was able to help you and your mom." She gave me a tentative smile and nod and then headed back to her mom's room, leaving me to catch up with the group.

Healing the next two patients was successful, but extremely challenging. Dr. Yates was the crystal conductor for our second patient who was a surly seventy-something-year-old man named Mr. Strable. It didn't take me very long to determine that he was very used to having things done his way and that he used fear as a means of controlling everyone in his life. I really didn't know if the treatment would work on him at all. He would be a really good test subject.

The value of the aura visioning system was proven once again. When we showed Mr. Strable how black his aura was, and then (with her permission) Carmen's healing, I guess a light bulb went off in his head. Dr. Yates commented to me that he had no idea how exhausting energy healing could be and passed on the crystal conducting to Nurse Stephanie for our last session.

Our last patient was a very young single mother named Lydia who had been in an abusive relationship. Apparently, her tormentor died of the Blue Flu a few weeks ago, so there was no doubt how she got infected. Leah and I took our usual positions in the corner of the room to observe the proceedings. Angeni silently followed us from room to room and was currently floating next to my mom and dad watching the aura on the screen. Thankfully, she doesn't talk to us too much when there are other people in the room, that way we don't look stupid talking to empty space.

"Mom told me that Lydia is also addicted to crack and alcohol," Leah whispered to me. "She's only twenty years old. She agreed to be a test subject because she doesn't want to leave her son alone."

"That's a whole lot of negativity and abuse to overcome. I can see it in the parts of her aura that aren't covered up by the disease. She may need some follow-up sessions," I whispered back.

Then Leah and I fell silent as the chanting began. I fixated on Nurse Stephanie's predominately turquoise light body as it expanded out further beyond her body and increased in intensity. *She has a real knack for this*, I thought, and then I watched the oil spill covering Lydia flow into the crystal in Stephanie's hand.

We're four for four, I said to myself as we all headed down the hall back to the meeting room where we first gathered. I looked out the windows and noticed that some clouds had covered the sky making it seem later than five o'clock, and the wind had picked up even more. The energy in the room was buzzing as the group animatedly discussed their thoughts and opinions on the procedures. For the most part, Leah and I had been forgotten as the adults discussed the next steps in getting the word out to the world. They decided to call the local news stations and do a press conference. Angeni faded out telling me it was time for her to go and that she would catch up with me later.

Dr. Yates made the call, and we didn't have to wait long for the news crews to show up. Lisa led the press conference and introduced me as the one who discovered the source of the Blue Flu through my ability to see auras. Thankfully there was no mention of the Fifth Dimension and the role they played in the discovery. We agreed that the fewer people who know about that the better. Leah's mom introduced the Aura Visioning System, played the videos, and then showed the four tarnished crystals. A few moments of stunned silence permeated the room after Lisa finished speaking. Suddenly, questions were shouted out fast and furious. Dad neatly deflected any further probing into my abilities and got the reporters to focus on the treatment. The questions were just beginning to die down when the enema man himself, Mr. Todd Black, barreled through the door.

CHAPTER TWENTY-ONE
Return to Akasha

"What the Hell is going on in here?!" Todd Black demanded, zeroing in on Leah's mom with an accusing stare.

"A press conference," Lisa replied stating the obvious as she looked directly at him not giving any ground. The reporters easily caught the tension radiating off of Mr. Black and eagerly swung their cameras in his direction hoping for some great drama.

"That much is obvious," Todd said with a sneer. His black pants and button-down shirt matched his dark and tormented aura. He wasn't infected, yet, but he's a perfect candidate. "Ladies and Gentlemen," he addressed the reporters. "This is an unsanctioned meeting and any information you were given by any hospital personnel has not been approved nor is it in any way affiliated with this hospital."

"So, Mr. Black, Reno General doesn't want to take any credit for potentially finding a treatment for the Blue Flu?" The reporter closest to Todd at the back of the room asked as he stuck a microphone into Mr. Black's face waiting for a response.

"A treatment for the Blue Flu? No. I know nothing about it except that Trader Pharmaceuticals has discovered a treatment that has been submitted to the FDA for final approval which is expected any day now," he replied. His statement was a surprise to everyone in the room. Registering everyone's intrigue, he pulled himself up to his full height, stuck his hawk nose up in the air slightly, and then looked down at all the hospital personnel at the front of the room. "Would any of you care to explain this treatment you've been working on behind my back?"

"I'd be happy to explain it to you, Todd," Dr. Ryan spoke up. A flash of irritation crossed Mr. Black's face at her use of his first name. Jennifer quickly summarized what Dr. Lisa had previously told the reporters and then showed him the crystals.

Todd had a look of incredulity on his face as he surveyed the room, I'm sure he didn't listen to a word Dr. Ryan said. "And you all believe this hocus pocus nonsense?!" He exclaimed to the group of reporters. Some nodded, others shrugged their shoulders. "If you want to believe the deranged rant of a brain damaged thirteen-year-old girl, that is certainly your prerogative. However, it is the policy of this hospital to base its treatments on sound scientific medical practices with treatments and medicines that have been approved by the FDA! Therefore, by showing such a blatant and public disregard for this hospital's policies and procedures, I have no choice but to relieve you all of your responsibilities here. Please remove any personal items from the premises when you leave today."

Without taking a breath he turned his focus on my dad. "As for you, Hawthorne family," Todd Black said as he spied us off to the side of the doctors and nurses. "We might have been able to prevent this unfortunate incident today had you brought your daughter back in for the testing that she needed after her coma."

I watched my dad's face flush as he took a deep breath and his back went rigid. Dad walked over to the Executive Director and put his face three inches from Todd's nose. "Mr. Black, your arrogance is equaled only by your ignorance. I will never allow my daughter to get anywhere near your grubby little hands for any reason. Now, step aside. With your arrival, the air in here became putrid." My dad's shoulder banged into Todd's causing the Executive Director to lose his balance. I was close enough behind dad to hear their interchange, but couldn't resist giving him a dig of my own. "Mr. Black," I said making him look down his nose at me. "I think it would be great if you personally attempted to prove me wrong."

"Oh, really? How's that?" He asked with a perfected patronizing tone.

"If you are so confident in Trader Pharmaceutical's new cure, why don't you go catch the Blue flu yourself. If their treatment doesn't work, well, then, you've done us all a favor!" I said, smiling.

Startled into silence, the Executive Director looked me up and down with an ugly look on his face. Then all Hell broke loose. Everybody started yelling and talking at once. I saw my mom take Leah's hand after she hugged her mom, and the two of them headed for the door after us.

The quietude in the hallway made me feel as if Dad and I had walked into a vacuum. I think my ears even popped. It had gotten dark outside and I realized I was really hungry. There was a moment of chaotic noise as Mom and Leah exited the conference room, only to disappear again as the door shut behind them.

"Well! That's something you don't experience every day!" My mom said as we started walking down the hall toward the exit.

"No kidding. Leah, is your mom okay?" I asked putting my arm around her.

"Yeah, she seemed to be. Told me not to worry, that she'd work it out and that I was to come home with you tonight. Your mom said it was okay," she responded quietly.

"Can we stop to eat on the way home?" I asked my parents.

"Yeah," Mom said smiling as she put her arm around Dad. "I don't feel like cooking."

We ate dinner at Hamburger House, and that was yummy, but we didn't get home until 9:30. Dad turned on the TV in the family room as soon as we got home to see what the Ten O'clock news would have to say. Leah and I sat on the couch together as Mom and Dad each took their favorite recliner. Channel 2 news put together a fairly comprehensive piece on our metaphysical treatment and even mentioned our website for more information. They also gave the YouTube address so people could see the healing videos. (Leah and I high-fived each other.) Then they showed Mr. Black debunking the whole thing and firing Leah's mom and the rest of the hospital staff who had participated.

The news stations even gave Mr. Black the privilege of being interviewed alone. His hawkish face filled the screen as he droned on. I did my best to tune into his nasally, monotone, voice.

> *Finding a treatment for the Blue Flu has been difficult because the disease targets different areas of the body. We do know that infected people are not producing enough red blood cells and, therefore, not enough oxygen. As the son-in-law of Mitch Trader, Chairman and CEO of Trader Pharmaceuticals, I have been authorized to reveal to you that the company has discovered a treatment to increase red blood cell production, and as a result increase oxygen levels in the body. This has proven to be an effective treatment for those infected with the Blue Flu. Trader Pharmaceuticals has submitted their treatment to the FDA and is currently awaiting their expected approval. I can assure everyone that developing a treatment for this pandemic has been Trader Pharmaceutical's number one priority since the outbreak in September. Reno General Hospital and Trader Pharmaceuticals have a long and prosperous history of working together to provide the community of Northern Nevada and our patients with cutting-edge treatments. We are working around the clock to ensure that our patients get the best care possible. You can count on us because we are*

committed to YOU! This is more than just my job. This is what I was born to do and why I was put on this planet.

"I've seen enough," Dad said with disgust as he pressed the off button on the remote. I continued to stare at the blank television for several moments while my brain processed what I had just heard.

"I have to go back," I said quietly, more to myself than anybody else.

"Back where, Honey?" Mom asked.

"Back into the Records. Back to Akasha," I said, now with more emphasis and conviction.

"Whatever for Salena?" Mom asked.

"Because we need to know if Trader's treatment is legitimate. I can go into the Records and watch what they've been doing for their testing. We know how the disease is spread, they clearly don't, but they think they've developed a treatment. I need to see what they've really done. While I'm there I can also find out what to do with the infected crystals. I'll go tomorrow after a good night's sleep."

"You'll miss the first day of public home school," Leah said. I kicked her foot with mine under the table. Mom and Dad nodded their heads in silent agreement.

"Yeah, I know, but I'll make it up on Tuesday. I promise."

I woke up Monday morning at 7:00 am to my cell phone softly playing Keia's special ring tone. Leah, who was still asleep on my floor, groaned and put the pillow over her head.

"Hey Keia!" I said softly answering the phone, trying not to disturb Leah as I navigated around her and out of my bedroom.

"Hey Sista! I think I got two hours of sleep. Sam was up all night monitoring Facebook and YouTube. We've got over 110,000 views already!! In just one night! Isn't that awesome!?"

"That's great," I said trying to sound enthusiastic as I stifled a yawn. "Sam's viral plan seems to be working."

"Most definitely. Don't ask me how, but he managed to find the footage of you and your dad telling off Mr. Black. That was awesome. Have I told you lately that I love you?!"

I laughed at her. "Did he post that?"

"Naw, he just showed it to me, Tim, and my mom. Mom says you're her hero now. That's two times you've showed Black his ass. Mom's mortified that he fired everyone. They're talking about setting up their own Blue Flu treatment center with my mom running it."

"Please tell Sam not to post that video, okay? That treatment center sounds totally awesome! I bet your mom's excited about that! Hey, I wanted you to know that I'm going back to the Fifth today. I've got to see if Trader's treatment is legitimate, and I need to find out what to do with the dirty crystals."

"You're parents are letting you go again?" She asked.

"Yeah, but they are sending Angeni along as my chaperone. She dropped in last night during our discussion and said she would go with me. That made them feel better. Is Leah going over to your house today since I won't be here?"

"Yeah, both she and her mom. I think the other doctors and nurses that were fired are also coming over. They are going to find a space to lease for their clinic."

"Cool. Have fun with public-home-school today. Let me know what I miss in Math, Science and English, 'kay?"

"Gotcha covered! Say 'Hi' to Jace!" Keia said, and I felt my ears get warm.

"Yeah, Okay. Say 'Hi' to Tim for me," I replied.

"Sure. Be safe Salena."

"I will. Later tater."

"See ya," Keia said as we hung up our phones.

Mom fixed me a huge breakfast and Dad took Leah over to Keia's house. I made sure to grab the five smoky crystals so I could ask somebody what to do with them, and I stuck them in the pocket of my jeans. I dressed in layers in case I had to go to the colony in the mountains and then to the Crystal Caves in Mexico. This time I decided to sit in the family room recliner for my journey to the Fifth. Mom watched over me as I vanished.

"I love you Salena," she said after I had

disappeared.

"Love you too, Mom," I said.

Nobody was waiting for me, so I decided to head to the colony first. I materialized in the center of the settlement. All of the buildings and homes were protected from the weather by some kind of energy field surrounding everything. I could see patches of snow outside the area, but inside the energy dome the air was temperate and dry.

Amalya, Jace, Diana, Chancellor Williams, and Chronoscenti Cosgrove exited the building where I sat through my Metaphysics lessons last Thursday and headed toward me. I got a hug from everyone except the Chancellor who shook my hand. The best embrace though, was from Jace who lingered longer and squeezed me tighter than anybody else.

"Welcome back, Salena," Amalya said. "I was shadowing you yesterday and knew you'd be coming over today, so we've been preparing for what you're going to do. As you know, Chancellor Hart Williams is the Fifth Dimension's foremost scientist and doctor. We thought he should join you and Chronoscenti Cosgrove in the Records because he is the best person to translate any medical-speak to you, and he will know immediately if what they have developed is legitimate."

"Sounds good to me."

"Salena, you and your friends did an excellent job in finding a treatment for the Blue Flu. I was very impressed," Chancellor Williams said to me.

"Thanks," I beamed. "Oh, before I forget what should I do with these?" I reached into my pocket and pulled out the crystals. To my surprise they were completely clear just like they were before the disease was sucked into them. "Uh, they were all dark and muddied when I put them in my pocket. Now they look perfect," I said frowning at the crystals in my hand and holding them out for the group to see.

"You changed their vibrational level when you brought them here, Salena," Chronoscenti Cosgrove explained. "Remember, negative energy can't survive here. So, as you ascended, the crystals were cleansed. Obviously that's not a practical solution for cleansing all the crystals in the world that are going to be contaminated, so my recommendation would be to soak them in salt water, sea water preferably, until they clear up. Then they should sit outside in direct sunlight for at least sixteen hours. After that the crystals should be ready to use on the next patient. See if that works when you get back home," the Chronoscenti told me.

"Does your remedy have anything to do with using the four elements?" I asked as I put the crystals back into my jeans pocket.

Lady Cosgrove's azure eyes danced and sparkled with my question. "What do you think?"

"Well, the crystals come from the earth, salt and water are purifying substances, sunlight comes from a fireball in the sky and the air outside isn't treated or processed. Am I close?" I asked curiously.

"You're better than close, my child. You nailed it," she smiled at me. I beamed at her praise. "So Hart and Salena are you ready to go?" Chronoscenti Cosgrove asked us.

I looked at Jace. "You're not coming?"

"Not this time," he said as he took both of my hands in his. "Don't repeat your last exit from the caves, okay? I won't be there to save you this time," he chided me.

"I won't. I promise," I said looking into his emerald eyes. "Can I leave these crystals with you for the time being? I'll stop back here before I go home."

"Sure! I'll be waiting," he said as he gave me a quick kiss in front of everyone. His affectionate display surprised, flattered, and made me slightly self-conscious. The adults didn't seem to care, though.

I took the Chronoscenti's outstretched hand. She clasped the Chancellor's hand with her free hand and the Sierra Nevada Colony vanished. We rematerialized inside the Crystal Cave this time. Just like last time it was warm, humid, and had that slightly rotten egg smell. I pulled off my sweatshirt and laid it across one of the selenite shards. I was slightly disappointed that I didn't get a chance to see the sexy Akashic Sentinels again. The other Chronoscentis welcomed me and greeted the Chancellor like an old friend as they exchanged pleasantries with him. I spotted two Third Dimensional scientists in orange jump suits entering the cave. *That's right. Today is Monday.* I giggled at the thought of what their reaction would be if I suddenly appeared in front of them.

"Are we ready?" Chronoscenti Cosgrove questioned me and the Chancellor, which brought me out of my reverie. The other Chronoscenti assumed their directional positions, and cast their circle. The vibrational energy of the music from the crystal bowls filled the cavern. Chronoscenti Cosgrove stood between the Chancellor and me facing the crystal lotus and took hold of my right hand and Hart's left hand. Chancellor Williams and I grabbed one of the crystal lotus petals with our free hands. The three of us closed our eyes and said out loud and all together, "I am entering the Akashic Records!"

CHAPTER TWENTY-TWO
Treatment or Torture?

The foggy marshmallow room with the twinkling soul stars appeared around us. I adjusted to the weightless disembodied feeling more easily now that I was a veteran. Chronoscenti Cosgrove didn't waste any time as she pulled us into a green star.

We came to a stop inside a laboratory. The person we were hitching a ride on was looking into a microscope. I was glad that the Chancellor was along for the ride because I had no idea what we were looking at. Lady Cosgrove's telepathic voice filled my head.

We are inside Shu Ming at the Trader Pharmaceutical Laboratory in Singapore one week after Trystan Jones delivered the samples he appropriated. Shu is one of their lab technicians. Shu's thoughts were loud and clear, and in what sounded like Chinese, which totally didn't help me at all.

Do either of you speak Chinese? I telepathized to my traveling companions.

Yes, we both do. Now don't distract the Chancellor so he can listen to what she is thinking and doing. Lady Cosgrove had such a pleasant way of telling me to shut up. So I bided my time in silence waiting for further instructions.

Once when Shu lifted up her head, I noticed she had one of those daily tear-off calendars on her desk. It indicated the day was September 26, 2012. *(That was only a week after I went home from the hospital.)*

I watched Shu go through several petri dishes and mark them with something when an Asian guy in a white lab coat entered the laboratory. He was small in stature yet stocky. His spiked black hair made him look like he wanted people to think he was a twenty-something badass, but he had too many lines etched across his saffron-toned skin to pull it off successfully. His security nametag said his name was Kasem Chang and that he was the Director of Product Development. Mr. Chang and Shu started talking to each other in yet another language I didn't understand. What I did understand was that Shu didn't agree with what the other guy was saying to her. Their voices were raised and the conversation was heated. Shu showed the guy a couple of her samples and he grunted. Not sure if it was a good grunt or a bad grunt. Then he said something more to Shu and walked out. She grabbed an empty petri dish off of the counter and threw it at the door. It shattered into a gazillion pieces. I guess it was a bad grunt.

Chancellor Williams took this time to fill us in on what he learned. *That man was Shu's boss. He told her that they have fifty test subjects waiting and that she was to have the first trial ready to go today. She was arguing that she couldn't come up with anything by then. He told her he didn't care what they actually injected into the test subjects; he just had to show Jones that they had something. Before he walked in, she was onto something with the red blood cells. They determined right away that the victims had died of Hypoxia, so they've been trying to intentionally increase the production of red blood cells. She was having some success, but it wasn't consistent. Let's move ahead in her timeline to see what she comes up with.*

I didn't even have a chance to think up any questions before I felt a tug and saw the streaming tunnel lights. We came to a stop. Shu was at the same lab station in the same lab coat although it looked more wrinkled and stained than it did when we'd been with her before. I was wondering if she slept there. The desk calendar now said it was October 15, 2012. This time, though, Shu wasn't alone. There were several other lab technicians all huddled over microscopes. Shu viewed several petri dishes which all looked to me to be very similar. Then she went back to a report and looked at it. She was excited about something and picked up the phone. She spoke briefly and then hung up. A few minutes later Mr. Chang, her boss, showed up again. He followed her over to her station and looked at her slides through the microscope. He came up smiling, shook her hand and patted her on the back. She went over to a drawer and pulled out a container of about twenty vials that looked like they were full of blood and handed it to him. He gave her a quick nod and then left. The eyes of all the technicians in the room were on his back, and then they lowered their gaze and went back to work. Something about the expressions on their faces really bothered me. My brain wanted to classify their body language as resigned fear, but that didn't make any sense if they had just discovered the cure. I was really confused and about to speak up when Chancellor Williams started talking in my head.

Well, this is disturbing on many levels. First of all, it appears that Shu was able to consistently replicate an unusual blood disorder called Polycythemia Vera, or PV for short, in which the body makes too many red blood cells. Since red blood cells carry oxygen throughout the body this method appears to counteract the lack of oxygen that was found in the blood of the victims of the Blue Flu. Alone, this is disturbing, because there can be some long-term negative effects from PV, not the least of which is Leukemia. They haven't performed, and don't have enough time to, a full study of this treatment. The more disturbing thing though is that the fifty test subjects Kasem referred to before were not animals or human volunteers.

If the test subjects weren't animals or humans, what were they? I asked completely confused. Chronoscenti Cosgrove and Chancellor Williams were silent for a very pregnant moment.

Well, Salena. This is a part of Third Dimensional existence that I'm sure your parents would want to keep you sheltered from for as long as possible. The Chronoscenti's response was loaded with resignation. I was suddenly very concerned with what the Chancellor was going to say next.

They are human, Salena, they just aren't "volunteers." Trader Pharmaceuticals has been using people as test subjects they purchased from a human-trafficking ring. I caught a stray thought from Shu that she hoped this saved the last fifteen. They apparently injected the blood of one of the early victims into the first set of test subjects, but none of them contracted the disease, so Shu and her co-workers were, and still are, completely baffled as to how it spreads. Therefore, they started inducing hypoxia through various methods into their victims, and then they tried multiple ways to increase their red blood cell count. Normal Hypoxia can usually be cured by putting the victim on oxygen, but they know that doesn't work for the Blue Flu. Thirty-five people have died so far from their various methods of inducing Hypoxia and the resultant failure of their attempted cure. I don't know if any of their test subjects are actual victims of the Blue Flu or not. We have stumbled into a rat's nest full of all sorts of nasty vermin that we weren't expecting.

OH MY GOD! What did you just say? I couldn't possibly have heard him right.

Trader Pharmaceuticals is using human trafficking victims as test subjects, he repeated.

No way! They couldn't be. That's . . . that's illegal!

Yes . . . it is. Immoral, unethical, reprehensible . . . I could go on and on, Chronoscenti Cosgrove interjected.

We . . . or I had to do something! What could I do? How could I help these people? I mean, for starters I don't even know where they are. My thoughts raced as I tried to come up with some logical next steps.

Can we follow Kasem to see where the test subjects are being held? I asked the Chronoscenti.

We can sure try, she said as she whisked us back to the cloud room and into a different green star.

Chronoscenti Cosgrove timed it perfectly as we hitched a ride on Mr. Chang right when he was leaving the lab with the vials Shu had given him. With his free hand he speed-dialed somebody and spoke a few curt words. The elevator doors in front of him opened up and he pressed the button for the fifteenth floor.

Mr. Chang used a card key pass and a retinal scan to get into the hallway. He walked a short way down the hall and then opened another door with his key card. We ended up in some kind of observation room. Eight people with tubes and wires connected to them were strapped down to beds on the other side of a window. All of them were unconscious. Two technicians sat in front of the window behind a glass counter that had computer screens mounted underneath them, and a man in a lab coat stood behind them looking over the technician's shoulders. To my relief, Kasem Chang started speaking in English, heavily accented English, but English all the same.

"Dr. Charles is everything ready?" Kasem asked the man in the lab coat. A short round Caucasian guy with small, closely set beady eyes and round spectacles —who creepily reminded me of the Gestapo Agent character from the Raiders of the Lost Arc movie, only with more hair—turned around to look at Mr. Chang and then looked down at the container in his hand. A massive amount of gel kept every combed back gray hair on his head glued in place.

"Yes, Mr. Chang, everything is ready," Dr. Donald Charles, as his nametag identified him, responded with a heavy English accent. That startled me since I was expecting a German accent. "The patients are in an induced state of acute hypoxia, so let's see how this treatment works, shall we?" He said as he took the vial container from Mr. Chang, and opened a door that led into the room with the patients.

Dr. Charles put on an oxygen mask and then

proceeded to introduce whatever was in the vials into the blood stream of four unconscious people strapped to the beds. Four were not touched. The control group, I guessed. Would they survive? Where were the other seven test subjects, since there were only eight here and Shu was hoping to save the last fifteen? None of these people were really infected with the Blue Flu. Their energy fields were weak and had a good mixture of gray with other colors, but nobody was infected.

When we saw Chang through Shu's eyes I noticed that his aura was tainted similarly to other Trader Pharmaceutical employees and family members. Dr. Charles' light body was likewise styled, so he was definitely part of the "in" crowd. However, neither Mr. Chang nor the doctor were infected. They must not have come in real close contact with Trystan Jones as Marc Malicki did.

The doctor finished up with the last patient and headed back to the control room. He left his oxygen mask in the patient's room upon exiting. Closing the door behind him he looked at Chang and said, "So now we wait."

While we waited, I watched the four people in the untreated control group die of Hypoxia. I so badly wanted to do SOMETHING, anything to help those people, but I couldn't because what I was watching happened three weeks ago. I've never felt so helpless. I'm sure that if I had a physical body at that moment, I would have felt tears running down my cheeks. I fidgeted and tried to focus my thoughts on something else. I couldn't save the four people in the control group who died, but a thought suddenly occurred to me. Maybe I could do something to save those who were still alive.

I studied the faces of the survivors. There were two males, one older and one younger, and two females, one older and one younger. Not feeling particularly creative, I named them One, Two, Three, and Four. Number One was a dark-skinned, middle-aged man who looked as though he could be from India. Number Two had white blonde hair and super pale, loose skin, like maybe he was a half-starved Viking descendent. I didn't think he could be more than twelve years old. Three was a woman in her thirties of African descent, and Four was a young Caucasian woman who wasn't much older than I was. I knew all of those people were victims of human traffickers, and I wondered how or why they ended up here. If I believed Chronoscenti Cosgrove, those people in that room, on some level, had created that existence for themselves. I couldn't imagine why they would do something like that on purpose.

Can we fast forward a little? This wait is killing me, I telepathized to the Chronoscenti.

Sure, she said and there was a momentary flash of light. *We should be about two hours ahead now of where we were.*

Mr. Chang and Dr. Charles were still in the control room, but the technicians were gone. "All four of the subjects who received the injection have pulled through very nicely. Their oxygen levels continue to increase and they seem to have stabilized. We'll keep an eye on them for the next forty-eight hours, but I expect that they will be fine," the doctor told Chang. "I think we can start testing this on patients who have been diagnosed with the Blue Flu. Have you had any volunteers?"

"Yes, although, before we get started testing volunteers afflicted with the virus, we need healthy people who match these surviving test subjects. We should have the authentic Blue Flu volunteers within a week's time," Kasem said.

"How long do you plan to keep these original subjects under observation?" The doctor queried.

"Once their replacements are in place, probably only a few more weeks. If you have anything else you need to test on humans, it would be a shame to let the leftovers go to waste," Chang said with a sneer as he laughed. I was frozen solid from shock and disbelief as I struggled to process that man's cold cruelty. He couldn't have just said what I thought he said. No way.

Chancellor Williams and Chronoscenti Cosgrove, I said trying to get my stunned and outraged thoughts in order. *Am I crazy or did Kasem just insinuate that he will use these people for random testing until he decides to kill them?*

No, child, you aren't mistaken. That is his intent, Lady Cosgrove responded with resignation.

I'm sorry to say that my understanding is the same as both of yours, said the Chancellor.

We have to do something! We can't just let Trader kill the rest of these people!

Remember, Salena, what we are witnessing happened three weeks ago. They may already be beyond any help we could offer, the Chronoscenti said.

Well, let's fast forward as far as we can to see if they are still alive. If they are, maybe there is something I can do.

Let's see, I am guessing it's about two o'clock 3D time outside of the Records here in Niaca, so that's going to make it about four am tomorrow morning in Singapore. Mr. Chang is most likely asleep, so I'll take us to his Monday morning. We'll see what sort of unsettling things Mr. Chang cooked up today.

At first, lights sped by as they have before, then when we approached the timeline destination the Chronoscenti decelerated us into a slow fast-forward where we could see what Mr. Chang was doing, but not hear what he was thinking or saying. It was just like when I fast-forward through the commercials on my DVR. We watched him scamper through his morning at the office, then get in his car and leave the building at just about lunch time. They drive on the opposite side of the road in Singapore, so I was totally distracted by his driving, especially experiencing this in hyper-speed, and I kept leaning to my left while wanting him to move to the other side.

Kasem Chang finally came to a stop at a guard gate. At that point the Chronoscenti slowed us down to the regular viewing mode, which was good, because I was feeling a little queasy.

Where are we now? I asked my companions.

The Port of Singapore. It is a very expansive shipping port that is comprised of a number of facilities and terminals. This port handles a wide range of cargo including containers as well as conventional and bulk cargo. You'll see all kinds of ships here like tankers, bulkers, military vessels, and container ships.

The Port of Singapore is one of the world's busiest ports for all kinds of trade, commerce, and shipping activity, the Chancellor informed me.

Chang showed some ID at the entrance and the guard waved him through. We drove for a little while through towers and rows of shipping containers that were all stacked on top of each other. I decided that this was a great place to hide something in plain sight. I felt like an ant in Lego Land.

Finally, after weaving in and out of the container maze, Mr. Chang parked his car outside an innocuous looking large, metal rectangular box that was covered in rust and had no discernible markings on it. It was about forty feet long by about eight feet wide, and unlike many of the others surrounding it, there weren't any other containers stacked on top of it. The only thing that was unusual about it was that there was a regular door with an electronic key pad and door handle. As he approached the entrance this huge Samoan looking dude approached him. He looked as if he should have been wearing a Sumo wrestling diaper as opposed to baggy, holey jeans and a dirty T-shirt. He was definitely keeping watch on this container from someplace, but I couldn't pinpoint where. Sumo dude and Chang exchanged some words that I didn't understand because they were speaking in either Chinese or Malay.

What did they say? I asked.

Chancellor Williams answered, *Chang told the other guy that this was his last visit to the container. He'll only be back to supervise it being loaded onto the freighter scheduled to be shipped out on Friday, and that the guard should continue the regular feeding schedule until then.*

After their exchange Chang turned to the container door and entered the access code. I watched him press the buttons 8-9-7-0-1-* slowly and deliberately. Each button made a beeping noise and then a green light lit up at the end of the sequence. He turned the handle and entered the container.

The light from the open door briefly illuminated the interior of the container before Chang pulled it shut behind him. I guess he trusted that Sumo dude would let him out. In the gloom of the container, the only light source came from three six-inch-wide by three-foot-long vents in the ceiling. Chang looked to his right, and along the wall with the door, I saw a counter with a stained sink and leaky faucet, along with a few trays of seriously unappetizing, picked over food. As he slowly surveyed the rest of the area, I saw that there were six narrow, rusted, military-looking bunk beds on each side of the container positioned head-to-toe lining the walls. I also saw what maybe looked like a port-a-potty stuck in between the beds at the far end of the "room." None of the top bunks were taken, but all the bottom bunks, except one were occupied. I guessed that these were the last eleven of the original fifty test subjects—the four survivors from the trials a few weeks ago, and the "lucky seven" who never got "volunteered" throughout the process.

Four of the six prisoners in the bunks on the right wore hospital gowns. I recognized them as test subjects One, Two, Three, and Four whom I had named earlier. They were curled up on their soiled sheet-less mattresses either sound asleep or semi-conscious. The other seven captives—of various ages, ethnicities, and genders—were in various states of undress and consciousness as well. I was very grateful that smells were not recorded in the Records because I was pretty sure that with the lack of provisions for hygiene and the proximity of the port-a-potty, the rank odors inside of this container would be gag worthy.

I didn't understand why these poor people were so complacent and lethargic. Maybe their food was drugged or something. Although all their auras were weak and dominantly ash colored, no one was infected with the Blue Flu. Even assuming that I could possibly save these people, I couldn't help but wonder if some of them would still end up dying from Dr. Charles' experiments anyway.

Chancellor, can you determine if the test subjects are going to contract Leukemia or some other disease as a result of the treatment they received? I asked reluctantly, not sure if I wanted the answer.

Not here in the Records I can't; but, if I were with them in real time, I have a way of diagnosing Third Dimensional people.

(Huh, that's interesting.) I'm always learning something new about cool things they can do in the Fifth Dimension.

Mr. Chang proceeded to do a cursory check of the vital signs of each of the four test subjects that survived Dr. Charles' experiment, after which his eyes briefly scanned over the remaining people. On his way out he checked to make sure the sink faucet was working. I decided they must have a water tank attached to either the side or the roof of this prison. He opened the food service hatch, and yelled something at Sumo Dude. Seconds later I heard the beeping of the code being entered into the lock and the rusty door screeched open. Sunlight momentarily blinded me as Chang stepped through the door and shut it behind him.

CHAPTER TWENTY-THREE
Shadows and Dreams

The finality of the clanging of the door and the clicking of the lock into place bounced around in my head like an echo bounces off walls. My companions' silence convinced me they were feeling as empty as I was. Unlike me though, they had no ability to intervene, but I did. I just needed to be smart about it, and I needed as much information as I could get.

Chronoscenti, I think we've learned all we can from here, but I was wondering if you could identify the soul stars of the people in the container and let me know what color they are?

Sure Salena. Let's head back to the portal room and I'll see what I can find out for you.

The light tug on my hand and the ensuing roller coaster lightshow told me that we were headed back. We came to a stop in the foggy soul star room and it felt as though I floated there for some time. Neither the Chronoscenti nor the Chancellor telepathized anything, so I tried to enjoy the sensation of being weightless as I do when I'm relaxing in a swimming pool.

Salena and Hart, Lady Cosgrove's voice inside my head grabbed my wandering attention. *I've located the soul* stars of the prisoners in the container. They are all green except for the four test subjects that received the last treatment we witnessed. Theirs are yellow.

Okay, just so I'm sure I remember correctly, the color of the soul star indicates the physical status and dimension of an entity or soul. So a yellow soul star means that those people are dying from some disease. It doesn't predict random deadly accidents or murder, correct?

That's exactly right, Salena.

Chancellor, you said you couldn't diagnose them inside the records, but that you have the ability to diagnose people inter-dimensionally in real-time? Yes?

Yes, that's correct.

I need to know what those people are dying from, I told them both. *If they are dying from the treatment they received for the Blue Flu then it is critical that I stop Trader Pharmaceuticals from getting that treatment approved.*

So, are you asking me to go to the container when we are back in the Fifth and diagnose those people? the Chancellor asked.

Yes, sir, and I'm going with you, I said. Both he and the Chronoscenti were silent. I couldn't tell if they were conversing privately with each other or if they were just thinking. Either way, neither of them answered me or commented on what I said for a very long quiet moment.

Let's discuss that when we are on the outside, Chronoscenti Cosgrove finally punctured the heavy silence with her telepathic voice. *Are we ready to leave?*

The Chancellor and I verbally agreed we were ready to exit. I looked up at the full moon portal and said in unison with my companions, *I am exiting the Akashic Records!*

I'd like to say that this exit was easier than before simply because I kinda knew what to expect, but it really didn't work out that way. I still felt like I had put a porcupine costume on inside out that was several sizes too small for me. My hands were feverishly scratching my arms and legs trying to get the burning and itching to stop their aggravating assault on my body. To my chagrin, neither the Chronoscenti nor the Chancellor seemed to be discomforted in the least. That's just so not fair.

I finally had the presence of mind to look up at the crystal lotus flower in front of me and saw the translucent sparkly body of Angeni undulating softly behind the portal console. She had a smirk on her face, her mouth was open and her lips were turned up. I got the impression that she was trying not to laugh at my scratching antics.

"Hey Angeni, been waiting long?" I asked.

"I don't think so," she said crinkling her eyes together and glancing around the room as if she were looking for a clock. She really didn't have any sense of time in the Third or Fifth Dimensions. I wondered if they ever had meetings or classes in the Spirit Realm, and if they did, how did everyone get to the location or class on time? I shook my head in an effort to clear it of any random and disjointed thoughts pertaining to time management in the other dimensions. It was hard enough to manage Third Dimensional time that is more predictable and less prone to interference from somebody else's thoughts. "Did you get the information you needed?"

"Yeah, and then some," I replied as I proceeded to fill her in on the events inside the Records. I watched her gaze darken and the swirling sparkles of her aura vibrate at a faster pace.

"That's dreadful," she commented.

"The Chancellor and I are going to go over to Singapore and into the container in a few minutes. He's going to diagnose what the last four test subjects are dying from," I told her.

"Is it really necessary for you to go, Salena? Why don't you just stay here, or above at the entrance where it's safer? The Chancellor can come back and tell you what he found out." Angeni's concern for my welfare was evident, but I dismissed it. I needed to go. I was compelled to go. She recognized the stubborn look on my face.

"Even if we, the Chronoscenti, Chancellor Williams, and I, disagree with you, you'll go anyway, won't you?" she asked.

"Yes, but it would be safer if I went with you. I really need to see this for myself, in person, and try to come up with some idea on how I can help those people. I can go there on my own since I know where it is, but I'd rather do it with you." Angeni frowned at my stubborn logic.

"We were hoping you'd be able to talk her out of going," Chronoscenti Cosgrove said to Angeni.

"Yes, well, I've known this young woman her whole life, and once she's determined to do something, she usually finds a way to do it," she said looking down at me and frowning. "Even when she knows it isn't good for her."

I began to sense that I'd won my argument. "So, I can go with you?" I asked the Chancellor. Angeni would go wherever I went.

"I suppose . . . ," he replied. "Just don't wander off, and don't take any candy from strangers," he said with a slight upturn of his lips as he shook his head.

Elated, I animatedly joined the conversation as we discussed our next move. The plan was that we were going to pop over to Singapore and into the container. Due to the fifteen-hour time difference, it was already early the next morning over there. The prisoners could still be sleeping. The Chancellor would do whatever he needed to do to diagnose the four terminally ill test subjects and hopefully be able to determine the cause as well. He didn't think it would take too long. After he was done, we'd go back to the Sierra Nevada Colony for a quick debrief and I'd be home before dinner. As strategies go, it seemed like a good one. Really, what could possibly go wrong?

Chancellor Hart and I clasped our hands together as we transported ourselves to the interior of the rusted shipping container at the Port of Singapore. Angeni followed me in the special way that she does. Test subject Four, still clad in her hospital gown, was whimpering and sniffling and curled into the fetal position on the stained mattress. Her back faced the center of the container. Pre-dawn morning light barely filtered through the ceiling vents reflecting dust specks that were floating around the openings. I gave my eyes a moment to adjust to the dimly-lit room.

There was more movement and grumbling coming from the captives than I noticed before. My nose crinkled at the warm, putrid air that permeated the container. A cocktail of body odor, urine, rust, mold, and stale food made me gag. I was glad that when in the Fifth Dimension, the temperature is more manageable. It had to be unbearably warm inside this container, especially if the state of undress of its inhabitants was any indication.

One skinny old Asian guy with white, thinning hair and a long beard, who wasn't one of the four test subjects, was sitting up, his scrawny legs protruding from thin and ragged boxers. He was studying his boney hand as if it held the secrets of the universe. He totally reminded me of one of those stereotypical frail spiritual gurus who was some kind of Jedi Master.

Chancellor Williams didn't waste any time and immediately went over to test subject Three's bed. Even though the thirty something lady with chocolate skin was thrashing around, she appeared to be fast asleep. Maybe she was having a nightmare. I watched the Chancellor place his left hand on (or, oddly, slightly inside) her forehead and his right hand over (or in) her heart. It was a little disconcerting being able to see only part of his hands because half the palm and fingers were inside her forehead and chest. Three's flailing stopped and she became perfectly still. I know she couldn't see him, but it was as if her spirit knew that something was happening to her. I could see the energy that he was channeling into her Third-Eye and Heart chakras. It was pretty cool.

"Have you ever seen this done before?" I whispered to Angeni who hovered next to me.

"No. I've never spent any time in the Fifth Dimension until now. Not a lot of call for spirit guides here. Most everybody knows why they are there and are fully aware of their life path and mission. All of my charges have been in the Third Dimension."

I digested that information as I continued to watch the Chancellor examine Ms. Three. His aura changed as his energy pulled away from the woman. There was a reflection of uneasiness in his eyes that wasn't there before he examined her. He moved down one bed to the girl I named Four. Ms. Four was still whimpering and facing the wall so the Chancellor had to lean over her and under the top bunk to reach her forehead and heart. He proceeded to allow his energy to flow into her as he sorted through whatever he was able to pick up by doing his thing.

Every time he pulled away from a person, his energy field depleted a little. I think he consciously was trying to leave a little behind. "These people are drugged, Salena. It makes their energies kind of thick and sluggish, like mucous. It's kind of a draining experience," he explained to me.

"I kinda figured they were drugged since they are so lethargic. Are you able to diagnose anything?" I asked suddenly worried that we wouldn't be able to get what we came for.

"Yes, but before I explain it to you, I want to check the next two." I watched as he proceeded to check on the last two surviving test subjects. I heard distant creaks and groans going on outside the container. Whatever shipping work was going on at this port was happening fairly far away from this container.

While I waited for the Chancellor, I wondered idly about the effect that ambient temperature has on scents. I couldn't smell anything inside the records, maybe because I didn't have a physical nose, or maybe because scents weren't recorded. In the Fifth Dimension I can smell some things from the Third Dimension, but not everything, and some aren't as strong as I think they should be. Curious, I decided I'd ask my dad when I got back if he had any "smelly" theories.

My gaze wandered back to the old Asian Jedi Master man. I have to admit that I was kinda captivated by him. *Why was he so fascinated with his hand? He hadn't stopped examining it since we arrived. What was he looking at?* I watched him a little longer, but none of my questions were answered.

My attention turned away from the man and focused on the dirty footprints on the floor. That these people had survived in here at least since the end of September, astounded me.

"Salena." The Chancellors voice startled me out of my reverie. "I've concluded my examination of the four people who received the Blue Flu treatment."

"And . . ." I prompted him to continue.

"And, they are indeed all dying as their soul stars indicated. The two oldest, who are also the least healthy, will go first. They are actually already beginning to show signs of stress in their bone marrow. There is no doubt in my mind they will develop some form of terminal Leukemia within a few years Third Dimensional time. I have seen this energy pattern before. The two younger ones are better, in that I don't see the signs of stress in their marrow just yet. Their bodies continue to produce an excess amount of red blood cells, and the mutation caused by the treatment is still active. I was thinking that the treatment might have included an inactivating agent after some period, but that doesn't appear to be the case. Nor could I find any evidence of such a possibility occurring. I believe that the two younger people will also develop Leukemia over time if the blood mutation isn't neutralized or stabilized. Simply put, this treatment may save some people from the Blue Flu, but it will eventually kill those who receive it."

I stared at the Chancellor with my mouth hanging open, blinking at him. His declaration rocked me to my core. I hadn't realized up until right then how much I didn't want to believe that Trader's treatment was actually a slow-acting poison. Todd Black's press conference flashed through my mind. He told everyone that Trader's approval for the treatment was almost completely through the FDA. My thoughts turned to the conversation Mr. Chang had with Dr. Charles about needing volunteers whose demographics matched the four surviving test subjects.

Oh my God! Trader is assigning the test data on the original subjects to new people who didn't receive the cure! The new volunteers won't die of Leukemia because they were never treated. The cancer link to this therapy may never be discovered! I realized, to my horror, that they must have submitted to the FDA the merged data from the original and the volunteer test subjects.

Fear hit me—breathtakingly fast. I couldn't control my emotional response. A full-blown panic attack for the future victims of Trader Pharmaceutical's greed and treachery washed over me. I started sweating profusely as I realized I had lost my grip on the Fifth Dimension and was reentering the Third. All it took for me to fully materialize inside the container in the Third Dimension was the realization of what a colossal screw up I was and how pissed my parents were going to be.

OW! OW! OW! OW! Water! I need water! I was so freaking thirsty, and hot, and nauseous. My legs gave out and I ended up on my rump in the middle of the dirty floor. I sat there for a moment, breathing heavily. My sudden appearance in the middle of the container didn't create much of a stir. Only the guy who was playing with his hand noticed me by giving me a quizzical look.

"Water?" I croaked to him. He pointed to the faucet in the corner. I crawled to the edge of a bunk bed and pulled myself up. Using the beds and frames as support I headed over to the corner and filled a small paper cup with water. I drank it down in practically one gulp, and then repeated the process two more times. The water was warm and had a little metallic taste to it, but it was water and I began to immediately feel better, lighter, and definitely not quite so stressed.

I found my way to the last empty bottom bunk at the far end of the container and sat down with my glass of water. Angeni materialized in front of me. Boy was I happy to see her!

"Salena! You have to get out of here! NOW!" She yelled. I don't think I've ever seen her so pissed.

"I know. I will. I just need a few minutes to recover. I'm exhausted. I didn't do this on purpose you know. I just lost my grip on the Fifth after I remembered that Chang had substituted these people with unsuspecting volunteers. They've tampered with the data they provided to the FDA. Angeni, if that treatment gets approved, everyone who receives it will eventually die. They can't be allowed to get it approved! You have to go back and tell Mom what I just told you. I'll rest here for a few minutes, and then I'll go back to the Fifth and catch up with you there or at home. I won't be long, I promise."

"I don't want to leave you," she said clearly distraught and torn between her responsibility to me versus her responsibility to humanity.

"I know, but I'll be fine, I promise," I said.

"Okay, but don't be long," she said.

"I won't."

Angeni faded away as I set my water on the floor, laid down on the thin, stained mattress, and cupped my hands behind my head. I took a deep breath to start my meditation so I could return to the Fifth Dimension. I was so tired. My heavy eyelids were relieved when I allowed them to close. It couldn't possibly hurt to shut my eyes . . . just for a little while.

I had the weirdest dream. Well, it was really more like a nightmare. I've had nightmares like this before where what you're dreaming feels so real, but it just can't be. There doesn't seem to be a distinction between reality and fantasy.

I was inside this really hot and smelly metal box. It was really big, and I was not alone. There were zombies in the box with me. They scared me. They wouldn't or couldn't talk to me. Their skin was pasty looking and saggy. Their eyes were haunted and hollow. They smelled like meat that had spoiled from sitting in the hot sun. Their hair, for those who had any, was clinging to their heads like greasy spaghetti strands. Occasionally they would shuffle toward me. Sometimes I felt their hands on my body, pulling and tugging on my legs and feet. At first I thought they might be hungry and I was their dinner, but after staring at me and mumbling something I couldn't understand, they moved on out of my nightmare or into their own.

I was pretty sure I was not a zombie, but I couldn't quite form coherent thoughts. Every now and then something would start to make a little sense, but then I'd get so thirsty, and soon after soothing my dry mouth with their water, nothing made sense again.

I kept seeing this sparkly-shaped woman. She tried to talk to me. I waved and smiled at her. When I touched her glitter my hand tingled and a fire trail of sparkles followed. Somehow my hand passed right through her. It reminded me a little of waving a sparkler through the air during the Fourth of July. There were times she seemed to be saying something, but I couldn't understand her. Maybe I was in a bubble of air inside this box that was actually in the water. The lady looked as though she was floating in water. She was pretty even though she was really unhappy about something. The zombies couldn't see her, which made me glad. I really didn't feel like sharing my sparkly friend with the zombies. They weren't any fun.

When the urge to pee suddenly hit me, I didn't want to go to the bathroom in front of zombies. That would be so gross! But, I couldn't figure out how I had done it in all the time I had been there. I began to wonder when I'd wake up from this dream. Sometimes it felt like a lot of time had passed; sometimes it seemed that no time had passed. At least the zombies didn't want to eat me. Something was gnawing at my tummy, though I was pretty sure something was trying to eat its way out, not in. I didn't like the way that felt, so I decided to get off of the cloud I was floating on inside this strange and fetid container that was my dream.

The pain in my belly forced my brain into some semblance of coherent thought, at least, I thought my head didn't feel quite as fuzzy as I emerged into a semi-conscious state. Maybe I felt a little better. The sparkly lady was there and this time I could hear her calling my name and saying something else.

"Salena! Salena!" I think she was actually yelling.

"Don't pink the waiter!" I looked at her, confused. *What is pinking the waiter? Was I in a restaurant? It sure didn't smell like any restaurant I could remember.*

"What?" I grumbled. My voice sounded like I was gargling with rocks and I had trouble forming words and making my lips and tongue work together. My eyelids were physically challenged with obeying my "STAY OPEN" command. I kept raising my eyebrows to help them out. Suddenly I remembered the name of the sparkly lady yelling frantically at me. It was Angeni.

"Salena, can you hear me?!" She yelled. "Don't drink the water! It's drugged. The water is drugged! Can you hear me?"

I rubbed my eyes and then opened them again to look at her. Yup, I could still see her, and I could see through her as well. That was weird. Slowly it came back to me. *Angeni is my spirit guide. She is only visible to me and mom. Mom! Uh oh. Where was I?* I tried to move my legs and arms. They felt like the rubber bands that held them together were stretched taut to the point of breaking and that somebody had filled my bones with lead. Slowly I rolled onto my right side and propped up my head on my right hand. I decided to whisper since my throat was so dry.

"Angeni . . . where . . . am . . . I?" The words sluggishly tumbled from my mouth. The relief in her face at my question sent a shiver of apprehension through me.

"You're in the test subject container in Singapore. You've been drugged and asleep for the last two and a half days. You have to get out of here. They are going to be shipping this thing out tomorrow."

I said nothing as I blinked at her struggling to push her words into my brain. Angeni wasn't making any sense. She was speaking English, but nothing was coherently connecting. I moved my lead-filled legs over the side of the bed and set my feet on the gritty floor. *Where are my shoes?* My gaze slid up from my toes to my legs. *Where are my pants? Why don't I have any pants on?* I shook my head rapidly trying to clear out the cobwebs and the cotton stuck in my brain. A rush of memories started exploding in my head like rapid machine gun fire. I struggled to tie them together, but had remembered enough to know I was in deep doo-doo.

A deep male voice, dripping with arrogant superiority penetrated through the metal walls that surrounded me. Chills raced up my spine and I started to shake. I'd recognize that voice anywhere. Mr. Kasem Chang, Director of Product Development for Trader Pharmaceuticals, had arrived to supervise the loading of the container onto the ship. His presence was all I needed to jerk my attention away from my memory puzzle. Chang was outside the box and loudly barking orders. I suspected I only had a few minutes to get out of there before I was discovered. I didn't have time to wonder why I hadn't been discovered over the last couple of days. Maybe, I had been and that's why my pants and shoes were missing.

"Salena, any time now would be good!" Angeni kept pressing me.

Every second, my thoughts were becoming clearer and clearer. The drugs were wearing off rapidly, but I was so thirsty! My gaze instinctively looked down at the empty cup on the floor. Squelching that thought, I looked around the container trying to orient myself. I was in the last bottom bunk bed at the far end of the left side of the container. A dirty shirt and a pair of pants hung from the top bunk, which blocked me from view of the door. I quickly realized that might be why I wasn't discovered earlier. I recognized the pants, they were mine, but the shirt definitely wasn't.

I looked around at my fellow captives to see if any were coherent. The old man who I had seen playing with his hands was sitting across from me in his bunk staring straight at me almost like he could see through me. It was kinda creepy. He was shirtless, but I didn't think it was his shirt hanging next to my pants. It would take three of him to fill that jersey.

"Angel Girl," the old skinny man across from me said in a quiet voice. "I save you, now you save us," he said nodding to the shirt and pants. So he was the one responsible for keeping me out of sight for the last couple of days.

I inclined my head toward him in acknowledgement to what he had done. "I'll do my best."

I couldn't understand what Mr. Chang was saying outside since he wasn't speaking English, but his voice was getting closer and closer to the door of the container.

Two loud beeps from the keypad echoed off of the metal box surrounding me. *He's coming in now!* My brain screamed at me and panic set in. I scrambled up onto the mattress, pushed my back up against the hot rusty wall, and hid behind the giant sweaty smelling shirt that had been my shield. Another two squealing beeps echoed away from the door. I tried to take deep breaths to calm down.

"Salena, stop fooling around and get centered. You are running out of time!!" Angeni scolded.

A car door slammed outside. To my relief Chang stopped entering the combination. I heard him start talking, still not in English, with the newcomer. I took a deep breath of the sour air surrounding me and relaxed a little.

"You're SO not helping, Angeni! I'm not fooling around. How can I get centered when you're yelling at me?!" I whispered fiercely at her.

"Sorry," she said and actually had the decency to look chagrined. "Here, I'll help you," she said and then did something she had never done before. She jumped into me.

It felt like every neuron in my body fired all at once, but it didn't hurt. I felt a rush of energy and love that gave me an instant sensation of connection to the Goddessence. I concentrated on my breathing. I actually wasn't as anxious as I probably should have been. Whatever was in that drug they put in the water seemed to reduce anxiety among other things. Refocusing, I imagined the divine masculine energy vortex swirling down from the heavens and the divine feminine energy vortex swirling up from the earth. They converged in my heart chakra filling it with the joyous power of unconditional love that only being at one with creation allows. I felt the heaviness of the Third Dimension slip away just as the beeping of the combination lock resumed, heralding the return of Mr. Kasem Chang.

CHAPTER TWENTY-FOUR
EPIC

Angeni slipped out of me when she felt I had a good hold on the Fifth Dimension. I looked at the frail old man across from me who was grinning an almost toothless smile and waving at me. I knew he couldn't see me now, but he did watch me disappear. He quickly turned his wave into the hand and finger examination thing he was doing when I first noticed him. Chang walked down toward the end of the container giving the old man a hard look and then he turned toward my bunk and narrowed his eyes, which lingered on my jeans and the extra-large T-shirt. My invisibility was complete, but his brutal scrutiny still made me slightly nervous. He had a surgical type mask on over his face. They hadn't cleaned the port-a-potty or the leftover food since I had arrived. Yuck. The stench permeated through to the Fifth Dimension.

Looking down I noticed I was still pant-less and shoeless. I quickly conjured a change of clothes and a brush to try to make some order out of my unruly and greasy hair. As I brushed through my tangles, I watched my savior act totally stoned as Chang turned away from my bunk. With one last sneer at the old man, Chang turned and headed back toward the entrance, no longer interested in my friend's antics. Realizing I was still ravenously hungry and thirsty, I conjured a large glass of ice water that I immediately made disappear the old fashioned way. I finally felt stabilized enough to figure out what to do next, knowing the first order of business was to get out of this putrid box.

"Let's go outside. I can't breathe in here," I said to Angeni as we transported to the other side of the metal wall. I took a deep breath of the humid ocean air tinged with a hint of fish, oil, and steel. I looked around, surprised that nobody from the Fifth Dimension was here waiting for me. Twilight had just taken hold of the sky pushing down the sun once again. "Where to now?" I asked.

"Your mom and dad are here in Singapore. I suggest going to their hotel room first."

"Mom and Dad are here?! In Singapore? Already?"

"Yes, they caught the first plane they could as soon as I told them what happened. They arrived early this morning. Your Uncle Jack is with them."

"Uncle Jack? What's he doing with them?" I wondered out loud as Angeni smiled an interesting smile that meant she was about to reveal a big secret.

"Well, you know he works for the government, right?"

"Yeah, he's always traveling for his job. Dad's told me he doesn't know where Jack goes, but I always thought they were teasing me."

"He wasn't traveling for the government, Salena, he was on military missions to save the Earth. He's the Director of EPIC, Earth's Paramilitary Intelligence Core. It's a highly specialized, covert worldwide organization made up of military agents from various countries whose mission it is to save the planet," she said, her voice flat and emotionless, but her eyes gave her away. She loved to shock me.

"WHAT?! SERIOUSLY? My Uncle Jack is some kind of James Bond secret agent? No Way!"

"Way," she said smiling at my reaction, which she had worked hard to achieve.

"Do Mom and Dad know?"

"Of course. They've known all along whom he works for, but they've never known about any of his missions . . . until now," she said with a smile. "Shall we? Don't want to be late to the family reunion. Intercontinental Hotel room 1605."

"I'm right behind you!" I said, my voice trailing after me as I left the prison box in my wake.

Mom, Dad, Uncle Jack and some badass looking chick I'd never met before were pacing in the living area of the hotel suite. Since everyone was standing, I decided to sit on the couch since I'd likely collapse anyway. Angeni beat me back by seconds, and she had materialized in the Third Dimension. *Show off.*

"She's here and will be materializing momentarily," Angeni informed mom. The relief that flooded my mom's face made me feel guilty instantly. As it turns out, that was all the negative emotion I needed to start my descent back into third-dimensional form.

The duration of this trip to the Fifth was pretty short comparatively, but coming back still came with the usual aches and pains, just not quite as severe.

"Hey guys," I gurgled out. I heard a yelp from Warrior Chick as she wheeled around to stare at me sitting behind her on the couch. She apparently hadn't been informed that I might materialize out of thin air. "Can I have a glass of water and maybe some room service? I'm starving!"

Mom rushed to me, fell to her knees and then tackled me on the couch in the most humongous bear hug. Then she started to sob, incoherent babblings of love and gratitude pouring out of her mouth as she pet my greasy hair. I couldn't breathe. Dad got down on his knees and wrapped his arms around the two of us. Uncle Jack cleared his throat, which caused Mom to release her grip enough to allow me to untangle myself and take the water he was offering me. Angeni was floating in the corner of the room by the expansive window that looked out into a darkening sky and an illuminated city. The warrior woman who was standing next to Uncle Jack was still staring at me even though the initial shock on her face had been replaced with stoic professionalism.

"Welcome back Salena," Uncle Jack said, which kinda broke up the sentimental family reunion. "You gave us quite a scare."

"I know. I'm sooo sorry. I didn't mean to. Honest. I had no idea the water was drugged. I thought it was the food. When I dropped out of the Fifth I was so thirsty, as usual, and I thought I'd give myself a few minutes to recover. I drank a glass of water and passed out. The next thing I remember was waking up a little while ago and Angeni finally getting through to me to stop drinking the water. I don't think I've eaten anything in the last few days, so I'm absolutely ravenous right now. But what are you doing here? Angeni told me you are the Director of EPIC? What exactly does that mean? And who is she?" I nodded toward warrior woman.

Uncle Jack smiled at me. "Yes, I am the Director of EPIC. I'll let your dad tell you all about it in a few minutes. She is Brighid Firestone and she is my first officer. Firestone, meet Salena Hawthorne, my wayward niece."

"Hi, it's nice to meet you . . . Fire . . . um . . . Brighid," I stuttered as I carefully stood up and extended my hand.

She laughed. "Brighid is fine. Firestone is what the team calls me. It's nice to meet you too, Salena. I have to say, you know how to make an entrance!" Brighid said smiling as she shook my hand. "I was all ready to storm the shipping docks to rescue you. It's nice to meet a young lady who is able to get herself out of sticky situations!"

I liked her. Similar to the Celtic Warrior Goddess she was possibly named after, Brighid had rust-colored hair that was long enough to be pulled back into a secure bun. Her five-foot-nine-inch frame was slender yet muscular and covered head-to-toe in black, tight-fitting clothes complete with something that looked like a Batman utility belt at her waist. This woman was definitely a force to be reckoned with. Her sparkling jade eyes reminded me of Jace, and I felt an unexpected pang of apprehension deep in my gut. I sent out a silent prayer that he was okay.

"You don't have to go get me out now, but I wasn't the only one in that nasty ass container. You aren't going to leave those other poor souls are you? Trader Pharmaceuticals is planning on having them killed! Did Angeni tell you?" I asked looking at Angeni, then to my mom, and finally resting on Brighid. They all nodded. "Well? What's the plan?"

"The first part of the plan, young lady, is to get you bathed and fed," my dad said. "I think you've done quite enough." As fabulous as food and a shower sounded, I still pouted. I wanted to help save those people, especially the old guy.

"Your dad will stay here with you, Moonling. Angeni said she could guide us to where you were being held through your mom," Uncle Jack informed me.

My lower lip still protruded out, but realistically I didn't stand a chance of being able to tag along with this group. Taking Mom was a big enough risk, but once inside the shipping port, navigating among the shipping containers would be like driving through an endless maze without help from somebody who had either been there before or who could see it from above, both of which qualified Angeni as the perfect navigator using Mom as interpreter.

Dad handed me the room service menu "Pick what you want and I'll order it while you shower." I scanned the menu. The cheeseburger and fries made my mouth water. I added fruit salad and a big slice of chocolate cake hoping that would tide me over for a while. I looked up at Uncle Jack who had a serious look on his face while his left hand was touching his left ear and he was talking.

"Roger that. We'll be down in three. Hammer out," he said and looked at Firestone and Mom. "Team one is in position at the rendezvous point awaiting our arrival. Let's move out."

Dad wrapped his arms around mom and kissed her. "You be careful," he said as he cupped her face with his hands and locked his eyes with hers. "Anything happens to her and you're dead meat," Dad said to his fraternity brother and best friend as Mom hugged me again.

"I'll guard her with my life," Jack replied putting his arm around Mom and smiling down at her. He was as big as a moose.

"I'll see you in the lobby," Angeni said to my mom as she misted away. Uncle Jack ushered Mom and Brighid out the door ahead of him. Just before he pulled the door to the suite closed behind him, he turned around and winked at me. I rewarded him with my best Cheshire Cat grin.

While Dad got on the phone with room service, I headed into the bedroom to explore the bathroom facilities. *Nice digs, I wonder who's paying for this place?* The shower was amazing. Five of my friends could fit comfortably inside it; granite tile covered the floor, three sides and the ceiling, which had to be ten feet up. A ginormous round showerhead jutted straight down from the ceiling. I stripped out of my conjured pants and shoes and the, now totally disgusting, T-shirt I had worn since Monday. Turning a likely knob on the shower wall, a deluge of warm water plummeted down. Testing the water, I stepped into what felt like a tropical downpour. A shower had never felt so good in my life.

I could have stayed in there forever, but I was starving. Reluctantly stepping out of the shower, I noticed that my dad had sneaked in and placed a clean pair of pajama pants, underwear and a clean T-shirt on the counter for me. I dressed quickly and wrapped my hair in a towel. I smelled dinner as soon as I opened the bathroom door.

Dad had our room service feast all set up for us. Turns out he ordered a hamburger for himself too. I took a long slug of my Diet Coke and tore into the fries. "So," I chewed a little. "Wanna tell me about Uncle Jack and EPIC?" I said around the food I had in my mouth.

"Don't talk with your mouth full, Salena," Dad said absently. Then he smiled. "Yes, EPIC is a pretty neat story." He took a bite of food, chewed it completely and then swallowed. I tapped my fingers on the table, waiting and chewing. "EPIC stands for Earth's Paramilitary Intelligence Corps. Your uncle was chosen to be its Director about six years ago. Jack was working for the CIA then. Before that, he was in Army Intelligence and spent part of his early career as a Captain of a Special Forces Team. That was when he got the call sign Jack Hammer," dad said smiling as a wistful look in his eyes told me he was reliving some long ago moment. "EPIC is partly backed by the US

Government, but not completely. Its members are handpicked from military and intelligence organizations from around the world. Their mission is to keep mankind from destroying Mother Earth. They've stopped countless countries, companies, and individuals from doing permanent damage to our eco-systems. Of course, accidents still happen, and they can't be everywhere, but they do one hell of a job."

"Have you known about EPIC since its beginning?"

"Yes, and I knew if there was one person I could count on to help us get you out of that box it was your Uncle Jack. As it turns out, they have been monitoring the Blue Flu because of the potential any pandemic has to disrupt the natural order of things. If it turned out to be a water or airborne pathogen that could impact plants, animals, or the oceans, they wanted to be ready to act. Going in and saving these people is a little out of their jurisdiction, but Jack has connections in governments all over the world. Turns out that Singapore was more than willing to allow them to take point on this mission." Dad paused to enjoy a bite of his hamburger and a swig of his drink.

After wiping his mouth with his napkin, he continued, "The accusations that you and Angeni are making toward Trader Pharmaceuticals are extremely serious and could have worldwide repercussions. Coming up with proof from some source other than a spirit and a teenaged girl is paramount before any government is willing to take action. EPIC was a perfect choice, as it turns out, to try to rescue you and gather that needed evidence. Regular commercial international travel is highly restricted now due to the pandemic. Jack was able to get your mom and me on his plane with his team. We owe him big time." Dad paused again for another bite.

"Angeni kept popping in to give your mom regular updates. She felt she had let us down by not keeping you safe and allowing you to go to Singapore with Chancellor Williams. She was so frustrated that she couldn't seem to get through to you."

I had almost managed to clean my plate while dad was talking. In order to give dad the opportunity to eat, I relayed what I remembered about my time in the container and what had happened in the Akashic Records. "The Chancellor confirmed that the four remaining test subjects will die from some form of Leukemia in the future, Dad. Trader Pharmaceuticals has 'replaced' their original test subjects with legitimate volunteers and assigned the study data to those they didn't even test. If they are allowed to use their treatment on the population, they may stop them from dying of the Blue Flu now, but they will die later. That's why Uncle Jack has to save those people, Dad. They are the best and really only proof we have."

"That's very true, Salena."

I then proceeded to tell Dad about the old Asian man who had removed my jeans and hung them up, with the big shirt, between my bed and the one in front of mine. I'm guessing that the stench was so rank in the box that the guard outside only opened the door to do a quick bed check from the entry way. He didn't even think to look behind the pants and shirt because nobody had been in that bed before. He probably didn't want to walk inside that container without wearing a gas mask.

I finished off my fruit salad and started digging into my chocolate cake as dad told a few crazy stories of him and Uncle Jack from their college fraternity days.

"Tell me the story about how you and mom met, again," I asked.

"Again, Salena? You've heard it a thousand times."

"I know, but I love it."

So once more, Dad told me that he had spotted Mom in one of their early undergraduate classes, but he was too shy to approach her. Jack, on the other hand had no such lack of courage. He approached mom out of the blue and told her that his friend was so love sick over her that he was afraid his friend was going to die.

"That insufferable man asked Mia if she would be willing to save a fellow student's life and grace us with her presence at dinner. Oh and bring a friend, he said." My dad shook his head. "If I had a gun, I would have shot him, but he was my best friend, and cleaning up after that would have been messy."

I continued to ask him questions about Jack and Mom and himself while we slid into an easy conversation. And, suddenly Angeni burst into existence between us.

"It's gone!" she said with distress. "I led them right to where that damn container was a little over an hour ago and it was gone! Jack has a driver bringing your mom back now, and he is regrouping with his team. They are going to try to find out what ship they put the container on, but chances are there isn't any paperwork or trace to follow at this point," Angeni told me in a rush. Just as she finished, my dad's cell phone rang.

"James here . . . okay . . . Damn, that's not good . . . Alright, keep me posted," Dad said and hung up. He looked at me expectantly. "That was Jack. The container is . . ."

"Gone. Yes, I know. Angeni just popped in and told me." I interrupted him and repeated what Angeni said.

"Well, that's pretty much what Jack told me," Dad replied.

"Angeni, do you know what ship the container is on?" I asked her.

"No, Salena, I don't. I've been with you or your mom the whole time. Chang must have had it moved out immediately after he arrived."

"Angeni doesn't know, Dad. But I might be able to find it, if I go into the Fifth."

"No, Salena. I am not risking you again. It's too dangerous. What if you materialize in that box again?"

"I won't, Dad. In fact, once I find it, I'll move out of it immediately. I need to find out what ship it's on anyway," I reasoned. I didn't think he was buying any of it.

He shook his head. "Let's give your Uncle Jack some time to locate it his way first, and keep you out of the line of fire for once, okay?"

"Okay," I said, but Angeni gave me a look that said she wasn't buying my complicity for one minute.

"Didn't you find out that they were shipping out on Friday when you were in the Records?" Dad asked me.

"That's what Kasem told the Sumo Wrestler dude who was guarding the container outside, but that was around noon on Monday. Who knows, maybe they were able to get it shipped out early. Either that or they just loaded the container tonight and the ship is still sitting in the port. I could just slip into the Fifth and check it out…"

"Knock it off, Salena." Dad said giving me his "I've had enough of your crap" look. I was just stubborn and defiant enough not to let it intimidate me… too much. I told Dad that I would wait for Uncle Jack to work his magic, so wait I did. I paced and fidgeted and fussed and asked annoying questions that earned me a few more of those same looks from Dad.

Finally mom showed back up, and I was able to pepper her with questions after she told us how there wasn't any cheese at the end of the rat's maze. "In fact, there was very little evidence to suggest that there was ever any cheese there to begin with. Jack's team is very loyal to him, but he didn't tell them how he had found the spot where the container was supposed to be, and he didn't explain how I was supposed to know where it was in the first place. Now it's a little like looking for a needle in a haystack, I'm afraid."

"I could find the container, Mom." The words were barely out of my mouth when my dad shot me a dirty look.

"Aw, Salena! Will you please give it a rest?" He said, his voice rising in frustration.

"What does she mean James?" Mom asked. So dad told her. I could see the same war between wanting to protect me and the need to save the imprisoned people flash across her face as it did Dad's. I was pretty sure at that moment that being a parent could really suck sometimes.

I tried another approach. I explained how the Asian guy had saved me and then asked me for help. "I feel like I really owe him. He needs my help," I pleaded.

Mom and Dad looked at each other and did that weird telepathic thing that totally in love married couples do. My arguments fell on deaf and protective ears. Mom ended up agreeing with dad that we should wait to see what Jack finds, if anything.

You would think that with all the sleep I had over the last couple of days, that I wouldn't be tired. But I was. I let the adults, Angeni included, wait up for word from Jack while I headed to the second bedroom I'd discovered in this massive and elegant two bedroom suite. I guess EPIC is a well-funded program. *Works for me.*

I didn't sleep well. I tossed and turned and had nightmarish dreams. Finally, the red numbers on the clock said it was 3:42 a.m. I decided I had had enough. I padded across the carpet in my bare feet to the slightly ajar door and looked into the living room. It was empty. Not even Angeni was hovering about. She must have gone to wherever she goes to recharge. The door to the master bedroom was shut, so I put my ear up to it. I could hear my dad snoring, loudly. I wondered how in the heck my mom slept through that. They had promised to wake me with any news, but now they were asleep. I thought that this would be my perfect opportunity to quickly locate the container and have the information ready to give Uncle Jack if he came up empty-handed. I decided it would be worth whatever punishment I got from Mom and Dad.

I slipped back into my bedroom and closed the door. I sat on the floor, crossed my legs, and breathed deeply in and out. I went through my ritual, and soon the heaviness of the Third Dimension peeled off of me like a wet blanket. I was back in the Fifth.

I was getting better and better at transporting. Closing my eyes, I focused my thoughts on the container and imagined myself there. I opened my eyes into a black void. I couldn't see anything at all. The only way I knew I was in the container at all was due to the smell, which hit me like a punch to the stomach and threatened to make me relive my dinner in a particularly nasty way. I had to get out of here.

I didn't exactly know if there was anything surrounding this box or not, and experimenting with Fifth Dimensional materialization inside Third Dimensional objects wasn't something I wanted to start doing now. I looked up hoping to catch a glimpse of the slits in the roof. My eyes had adjusted enough to spot them so I floated up and gazed out. Nothing was sitting on top of the container, but it did look like it could be inside some kind of cargo hold. Cautiously, I slipped up to the top of the container and looked around. There was a very dim light at one point in the distance and I headed toward it. As I approached the light it turned into a green button at the top of a ladder that was covered with a closed hatch. I shivered as I moved through the steel hatch cover. The cold, dead metal prickled my skin like I had fallen into a bush of stinging nettles. Thankfully, once I was through, the sensation stopped. I looked around. I was definitely on a freighter, and the ship wasn't docked. I could see the lights of Singapore fading away in the wake of the big ship. I zapped myself to the stern and then floated gently up, letting the boat pull ahead of me. I looked at the name painted in large white letters across its stern as the Tomi Maru plowed her way through the waves away from the fading lights.

I have to find Uncle Jack.

CHAPTER TWENTY-FIVE
Tomi Maru

As I floated in the air watching the ship move slowly away from me, I closed my eyes and concentrated on everything I knew about my uncle, the way he looked, smelled, smiled, and laughed. "I am with my Uncle Jack!" I said out loud with purpose and intention. I opened my eyes and found myself standing behind him. He was lying down on a couch in a wood paneled room that smelled of stale cigarette smoke. There were no windows. The only door was opposite the couch with an eight foot round metal-legged table with a wood veneer top between them. Brighid was sitting at the table in a plastic folding chair, coffee cup in hand, scouring a stack of papers. Another beefy dark-skinned guy with a flattop buzz cut, dressed in all black like Brighid, frowned at a computer screen. Two other people, one man and another woman, were sitting on the floor with their backs to the wall with their eyes closed. All of them were armed. I decided that materializing in front of all of these edgy warriors might prove hazardous to my health. *Might be better to knock first.*

I sieved myself through the door. For some reason passing through Third Dimensional wood is not nearly as uncomfortable a passing through Third Dimensional metal. Oddly enough, nobody was standing guard outside the door. The room Uncle Jack and his team occupied was upstairs inside a larger wood structured warehouse. There was a landing outside the door with stairs going down to the floor on one side. Nobody was patrolling at the bottom of the stairs either. The warehouse below the room was fairly empty. Just a few pallets with boxes strapped to them and a couple of fifty-gallon drums were pushed up against the edges. There were two opaque skylights that told me it was still pretty dark outside. It was time.

Maybe the Tinkerbell P.J. pants with the matching "Looking for Lost Boys" cami top should go, I thought. I manifested a pair of black jeans and a black tight fitting sleeveless shirt like I wear when I work out. Matching sneakers went on my feet, and I pulled my hair back into a ponytail. I could do badass too, if I wanted.

Thinking about how much trouble I'd be in if my parents found my bed empty, I began to feel the heat and heaviness of the Third Dimension envelope me. The usual disorientation thing hit and I grabbed the peeling paint wood rail of the landing to steady myself. I hadn't been in the Fifth long, so it didn't take much time for me to stabilize. Letting go of the railing, I confirmed my balance and knocked on the door. I heard the sounds of people rustling, chairs scraping, and muffled voices coming from behind the door.

"Yeah?" I heard Brighid's voice ask.

"Brighid? It's me, Salena. I've got to talk to Uncle Jack!"

"Salena?! What the Hell?!" Brighid exclaimed as she turned the deadbolt and opened the door. "How in God's name did you find us?" She said frantically scanning the warehouse for signs of any other intruders.

"It's okay, Brighid, I can guarantee you I wasn't followed. I came here via the Fifth Dimension. I didn't want to materialize inside the room. Thought I might get shot," I said with a lopsided grin.

"Don't just stand there, ladies, come in and close the door," Uncle Jack said from behind Brighid. "Do your parents know you're here, Salena?"

"Uh, not really, no." I looked down at my feet and kicked at a little pebble I spotted on the floor. "I couldn't sleep. I assumed that you hadn't had any success because Mom and Dad promised that they would wake me up if they heard back from you. I knew I could find the container by going to the Fifth, so I did. The ship isn't in port anymore, Uncle Jack. It's already headed out to sea. The name of the ship is the Tomi Maru."

"I'm on it!" Firestone said sitting down at the table and pulling the laptop away from the big guy with the buzzcut who was staring at me, with an open-mouthed astonished expression on his face.

"Got 'em. Salena's right. They're not in Kansas anymore!" Brighid confirmed.

Uncle Jack looked like he was talking to himself, but it was probably more likely that he was using some high-tech gadget to communicate with the rest of his team. There were only six people in this room, and I think dad told me that they had twelve.

"We're moving out in three!" The EPIC Director bellowed commanding the attention of his team. He walked up to me and put his big hands on my biceps, freezing me in place. "You are absolutely positive about this Salena? I am trusting your information implicitly because there is absolutely no justification for what we are about to do, nor do we have any jurisdiction over that ship. You are risking my life and the lives of this team." His eyes bored into me, challenging me to take responsibility for my information and for what I was asking them to do.

"I swear to you that I was just inside that container while it was on that freighter. I moved through the box and up onto the deck, and then I went to the stern of the ship and looked at the name. As long as you arrive before they unload the container, they *WILL* be there! It's in the forward cargo hold with a bunch of bags of something piled up on either side of it. I know you are putting a ton of faith in me Uncle. I promise what I'm telling you is the God's honest truth. Please save those people." I looked back at him with my eyes and heart open showing him the veracity of my words.

"Alright. Firestone, you have the coordinates?"

"Yes Sir!" She said as she closed up the computer and slipped it into a backpack that she pulled out from under the table.

"Salena!"

"Yes, Uncle?"

"Go back to your hotel room, the same way you came, before your parents wake and find you missing. Thank you for your assistance. I'll take it from here."

"Yes, Sir," I said, looking down at my feet again. I really wanted to tag along, but this was a military operation. *There was no way in hell they would knowingly allow me to go along . . . The key word there is knowingly. I could watch them from the Fifth. That way I could be sure they found the right container . . .*

"MOVE OUT!" Jack bellowed and the five team members exited the room. Just before he closed the door behind him, he looked at me. "You'll be okay getting back the way you came?"

I smiled at him. "Don't worry. I've got this. I'll be fine."

He moved back into the room and reached into his pocket pulling out some cash. He picked one out of the stack and slapped it onto the table. A twenty Sing dollar bill stared up at me. "Just in case you need to take a cab. Be careful."

"You too," I said as I picked up the bill from the table and shoved it into my pocket. I'd give it back to him later. He headed out the door and closed it softly behind him.

My nose twitched in anticipation of a sneeze as the old and musty smells of the suddenly abandoned room closed in around me. I hadn't realized how the intense energy of the EPIC Team had filled the room. I decided to leave the light on, figuring somebody would eventually show up to turn it off, and headed toward the couch where Uncle Jack had been sleeping.

I sat down on the sofa, which immediately sent a poof of dust into my nose causing me to sneeze. Feet planted on the floor, one palm facing up and one palm facing down, I took a deep breath and imagined my divine vortexes converging into my heart chakra. The Third Dimension slipped away, and I quickly conjured a glass of water. I had forgotten to ask Uncle Jack for some.

I stood up, closed my eyes, and focused on the leader of EPIC. When I opened my eyes I was in the back seat of a vehicle moving very quickly through the shipping port. Thankfully, I had managed to arrive in the empty seat and not the one with Buzz Cut in it.

I quickly made my root chakra tether the way Jazwynd taught me in Disneyland. Being reminded of the Haunted Mansion, I felt like I was haunting the car. I amused myself by thinking about rattling chains and making spooky noises, but they wouldn't hear me anyway.

Huh, I wonder why Amalya hasn't shown up? I know she can sense when I enter the Fifth. Maybe something more important than babysitting me has come up.

Our car stopped and so did the one behind us. We were in the ginormous Port of Singapore, but not where they moor the freighters. The boats docked here looked like military and Coast Guard type vessels in various shapes and sizes. The team gathered their bags of gear out of the trunks and headed down to the pier. Gliding along behind them I noticed a very faint glow off to the east. I figured maybe an hour had passed since I left my hotel room.

The team stepped onto the stern of one totally bad to the bone looking boat. EPIC had some serious financial support. Batman would so totally be hella jealous of this baby. She was close to sixty feet long with a dark charcoal finish. The bow was long and deep, which looked like it would take the ocean waves really well. We climbed up the stern ladders and met up with the other team on the back deck. After all the usual greetings between people who worked closely together, Uncle Jack told everyone to go below deck for the briefing. This vessel came with her own Captain and crew, because the whole EPIC team headed inside. I felt the engines rev up and looked around to see a growing expanse of water between the dock and us. *Wow! They sure don't waste any time!*

I followed the group down into a state of the art control room. Suddenly, I realized that my well-practiced tethering system might not allow me to move freely around the boat. Chewing on my lower lip, I tried to figure out a way to instantly connect with the vessel with each step I took. After discarding a couple of really useless ideas, the image of a burglar using suction cups to climb up the outside of a skyscraper popped into my head. Smiling, I attached energetic suction cups to the bottom of my feet, and tested my "portable" tether while we slowly headed out of the harbor. It worked perfectly! After congratulating myself for my inventiveness, I took a look around the command center. There were monitors banking both the port and starboard sides with a big monitor table in the center. That was so cool. The whole set up reminded me of the main office in Hawaii 5-0. Brighid pulled up a digital chart of the area we were in.

"Welcome aboard the Excalibur, everyone. Firestone please brief us on the status of our target." the Director of EPIC instructed.

"The Tomi Maru is here," Brighid said as she pointed to a red dot on the map. "They left port at 0230 hours, so they have a two and a half hour lead on us. Assuming they don't change their speed we should catch them in a little over an hour. The seas are calm and this lady has a top speed of fifty knots."

The group gathered around the table and they all started talking and asking questions. I tried to pay attention, but the military speak bored me. I wandered around the yacht checking it out. The coolest thing was the "garage" in the back that opened up. Inside was an inflatable Kodiac speedboat that I assumed was used for stealth attacks. Up on deck, I could see the Excalibur slicing through the ocean waves the way I imagined Arthur Pendragon would have wielded the sword in battle. I still had an hour to kill, so I let go of my energetic tie to the Excalibur and popped back to my hotel room to see if my parents had awakened and discovered my absence.

Everything was quiet in my bedroom. It looked just as I left it. Moving into the living room I could hear my dad snoring through the door. I was sure they had to be exhausted from the stress of my disappearance and captivity. So hopefully they would sleep for a while longer.

Concentrating on the Excalibur and my Uncle, I

closed my eyes. When I reappeared inside the operations room on the Excalibur, only half of the EPIC team was still present. I guessed that they were getting ready. Brighid stared at a computer screen while Uncle Jack paced in thought.

"Commander! Target has slowed. Estimated time to intercept at our current velocity is ten minutes!" Firestone said. The EPIC Director quickly moved over behind Brighid's back while she pointed out our position relative to the Tomi Maru on the screen.

Wow, only ten minutes! That was fast! My boat tour and side trip home must have taken longer than I thought. I figured I could head over to the Tomi Maru now and wait for the EPIC Team to arrive. I closed my eyes and pictured the stern of the freighter in my mind. I didn't want to risk going back inside that rotten container again.

The ship had indeed slowed down; in fact, it had stopped. It was floating quietly in the middle of the ocean like a cork bobs in a bathtub. I headed up toward the front of the ship where the metal prison box was stored inside the hold. The ship had to be about four hundred feet long. There were three storage areas, each one with its own crane that stuck up from the deck like a misshapen mast. I spotted only a few sailors on the deck. They were armed and pacing back and forth in various posted positions. I guessed that the fewer people who knew what they were doing, the better. Two of the three compartments were closed, but the front one was open and the crane's arm was centered over the open hold. Big rusty cables extended down from the horizontally protruding arm of the crane. Screeching and clanking reverberated throughout the ship. I quickly moved myself toward the front of the ship so I could see what they were doing. I had a sinking feeling that EPIC's team would be cutting it pretty close. (No pun intended.)

I looked down into the opening. The single cable had a container length metal contraption that was covering the top of the prison box. I watched two sailors align the brace to the top of the container and then I heard a loud snapping cracking sound as the corners of the contraption clamped onto the corners of the metal container. The groaning and clanking of the stretching cables made shivers go up my back, but the screaming and yelling that came next from inside the box made the hairs on the back of my neck stand on end. *Hell! What was I going to do now?!*

I watched the two men scramble up the ladder and out of the hold. Following the cable up from the container into the arm of the crane and down the support beam, I spotted the small operator's room where a guy was sitting and controlling the crane. He looked to be in some kind of space capsule. A dome shaped bubble of glass enclosed the crane operator's cabin giving him a 180° view of the ship. It reminded me of a bug-eyed Cyclops. Closing my eyes, I pictured myself on top of the operator's cabin.

Leaning over the top of the capsule, I peered through the side window. The Caucasian guy operating the crane was bald, beefy, and had a goatee. Tattoos of dragons and snakes wrapped around his leathery Popeye arms. He probably smelled as bad as he looked. Thankfully, I was outside the cabin. I paid close attention as he maneuvered the controls. The box imprisoning the victims slowly rose from its resting place.

He's going to dump that container overboard! I thought frantically. The crane operator continued to lift the container until it was above the hatch. It paused, hanging above the open chasm, slightly swaying with the pitch and roll of the ship. The man took his hand off the control and wiped his palm on his pant legs. Then he gently tapped the joystick, slowly moving the boom to his right. The metal box began inching its way toward the edge of the ship.

It's now or never! I have to do something! Half of the container was now floating in the air above the ocean. Frantically running through potential options in my head, I almost missed the shouts coming from the stern of the ship. There was no mistaking the sound of rapid gunfire though! *The Calvary has arrived!!! Yes!*

The tattooed crane man had heard the gunfire as well. He took his hand off of the control stick just as the last part of the container edged over the starboard railing. It hung in midair, swaying over the water. Crane man got out of his chair, pressed his face up to the window and tried to look behind him where the shots were being fired. I guess he wasn't able to see very well, because he headed out the door behind the cockpit seat and started to climb down the ladder to the deck of the ship. Seeing my opportunity, I sieved through the cab walls and settled myself into the control seat. Hoping to stave off some of the negative effects of rematerialization, I manifested a large glass of water and downed it all. It wasn't difficult to come up with a fear thought as I looked at the swinging container hanging over the ocean. The heat and heaviness settled over me as I materialized into the Third Dimension.

My legs were shaking, and perspiration beaded up at my hairline. I gently placed my jittery hand around the control rod and cautiously began to maneuver the crane and its cargo back over the bow of the ship. The joystick was really touchy and the boom started moving too rapidly, causing the container to swing wildly. The cables groaned with stress. Completely freaked out, I jerked my hand away from the control like it was a hot potato. I chewed on my bottom lip, petrified, while I watched the container swing wildly back and forth. The out-of-control box had gained momentum not only from my novice abilities, but also from a sudden lurch the ship took as a result of a random ocean swell.

God! I hope the prisoners are all holding onto something inside there, and that the beds aren't falling on them! As I waited for the swinging to settle, I wiped my sweaty hands on my pants, hoping that I'd do better the next time. Once again, I very gently and ever so slowly started moving the boom back over the ship. Deep in concentration, I practically jumped out of my skin when the cab door slammed open and a deep, angry voice boomed behind me, "How the hell did you get in here?!"

I whipped my head around and found myself face to face with the Crane Man. I bolted up out of the seat and pressed my back into the front window of the cab. Not taking his eyes off of me he leaned down and grabbed a very large gun and some rope from under the control seat. The pistol looked like it grew even bigger when he pointed it at me.

"Uh . . . Uh . . . " I stammered putting my hands up in the air like I was getting ready to do air push-ups.

"I asked you a question little girl," he said fiercely. "You speak English?"

"Uh . . . yeah . . . yes . . . I . . . uh . . . speak English," I stammered. The sweat on my forehead started trailing down toward my eyes.

"How'd you get in here?! Where did you come from?!"

"I . . . um . . . um . . ." My answer was interrupted by sounds of more shots and shouts from the deck below.

"Never mind. I don't have time for this right now. Come here!" he commanded with a wave of his gun.

Slowly, with my hands still in the air I took two steps forward around the console chair and faced his chin. I was right. He did smell as bad as he looked. I crinkled my nose and tried not to breathe too deeply.

"Turn around!"

I turned.

"Put your hands behind your back."

I lowered my arms and brought them behind me. Crane man momentarily set down his gun, and expertly wrapped and tied the rope around my wrists. He closed the cabin door, grabbed me by my upper arms, and shoved my back against the entrance.

Picking up his weapon he said, "Sit!," again directing me with the gun he held on me.. I slowly lowered myself down, never taking my eyes off of him.

My captor then turned his back to me and sat in the operator's chair. Gun in his left hand and joystick in the right, he once again started moving the container toward the water. The cables loudly complained as I watched the container of innocents, once again, inch closer to the rolling waves of the South Pacific Ocean.

"There's people in there! You can't drop that container into the ocean! You'll kill them!"

Crane man laughed.

He laughed! That ass-wipe laughed! I glared back at him.

Holy Crap! I am stuck inside this bubble with a stinky, diabolical murderer. Way to go, Salena. I shook my head at myself. *You really did a doozy this time.*

Yeah, so NOT my best moment!

CHAPTER TWENTY-SIX
Firefight

"Yes, little girl. That was the plan. That's why I get paid the big bucks! If you are really lucky, maybe I'll let you hit the release button!" He laughed some more.

I decided now would probably be a good time to shut up. I obviously wasn't going to be able to appeal to his better nature. Instead, while he was concentrating on moving the container, I closed my eyes and focused the whole of my being on releasing my fear and concentrating on love. The energy responded quickly and I felt the familiar tingling sensation of my body's frequency rising. I was so focused and intent on going back to the Fifth that I barely heard the battle heating up on the decks below.

Crane Man heard all the commotion, though. "What the hell!! What *are* you!?" He exclaimed. Opening my eyes, I looked into his and noticed that they were bugging out of his skull with shock and fright. He pointed his gun at me, his hand shaking. I can only assume that I looked like a ghost. He caught a glimpse of me just before my frequency was out of Third Dimensional visual range.

He squeezed off three rapid shots at my apparition. The bullets burned like dry ice when they zipped through my Fifth Dimensional form. I quickly looked down at my abdomen. Relief flooded through me. I was fully in the Fifth and completely intact. *I can't lose my grip on the Fifth now!* I reminded myself, so I closed my eyes and visualized my meadow with the peaceful loving energy flowing through me. I decided I wasn't going to think about what just happened until I wanted to go back to the Third Dimension.

Hastily scrambling to my feet, I dissolved the ropes that had made the transition with me and quickly stepped around to the other side of the chair from the crane operator, who was still stunned and attempting to recover from the shock. He finally snapped out of it, opened the door, and stuck his head out of the cabin looking up and down the ladder for any sign of me.

A frantic voice from the decks below yelled up at Crane Man, "Ruddick!! What the hell are you doing?! Get your ass down here, NOW!"

With one last longing look at the container swaying above the sea and the empty cabin, Ruddick exited through the now bullet ridden door. Slamming it in frustration behind him, he shoved the gun down the back of his pants and proceeded to scramble down the crane ladder.

I waited, giving Mr. Ruddick plenty of time to get down to the deck. Absentmindedly I rubbed my wrists as I stuck my head through the glass dome of the cab scanning the ship to see if I could tell what was happening. There were black clad people running toward my direction with machineguns in hand. I watched the bald head of Ruddick engage one of the EPIC team members in a firefight. The crane operator thought he had a good advantage being higher than his enemy as he stopped a few rungs up from the bottom. He just didn't have very good aim. The EPIC commando easily dodged Ruddick's bullets and then shot back at him with far better accuracy. I don't know where my captor got hit, but he slid down the last few rungs and sat limply on the deck at the bottom of the ladder.

Trusting that EPIC would prevail and that Ruddick wouldn't be climbing back up to visit me again anytime soon, I sat back down into the control seat. Taking a deep breath, I conjured another glass of water, which I promptly guzzled down. Ready to go back to the Third Dimension, I decided to recall the moment when Crane Man shot me.

The Third came on me quickly. So fast, in fact, that I was a little dizzy and disoriented at first. I held onto the arms of the chair and breathed deeply until it passed. Then once more, I tried to move the container back over the ship and toward the open cargo hold. The sun was beginning to rise, bathing the deck in an early morning light.

More shots rang out from the other side of the ship. Sparks flew off of the beam holding the container. *They're trying to shoot apart the cables!* Gunshots continued to fire as I slowly handled the controls. Bullets zinged and sparked off of their targets. I screamed as one of the cables broke free thrashing around like a loose high-pressure hose. The metal box swung wildly as one corner dipped toward the ocean. I couldn't stop shaking as I continued to try to navigate the unruly deathtrap back over the side of the ship. The gunfire stopped as suddenly as it started. I hoped that one of my Uncle's team had captured him, and that he wasn't just reloading. One of the EPIC warriors saw the container moving and looked up at me. His eyes opened wide in shock and recognition. *Uh Oh! I am so totally busted!*

The EPIC guy caught Uncle Jack's attention and pointed at me. My uncle just stared at me shaking his head as I cautiously maneuvered the container to the center of the hold and started lowering it down. It hit the bottom of the hold with a loud jolting clang and totally catawampus with one end elevated on top of some of the surrounding cargo bags and the other end on the floor, but at least it wasn't dangling above the sea anymore. I was pretty proud of myself for maneuvering the dang thing as well as I did, considering I only watched the Ruddick guy for a few minutes, and especially now that it was totally lopsided. I didn't know which button would disengage the clamps, so I just decided to leave it.

Another eruption of semi-automatic weapons exploded on the deck. The sound reminded me of a big eighteen-wheeler diesel truck down shifting after cresting a hill. Several bullets suddenly slammed into the cab, one piercing through the corner of the front window.

They missed me, but I still let out a startled scream and started shaking all over again. Scrambling out of the seat, I sat on the floor with my back to the cab door, breathing heavily. Listening to shouts coming from the deck of the ship, I tried to get my heart rate to calm down.

I focused on my breathing and felt the familiar calm settle over me. The noises coming from the deck of the ship finally quieted down and I didn't hear any more gunfire. Slowly and cautiously, I crawled back to the front of the cab and looked down at the deck. The EPIC team had dragged the crew of the Tomi Maru into a tight circle. There were a couple of injured crewmembers, the bald crane operator among them. It looked like he'd been shot in the leg.

From my perch in the crane cabin my gaze shifted down into the hold of the ship where I watched Uncle Jack key in the code to the door that I had given him earlier in our adventures. Uncle Jack turned the handle of the container's entry door, but before he opened it, he turned around and looked up at me. He smiled, gave me a thumbs-up, and stepped inside.

Two of his team members followed him in. I thought I recognized Brighid, but it was kinda hard to tell. I stayed inside the control cab watching for the emergence of the test subjects. It wasn't long before they started to come out with the assistance of the EPIC leader and his comrades. None of the victims had the physical strength to climb the ladder out, so they rigged up a rescue stretcher and hauled them up to the deck of the ship one by one. The Excalibur had pulled up alongside of the Tomi Maru, and the victims were loaded onto the fast attack cruiser for the trip back to

Singapore. The old Chinese guy came out of the container last. Stopping just outside of the door, he let his eyes adjust, and then, somehow, his eyes found me and he gave me a huge toothless smile. How he knew I was there, I had no idea, but it sure made me feel fulfilled and accomplished. For the first time in my life I was truly happy that I wasn't "normal."

It was time for me to get back to my bedroom in the hotel. I knew that Uncle Jack and his team would handle it from here, and I needed to get out of the way. Closing my eyes, I focused on my breathing and visualization. I could feel the powerful energy racing through my body as the Third Dimension slipped away.

Once again, I was fully in the Fifth Dimension. I glanced down at the container and noticed that Uncle Jack had stepped out in time to see me disappear. He smiled and waved. Eyes shut once again, I pictured my bedroom at the Intercontinental Hotel and the muggy, smelly confinement of the crane cab vanished.

Oh, my bed looks good! I can't wait to crawl into it! Before I descend back to the Third Dimension, I better go check on Mom and Dad first to make sure they are still asleep, just in case. The clock beside my bed said it was 6:36 am. I had no idea what time my parents went to bed last night, so they could sleep for a little longer. Moving through my door into the living room, everything looked like it had when I left. I poked my head through my parents' door. *Yes! They're still conked out!*

Back in my room, I conjured a protein shake and a large glass of water. After scarfing those down, I dematerialized my ninja outfit and rematerialized my

Tinkerbell P.J.'s and went into the bathroom. Placing my hands above the counter, I let go of the Fifth Dimension for the fifth time in three hours. The water and the shake helped the reentry process, but now I really had to go!!

When I finally melted into the soft sheets of the queen size bed, I exhaled loudly, releasing the intensity of the last few hours. Rolling on my side, I stuffed a pillow between my knees and put my arms around another. I was asleep before I finished yawning.

The excited voices coming through the door from the living room broke through to my dreams. *Captain Jack Hammer was shouting commands at me while he and I fought pirates on a black ship in a dead calm. Against our enemy he wielded a jackhammer while I battled only with a purple crystal.* I slowly awakened to the sound of the TV and loud talking. Groaning with the absurdity of the dream, I rolled over and opened one eye to check the time. No wonder I was hungry! It was time for lunch! I'd been asleep almost six hours!

Crawling out of bed I padded over to the slightly open door. No wonder their voices were so loud! Peeking out of the crack in the door I spotted Mom, Dad, Uncle Jack, Brighid, and Angeni. *The gang's all here!* After smoothing out my bed head with my hands, I opened the door and entered the cacophony.

"Mornin'," I croaked. They all turned to stare at me, and then smiled.

"There she is! Secret Agent Salena! The girl who saved the world!" Brighid announced. *Uh Oh. I guess they told my parents what happened. I'm totally gonna get it now.* I just returned a rather tentative smile, not sure about the severity level of the imminent tongue-lashing.

"Jack told us about your exploits this morning, Salena," my Mom said more calmly than I was expecting.

"Uh, huh. So, how much trouble am I in?"

Mom sighed and looked at Dad. They don't have to speak to communicate with each other. "Well, honestly we're not quite sure what to do with you. You blatantly disobeyed us, but if you hadn't, those people would be dead. Your actions saved more than just those eleven prisoners. Do you know that?" Mom asked.

"Umm. No. Honestly, I hadn't given it much thought. Once I saw that Uncle Jack had evacuated the people, I came back here and went right to bed."

"It's back on again," Brighid said pointing at the CNN Newscaster. I turned my attention toward the TV.

Early this morning an elite paramilitary rescue force seized a freighter that, according to manifests, was shipping rice to America. However, it was discovered that the cargo included eleven victims of human trafficking. They were rescued from certain death as the shipping container in which they were imprisoned was prevented from being dumped into the ocean. The Tomi Maru was seized and brought back to Singapore, its Captain and crew brought in for questioning by the Singaporean authorities.

The eleven survivors were originally part of a group

of fifty people abducted and subsequently sold. Purportedly bought by Trader Pharmaceuticals last September, some of the victims claim they were stored in this container until they were picked to be a test subject for the Blue Flu treatment. Once a treatment was finalized, the surviving subjects, and those who were never picked, were no longer needed. They were rescued just before their captors dumped the container overboard. All of the victims have been taken to a local hospital in Singapore for treatment.

Mitch Trader, majority stockholder and Chairman of the Board of Trader Pharmaceuticals cannot be reached for comment. Trader Pharmaceuticals' President, Jude Bonaparte, and their Vice President of Public Relations and Marketing were also unavailable for comment, due to illness. The Singapore office of Trader Pharmaceuticals has declined to comment as well.

Coincidentally, early Thursday morning in the US, Trader Pharmaceuticals received approval from the FDA for their anxiously awaited Blue Flu treatment. CNN just received word that the FDA has rescinded their approval due to the events that have unfolded today in Singapore.

In a related story, the viral explosion of the metaphysical treatment for the Blue Flu that was launched on the website www.BlueFlu.edu last Monday has received record exposure and interest.

The first clinic of its kind, "The Body of Light Clinic" in Reno, Nevada is directly connected to the BlueFlu.edu website. CNN News reporter, Tiffany Evans, is on the scene now.

"Thank you, Joe," a young woman with shoulder length brown hair and blue eyes filled the screen.

What is happening here in the "Biggest Little City in the World" is truly remarkable. The BlueFlu.edu website that just launched on Monday is directly connected to this clinic that opened its doors on Tuesday. Owned and operated by a group of medical professionals previously employed by Reno General Hospital, the clinic has developed an amazing and proven process for curing the Blue Flu, which they are sharing with the community and the world.

This treatment doesn't require the use of any drugs or conventional forms of western medical treatment. It uses ceremony and crystals to cleanse people's auras that have been infected with this disease. The response has been tremendous, not only locally, but globally as well. As you can see behind me there is a line out the door and up the block. The doctors and staff have been working twenty-four hours a day since they opened. There is talk about moving the operation to the Convention Center here in town to attempt to meet the demand.

It was dark in Reno, but I could see the trail of

people wrapping around the small office complex that Lesley had found to lease for Dr. Lisa and the rest of the doctors and nurses from Reno General. Everyone in line had surgical masks on even though those things did absolutely no good. Tiffany continued her report,

> *Copycat clinics are popping up all over the world as people follow the instructions from the video posted on the website and YouTube. There are plenty of critics, but those who have been cured, of which there are thousands now, sure are believers.*

The anchorman asked if they knew how they discovered the unconventional cure. I cringed as Tiffany reported my role in the discovery. Again, so NOT what I wanted to happen. I guess there was no avoiding the spotlight now. I just stared open mouthed at the TV.

"You're a hero, Salena. Hard for us to punish you for saving the world, and they don't even know that you were the one responsible for thwarting Trader's plans to hide the evidence of their misconduct," Dad said gently. "We are very proud of you for your courage and determination."

"I could use you on my team, Salena! Wanna come work for me?" Uncle Jack said half joking. My mom shot him a dirty look. Dad gave his best bud a "Don't even go there" look and just shook his head.

"You've got my vote! I like your moves, girlfriend!" Brighid chimed in and raised her hand for a high-five. I laughed, slapped her hand with mine and then looked at Angeni who had been very quiet thus far.

Her expression told me she didn't think that this would be my last mission with Uncle Jack. I decided I really didn't want to think about that too much.

"Angeni, do you have anything to say?" I whispered to her.

"Not really, other than I'm realizing that signing up to be your spirit guide has turned out to be a bigger job than I expected," she responded wryly. "But, I wouldn't give it up for anything!"

CHAPTER TWENTY-SEVEN
Soul Crystal

I was *SO* ready to leave Singapore. Every time my mind drifted to the Sierra Nevada Colony, my heart felt heavy. I only got that feeling when something was wrong, and I couldn't imagine what could possibly be "wrong" in the Fifth Dimension. Pushing aside the unwelcome dread and worry, I focused my thoughts on what we had accomplished and the good things to come.

We ordered room service for a lunch celebration, but after that there wasn't anything left to do. Uncle Jack and his EPIC team had to stick around for a while to be available for the investigation into their raid of the Tomi Maru and the subsequent investigation into Trader Pharmaceuticals. I told him that Kasem Chang was the one in charge of the prisoners, but that there were a lot of people at Trader who knew what was going on. The fallout from all of this was going to be tremendous. They may even make some headway into the human-trafficking ring that has been plaguing this area. I was glad I was able to help in some way.

Due to my lack of a passport, the group decided I should return home the same way I came. Uncle Jack arranged for more conventional transportation for my parents, but that wouldn't get them home until sometime Saturday morning. I told Mom and Dad that I was going to detour to the Sierra Nevada Colony on the way and that I'd email them when I got home. They'd still be en route, but hopefully their plane had Wi-Fi so they would get the notice.

I arrived in the center of the colony in almost complete darkness. Lights coming from a few windows of homes plus the light of the moon helped my eyes to adjust more quickly. Slightly disoriented, I belatedly remembered the sixteen-hour time difference between Singapore and Reno. The vibration of my arrival brought out the welcoming committee. Amalya, Diana, and Chronoscenti Jacqueline came out of Jace's house to greet me. *What was the Chronoscenti doing here? Where was Jace?* I looked around them to see if he came out behind them. He wasn't there.

"Salena! It's so great to see you! We are so glad you're okay!" Amalya rushed to hug me.

"It's good to see you too!" I said looking past her to see if Jace had come out.

"You provided us with quite a challenge young lady," Chronoscenti Jacqueline said. *Uh oh, what did she mean by that?*

Diana looked at me with a hint of regret in her eyes. *What is going on? Nobody in the Fifth Dimension has any regrets!* "Why don't you come join us at the Stanton's house. Jace's parents have something to tell you," Diana said.

My stomach leapt up to my throat. Something

was wrong, very wrong. Panic started to seep through me when I felt Amalya grab my arm. A rush of energy came through her hand and traveled throughout my body. After a few deep breaths I felt stabilized, but Amalya didn't let go. She, Diana, and the Chronoscenti led me toward the house. The large front door was still ajar from when the ladies had left to greet me, so we just walked in. Jace's parents were not alone. Standing between them with one of her parent's hands on either shoulder, Jazwynd looked at me with an expression I couldn't read. Zander and Illiana were there too, standing on either side of Cherie and Gregg touching them gently. Opal, sporting a purple mop today, was already seated.

"Welcome, Salena!" Jace's mom, Cherie, said. "Please, have a seat." She motioned to a large half-circle-shaped overstuffed couch that I was sure could accommodate at least six people comfortably. Cherie and Gregg took a seat across from the couch in matching overstuffed chairs. Amalya and I sat on the couch, while Lady Cosgrove stood behind Cherie, and Diana stood behind Gregg, each one put their hands on the shoulders of the person in front of them. Amalya was still holding on to my arm sending me a steady stream of energy. Jazwynd sat at the opposite end of the couch between Opal and Illiana and Zander stood behind them.

I was having trouble deciphering the looks of hope and guilt that were warring for real estate on Jaz's face.

"It's nice to see you again Mr. and Mrs. Stanton.

Can you please tell me where Jace is? Why isn't he here with you?" I said trying to deny with my voice the dread I felt in my heart.

"Well, that's what we wanted to talk to you about," Cherie said. Her voice cracked a little and she gave a pleading look to her husband. I could see the energy that Lady Cosgrove was feeding Cherie. I knew what was coming next wasn't going to be good.

"Jace didn't handle your captivity very well at all," his dad started to tell me. "Fear for your life and safety hit him so hard and so fast we barely got him to the Chronoscenti in time."

"I . . . in . . . in time for what? D . . . did Jace evanesce?" Even with the steady stream of energy from Amalya, I knew I was barely holding it together.

"No, no he didn't. Well, he almost did which is why we made the decision we did. He had lost his ability to maintain his physical form, but he didn't want to evanesce, he didn't want to leave you." Cherie's voice cracked. She stopped for a moment and looked down at her hands. After conjuring a glass of water, she drank about half of it down.

In order to give his wife a break, Gregg picked up the explanation. "There is this ancient ritual that the Chronoscenti can do that allows a person who is involuntarily evanescing to be placed into a kind of stasis to keep them from moving on to the spirit realm. Nobody has chosen this particular path in a very long time. It was Jace's only option . . ." His voice trailed off as he shook his head and looked down.

"What was Jace's only option?" I asked quietly,

dreading the answer.

Cherie cleared her throat, "We told Jace that the soul stasis ritual would give him the time to process his fears around you without evanescing. That was enough for him. He didn't care about any of the risks. He asked to be put into stasis inside a soul crystal." Cherie said as she held out a sparkling, one inch long crystal that looked like an amethyst gemstone. It was about three quarters of an inch in diameter and shaped like a pendulum with a point at the bottom. There was a silver cap on the other end that had a silver chain going through it.

I looked at the glowing amethyst colored crystal, and then at Cherie, and then back at the stone. "You're telling me that Jace's soul or spirit is inside that crystal?"

"Yes, that is precisely where he is," Gregg replied.

"So, he can come out now, right? I'm okay. I'm here. He doesn't have to worry about me anymore. How do we get him out of there?"

"We don't, or can't, until he's ready. The stone will turn a brilliant turquoise blue when he is ready. Until then, we wait," the Chronoscenti responded.

"Seriously? Isn't there a way to communicate with him? To tell him to get ready?" I refused to believe that Jace was stuck inside that rock until some unknown time in the future.

"We don't really know the answer to that, Salena. We haven't performed the soul stasis ritual in hundreds of years. There hasn't been the need to do so. The Chronoscenti are all taught it as part of their training, but none of us have ever performed it, until now. We do know that once in the crystal Jace is still sentient, but kind of like in a dream world. Choosing consciousness is a process and then learning how to cope with the reason he's in the crystal in the first place is another process. When he is ready to come out, the color of the crystal turns to alert us and we will perform another ritual to get him out. Beyond that, I'm afraid we don't know much," Chronoscenti Cosgrove admitted.

"I assume those were the risks that he didn't care about? That some unknown amount of time might pass before he regains consciousness?" I asked.

"Yes, but Jace has so much faith in you. He asked us to give you his soul crystal. We know that you two are twin flames, and are therefore connected spiritually and energetically. We all, Jace included, figured if anybody had a way to reach him once he was inside, you would," Cherie replied as she picked up the chain. The crystal swayed back and forth.

"We thought if you wore this around your neck, and close to your heart, maybe he would be able to sense you or feel your energy through the crystal. If he can sense you, then he'll know you're okay, and maybe then he'll be ready to come home," Cherie said holding the crystal and looking from it to me, her eyes begging me to help her. I swallowed and blinked back more tears, totally overwhelmed.

I looked over at Jazwynd, and she nodded slightly. I understood the expressions on her face now.

"You want me to wear Jace around my neck? Will he . . . it survive the transition to the Third Dimension and back again?"

"Yes, and yes. The Akashic records exist in every dimension with the energy of billions of souls in them. The crystal will keep him safe no matter what dimension he's in," Lady Cosgrove responded.

"The crystals from the Blue Flu healings made the transition okay, but the energy inside didn't," I noted.

"That's because the energy inside the crystal was negative and vibrating at too low a level to exist in this dimension. Jace's energy is high vibrational energy. Inside the crystal, he'll be protected while it is in the Third or the Fifth Dimensions. Once the soul crystal turns turquoise though, you'll need to bring him back here for the extraction ceremony. His Fifth Dimensional Form can't exist in the Third Dimension. Only you have the ability to go back and forth in your physical form," the Chronoscenti explained with a soft nurturing smile.

"The metal is white gold, so it won't tarnish, and you don't need to worry about cleansing this crystal. It can't absorb any more energy than it already had inside of it," Cherie explained with a little smile.

Shaking, I reached over the coffee table and let Jace's mom place the crystal into the palm of my hand, its chain following behind it like a trickle of water. It was warm, body temperature warm, not cold as I expected, and the energy thrummed through my hand, up my arm, into my core harmonizing expertly with my own vibration. *Wow! What a rush!* I held the crystal against my chest while Amalya clasped the chain. I no longer needed her to feed me energy, what I was getting from Jace was plenty. Putting my hand over my heart with the crystal sandwiched between, I locked gazes with Cherie.

"I promise I will wear this crystal and never give up trying to communicate with Jace so long as it remains purple. I will do my very best to bring your son back to you," I pledged as my eyes welled up and crested over, again. She smiled at me in deep gratitude

"Thank you, Salena. Because of you, I know that he will come back to us," she said.

Did you hear that Jace? You better come back to us, really soon! I thought, but refrained from saying so out loud. I stood up, walked around the table and gave Cherie and then Gregg a hug. Their doorbell rang just as I reached over to Jazwynd to give her a hug as well.

"I'll get it," Amalya said heading towards the door.

"Kind of late for visitors, isn't it?" The Chronoscenti questioned to nobody in particular.

"Chancellor Williams! What a nice surprise!" Amalya exclaimed from the foyer. My gaze moved to the front door. I hadn't seen the Chancellor since I dropped out of the Fifth and into the nasty Third Dimension prison container. I hoped he wasn't mad at me.

"I'd heard that Salena was here, and I have something for her," he told Amalya. Gregg Stanton stood up and went to greet the Chancellor.

"Hart! Good to see you!" Gregg enthusiastically shook his hand.

"Excellent to see you too, although I wasn't sure you'd feel the same. I'm afraid I wasn't aware of young

Jace's feelings toward Salena here. If I had known, I would have been more careful about how I delivered the message of her captivity. I feel very responsible for his current predicament," the Chancellor said looking at me and then down at the amethyst crystal sparking against my chest.

"Hart, you know as well as the rest of us that this experience was something we all chose before this incarnation. It will be a learning experience for all involved. Salena wasn't so much the cause as the catalyst. For all we know, it was absolutely necessary for Jace to go into that crystal in order to better help Salena with her next Third Dimensional challenge, whatever that may be," Chronoscenti Cosgrove explained.

"You mean, this wasn't it? There's more to come?" I said suddenly feeling very overwhelmed and heavy, like once again the Earth was sitting squarely between my shoulders.

"Oh, sweet child, I'm afraid you're just beginning. But you are not alone. You chose this path for yourself, but we all chose to help you accomplish the tasks your destiny puts in front of you. You are the bridge between the worlds, the Quantum Spirit who will lead the Third Dimensional world into the new Age of Enlightenment."

"Do I still have to take Algebra?"

"'Fraid so, kiddo!" Amalya said laughing.

"Since your abrupt departure from the Fifth Dimension last Monday, Salena, I've been working on the cure and or treatment for PV, the blood disease contracted from Trader Pharmaceutical's Blue Flu treatment," he told me. "I don't know how many people they actually infected, but if you give this treatment to your father, he'll get it to the right people. At the very least it will cure the four test subjects you rescued. So you'll have saved their lives twice." He reached down into the outer pocket of a brief case that suddenly materialized and handed me an envelope.

"Thank you," I said as I looked at the envelope and then tucked it under my arm.

Before I left I needed to know one more thing. "I just have one more question, unrelated to Jace." I said to the group as I walked back into the living room.

"Yes, Salena?" Diana replied.

"Have you given any more thought as to how to release all of the trapped souls of the deceased Blue Flu victims?"

"No, we haven't at least not at this colony. Like you, we've been focused on the living. I believe that Hierophant Jana Tarini went back to her colony after your Metaphysics class with the intention of working on that problem. We haven't followed up with her since she left," Diana said with a slight shake of her head.

"Oh, that's okay. I've been a little busy too. I was just curious," I said with a smile. At this point, I was totally okay with Hierophant Tarini taking all the time she wanted.

CHAPTER TWENTY-EIGHT
Reunion

"Salena, you really kicked ass over the last couple of days. You're one badass chick!" Zander exclaimed after I related to the group what happened to me while they were dealing with Jace.

"Yeah, the Thir-Ds totally owe you big time!" Opal agreed.

"How many times did you go back and forth between dimensions? Five? Six? I totally lost count. That's some serious mojo, girlfriend!" Illiana chimed in giving me a high-five.

"You are definitely getting the hang of inter-dimensional travel," Diana said.

"What Angeni did for you was incredible!" Jazwynd stated coming out of her funk just a little.

"I agree, Jaz. I didn't know that could be done!" Amalya commented.

"Yeah, I owe her big time. She totally saved my butt!" I said and then stifled a yawn. Even though my internal clock said it was early evening, I was still tired. My body was assimilating all the stress and activity from the last few days, not to mention crossing time zones and dimensions. I had some serious cosmic jetlag creeping up on me.

"I'm not surprised that you are tired, Salena. You've been through a lot over the last couple of days. I'll keep you company on your way home," Amalya said.

"Please come back often to visit us and give us an update on Jace. Especially if you notice any changes in the crystal," Gregg said as Cherie and Jaz nodded in effusive agreement.

"I will, I promise."

"It was good to see you again, young lady. Let me know how that treatment works for the PV. We will continue to monitor the spread of the Blue Flu from here and keep you up to date whenever you visit. I'll keep in close contact with Diana and Chronoscenti Jacqueline," Chancellor Williams shook my hand. "Good evening, everyone!" He said and then he and his briefcase vanished.

"It's time for me to be on my way too, Salena," Lady Cosgrove said as she gave me a hug. "I'm sure I'll see you soon."

"Thank you for everything," I said returning her embrace.

Chronoscenti Cosgrove said goodbye to each person, and then she too disappeared. Diana just lived across the street, so she and Opal decided to walk instead of popping back home. I understood now why Opal had purple hair today. Zander followed them out.

"Take care of yourself, young lady. We look forward to your next visit," Gregg clasped his hand over my shoulder while Cherie and Jaz encircled me in a group hug.

"I will, and I look forward to coming back."

"Let's get you home Salena!" Amalya said. "Illiana, I'll see you at home?" Illiana nodded, waved at me, and then teleported.

"I'm ready."

My house was dark and cold when Amalya and I arrived home in the foyer. It was after midnight Friday morning—again. I had gone back in time, sort of. It was so weird to think about gaining almost a whole day once more.

"You good to descend to back to the Third from here?" Amalya asked me.

"Yeah, thanks. Amalya?"

"Yes, Salena?"

"I feel terrible about Jace. What I put him through, that he's in this crystal because of me! I can't believe that the Stanton's don't hate me. They were so nice. How can they not resent me even a little?"

Amalya took both of my hands in hers. "They don't blame you or resent you. Your reason for everything you did was to help other people. Jace's reaction to your captivity was unexpected. It's time to move on. I think the resolution is a good one."

"Thank you, for everything." I said as I let go of her hands and put my arms around her.

"You're welcome!" She said, giving me a peck on the cheek. "Oh, I almost forgot. Chronoscenti Cosgrove and I thought you might want this back," she said as my Lake Tahoe sweatshirt materialized in her outstretched hands. "You left it in the Crystal Caves."

A delighted smile lit up my face. "Thanks! I love that sweatshirt! I totally forgot all about it."

"You're most welcome, my young friend," Amalya replied before she dematerialized out of my foyer.

I walked over to stand in front of the burglar alarm pad, and then easily found a fear thought to drop me back into the Third Dimension. *What if Jace never decides he wants to come out?*

The familiar sensation of descending back down into the Third gripped me. I held onto the wall with my head down, breathing hard, waiting for the disorientation to stop. I heard the slow steady beep of the alarm panel go off just after I rematerialized in the foyer and moved slightly, triggering the motion detectors. After quickly silencing the beeps, I pulled my sweatshirt over my head and made my way down the hall toward my bedroom using the doors and walls for stability.

Once in my room I found the way to my bed and laid down. My cell phone was fully charged now and sitting there waiting to be used. I mass texted the Society of the Silver Moon and emailed my parents, letting them know I was okay and home safely. Closing my eyes, I promptly fell asleep.

The incessant ringing of the doorbell jolted me out of my sleeping stupor. Still fully dressed, albeit wrinkled, from the night before, I made my way to the front door to see who was making such a racket. The expanded Society group poured through the front door practically knocking me over. *Oh God! Tim's here! I probably have a case of morning breath that would stop a freight train!*

"Holy Moley, Salena! Where did you get that amazing necklace!" Keia blurted out. The memories of the night before came flooding back to me, as I grabbed the crystal with my right hand feeling a rush of warmth and vibrant energy fill me up.

Quickly smoothing my hair with one hand and then covering my mouth with the other, I said "That is a long story! What time is it? Better yet, what day is it? I'm so discombobulated!"

"It's a little after ten a.m. on Friday, November 9th," Sam informed me.

"That's so weird. It takes over twenty plus hours to fly back from Singapore, but the way I traveled, I got back here before I left there. My parents won't be home until tomorrow morning," I said shaking my head. "This is my second Friday, November 9th!"

"That's kinda freaky. We brought bagels, cream cheese, some totally awesome apple Danish things, croissants, and . . . TA DAAA! A Starbucks caramel mocha for YOU!" Leah pronounced bringing her hand carrying my drink from behind her back with a flourish. As she handed it to me, she gave me a hug. "I was so worried about you! We all were!" Enormously grateful for the chocolaty-caramely coffee, I took a huge swig hoping it would ward off some of the negative effects of my morning breath.

"Hey, Salena, it's good to have you back," Tim said putting his arm around me, and squeezing.

"Yeah, Girlfriend, Mom and I were praying every day for you. We were so worried!" Katrina said as she and her mom moved in to embrace me too.

"We missed you! That's for sure!" Lesley said.

"We certainly could have used your help at the clinic the last few days! It's been totally crazy!" Lisa added.

"I want to hear all about everything that's been happening since I left on Monday. Let's go into the kitchen so we can sit and eat," I said, slowly moving the herd toward the kitchen. "I heard on the news that Sam's website and video had record breaking hits. That's SO COOL, Sam," I said beaming at him, and he blushed.

"Yes, that's true! His viral internet campaign worked better than we could have ever imagined. More and more people every day are realizing it is fear causing the illness; so many are using Trinity's video to strengthen their aura and mitigate the risks of contracting this disease. The daily death toll has stabilized and we expect it to start dropping soon," Lesley informed me.

I took a sip of my caramel mocha and bit into a chocolate croissant; the buttery flakes of pastry melted in my mouth. I involuntarily groaned and closed my eyes savoring the chocolaty deliciousness. Recovering from that momentary bliss, I found a seat at the kitchen table where Leah, Keia, and Katrina joined me. The moms sat on the sofa in front of the table and the boys found room at the counter. The bags of bagels and pastries were passed around as we caught up.

"On the news I saw lines at the clinic that extended out the door and up the street. They said there was talk of moving it to the convention center," I asked Lesley and Lisa.

"It's true, we've been totally swamped. Thankfully, we have an amazing group of metaphysical healers in this area who have all stepped forward to help. Your mother contacted a Native American medicine woman who has been heading up the training and development of the local alternative healing practitioners. They are the ones who have set up shop in the convention center," Lesley said.

Lisa picked up the conversation, "They have an area for training, and other rooms for the actual ceremonies. It has been fascinating to watch people embrace this process and start to wake up and raise their conscious awareness. The Blue Flu has shown the world how deadly living in fear and using fear to control others can be."

"How many people have died so far?" I asked.

"About four million have died, and about one million more are infected. Interestingly, the most impacted demographic has been men between the ages of thirty and seventy. There is a high concentration in areas that are dominated by military or religious control. There have been all sorts of media reports calling the Blue Flu the 2012 end-times apocalypse supposedly predicted by the ancient Mayan calendar. Some of the world's major religions are scrambling to find a way to reframe their public image to one that promotes tolerance and peace. It's been rather amusing to watch,"

Lesley smiled wryly.

"Apocalypse doesn't just mean the end of the world," Sam added. "It also means an unveiling or revelation. I think the Blue Flu could be the apocalypse in that regard. It is becoming the catalyst to help humanity begin their spiritual awakening by revealing to us the risks of fear and the power of compassion, forgiveness, and love."

All of us stared in open-mouth surprise at Sam for so long that he turned beet red and looked down at his lap.

"Alright Sam! That was incredibly well put!" Lisa exclaimed.

"Dude, that was awesome!" Keia agreed.

"Somehow, I don't think that some of those die hard fear mongers are going to let go of their control that easily," Connelly commented.

"You're right, Connelly," Lisa replied. "That is why we will never be able to completely eradicate the Blue Flu from existence on this planet. It will be an ever-present reminder of the damage fear can cause."

"It will disappear one day," I said. Everyone looked at me, questions in their eyes. "When all of humanity shifts to the Fifth Dimension, the Blue Flu will be eradicated. All negativity will be. There will be no more lack, no more disease, no more haves and have-nots. When I took the smoke filled crystals to the Fifth Dimension, they were completely cleared. By the way, I know how to cleanse the crystals here in the Third Dimension now. The Fif-D's gave me the process. How many are there to be cleansed?"

"We have thousands here alone. I have no idea how many there are around the world," Trinity said. "I've been collecting them until we figured out what to do with them."

"Ok, I'll help you with that, Trinity," I said.

"I'll put an update on the website," Sam volunteered.

"Salena, we want to hear what happened to you. How did you end up in that shipping container? Were you involved with the seizing of the freighter at all?" Connelly prodded.

"Yeah, were you? That was a pretty incredible story they had on the news," Tim added.

I took my last bite of croissant and another couple of swallows of my mocha, and then I settled in to tell my story to my best friends. No one took their eyes off of me as I described the events of the past few days. I left out the skirmish with the crane control operator because I didn't want the grown-ups to know about that. I decided I'd tell the kids later. Even Uncle Jack didn't know the crane operator had taken a shot at me.

When I had to tell them about Jace, though, I broke down. Between hiccups and sobs I described the evanescence process that happens in the Fifth Dimension and how Jace had chosen stasis over evanescence. Tears tracked down my cheeks as I held the amethyst crystal in my hand, and closed my eyes.

"Jace's parents think that if anybody can communicate with him inside this crystal, then I can. It'll change to a vibrant turquoise blue when he is ready to come out, until then it looks like this," I said holding up the pendulum shaped violet crystal.

"Dang, girl. Who picked you to be the Savior of the world and a star-crossed lover?" Keia said reaching out and wrapping my hand in hers on top of the table.

"That's just it," I said pursing my lips together. "Apparently, I did. At least that's what the Chronoscenti told me. And . . . this is only the beginning."

"Well Girlfriend, you're not alone, whatever may come. You've got me!" Keia proclaimed.

"Me too!" Leah said as she put her hand on top of Keia's.

"Me Three!" Katrina said smiling placing her hand on top of Leah's.

"Count us in!" The boys said in unison as each placed his hand on top of the girls'.

The moms surrounded the group holding hands as they encircled us. "You all have our love and support!" Trinity said.

Nobody else saw it, but Angeni materialized in the middle of the table, above, below, and through our hands; she was a bright beam of light, a magnificent blinding star, a column and conduit of pure love coming up from the Mother and down from the Father in perfect harmony. She smiled down upon us showering the group with the sparkles of pure Goddessence.

Epilogue
Three Months Later ~ Off the Coast of Puerto Vallarta

The swells coming into Banderas Bay from the Pacific Ocean rolled underneath the midnight colored hull of the 150-foot *Trader Empress* causing her to only slightly rock from side to side. A February storm was building off the coast promising to bring rain and wind. After being on the mega yacht since October, seventy-two year old Mitch Trader didn't even notice the swaying anymore. His attention, at the moment, was completely on his two sons-in-law who had just boarded. Impatiently, he ran his hands through the few remaining white hairs that filled in about one inch above his ears and encircled his head like a fallen headband. His hairless crown was covered in age spots, the result of too much exposure and not enough sunscreen. Not seeing the need to shave while on the boat, a full white beard covered most of his face.

"It's good to see you, sir. Your daughter misses you, and wishes you well," Todd Black reached out and shook his father-in-law's hand.

"Yes, yes. Well, tell her that I miss her too," Mitch replied. "And the grandchildren, give them my love, too," he added as an afterthought because it was expected.

"Mitch, thanks for bringing me out." Brad Killigan, son-in-law number two, extended his hand toward the old man. At forty-two, Brad was four years younger than his brother-in-law. He had a full head of almost jet-black hair that he wore long enough to cover his ears and contrasting pale blue eyes. Easily the shortest of the group, he stood at only five-ten versus the six-foot-two inches of his in-laws. Mr. Trader gripped Brad's hand and squeezed it like a vice clearly communicating who was boss.

"Stacey and the kids send their love," Brad said while he unobtrusively wiggled his hand trying to shake off the lingering effects of Mitch's python grip.

"Sir, may I bring you and your guests a drink?" A steward, one of the five crewmembers on board, appeared on the aft deck.

"Yes, Randall, that would be very nice. Please bring them into the salon when they're ready. I'll have my usual. Gentlemen, what would you like?" Mitch asked his guests. They ordered and then followed their father-in-law into the salon.

"Any more news about the federal investigation?" Todd asked.

"Nothing too new. I assume you've kept up with all of the media reporting," Mitch said waving at the papers and magazines that were strewn around on the tables and counters, their headlines shouting out the latest news on the Trader Pharmaceuticals investigation.

"You know that the damn U.S. Government has seized every company asset they could find. They're hoping to draw me out, but I'm staying put. Being exiled on the Trader Empress isn't the worst way to live. I assume you two weren't tailed?"

"We followed your instructions, Sir. We kept a close eye on our surroundings throughout the trip. We didn't see anything suspicious," Brad replied.

"Good. How's Candice holding up?"

"As well as can be expected under the circumstances, since you left her behind to handle things. She's not very happy with you, you know. I'd say your marriage is as unstable as the company," Todd asserted.

"She hasn't been happy with me for a very long time, but I don't see her doing anything about it. Do you?" Mitch smirked. Both of his sons-in-law mutely shook their heads side-to-side. Candice Trader would put up with practically anything to maintain her marital and social status. "How were Bonaparte's and Malicki's funerals?"

Todd and Brad grimaced as they took turns relaying the events that surrounded the services for Trader Pharmaceutical's late President and Vice President of Global Marketing. The media went crazy speculating on why so many of Trader Pharmaceutical's top management had died of the Blue Flu. They hadn't yet tied the initial spread of the Blue Flu to the company, but the probing continued. Malicki was a master alchemist at spinning public relations crap into pure gold. With the loss of their spin master, Trader Pharmaceuticals had nobody to speak for them in public except for a couple of weak-minded board members who were simply there to vote how Mitch told them to vote. They were practically useless.

After the steward delivered their drinks and then quickly left the room, Mitch continued the conversation. "Well, I have no desire to be questioned about anything. Period. Which is why I'm staying here, in international waters. Although their deaths may look suspicious, Malicki and Bonaparte and Mr. Jones in Singapore are perfect scapegoats for the other operations that the Singapore office was involved in. Laying the blame at their feet will hopefully help to clear my name and the company's name. And that brings us to the reason I've asked you two to fly down here to meet with me," Mitch said. The yacht lurched from side to side in the wake of a passing boat. The wind outside picked up. The breeze coming through the open window caused some of the newspapers to flutter to the floor.

 Mitch stood up and closed the window just as the mid-afternoon sun vanished behind some dark clouds. "As you are aware, the stock of Trader Pharmaceuticals has plummeted in the last three months since the test subjects were freed from the shipping container. Before November 9th our stock was trading for $92.00 per share. Today it's almost worthless. Also, you know the corporate attorneys have categorically denied any knowledge or complicity on my part in the actions of Jude Bonaparte and Marc Malicki, especially in this whole human-trafficking mess. Trader Pharmaceuticals needs new leadership and we need it now. The stockholders are clamoring for a change, and the board continues to encourage me to resign as Chairman. So, I have decided to hire the two of you," Mitch explained to Todd and Brad as he sat back down on the supple leather couch.

 That got the younger men's attentions. Both of their heads popped up, and they looked Mitch in eyes, holding his gaze. "I have already spoken to the Board, and they agreed to my proposal. I will step down as Chairman if they vote you, Todd, President, CEO and Chairman of Trader Pharmaceuticals. I am staying on the board in the position of Chairman Emeritus. Brad, I would like you to take on the position of VP of Global Marketing and PR," Mitch informed them.

"What about my job and responsibilities at Reno General?" Todd asked.

"Your first action as President of Trader will be to sell off that asset to either the Von Housen Family, or to another investor. Trader can no longer afford to keep it." Todd's eyebrows and lips pursed together in concentration. Although he tried to keep his face impassive, he was already thinking about what kind of raise he could expect.

Brad watched the emotions play across his brother-in-law's face as he desperately tried to keep the heat of his jealousy from showing up on his countenance. *Just because Todd is older than I am and married to the oldest daughter, doesn't make him a better leader*, he fumed. All in all though, he didn't mind giving up his boring job as a marketing manager for a major pharmacy chain. Going to work for Trader would be a great opportunity to make more money and keep an eye on the brown-nosing husband of his wife's big sister.

"Brad, your first job will be to hire a PR firm. We need to do some serious damage control. Do you have any questions or comments?" Mitch asked.

Shrugging nonchalantly, he said, "No, not really. Sounds like a great opportunity. I look forward to helping Trader Pharmaceuticals once again become world's leader in medical research." Smiling, he reached down, picked up his beer, and toasted his father-in-law and his brother-in-law.

The white caps splashing against the hull of the yacht were barely audible in the salon, but the nautical flag on the stern of the ship, flapping furiously in the wind, could easily be heard.

"All right, then. Congratulations to both of you on your promotions!" Mitch said as all three of the men raised their drinks. "Todd, I know you have been spending some time with our own internal investigators and attorneys. Do you have any information as to how this whole debacle even happened? What I really want to know is who's to blame, and, most importantly, HOW THE HELL DID WE GET CAUGHT?" Mitch bellowed his voice getting louder and more frustrated with each question.

Todd reached down to a briefcase he had carried aboard, unzipped it, and opened a large envelope. He pulled out a dozen eight by ten photos, all of a young girl who was about thirteen or fourteen years old. He spread out the photos of the girl on the coffee table between the three of them.

"Who's that?" Brad asked, only mildly curious.

"Her name is Salena Hawthorne. I believe she is the one behind the downfall of Trader Pharmaceuticals."

"How in the world could a teenage girl be responsible for the downfall of a multi-billion dollar world-wide organization?" Brad asked amazed that his brother-in-law would make such a preposterous statement.

"I don't know exactly how she did it, but I have several reasons to believe she is responsible. She is a very special girl who may have some very unique abilities that could be useful to us in the rebuilding of this company," Todd explained.

"Go on," Mitch prompted.

Todd explained to his family how he first met Salena at the hospital. He pulled out a copy of her MRIs and showed them to Mitch and Brad. "I know that none of us knows exactly what we are looking at here, but I have had several neurologists check this out, and the activity in her brain is off the charts. They have never seen anything like this. I made several attempts to get her back to the hospital so I could run more tests on her, but her father flatly refused. Shortly thereafter, the Blue Flu set in and the hospital was too busy for me to pursue them. She was also at the hospital with the team of doctors and nurses performing the ridiculous metaphysical treatment. In asking the patients about their treatment they received that day, they confirmed that Miss Hawthorne was in the room with the doctors and nurses. One woman told me that Salena had admitted to having some kind of gift."

"That's mildly entertaining, Todd, but it doesn't make her responsible for the company's downfall," Brad smirked.

Flashing an annoyed look toward his brother-in-law, Todd continued. "You're right, but she was also in the crane operator's cabin on board the Tomi Maru. She is directly responsible for bringing the container back aboard the ship during the raid."

"What the hell?! How is that possible?" Mitch exclaimed.

"I don't know sir, but I spoke directly with the crane operator, a man named Ruddick, who is now in prison in Singapore. He confirmed that he had left the cab in a hurry to help his crewmates after he heard gunfire. He realized he had forgotten his weapon after he was halfway down the ladder, so he went right back up to get it. When he opened the door to the control room, there was a young girl sitting in the chair moving the crane arm back over the ship! There was no way she got up there using the ladder because he was on it. I showed him a dozen pictures of young girls, and he positively identified Salena out of the pile. She did not travel to Singapore in any conventional way. There are no records of her entering or exiting the country. And, here is the kicker, Ruddick swears he saw her *disappear* right in front of him. He thought she was a ghost and was so freaked out that he shot at her."

"He shot her? What happened after he shot her?" Brad asked.

"Nothing to her, apparently. Ruddick said he stuck his head outside the crane cabin to look for her. She wasn't anywhere to be found. Here are a few photographs of a very alive, unharmed Salena Hawthorne taken during her interviews pertaining to the development of the Blue Flu treatment in the weeks following the Tomi Maru raid," Todd said as he laid a few more photos on top of the other ones.

"Has there been anything we've been able to find

that connects this child to the Tomi Maru raid other than the crane operator's story?" Mitch asked.

"The raid on the Tomi Maru was executed by a paramilitary group called EPIC. Coincidentally, the director of EPIC is a very good friend of the Hawthorne family, but other than that, no. Nobody on the EPIC team or any of the freed prisoners mentioned Salena in any of their testimony regarding the events aboard the Tomi Maru."

"So you're theory is that this thirteen-year-old girl has a vendetta against Trader Pharmaceuticals and used her super-power abilities of disappearing and teleportation to destroy the company," Brad smirked. Todd shot him a dirty look.

"What I do know is that his young lady somehow found out about the prisoners who were onboard the Tomi Maru and managed to prevent the crew from delivering their cargo. She was also behind the development and dissemination of the metaphysical Blue Flu treatment. I don't have the proof, but I have plenty of circumstantial evidence that points to Salena Hawthorne being behind Trader Pharmaceuticals current, uh . . . difficulties. There's something unusual about that girl—something that, given the right set of circumstances, we might be able to capitalize upon." Todd defended.

Mitch Trader rubbed his beard as he scrutinized the new President and CEO of his company. Dark angry clouds blotted out the sun as large raindrops fell heavily upon the outside decks of the Trader Empress and knocked randomly against the windows. The yacht groaned as it pulled against its moorings, resisting the wind.

"You're absolutely sure about this?" Mitch finally asked Todd.

"Yes, Mitch, I am. I've met this little girl, and I know that either in her brain, blood, or genetic code, she holds the key."

"What key?" Brad asked.

"The key, my dear brother-in-law," Todd said, a maniacal glint igniting in his eyes, "to our revenge or our redemption."

Color Exposition

Black - *Aura Meaning* - The color of negativity. Black draws or pulls energy to it, and in doing so, transforms it; captures light and consumes it. The presence of black usually indicates long-term lack of forgiveness collected in a specific area of the body, can lead to health problems.

Blue - *Aura Meaning* - The color of a cool, calm, and collected nature; characteristics are: caring, loving, helping, sensitive, and intuitive.

Chakra - Throat – governs the Thyroid Gland bronchial and vocal apparatus, lungs and alimentary canal.

Soul Star Meaning - Fifth Dimensional.

Elements and Directions - Water - West

Blue (Bright Royal) - *Aura Meaning* - Indicates clairvoyance, highly spiritual nature; individuals who are generous, on the right path, new opportunities are coming.

Blue (Dark or Muddy) - *Aura Meaning* -Indicates a fear of the future, fear of self-expression, fear of facing or speaking the truth.

Blue (Soft) - *Aura Meaning* - Indicates peacefulness,

clarity, and communication; individuals who are truthful and intuitive.

Blue (Turquoise) - *Aura Meaning* - Indicates sensitive, compassionate, healer, therapist.

Brown - *Aura Meaning* - The color of soil, wood, minerals, and plants. These colors in an aura represent a love of the Earth, of being grounded; often found in people who live and work outdoors.

Elements and Directions - Earth - North.

Brown (Dirty Overlay) - *Aura Meaning* - Indicates insecurity, inability to release negative energies.

Gold - *Aura Meaning* - The color of enlightenment and divine protection; found in a person being guided by their highest good--divine guidance. Indicates protection, wisdom, inner knowledge, spiritual mind, intuitive thinker.

Soul Star Meaning - Angelic Realm.

Gold - (Clear, shiny bright metallic) *Aura Meaning* - Indicates spiritual energy and power activated and awakened; an inspired person.

Gray - *Aura Meaning* - The color of fear accumulating in the body, with potential for health problems, especially if gray clusters are found in specific areas of the body.

Gray (Dirty Overlay) - *Aura Meaning* - Indicates a presence of guardedness; an individual who is blocking external energy.

Green - *Aura Meaning* - The color of growth and balance, and most of all, something that leads to change. Found in individuals with a love of people, animals, nature; teacher; social.

Chakra - Heart – Governs the Thymus, heart, blood, Vagus nerve, and circulatory system.

Soul Star Meaning - Healthy Third Dimensional.

Elements and Directions - Earth - North.

Green (Bright Emerald) - *Aura Meaning* - Found in a healer, also a love-centered person.

Green (Dark or Muddy) - *Aura Meaning* - Indicates jealousy, resentment, feelings of victimization; blaming self or others; insecurity and low self-esteem; lack of understanding personal responsibility; sensitive to perceived criticism.

Green (Yellow) - *Aura Meaning* - Indicates a creative with heart, communicative.

Indigo - *Aura Meaning* - The color of an intuitive, sensitive, deep feeling nature.

Chakra - Third Eye – Governs the Pituitary Gland, Lower brain, left eye, face, ears, and nervous system.

Orange - *Aura Meaning* - The color of vitality, vigor, good health, and excitement. Indicates high energy and stamina. Found in individuals who are creative, productive, adventurous, courageous, outgoing; often experiencing stress related to appetites or addictions.

Chakra - Sacral – (Belly) Governs the gonads, reproductive system.

Orange (Red) - *Aura Meaning* - Indicates confidence, creative power.

Orange (Yellow) - *Aura Meaning* - Indicates creative, intelligent, detail oriented, perfectionist, scientific.

Pink (Bright and Light) - *Aura Meaning* - The color of love, tenderness, sensitivity, sensuality, artistic, affectionate, purity, and compassion. Indicates new or revived romantic relationship; can indicate clairaudience.

Pink (Dark and Muddy) - *Aura Meaning* - Indicates immature and/or dishonest nature.

Purple - *Aura Meaning* - The most sensitive and wisest of colors. This is the intuitive color in the aura and reveals psychic power of attunement with self. Characteristics are: intuitive, visionary, futuristic, idealistic, artistic, magical.

Chakra - Crown – Governs the Pineal Gland, upper brain, right eye.

Soul Star Meaning - Evanescing Fifth Dimensional.

Elements and Directions - Center of Circle - Spirit.

Purple (Lavender) - *Aura Meaning* - Indicates imagination, visionary, daydreamer, etheric.

Red - *Aura Meaning* - The densest color, the color of friction. Indicates friction that can attract or repel; money worries or obsessions; anger or unforgiveness; anxiety or nervousness.

Chakra - Root – Governs the Adrenal gland, spinal column, hips, legs, lower back and kidneys.

Soul Star Meaning - Third Dimensional Ghost – Hasn't crossed over.

Elements and Directions - Fire - South.

Red (Clear) - *Aura Meaning* - Indicates powerful,

energetic, competitive, sexual, passionate nature.

Red (Deep) - *Aura Meaning* - Indicates grounded, realistic, active, strong will power, survival-oriented.

Red (Muddy) - *Aura Meaning* - Indicates anger.

Silver - *Aura Meaning* - The color of abundance, both spiritual and physical. Lots of bright silver can reflect to plenty of money, and/or awakening of the cosmic mind.

Silver (Bright Metallic) - *Aura Meaning* - Indicates individual receptive to new ideas; intuitive; nurturing.

White - *Aura Meaning* - Reflects other energy. A pure state of light. Often represents a new, not yet designated energy in the aura. Indicates spiritual, etheric and non-physical qualities; transcendent or higher dimensions; purity and truth; angelic qualities.

Soul Star Meaning - Spirit Realm.

Elements and Directions - Center of Circle – Spirit.

Yellow - *Aura Meaning* - The color of awakening, inspiration, intelligence and action shared, creative, playful, optimistic, easy-going.

Chakra - Solar Plexus – Governs the stomach, liver, gall bladder, pancreas, and small intestine.

Soul Star Meaning - Sick or Dying Third Dimensional.

Elements and Directions - Air - East.

Yellow (Dark Brownish) - *Aura Meaning* - Indicates a student or one who is straining at studying; overly analytical to the point of feeling fatigued or stressed; trying to make up for "lost time" by learning everything all at once.

Yellow (Bright Lemon) - *Aura Meaning* - Indicates struggle to maintain power and control in personal or business relationship; fear of losing control, prestige, respect, and/or power.

Yellow (Light or Pale) - *Aura Meaning* - Indicates emerging psychic and spiritual awareness; optimism and hopefulness; positive excitement about new ideas.

GLOSSARY

Aetheric – A blanket of energy that weaves itself through everything on earth; divine intelligence and love; synonymous with Goddessence.

Akashic Records – The energetic recordings of every soul's journey from the time it decides to leave its point of origin and experience life as a separate entity until it decides to return home. Every thought, word and deed are recorded in these records for every incarnation of every soul.

Akashic Sentinels – Keep watch over the access to the Akashic Records, and like to dress as Aztec Warriors to add an air of mystique and ceremony to the job, but basically they just function as receptionists for the Chronoscenti.

Aura – A field of subtle, colorful, luminous energy surrounding a person.

Chakra – A swirling energy center that permeates through a spot on the physical body. They are considered to be the focal points for the reception and transmission of energies throughout the physical and auric fields.

Chronoscenti – The master chroniclers and keepers of the Akashic Records.

Evanesce – To turn to vapor; the Fifth Dimension version of ceasing to exist, transcendence to the spirit realm.

Fifth Dimensionals – Humans who vibrate at extremely high frequency that they are not visible in the third or fourth dimension. Everyone has the ability to manifest anything instantly. They shape and mold the energy they require to meet any of their physical needs so that they can spend the rest of their conscious time on intellectual, artistic and spiritual pursuits.

Fourth Dimensionals – People who live in the Fourth Dimension are more loving, tolerant, open-minded and forgiving. They don't try to exert their will on others or try to control them for their own purposes or personal gain. Shares space, time and matter with the Third Dimension.

Goddessence – A blanket of energy that weaves itself through everything on Earth; divine intelligence and love; synonymous with Aetheric.

Hyperphotonic Emissions – The magnitude and force of the light and energy that comes off of organic materials, plants and trees. Can only be seen in the Fifth Dimension.

Ocular Dynamic Resonance (ODR) – The ability to

see auras and Fifth Dimensional hyperphotonic emissions. Allows Fifth Dimensionals to identify and classify the energy of everything in their environment.

Soul Group – A group of souls, like a family, that work together in the spirit realm to coordinate their next incarnations together. Members of the same soul group will often change roles with each other as family members, friends, or lovers in different incarnations.

Soul Mates – Two members of the same soul group who fall in love during an incarnation.

Soul Stars – Inside the Akashic Records the soul star resonates the colored energy of the spirit depending on which dimension they currently inhabit and where they are in their cycle of existence within that dimension.

Surdo Mallet – A Surdo is a Brazilian drum. A mallet is also used specifically to refer to a hand-held beater, like drum sticks, except a Surdo Mallet has a wrapped head connected to the thin shaft of wood. The tool used to play crystal bowls looks like a Surdo Mallet. It can also be called a striker or a wand.

Symbing – The Fifth Dimensional method of creating new life. Derived from the word symbiosis, which literally means 'together life'. Achieved by a joining the mind, body and spirit with a willing partner.

Third Dimensionals – People who are polarized by humanity's differences and stuck in their own limiting beliefs about their own separateness.

Twin Flames – Initially created at the same time, they are, simultaneously, the other half of each other's soul and a complete soul individually. This is similar to the way identical twins are formed from the same egg and sperm that split off into two separate people.

About the Author

As the great-granddaughter of the inventor of the drinking fountain, Sallie Haws spent 26 years using her Organizational Psychology degree to make a positive impact on her family's business where she held jobs from file clerk to President. Her passion for writing was fed by taking creative writing classes and by a voracious reading habit of paranormal, sci-fi, fantasy novels.

Quantum Spirit – Apocalypse is the culmination of years of personal and professional life experience combined with the desire to entertain and inspire adults and teenagers. Sallie lives in Reno, Nevada with her husband, son, daughter and a spoiled black cat.

Connect with Sallie on the web at www.QuantumSpiritBooks.com, on Facebook at www.facebook.com/Quantum.Spirit.Books or on Linked In at www.linkedin.com/pub/sallie-haws/2a/b07/ab4.

Quantum Spirit
Redemption

CHAPTER ONE
Rude Awakenings

My pillow smells funny . . . I scrunched my nose and stretched the achy sleepiness out of my legs before I opened my eyes. A yellowish popcorn ceiling with old water stains stared back at me. What the hell? That's not my bedroom ceiling! Where am I?!

It wasn't just my pillow that smelled bad; it was the whole room. A noxious blend of rust, dust, stale sweat, urine, and body odor stung my nose as I sat up in the foreign bed and tried to make sense of my surroundings.

"She's awake," a deep, gravelly voice said from the corner of the dimly lit room. I spun my head in the direction of the sound and rubbed my eyes.

"Who are you? Where am I? What am I doing here?" I asked, staring wide-eyed at the man responsible for the body odor. He was doing his best interpretation of a lumberjack, complete with plaid shirt, ball cap, and jeans. A full, unkempt dirty red beard covered most of his large face, which made his beady black eyes difficult to see. I tuned in my Sight to read his aura, and sure enough, most of his blue, green, and brown colors were dark and muddied. He had his share of charcoal as well. How he had avoided getting infected with the Blue Flu was a mystery.

In one hand he had a walkie-talkie, and in the other hand a plastic cup was half-filled with some yellowish-brown substance I didn't even want to know about. I noticed the butt of a gun poking out of the waist of his pants. Yeah, that caught my attention. Putting that together with his aura, there was no doubt . . . I was in big trouble . . . again.

Suddenly grateful that my normal sleeping attire consisted of PJ pants and a T-shirt, I noticed I was still in the clothes I had worn to bed last night. Instinctively I reached for my purple crystal necklace, but it wasn't there. Oh, yeah. I had taken it off and set it on my bedside table before going to sleep. Despite being fully clothed I still pulled the scratchy, musty wool blanket up to my chin and desperately tried to remember how I had gotten here, wherever here was. But all I could remember was a fairly normal Friday night. Mom, Dad, and I went to dinner and a movie, and then I came home and went to bed. Somehow this guy bypassed my parent's alarm system, broke into our house and kidnapped me. Do Mom and Dad even know I'm gone? We were all planning on sleeping in today.

My captor smiled in response to my questions. What a dreadful thing that was to behold, even in the dim light. His corroded grin only contributed to the nausea that was building since I had woken up. Add a serious case of cottonmouth, morning-breath, and a sudden wave of dizziness compounded by a dash of disorientation, and I was definitely having the rudest awakening ever!

"Salena Hawthorne?" He asked. I nodded my

head slightly, wondering what he would have done if he thought he had abducted the wrong girl. "You can call me Mr. E.," he said, and then moved the tobacco plug to the other side of his mouth. Gross. That explained the attractive teeth. "We've provided these nice accommodations while we wait for you to be picked up."

"Who are 'we'?" I asked looking around at my "nice accommodations" which consisted of the tired and lumpy double bed I was currently sitting upon, and a stained, dented bedside table that housed a lamp and an ancient TV remote. I didn't see a phone. I gazed down at the carpet . . . it was brown. I couldn't tell if that was its original color, and was sure it would be as rough as the blanket. There was a lopsided, half-open accordion door across from me that seemed to be concealing a closet. Another door was slightly ajar opening to what had to be a bathroom. What interested me the most, though, was the door that undoubtedly led outside. Thick rust colored curtains hung heavily over the single window to the right of the exit and only let in a thread of early morning light.

"My pardner, Mr. D. be making sure we ain't disturbed," Mr. E. explained.

"Why did you kidnap me? I don't know you. What do you want?"

"Yer sure full of questions for such a tiny little thang. Mebee you should be quiet now. Don't cause no trouble, or I'll hafta tie ya up and tape yer mouth," he threatened. My best weapon was my mouth. I really didn't want him to tape it up. I mimed zipping my mouth shut.

"E. Transfer confirmed. ETA thirty minutes," a disembodied voice said over my captor's radio.

"Ten-Four D," Mr. E responded, still grinning.

Thirty minutes. I had thirty minutes before I was transferred. To whom and to what, I really didn't want to find out. I scooted over to the edge of the bed closer to the front door futilely trying to put more distance between me and Mr. E. Swooning again, I dropped my feet on the floor, I placed my hand on the sticky nightstand to regain my balance. What was wrong with me?

I took a couple of deep breaths to calm my nerves and swirling stomach. It didn't help. I could feel the lumberjack's eyes boring into the back of my head before I saw something black and rather large scurry under the bed. Shrieking, I quickly drew my legs back under me and scrambled over to the other side. I tentatively peered down. Nothing came out. Not good. I really didn't want to know what had crawled under the bed, or if it had any friends.

"Wassamatter, little girl? Did you see a critter?" E guffawed, totally amused by my antics. I decided to ignore him and see how much of the room he'd let me explore.

I leapt off the bed, took two long steps to the door, grabbed the handle, turned and pulled. Nothing, it didn't budge. I pulled harder. Still nothing.

"We ain't stupid, chickie," E informed me. "D locked it from outside. You ain't goin' nowhere."

I turned to the window after glancing behind me

and giving him a dirty look. Peeling away the curtain I tried to see outside. I was greeted by the backside of a piece of plywood that only allowed light to enter from the top and bottom of the window. After sneezing three times from the dislodged dust, I decided I was probably being held in an old motel that had undoubtedly been shut down years ago. I flicked the light switch. Yup. No electricity. I doubted the water in the bathroom worked either and, frankly, I was terrified of what might be growing in there, but I really had to pee.

I turned around to glare at E. He hadn't taken his eyes off of me. As scared and nervous as I felt, I was actually relieved to notice that he wasn't leering at me like some perv. Instead, he seemed to watch me like I was some kind of entertaining lab rat.

"She s'ploring the room now," E informed his accomplice through the walkie-talkie, never taking his eyes off of me. "Naw, not causin' no trouble."

"Good. Don't let her out of your sight. I'll be back when our contact arrives," the device replied.

God! I hope he doesn't want to keep an eye on me while I pee. I crossed my legs and squatted a little. "Um . . . Mr. E?" I sheepishly asked. "I have to go to the bathroom," I said nodding my head in the direction of the slightly ajar door.

"Window'n there's boarded too, chickie. You ain't 'scapin'."

"I'm not trying to escape," I lied. "I just really need to pee."

E set the two-way radio in his lap so he could rub his beard and stare at me with a hard, implacable expression. "Didn' you just hear D? He tol' me to keep mine eyes on ya."

"Yeah, I heard him, but you just said there was no window in the bathroom. Where could I go?"

"Dunno," he said still rubbing his beard and continuing to glare. I was growing a little concerned that he may somehow know of my "special ability," and that could be the reason I was kidnapped in the first place. I didn't want to try to ascend in front of him. The last time I did that in the same space with a gunman, he shot at me.

"Look, I'm sure that wherever your transport people will be taking me, they won't want to stop for me to go to the bathroom, nor would they want me to wet my pants." At least I hoped that was the case. I started inching toward the bathroom door. My eyes locked with E's. I could tell he was trying to weigh the risks. If he knows for sure what I can do, he wouldn't be wavering.

"Okay, girlie. You can go in there, I s'pose. But no closin' that door! I want t'hear everything yer doin'!"

"Umm, creepy, but okay," I murmured keeping eye contact all the way to the entrance. Geez, I hope I don't get performance anxiety once I get in there.

The stench hit me immediately. Apparently this is where E had been relieving himself during his watch. I breathed as shallowly as possible through my mouth, wiping my watering eyes. Tiptoeing across the gritty, yellowed linoleum floor, I tried to flush the toilet, but as I suspected the water had been turned off. I dropped the seat loudly for E's benefit, only to discover several rust colored stains that totally grossed me out. I don't care how badly I have to pee, I so totally cannot sit on that! I gotta get out of here now!

Identifying the least offensive section of the rim of the moldy, yellow tub that extended the length of the back wall of the bathroom, I gingerly sat down on the edge and closed my eyes. My Fifth Dimension visualization came quickly and effortlessly. Taking a deep breath, I relaxed for the first time since I woke up in this wretched place. It was time to go home.